A BULLET FROM
DOMINIC

Also by Giacomo Giammatteo:

Fiction:
Friendship & Honor Series:
MURDER TAKES TIME: Friendship & Honor: Book I
MURDER HAS CONSEQUENCES: Friendship & Honor: Book II
MURDER TAKES PATIENCE: Friendship & Honor Book III

Blood Flows South Series:
A BULLET FOR CARLOS: Blood Flows South: Book I
FINDING FAMILY: Blood Flows South: the Beginning (A Novella)

Redemption Series:
Necessary Decisions
OLD WOUNDS (Coming late 2014)

Non-Fiction:
No Mistakes Careers
NO MISTAKES RESUMES: Book One of No Mistakes Careers
NO MISTAKES INTERVIEWS: Book Two of No Mistakes Careers

Sanctuary Tales (True Stories From An Animal Sanctuary)
WHISKERS & BEAR (Coming soon)

BLOOD FLOWS SOUTH: BOOK II

A BULLET FROM DOMINIC

Giacomo Giammatteo

INFERNO PUBLISHING COMPANY

A BULLET FROM DOMINIC
by Giacomo Giammatteo

© Copyright 2014 Giacomo Giammatteo

INFERNO PUBLISHING COMPANY

For more information about this book, visit
www.giacomogiammatteo.com

ISBN: 978-1-940313-06-1 (ebook)
ISBN: 978-1-940313-07-8 (print)

NOTE TO READERS:

Welcome back to the Blood Flows South Series, featuring Detectives Connie Gianelli, Tip Denton, and a special guest appearance by Hector "Ribs" Delgado.

This is the second book in the series and it picks up six months after *A Bullet For Carlos* left off.

I hope you enjoy it,
Giacomo

Na famigghia può esse distrutta solo dall'interno
A family can only be broken from the inside.

~ Dominic Mangini

Chapter 1

HOME AT LAST

Brooklyn, New York

I crawled out of bed, reluctant to start another day. It had been six months since the incident in Texas, and I still couldn't take five breaths without thinking about it. Or asking God why it happened to me. All my life I'd tried doing the right thing, going out of my way and putting myself through hell just to make sure I didn't end up on the same side of the law as Uncle Dominic.

And what did I get in return?

I got "the incident." That's what I called it. Too afraid to speak the word, or even think it.

I put the pot on the stove so I could get my daily shot of espresso. While I waited for the water to boil, I did a few dozen push-ups and then stretched my legs.

Rape, Gianelli. Spit it out.

That's what it was. Rape. I cracked my knuckles, did a few back bends, then closed my eyes and worked the kinks out of my neck. Whoever was talking inside my head was right. It *was* rape. And my only consolation was that Tip had killed the son of a bitch on the spot—five shots to the chest.

I turned just as the water boiled, grabbed the pot and poured a cup of espresso. Somehow I had inherited the genes from Uncle Dominic to *sense* when a pot of espresso was ready. The odd thing was, I got the genes even though he wasn't really my uncle.

I spoiled myself with a few melon balls while I sipped the espresso and wondered what the wise psychologist would find wrong with me today. It wasn't enough that I had damn near been killed twice in a matter of two months, and that my ribs were broken, jaw smashed, and I was raped. He seemed intent on finding some deep-seated reason for my depression. I guess what happened to me wasn't enough. Shrinks seemed to need a *deep-seated* reason.

As I thought about that I made up my mind. I wouldn't be meeting with Dr. Nutbag today; Uncle Dominic probably had better advice. I cleaned the dishes, dressed and headed out. Before long I was crossing the Willis Avenue Bridge into the Bronx. Uncle Dominic's house was minutes away.

I parked at the end of the street and went through the ritual of entering Mr. Gallo's house and making my way through Dominic's secret tunnel. It had been six months since I'd been on the job, and it was looking doubtful if I'd ever go back. But there was no sense in taking chances, so I kept up the ruse of non-association where Uncle Dominic was concerned. I felt sure the Feds still watched him, and anyone who associated with him.

I came up the steps into his kitchen, the half-man, half-tiger known as Fabrizio having led the way. I was relieved to be out of dark closed-in spaces with Fabrizio. I didn't want to like Fabrizio, knowing—or at least assuming—what he did, but he was so damn sexy that no matter how hard I tried, I found myself moving closer to him at every chance. To top it off, he was polite and charming. Oh, and a hit-man. I felt sure. Just what I needed in my life. Dr. Nutbag would have fun with that.

"*Buon giorno, Zio Domenico.*"

One of Dominic's famous smiles popped onto his face. He squeezed me and patted my back. If I still had chubby cheeks he'd have pinched them, but—thankfully—the chubby-cheek days were long gone.

"Concetta, you look fantastic. I'll put espresso on."

I laughed. No matter what happened—good, bad, or indifferent—in Uncle Dominic's house it was cause to put espresso on the stove.

"Thanks, Uncle Dominic, but I had some before I came over."

"Then I'll make some for me. How can we have a discussion without espresso?" He prepared the pot and started grinding the beans. After the whirr of the grinder stopped, he scooped coffee into the pot. "What brings my favorite person on earth to see me?"

I looked to the side, where Fabrizio stood. He took the hint and walked out of the room. Dominic waited until he was gone, then asked again. "What brings you? Troubles?"

I didn't know where to start, or how. I never was good at talking to people about my problems. When I got the nerve to speak, I avoided Uncle Dominic's probing gaze. "It's been six months and I still…"

"You are still ashamed," Dominic said.

His words stung. "I'm *not* ashamed."

Dominic reached for a biscotto and took a bite. "Yes you are. You don't want to admit it, but you blame yourself for what happened."

"That's *bullshit.*"

Uncle Dominic set the biscotto down and sipped his espresso. "Yes, it's bullshit. I'm glad you see that. But it's also what you're doing to yourself, and the sooner you admit that the sooner you'll get better."

I wiped a tear away before he saw it. "Why did this happen to me, Uncle Dominic? I try so hard to do the right thing… *Why?*"

Uncle Dominic set his cup down, and pushed it to the side. He reached across the table and pulled my hand toward him. He rubbed the rough knuckles and toughened skin. Then he leaned close and looked me in the eyes.

"Sometimes God makes good people suffer—like you and your mother—and He lets people like me have a smooth ride. I think He is preparing you for heaven, and He tricks fools like me into thinking we got away with something."

I thought I saw tears in his eyes, but he must have willed them to stop. "If anything, Concetta, you're the lucky one. When something bad happens to you on earth, think of it as one less day you'll have to spend in purgatory."

What he said shocked me. "I didn't know you were so religious."

He let go of my hand and leaned back in his chair. "You didn't know my father. He was *not* a good man. He wasn't even a nice man. But he told me one thing I remember. He said, 'A criminal never worries about getting caught until he hears the sirens.'"

Dominic nodded his head, as if he were considering this bit of wisdom, and not for the first time. "I'm getting old, and I can hear the sirens off in the distance."

"Then quit! Quit before they catch you."

Dominic laughed. He reached over and pinched my cheeks. "My dear sweet Concetta, I'm not talking about the police. And I don't think I can hide from these sirens."

He cleaned the table and rinsed the dishes in the sink. "You should go back to Texas," he said. "You have a clean reputation and you have a good friend. There's not much more to ask for."

"I don't know about that."

"Think about it," he said. "It would be good for you."

I grabbed a dish towel and dried the dishes.

After a moment of silence, he hugged me and gave me a peck on the forehead. "I'll finish. Go home and pack."

"I haven't said I'm going."

"You will," he said, and began drying one of the coffee cups. "You always make the right decisions."

"I'll think about it."

Dominic turned to me. "One thing to remember, leave the drugs alone."

"What are you saying?"

"I mean Carlos Cortes. When you get to Texas, stay away from him. Those people have no respect. They will kill a neighbor just to make a point. They will even kill children." Dominic wagged his finger at me. "They will do *anything* to frighten people into cooperating. They don't play by the same rules."

"I know all about *El Jabato*. I've seen firsthand what he's capable of."

"Good, then it's settled. You'll stay away from him."

I almost got pissed, but laughed instead, and then I hugged him. "Uncle Dominic, I love you."

He rubbed the back of my head, and said, "*Ti voglio bene.*"

I grabbed his espresso pot and took it to the sink.

"Leave it," Dominic said. "I'll be making more soon. Now do what I said. Go home and pack."

I kissed his cheek, and grabbed my purse. "We'll see."

***

Dominic waited until he heard the door close in the basement, and then he hit the button on the intercom system. "Fabrizio."

Fabrizio came to the kitchen a few seconds later. "Si, signore."

"Find out who owes us favors in Texas, especially in Houston. We need someone to keep an eye on Concetta."

"Is she going to Houston?" Fabrizio asked.

Dominic nodded. "She doesn't realize it yet, but she will."

Chapter 2

Breakfast In Monterrey

Monterrey, Mexico

Carlos Cortes fastened the last button on his shirt, tucked it into white linen pants, then bent to tie his shoes. No matter the inconvenience, he preferred shoes with laces. It would be a cold day in hell before he ever wore shoes called loafers. The name said it all as far as Carlos was concerned.

Echoes of hard leather heels slapping against the flagstone patio bounced off the stucco walls as Carlos took his seat at the table, a round glass top supported by wrought iron legs. Four chairs surrounded the table. They were wrought iron also, but the seats were covered with cushions featuring bunnies and flowers—compliments of Carlos' daughter, Adalia.

A servant brought a carafe filled with coffee. He poured a cup for Carlos and one for Tico, then set a sweet roll onto a plate beside each cup. A tall glass of freshly-squeezed orange juice sat to Carlos' right, accompanied by two packets of sugar. The servant walked to the other side of the patio and stood, out of earshot.

"Tell me the bad news from the States, Tico."

Tico reached for his coffee, steam rising from it into an unusually cool November morning in Monterrey. "It's not all bad, señor. Atlanta and St. Louis are running as planned. Austin and San Antonio are under control. And we have made good progress in Dallas."

Carlos smiled as he poured sugar into his orange juice. "I hear no mention of Houston or little Wilmington, Delaware."

"You know what happened in Houston, señor. And in Wilmington…" With no response from Carlos, Tico continued. "We can fix Wilmington, but we have bigger problems in Houston."

Carlos set his glass down and looked at Tico. "What kind of problems?"

"Distribution and laundering. Not to mention your legal complications."

"We had good people. What changed?"

Tico pushed his plate aside. "Much has changed since your visit to Spain. Our banker is afraid of the increased investigations. And the transportation is suffering because of the battles in Nuevo Laredo; the scum from the West have frightened him."

Carlos brushed a crumb from his shirt, smoothed a crease in his pants, and stared at Tico until the other man turned his head. "I see disapproval in your eyes, my friend. You think I was gone too long?"

Tico shrugged. "People need discipline."

"Nothing truer has ever been said." Carlos took a sip of his drink. "I think our discipline will have to start with our legal associates. As to our distributor…if he is afraid of a few bodies hanging from the bridge and a couple of heads in the backseats of cars, perhaps he doesn't understand *El Jabato*. We will have to remind him."

"Shouldn't we wait? It hasn't been long since you were in Houston and had trouble with those cops."

Carlos took a Fortuna cigarette from his pack, waited for Tico to light it, and then lifted his head to stare at the smoke rings he blew. He nodded as one ring split the center of the one before it. "I remember those cops. But our business dictates our actions, and our business demands we pay a visit to Houston; besides, I now have protection of a corporation in league with our government. I'm almost a diplomat." Carlos laughed and took a final sip of coffee. "Tomás is who everyone is after. He's the horrible drug lord. I am nothing but a telecommunications executive."

"That might be on paper, señor, but the authorities know who you are."

"Knowing who I am and being able to do something about it are quite different." Carlos blew a few more smoke rings, and then he said, "We might have need of *El Terrible* on this trip."

Tico raised his eyes, brow wrinkling. "*El Terrible?*"

"Yes, Tico. Make the call."

"We have more to discuss," Tico said, as Carlos stood.

"What?"

"Transportation for the new product. Pricing, and what the dealers will get. And the Chef had questions about the formula—"

"We will discuss that on the way," Carlos said as he walked toward the door. "Gather the men and make that call. It's a long drive to Houston."

While Tico made plans to depart, Carlos said goodbye to Adalia and Julio, and his wife, Marianna.

"How long will you be gone this time?" Marianna asked.

"It depends on how quickly the lawyers prepare the papers. It takes time to arrange this much financing."

She rested her head on his shoulder. "Hurry back."

"I will think of you every night," Carlos said, and kissed her softly.

Tico was waiting on the patio. "Our people in Laredo think we should fly."

"And what do you think?" Carlos asked.

"With the situation in Nuevo Laredo…I think we should fly."

Carlos nodded. "That situation is under control, though? We are making progress?"

"Si, señor."

"Good. We cannot afford to lose control. Nuevo Laredo is the busiest border crossing for trucks."

"Si, señor. We know that."

Carlos fixed him with a hard look. "I know you *know* that, Tico. I'm reminding you. Whoever controls Nuevo Laredo makes a lot more money. Texas is home to six of the top twenty cities in the country. That's a lot of product, my friend."

Roberto brought the car to the gate. Chaparrito got out of the front seat and opened the door for Carlos. "*Buenos días, señor.*"

"English, Chappo. Practice your English."

"Good morning, Señor Carlos," Chappo said in a thick accent.

"Much better," Carlos said. "Keep practicing."

Roberto drove the speed limit all the way to the airport, something Carlos insisted on. Tico and Chappo were in the back seat. Carlos sat in the passenger seat and glanced through the rear-view mirror at Tico. "Tell me one more time about the Houston situation."

"Coming along," Tico said. "San Antonio and Austin are good. The Dominicans are giving us trouble in Dallas."

Carlos leaned to his left and turned to face Tico. He wore a smile. "You already told me about San Antonio and Austin. And I know about the Dominicans in Dallas. I asked about Houston?"

"Many small gangs moved in when we lost control. It has been more difficult than we thought to regain that territory."

Carlos lost his smile. "Is the new distribution not going well?"

"Si, señor, it is. But we have more than distribution problems in Houston. The new product needs protection."

"Do we still have friends in the department?" Carlos asked.

"Si."

"Use them. Tighten the grip. And find more cops who are vulnerable. Before this is over, we'll need a lot more."

Chapter 3

A Rectal Affair

Houston, Texas

Forrest Lipscomb finished typing the email to his partner, straightened the papers on his desk, and grabbed his suit jacket from the coat rack behind the door. He loosened the knot on his baby-blue Kiton tie as he closed the door to his office.

"Goodnight, Mr. Lipscomb," Gretchen said, as he passed her station. "Have a good evening."

"Thank you. It will be a short one." He wondered why Gretchen worked so late. She was too old for affairs. Not even his partners would stoop that low, except maybe Griffin. Lipscomb almost laughed at the thought of her with Griffin, but he chased that image away and punched the button to call the elevator. There were more important things to consider—like whether he should go to his apartment and work, or go to the bar and find a willing, nubile partner.

The elevator door opened. Lipscomb got in and rode it down, non-stop for 25 floors. He walked outside, and dialed his wife while a parking attendant went for his car.

"What is it, Forrest?"

Her voice betrayed her breach of sobriety. "I was just checking on you, dear. Are you all right?"

"And if I'm not? Will you rush home to care for me?" Her laughter answered her own question. "Go ahead and screw someone. I won't mind."

A short pause, then, "That *is* why you're calling isn't it? To make sure I'm here, and to ease your conscience?"

Lipscomb closed his eyes and sighed. "I was calling to say goodnight."

"Now you've said it. Please resist the urge to call me after your romp. I'll be asleep."

The line went dead, and he wished for the millionth time Margaret had gone with it.

Lipscomb drove down Texas Avenue to a jazz bar he frequented. He hated jazz, but it drew the right kind of women, the young horny ones looking for a more *mature* companion, preferably one with money. It drew some of the over-the-hill hard-drinking, chain-smoking women too, but those he didn't care about. Once a woman hit her early twenties, her skin started down that inevitable road to wrinkling. It was all bad news after that.

Lipscomb pulled to the curb in front of the club, and had an attendant park the car. Then he went inside, straightening his collar as he tipped the doorman.

A blaring sound from a trumpet sent a shiver up his spine. It reminded him of Margaret's whining, nagging voice. He prayed he found a girl quickly, as he didn't know if he could take a whole night of this noise.

"Good evening, sir. Would you like a table?"

Lipscomb shook his head, never bothering to make eye contact. "I'll sit at the bar." He should have added, *like I always do,* but he kept that thought to himself and made his way across the room.

The bar seated about twenty people, and there were five open spots toward the right side. He took the third seat from the end, next to a half-full strawberry daiquiri with a straw peeking over the rim. *Has to be a woman.*

He ordered a glass of pinot noir and waited. Before long a woman plopped on the seat in front of the drink. Her perfume carried the sweet smell of lilacs. She set her purse on the bar, took a sip of the drink, then looked at her cell phone as if it would speak to her.

Someone stood her up. Perfect! And she was exactly Forrest's type—perfectly tanned, smooth complexion, short dark hair, and most important of all—young.

She punched a text out on her phone then held it in her left hand. After a few minutes—and numerous glances at her phone—she set the phone down, put her gorgeous lips around the straw and sucked the last of the daiquiri from her glass. A nod of her head signaled the bartender for a refill.

Better and better, Lipscomb thought, and cast a sideways glance at her legs. When she shifted in the seat the skirt rode up toward her ass. He quickly shifted his gaze, not wanting to be caught staring. The last thing a woman wanted was to be ogled, or so they said. *They should think of that before undoing the top three buttons of their blouses.* He risked another glance to her tits, and sighed.

Lipscomb watched for more than half an hour, nursing his own drinks while she put down two more. She checked her phone one more time, then stuffed it into her purse with a finality that said she'd given up. The problem was Lipscomb hadn't made a move, and she looked ready to leave.

The bartender was in front of her. Lipscomb saw his chance. "Give me one more glass before I go. Looks like she's not showing."

"You got it," the bartender said.

Lipscomb focused on not looking directly at her, not wanting her to see his desperation. She placed a few bills on the counter and turned in his direction.

"Me too," she said.

Lipscomb hid his smile. Twisted in his seat and stared at her, as if seeing her for the first time. "Pardon me?"

"I said, 'me too.' I heard you say someone didn't show. I was waiting for someone who didn't show."

Lipscomb shook his head. "Guess it's a bad night all the way around."

"Guess so," she said, and started to leave. She stopped a few feet away. "Shit!"

"What's the matter?" Forrest asked.

She turned to the bartender. "Can you call me a cab?"

Lipscomb couldn't believe his luck. "I'm leaving in a minute. If you need a ride, I'll drop you off."

She looked at him, perhaps sizing him up. "I don't know…" Just then her phone rang. She looked at the caller ID, then, "Andy, where the hell are you? I've been waiting forever."

She turned away from Lipscomb and whispered into the phone, "I almost had to catch a ride from a stranger.

"No, a guy I met." She laughed, then, "Yes, Andy, he's cute."

More laughter. "No way." Then she turned to Lipscomb. "My friend wants to know…" she broke into embarrassed laughter and put the phone to her ear again. "No way I'm asking that."

Lipscomb shook his head and started to leave, but she grabbed his arm. "Wait." She giggled, then, "My friend wants to know if you like threesomes."

Lipscomb kept his smile, but inside he was seething. Just his damn luck. "No thanks. Maybe another time."

She smiled at him and struck a sexy pose. "Two of us too much to handle?"

"Not that," Forrest said. "I'm not into guys."

She grabbed Forrest's hand. "Andy is short for Andrea. And trust me, she's *definitely* not a guy."

Lipscomb's genuine smile returned. "In that case…"

She held out her hand. "I'm Sahrina."

He shook her hand. "Forrest Lipscomb."

"Forrest? I like that name." She looked at him for a moment then said, "Do you dance? There's a club not far from here."

She took him by surprise with that question. "I…uh…"

"Oh, the hell with it." Sahrina leaned close and whispered, "Do you want to just cut straight to the night of wild sex?"

Lipscomb almost fell down. "Yes," he said. "A lot more than dancing." He reached for money to pay the tab.

"There's a hotel a few blocks from here," she said. "I'll have Andy meet us there."

Lipscomb went back and laid a fifty on the bar, then walked with her to the door. "Hotel it is," he said, and handed his parking stub to an attendant.

Ten minutes later they arrived at the Four Seasons Hotel. "There she is," Sahrina said to Forrest.

She approached a blonde waiting outside the entrance. "Andy, I can't believe you're here already."

Andy hugged her. "I was only a couple of minutes away when I called."

Sahrina took her hand and turned toward Forrest. "This is my friend, Andy. Andy, this is Forrest Lipscomb."

Lipscomb couldn't keep his eyes off her. She wasn't his type, but she *was* sexy. "Nice to meet you, Andy."

"Same here," she said, and then she held up a small brown bag with a recognizable red label.

"Is that what I think it is?" Sahrina asked.

"Baccardi 151," Andy said. "We might be staying the night."

Sahrina laughed, and said, "Why don't you two check in. I have *got to* run to the bathroom."

***

Sahrina made sure to steer clear of the surveillance as she made her way to the ladies' room. She pushed the bathroom door open with her foot, glanced around to make sure no one was inside, then set her purse on the counter and unzipped a side compartment. Inside lay two vials, each one contained 200 milligrams of sildenafil, enough to keep Mr. Lipscomb stiff for a long time. In the second compartment were enough *poppers* to get him started.

For back up, a syringe lay tucked into the back, wrapped in a small leather pouch. She pulled it out and checked it, holding it up to the light, then withdrew 20 milliliters of potassium chloride. She didn't want to use potassium chloride, but if necessary she would. After replacing the cap on the syringe, she put it back inside the leather pouch and set it inside the compartment of her purse. Then she waited.

Within a few minutes, the door cracked open and Andy popped her head in. "We're ready."

Andy grabbed hold of one of Forrest's arms and led him to the elevator. Sahrina made certain to stay behind them, clear of the cameras.

Thirty minutes later, Lipscomb and Andrea had showered and were lying on the bed, naked.

Sahrina reached into her purse and tossed a few of the poppers to Andy. "Get started with these. I'm taking a shower, so start without me."

"What are those?" Lipscomb asked.

"Just a few poppers," Andy said. "You never used them?"

"Is it a drug? What does it do?"

Andy laughed. "No way. I don't do drugs. This is more like Viagra, but for both of us." She reached between his legs and rubbed. "Don't worry. In a few minutes, you'll be a super stud."

They inhaled the poppers, and then Lipscomb started kissing her back. "I don't know what I did to deserve this night, but if I find out I'll make sure to do it again."

"I'll let you know if I feel the same way when you're done."

"I guarantee satisfaction," Lipscomb said.

Andy turned her head and looked at him. "Then you better stop kissing my back, and start kissing my ass."

***

After Lipscomb satisfied her, Andy worked him hard. Three times, she brought him close to climaxing then eased off. The fourth time she let him explode.

Panting, Lipscomb rolled to the side. "Good God, you almost killed me."

"Almost?" Andrea let her hand slide down his stomach. She fondled him. "I must be losing my touch."

"Room for one more?" Sahrina asked.

"Plenty of room," Lipscomb said.

Sahrina handed a glass to Andy and one to Lipscomb. "I poured us all a refresher," she said, and downed the drink she held. Andy and Lipscomb followed suit.

"Damn! That's strong," Lipscomb said, and shook his head.

"Who wants another?" Sahrina asked.

"Not yet," Andy said. "Maybe after Forrest finishes what he promised." She reached to rub him, but he didn't respond. "I hope you're not worn out."

"Not by a long shot," he said.

After a few minutes, Forrest slowed down, and then he stopped.

"What's wrong?" Andy asked.

"I feel dizzy," he said. "Very dizzy."

"Maybe you should stop," Andy said.

Forrest sat on the edge of the bed, breathing quickly.

Andy sat beside him. "Are you okay?"

He put his hand to his chest. "I'm not sure. I feel kind of strange."

"It might have been the popper," Sahrina said, and handed him a glass of rum. "Take a drink. It will help."

"Are you sure?" Lipscomb asked.

She nodded. "I've seen it before. Take a few sips and see if it helps."

He seemed reluctant, but then he took one sip, and then another. And then he dropped the glass. "Goddamn!" he said, and fell to the floor, holding his chest and gasping for breath.

Andy knelt beside him. "Are you okay?" she asked, and then looked up at Sahrina. "Call 9-1-1."

Sahrina got on the floor next to him and felt for a pulse. Lipscomb appeared to have stopped breathing. "He's gone," she said.

Andy listened for a heartbeat. "Hurry up and call."

"I think he had a heart attack," Sahrina said.

"Oh my God. What did you give him?"

"Just a little Viagra."

Andy started for the phone but Sahrina stopped her. "Don't. We could be in trouble."

"We didn't do anything. We—"

Sahrina grabbed her and shook. "Didn't do anything? We're prostitutes, and we gave him Viagra. And now he's dead."

Andy grabbed her clothes and started dressing. "We've got to get out of here."

"Not before cleaning up," Sahrina said. She handed Andy a washcloth. "Wipe everything down out here. I'll get the glasses and the bathroom. Empty his pockets, and take his wallet."

Andy rifled through his pants. He had a few hundred in cash and a half a dozen credit cards in the wallet.

"On second thought, leave the wallet," Sahrina said. "We need to get out of here."

"I can't believe this is happening," Andy said.

"Get hold of yourself. You go down first. I'll follow. Wait for me in the car."

Sahrina waited for her to leave, and then wiped down the bathroom. She left a few spots where she knew Andy's prints would be. Afterward, she put on a blonde wig and sunglasses. Sahrina wiped the doorknob, took a final look at the room, making sure she didn't forget anything, then turned the "do not disturb" sign facing out. No sense in having him discovered too early. She rode the elevator down and waited until she saw a man in a suit leaving the hotel. She stepped in behind the man and walked out the door, careful to avoid cameras.

Andy was sitting in the car, shaking. "What are we going to do?"

"You'll have to clean out your apartment. Get everything you need for at least a week because you'll be staying with me for a while. At least until this blows over. Get your clothes, money, anything that you would take on a trip. And don't tell anyone. Just pack up and leave."

Chapter 4

A FRIENDLY VISIT

Houston, Texas

Tip finished his cereal, strained the teabags, and added a spoonful of sugar to his cup of tea. Some mornings he had coffee, but on days like today, days when he had serious thinking to do, he preferred tea. Flash nudged his leg and gave Tip a few of her mandatory good-morning barks, and then Sacco, the new dog, joined in. His bark was deeper but he only barked once.

"Hey, Flash. Morning, Sacco. How are my best dogs this morning?"

Flash barked a few more times, and then her lips curled up in a snarl.

"I hear you, girl," Tip said, and then he let them outside before sitting down with his tea.

It had been six months since he helped Gino with the kidnapping case, but no matter what Tip tried, he couldn't clear his mind of Ed Harbough, the scum-sucking son of a bitch who more than likely had a lead on who killed Tip's mother. Gino had Harbough dead to rights, too, and he hadn't even given Tip a shot at breaking the guy. In hindsight, it was probably a good thing. Tip might have killed Harbough if he hadn't given up the information. Now Harbough was safe—at least from Tip—tucked away in a cell at Huntsville.

Tip grabbed his phone and dialed the first six numbers of Gino's cell, like he'd done a hundred times since that last case. Tip's finger hovered over the last digit for what seemed like a minute. "Fuck it," Tip said, and punched the number.

"Cataldi."

"I need to know what the fuck Harbough told you, and I need it now."

"Good morning, Tip."

"It's *not* a good morning."

"You know I wouldn't mess with you on something like this. Harbough didn't tell me anything. *Niente. Nada. Nothing.* Did that sink through your thick head in any language."

"You had him for twenty minutes and you didn't get anything? I'd have—"

"Tip! Are you listening? I told you before, I wasn't grilling Harbough about your mother's case. I had a kidnapping to solve. We had a girl missing. *That* was my focus."

There was silence, then Gino said, "What's going on? What got you thinking about it again?"

"I haven't stopped thinking about it. I'm going up to Huntsville, and I plan on getting something out of that son of a bitch."

"Let me know if I can do anything. I'm tied up on a strange case now, but when I finish I'll have time to help you."

"All right. Thanks."

Tip hung up and headed to his car. Huntsville was about 50 miles from his house. He'd be there in an hour.

Once Tip got on the freeway, he dialed Connie's number. She answered right away.

"What's going on, girl? It's been a while."

"Been a while? You pester me every week."

"Are you ready to come home?"

"In case you forgot, Texan, I *am* home."

"Nah, you're a Texan now. You don't know it yet, but you are."

Connie laughed. "Whatever you say."

"By the way, Gianelli, you still got that crooked nose?"

"It's not crooked. It's a little bump."

"Same thing," Tip said.

"If you ever wonder why you're not married yet, it might be your idea of sweet talk and flattery."

"I've heard it all before," Tip said.

"How's your new partner working out," Connie asked.

"You mean Gino? I got rid of him. He was a damn troublemaker."

"*He* was a troublemaker? Somehow I don't believe that."

"He got me a lead on my mama's case. In fact, I'm on my way to check on it."

"Tell me about it," Connie said.

"Gino found a guy who might know something. And it ties in with a few other leads I had. Reliable leads."

Connie was silent for a moment, then, "Now I wish I *was* there with you."

"Plane flight's only a few hours. I'll wait."

"Fill me in on what you find out. You never know, I might decide to come down."

"All right. See ya'."

Half an hour later Tip exited the freeway and pulled into the prison. He'd called ahead of time and let the warden know he was coming. They were old friends. Tip checked in both of his guns, his cell phone, and a wad of cash big enough to bribe a guard or two, if it came to that.

The guard recording the items looked at him. "Still the Tipster, huh?"

"Guess so," Tip said.

By the time Tip got to the holding cell Ed Harbough was waiting, sitting at the table like a real human being, as if he belonged or had a right to. He kept his eyes focused on the table in front of him. A bottle of water sat to his right.

"Mind giving us a few minutes?" Tip asked the guard.

The guard cleared the room, locking the door behind him. Tip pulled up a chair and sat across from Harbough. "You remember me?"

Harbough looked up. His eyes opened wide, then his head darted from side to side. "Where're the guards?"

"Where I told them to go," Tip said.

Harbough stood and smacked his hand on the table. "Guard!"

"Sit down," Tip said. "I'm not keeping you here, but if you leave you better watch your back, or should I say your *ass* from now on."

Harbough took another look at Tip before sitting. "What do you want?"

"Information. If you tell me what I need, I can do you some good."

"What kind of good?"

"I know it can't be easy for you, being an ex-cop in prison. Gotta be a lot of guys waiting to shiv you just to start their day off."

Harbough scoffed. "What're you gonna do about it? Get me out?"

Tip shook his head. "I can't do that, but I might be able to make it easier for you." He looked around, leaned close and whispered, "Me and the warden go way back. We shared six nasty months together on the East Side, patrolling Mexican gangs in the Navigation area. So the way I figure it is this, I can either whisper suggestions to some of the Mexican Mafia, or I can talk to the warden about putting you in protective custody."

"I'm already scheduled for that," Harbough said.

Tip laughed. "Yeah, I hear you. But there are different levels of *protective*. I think you know what I mean."

Ed Harbough didn't take long to decide. "How's this going to work? I tell you something and you get me moved?"

Tip shook his head. "You tell me everything. If it checks out, *then* I get you moved. I only have one favor to call in. If I move you once, I won't be able to do it again, so whatever you tell me better be good."

"It'll be good."

"Remember, if it doesn't check out, I practice my Spanish."

Harbough looked around the cell again, his eyes shifty and filled with fear. He started to talk, checked the cell again, then leaned close and whispered, "You're looking for a guy named 'The Ranger.'"

Tip scoffed. "Shit, I already knew that. I need something new. Who paid him, and why?"

Harbough slapped his hand on the table again. "Listen, I'm telling you what I know. Don't fuck with me on this."

A guard poked his head in. "Everything all right?"

"We're good," Tip said, then he turned to Harbough. "Go on. I'm listening."

"I don't know who wanted her dead, and I don't know why, but whoever it was had money. From what I heard the Ranger was paid fifty thousand to do her."

"Bullshit!"

"I'm telling you, Denton. Fifty grand."

"Who would pay that kind of money to kill a waitress?"

"I have no idea who'd pay that kind of money, or even who wanted her dead. Are you gonna listen to the rest or not?"

Tip set his elbows on the table and leaned in close. "Go on."

"I got called to the scene. I thought it was odd because it wasn't my rotation, but I did what I was told. When I showed up, I found the fake ranger badge."

Tip knew the stories. Any cop who'd been in Houston more than ten years had heard them. The brass tried to hide the stories now, but you can't hide a legend. And if one thing was true, the Ranger was a legend. His case file took up a whole drawer. It was a case that every cop dreamed of solving even though deep inside they were probably scared shitless. Tip didn't blame them. If the tales were to be believed, the Ranger killed anywhere from 20-50 people and nobody had a clue who he was.

Tip looked Harbough square in the eyes. "You find the badge under the body or beside it?"

Harbough took a sip of water, and then wiped his mouth. "Under it."

Tip nodded. The Ranger always left the badge under the bodies. "What else?"

Harbough looked around the room again, eyes darting toward the door and then the corners.

"Nobody's here," Tip said, "and nobody's listening. It's just you and me."

"I was told to keep it quiet." Harbough whispered this.

"Keep what quiet? Who told you?"

"They told me not to put the Ranger in the report."

Tip's heart beat faster. This was more than he'd gotten in all his years of searching. "Who told you?"

Harbough looked at Tip and cocked his head. "You're getting me transferred, right?"

"I said I would."

"It was my captain, Henry Richardson."

Tip closed his eyes for a second and squeezed his fists together. "What'd he tell you? Exactly."

"He said 'write up the report exactly as it is,' and then he grabbed me by the collar and pulled me close, and he said, 'but leave out any mention of the Ranger.'"

"Why?"

Harbough shook his head. "No idea."

"You didn't ask?" Tip said.

"Denton, you don't know what it was like back then. Things were different. If your captain said to forget something, you forgot it."

"What else?"

"That's it," Harbough said. "That's all I know."

"What about the money?" Tip asked.

When Harbough didn't answer, Tip asked again. "Let's get back to the money, Harbough. Who would pay fifty thousand to kill a waitress? It doesn't make sense."

"I agree. It doesn't," Harbough said. "Maybe she was more than a waitress."

The *way* Harbough said it implied more than the words said. Tip hit him—hard. Knocked him off the chair onto the floor.

"Guard. Guard!" Harbough curled up, his arms protecting his face.

The door burst open and two guards rushed in. "This maniac is trying to kill me," Harbough said.

Tip straddled Harbough and hit him.

One of the guards grabbed Tip by the arm. "You need to go, Officer."

"We have a deal, Denton," Harbough said. Tip didn't answer so Harbough yelled louder. "Denton, you hear me? We got a deal, right?"

Tip turned when he got to the door. "You'll get your deal. I gave my word on that."

Tip made arrangements with the warden to have Harbough put into protective custody at the highest level. He told the warden that besides being an ex-cop, he might be a witness in another murder. "I need him alive. Transfer him to the safest prison and keep him safe. I'll have more questions for him later." Tip looked at the warden. "Do this and we're even."

Twenty minutes later Tip was heading south on I-45, thinking through all that he'd learned. It wasn't much but it confirmed the lead he'd gotten from Cybil. Every little bit helped. He made a few voice notes on his phone and thought about how he could move forward on this. It would take an hour to get back to Houston; he had time to kill.

As he drove through Conroe, the phone rang. Caller ID showed it was Captain Gladys "Coop" Cooper, scourge of the Houston Police Department.

"Denton, where the hell are you? I've been trying to reach you for an hour."

"Sorry, Coop. I'm up near Huntsville. Must have had bad reception."

"Huntsville? What are you doing up there?"

"Felt like going for a drive."

Cooper was silent for a few seconds. "A drive? To Huntsville?"

"Scenery's great up here. They even have hills."

"I don't have time to figure out what line of shit you're giving me, or why, so just get back to civilization and find out why a poor middle-aged male is dead in a room at the Four Seasons."

"Four Seasons? Dead or not, at least he went out in style."

"Just get there," Coop said.

"On my way, Cap. And don't think I'm ungrateful, but the least you could've done was given me a female body. I hate looking at dead guys."

"You're a pervert," Coop said.

"I know, but it's fun. Besides, I was beginning to feel like I wasn't needed anymore."

"Get down there quick," Coop said. "I'll pair you up with Branch."

"Like hell. I have a partner." When Coop didn't say anything, Tip said, "We know who the body is yet?"

"He's a lawyer, so we'll be getting press. And I hate to tell you this, Tip, but we haven't enabled our long-distance homicide investigation, so Connie Gianelli is out of the question as your partner."

"How about Gino?"

"Busy."

"Give me Delgado then."

Long pause. "He's on a case…"

"It can't be that important if you put Delgado on it, and it's only until Gianelli gets back."

"When are you going to realize she's not coming back?"

Tip was silent. Coop sighed. "I'll see how busy Delgado is."

Tip hung up and dialed the phone.

"Gianelli."

"How cold is it up there?"

"What are you doing calling again. And why are you asking about the weather?"

"Just wanted to let you know that on this fine November day it'll hit 70 degrees down here in Houston. Sun's shining. No clouds in the sky."

"And I'm sure the birds are singing and money is falling like raindrops. Didn't we just talk a few hours ago?"

"Did we?" Tip said.

Connie sighed. "What do you need?"

"I need help."

"You mean you finally caught a case."

"The captain just called with a body. A lawyer, for God's sake. It doesn't get much better."

"Can't argue that."

"Are you comin' down?"

Connie didn't answer.

"Well? Are you comin' or not?" Tip asked.

"I don't suppose you've got any friends who have apartments open?"

"No, but you can sleep with me and Elena."

Connie laughed. "Go to hell."

"I miss hearing you laugh," Tip said.

"All right, for God's sake. It'll take me a few days to get there. I have to pack and I'll need to drive down so I have a car."

"Like hell. Pack a few things and get a flight. You can go back later and get your car. I'll even go with you."

Connie laughed again. "All right, you made up my mind. I laughed twice talking to you and that's more than in the last month."

"I can't wait," Tip said.

"I'll call with the flight information as soon as I get it," Connie said. "See you soon."

"See you, Gianelli. You better hurry or I'll finish the case without you."

Chapter 5

A Legal Corpse

Tip exited the freeway into downtown Houston and headed to the Four Seasons. The last time he was here it was to listen to a speech by some bigwig. He parked and headed inside, making his way to the sixth floor. Detective Hector "Ribs" Delgado was pacing the hall in front of room #614.

"Tip, what are you doing here? I thought I was getting a real partner."

"Go to hell. But first tell me what we've got. I heard it's a lawyer."

Delgado lowered his head and shook it, a grim expression on his face. "Not good, amigo. You know I don't like lawyers, but this...nobody should go like he did."

Tip pushed him aside. He walked in the room, nodded to one of the medical examiner's assistants, and made his way toward the bed. "Ben, what's it look like? Delgado said we got a nasty one."

Ben Marsh, the M.E. turned around. "Nasty? Looks like a heart attack if you ask me."

Delgado was already laughing when Tip looked at him. He shot Delgado an I'll-get-you-back glare and turned to Ben. "Are you sure? The guy's a lawyer; that gives us plenty of suspects with motive."

"As much as you want to make this a murder, I'm tempted to say this is a case of a man having too much fun and suffering the consequences of an unhealthy lifestyle." Ben lowered his head and looked at Tip over the rim of his glasses. "You know what I mean?"

"You can go to hell with Delgado."

Delgado stepped up alongside Tip. "You didn't ask the big question. *Who* was he having fun with?"

"Who was it?" Tip asked.

Delgado shook his head. "Not yet, but Officer Griggs said the clerk saw the guy checking in with a blonde. A young blonde. And the concierge said he thinks he's seen her here before, but not with Lipscomb. He thinks she's a pro."

"Lipscomb? That's his name?"

"Forrest Lipscomb," Delgado said.

Tip stepped to the side, where the victim's clothes lay. "This wasn't a sheister," he said. "This suit cost a fortune."

"Everything about the guy screams money," Delgado said. "It was probably a high-end hooker, too."

"We need to get surveillance from—"

"Already ordered it."

"Okay, good," Tip said, then to Ben, "What's the TOD?"

"Best guess is about 10 last night."

Tip looked at his watch. "Four o'clock. Why are we just hearing about this?"

"Whoever his companion was put the 'Do not disturb' sign on the door when she left. Probably to give her time to disappear."

"Did she take his wallet?"

"She left his wallet, including credit cards and license. And his cell phone," Delgado said. "I have the phone records being checked."

"I'm guessing a guy like this must have had cash with him," Tip said. "Which means somebody's having a party."

"Or buying a bus ticket to Atlanta."

"Atlanta?"

Delgado shrugged. "It's the first city I thought of."

"I hate working with you," Tip said.

Ben plucked a few hairs from the pillow case and the sheet and placed them in an evidence bag. "While you boys are arguing, you might like to know that your vic had sex with *someone* last night. And she didn't bother to clean up. Oh, and she *was* blonde, as the hotel clerk said."

"So she didn't clean up but she was smart enough to not want the body found right away." Tip tapped the uni on the arm. "Griggs, get a picture of her from the cameras, see if the concierge knows anything about her, and then grab a couple of helpers and head down to Main Street. Let's see if we can find Little Miss Prostitute."

"That's why people love you," Ben said. "You're so…warm hearted."

Tip laughed. "You know we're going to need the DNA on the girl as soon as you can. If she's a pro we'll probably find a match in the system."

"We might not need to wait on DNA. It looks like we have a few prints. She tried to wipe them away but missed some. She might be a pro at something, but not cleaning up a crime scene."

"Don't forget to turn off the lights when you leave," Tip said, and headed for the door.

"Are you going somewhere?" Ben asked.

"I guess we gotta tell this guy's wife or kids, or somebody."

"It's a wife," Delgado said. "Coop texted me the information."

"Texted *you*? You mean even Coop doesn't love me?"

Delgado headed for the door. "Let's go, temporary partner. But I'm driving."

"Ben, call if anything changes on your report," Tip said, and then he followed Delgado out the door.

"Doesn't your car go faster than 70?" Tip asked.

"If I pressed harder on the gas it would, but I don't see the need. I'm not in a hurry, amigo."

"Would you cut with the 'amigo' shit. I'm beginning to wonder if you're even Mexican. I think you're faking it."

"Why would someone fake being Mexican?" Delgado asked.

"I don't have the answer to that, but if anyone would fake it, it'd be you."

"Where does this *gringo* woman live?" Delgado couldn't hold in his laughter when he said it. Tip joined him.

"I'm glad my real partner's coming back. I'd hate to be stuck with you."

"Don't lie," Delgado said. "We shook the world on that last case."

"I don't know if we shook the world," Tip said, "but we scared the hell out of some white-collar criminals."

Delgado laughed again. "That we did, my friend. Now tell me where I'm going before we get to Dallas."

"Exit at Cypresswood. It's not far from there."

Delgado exited the freeway and headed west on Cypresswood. About six miles later he turned into one of the upscale neighborhoods and made his way to the Lipscomb house.

"Nice house," Tip said. "If the lady who answers is young and blonde we might have a case."

The lady who answered the door was middle aged, with dyed brown hair—from the looks of it—and jewelry dangling from all the normal spots.

"May I help you?" she asked.

Tip bowed his head a little. "Ma'am, I'm Detective Denton and this is Detective Delgado. Would it be—"

"Has something happened to Forrest?"

"Would it be all right if we came in, ma'am?"

She stepped aside, letting the door swing open. "I assume by your demeanor and the way you answered, that Forrest is dead."

Tip didn't know whether to reach for her and offer support or ask her if she did it. "Maybe we should sit."

"If you insist," she said, and led them into a formal living room. "I assume you don't drink on the job so I won't tempt you. Would you care for tea or coffee."

"No thanks," they both said.

She sat on the edge of a small sofa that appeared to be as rigid as she was, and reached for a half-empty glass of what looked to be scotch. She focused on Tip. "Well, get on with it. Is he dead?"

Tip searched for the right words, but then realized it probably wouldn't matter. He looked her in the eyes, and said, "Yes, ma'am. I'm afraid he is. He was found this afternoon."

She raised herself up a little straighter, and nodded.

Delgado said, "Would you like us to call someone, ma'am? A relative or friend?"

Mrs. Lipscomb took a sip from her glass and shook her head. "I'll be fine, Detective. And as I'm sure you can tell, this is not a shock to me. I am curious, though. How did he die?"

Tip leaned forward a little. "It appears to be a heart attack."

"Was he found in a hotel room or his apartment?"

Delgado cleared his throat. "The Four Seasons, ma'am."

She gave another nod. "He liked them young. That's what attracted him. He stopped caring for me years ago." She held out her arm. "As you can see, my skin isn't smooth anymore. Once the wrinkles set in, Forrest was gone. He would barely hold my hand."

"When was the last time you spoke with your husband?" Tip asked.

"Last night," she said, and paused to think. "I don't remember the time exactly. It was sometime after 8 and certainly before midnight. I'm sure if you check his cell phone you'll have the time."

"He called you?"

She laughed. "Yes, Detective. He called me every time he was going to be with another woman. I'm sure a psychiatrist could find a deeper meaning in it, but it never fooled me. Not even the first time."

"You think he was with another woman?" Tip asked.

"I *know* he was. And she would have been young. Maybe that's what killed him, trying to keep up with...whoever she was."

"Do you have any idea—"

"...who it might be?" she asked. "No. And I don't care." She took two swigs from her glass and stood. "And now, Detectives, if you'll excuse me, I have a funeral to prepare."

"Yes, ma'am," Tip said, then he and Delgado followed her to the door.

Delgado headed back down Cypresswood Drive toward the freeway. "I think we about wrapped that up."

"I'd like to talk to that prostitute," Tip said.

"*Corpus delecti,*" Delgado said.

"What kind of garbage are you spitting out now?"

"No garbage. *Corpus delecti.* It means you can't try a person for a crime unless you can prove a crime has been committed. I don't see a crime here."

"Don't think you fooled me with that bit of wisdom, Delgado. I know you've probably had that memorized for years, just waiting to use it."

While Delgado laughed, Tip cracked his knuckles. He intended to find out whether somebody killed this guy on purpose.

And that prostitute is the key.

Chapter 6

PRINTED MONEY

Delgado's phone rang as he neared the exit. "It's Coop," he said to Tip, and put it on speaker. "*No hablo ingles.*"

"Delgado, I don't have time for your shit," Coop said. "This is why I didn't want you and Denton working together."

"What's up, Cap?"

"I'm getting pressure on the sticker investigation. It's not just a matter of money anymore; we've got a guy in intensive care that might not make it, and we found boxes of stickers in his apartment."

"Territory dispute?" Delgado asked.

"Right now that's all we know. Finish up whatever you're doing with Tip and get back on it. The Chief approved the budget. And we need somebody who speaks Spanish."

"Who do I get to work with?"

"Take your pick—Rodriguez, Hernandez, Cruz…"

"Okay," Delgado said. "I'll let you know. We're on our way."

"Tell Tip to see me when he gets in."

"Leaving me in the cold, darlin'?" Tip asked.

"I talked to Ben. How much help do you need to investigate a heart attack?"

"We don't know what killed him yet, and besides, Gianelli's coming down."

"You better get clearance," Cooper said.

"John already okayed it."

"Stop calling him John. He's the Chief of Detectives."

"I know who he is, Cap, but his name *is* John."

"I'm hanging up," Coop said. "See me when you get in."

"See ya', Cap," Tip said, and then to Delgado. "What's this about a sticker investigation?"

"Bunch of crazy fucks counterfeiting inspection stickers for cars. Not to say we don't need a criminal enterprise like that; damn stickers are expensive."

"Can I quote you on that?" Tip asked.

"You heard it first from Ribs Delgado."

"That's sure to impress the media," Tip said, and then, "What's the big deal with the stickers? Why the heat now?"

"It wasn't a big deal until somebody realized they're making millions. Now our good mayor is going nuts. That man hates to lose tax revenue."

"I'm sure he does," Tip said. "It leaves him less to spend on whores."

"You're right about that," Ribs said, as he came to a stop at a traffic signal. "Is your old partner really coming back, or did you say that to taunt Coop?"

"She told me this morning she was. I'm waiting on her to call with flights."

"How did you get that cleared?"

"John's been working on it for a while. She impressed him on that last case."

"Speaking of that case, how's she dealing with things?"

"I don't know," Tip said. "She's not much for talking about personal issues, but I'm guessing she's all right. She's a tough one."

"And how about you?" Delgado asked. "Have you forgiven yourself?"

Tip pressed his forehead against the side window and stared at traffic. "I'm still thinking on that. I should've put that case together sooner. I shouldn't have missed those clues."

Delgado nodded, and then focused on driving.

A few minutes later Tip's phone rang. He listened for a few seconds, wrote something down in his notepad, and then said, "I'll pick you up at baggage."

Ribs looked over at Tip. "I guess she's coming."

"Tomorrow morning," Tip said. "It'll be good to have her back."

Delgado pulled into the station and parked.

"Are you going to see Coop right now?" Tip asked.

"She'll have my ass if I don't."

"Tell her I'll be by later, or else in the morning. I gotta find a place for Connie to stay."

"You got it, Tip. See you later."

***

Captain Cooper was sitting behind the desk when Delgado walked in. "You wanted to see me, Coop?"

She took off her glasses, rubbed her eyes, and said, "Have you thought about who you want with you on this?"

"Not Rodriguez; she'd get me killed in an undercover situation. I think I'll take Cruz."

Coop nodded. "He's good. And he knows the streets."

Delgado sat in the chair across from her. "Tell me what's going on."

She opened a folder and set six inspection stickers on her desk. "Point out the fakes."

He stood, looked down on them, moved a few around. Walked to the side to get a different angle. "Damned if I can tell. These guys should be working on fifties or hundreds, not inspection stickers."

"They're playing it smart," Coop said. "If they get caught counterfeiting money it's a federal offense."

"From what I've seen it's going to be tough finding a jury where half of them don't have these stickers on their cars."

"Exactly," Coop said, and pointed to a stack of boxes sitting on the floor.

"Are they filled with stickers?"

"To the brim," Coop said.

Delgado whistled long and low. "That's a lot of money."

"A lot," she said. "They found them in the apartment of Edward Martin, who is now recovering at Hermann Hospital."

"Does Martin have a sheet?"

"He's clean. And I suspect his real name is more like Eduardo Martinez, seeing as he doesn't speak English. Or at least he says he doesn't."

Delgado looked at the stickers on the desk again. "I guess you want me to go beat it out of him while he's in ICU."

Coop laughed. "That's exactly what I *want* you to do, but since we can't…how about you find Cruz and go speak to Mr. Martin in his native language. See what you can find out."

"We'll have this case solved in two days."

"You solve this in two weeks and I'll buy you dinner."

"Write that down, Cap. I'm gonna hold you to that promise."

"Where's Denton?"

"He said to tell you he'd be by later or in the morning. He's working on getting Connie a place to stay."

Coop put her glasses on and looked at Ribs. "Is she really coming down?"

"She called him half an hour ago."

Coop shook her head. "I wish somebody would fill me in on some of this shit."

"Go easy on Tip; he's got a soft shell."

"Get out of here, Delgado."

He grabbed one of the stickers from the desk and headed for the door.

"Where are you going with that?" Coop asked.

"Interrogation technique," he said. "And besides, Rosalee's car expires next month."

Coop threw a pen at him. "Call me when you get something," she said.

Delgado picked up Cruz and they went to the hospital. Edward Martin, or whatever he called himself, was awake but not willing to talk. Delgado and Cruz stood on opposite sides of the bed. "There's no sense in saying you don't speak English, Martin, because we both speak Spanish. One way or another, you're talking."

"*No hablo ingles*," Martin said.

"*Hablo español*," Cruz said, and leaned close to Martin's face. "I don't care what language you use, just start talking."

Martin stared at Cruz, then at Delgado. "I guess I'm fucked."

Delgado smiled. "I guess you are. So tell us who beat the shit out of you and left you for dead."

Martin shook his head in such a way that he didn't have to speak to get his message across.

"Somebody did this to you and you're protecting them?" Cruz said.

"Are you afraid?" Delgado asked. "We can get you protection."

Martin looked up. "There's nowhere to hide."

"Once they find out we got your stickers, they'll be back," Cruz said. "You know that, right?"

"They'll be back no matter what."

Delgado pulled a chair up close and sat. "Let us help you."

"Lawyer," Martin said.

"Do you have a lawyer?" Cruz asked.

Martin managed to shake his head. "Get me one."

Ribs headed for the door. "I'll tell you what, amigo. How about you get your own."

"Tell the nurse to get me a phone," Martin said.

A nurse greeted Delgado in the hall. "Did you get anything out of him?"

"Lawyer," Ribs said, and then hugged her. "How's my favorite cousin?"

"I'm fine, but I see you're still full of it. Or is everyone your favorite cousin?"

"Danette, this is my partner," Ribs said. "You can call him Cruz."

Danette shook hands with Cruz and then turned to Delgado. "I don't know if this means anything, but when he first came in he kept mumbling something. It sounded like he was saying '*El Terrible*.'"

"*El Terrible*? You're sure?"

"I'm positive. I remember thinking, he's right. Whoever did this to him must have been a terrible person."

Ribs shot a glance at Cruz. "Does that mean anything to you?"

Cruz shook his head. "I never heard the name, but I'll ask around."

Delgado kissed Danette on the cheek. "Tell that no good husband I said, hi."

"Say hi to Rosalee," Danette said, and walked down the hall.

"Come on," Delgado said to Cruz. "There's a waiting room down the hall."

"I'm getting coffee," Cruz said. "You want any?"

"Hang on and I'll go with you. I need to call Tip first." Delgado punched in the number and waited for Tip to answer. "Did you find a place for Connie yet?"

"Still looking."

"Don't be trying to sneak her into your house. I'll tell Elena."

"I bet you would too. Jealous shit."

"Tip, have you ever heard anybody mention a person named *El Terrible?*"

"No. Why?"

"We've got a guy down here in ICU. He's probably on his way to the morgue but he won't talk. One of the nurses said when they brought him in he kept mumbling about *El Terrible*, but he hasn't said shit since. Except 'lawyer.'"

"That figures."

"Just thought I'd check. Hope you get a case soon."

"At least I don't have Cruz as a partner."

"I heard that, Denton," Cruz said.

"Imagine that, and I didn't even say it in Spanish."

"See you later," Delgado said. "I gotta call Coop."

Cindy answered. "Captain Cooper's office."

"Is Coop busy?"

"She has people with her. You want to leave a message?"

"Tell her we're at the hospital but Martin lawyered up."

"I'll tell her."

"Thanks, Cindy, and will you transfer me to Julie?"

"Detective Hector Delgado," she said, "What can I do for you?"

"If I didn't know better I'd swear you had Tip Denton behind you writing down what you should say."

Julie laughed. "What's up, Ribs?"

"See if you can find anyone who goes by the name, *El Terrible*? Check local, but check the FBI, and even international, especially Mexico."

"What have you got?"

"Probably nothing, but we have a guy in the hospital who came in mumbling something about *El Terrible*. I don't even know if it's a person but it's worth checking out."

"I'll get right on it."

"Thanks."

Delgado and Cruz got coffee, and then went to the waiting room and settled in. Cruz played video games on his phone while Ribs kicked his feet up on the chair beside him and tried to catch a nap. "Wake me if Martin's lawyer gets here," Ribs said.

Two hours later Delgado's phone rang. It was Julie. "You find something?"

"I hope you and Cruz are carrying a lot of ammo and wearing vests."

Ribs perked up. "Tell me."

"I found your friend, *El Terrible*. He's a hit man from Mexico, and from the reports I've seen so far, he's responsible for a lot of bodies. No one has ever had reports of him working on this side of the border though."

"Did you get anything solid on him? Name, pictures, description?"

"Nothing. Whoever this guy is, he's invisible. No one has ever seen him. Not even a glimpse."

"Shit! Gather up whatever you can find. I'll pick it up tomorrow."

"It'll be waiting for you on the desk."

Ribs filled Cruz in on what Julie said, then he stood and started toward ICU. "Let's go, Cruz. We need to see if we can get Señor Martin to talk."

The doctor was just leaving when Ribs and Cruz arrived. "How's he doing?" Ribs asked.

"Good improvement. He'll be hurting for a long time, but he should recover without major problems."

"Thanks," Ribs said, and they went to stand beside Martin.

"Lawyer get here yet?" Cruz asked.

"Who's *El Terrible*?" Ribs asked.

Martin's eyes opened wide. "I said I wanted a lawyer."

"I know that. And we're not asking you anything about the crime. I just want to know who he is. Is he the one who did this to you?"

Martin's face cracked into a smile. "If I had met *El Terrible*, I'd be dead. If I knew who he was, I'd be dead. If I say his name, I'll be dead. Get me a lawyer."

"Whoever did this to you isn't through. You know that, don't you?"

"You can leave, Detectives. I'm not talking."

Ribs shook his head. "Come on, Cruz. We're talking to a dead man."

Chapter 7

ANOTHER GOODBYE

Brooklyn, New York

Tip's call convinced me I was heading back to Texas, and I didn't even know why. I had no family there. No friends, except Tip. And the last time I was in Texas I'd damn near been killed.

Part of me was afraid to go back. Almost like Texas was the one that hurt me. I sighed. But it wasn't Texas that raped me, and I had to face that fact sooner rather than later. Uncle Dominic's lessons always mentioned facing your fears. This was a big one for me, and I felt certain that was why he wanted me to go back. He *knew* if I was ever going to be the old me, I'd have to scrape myself off the streets of Laredo, or in this case, Houston.

There were good things about Texas, too. No one whispered that I was dirty because of my association with Uncle Dominic. No one questioned my loyalty to the department. On one hand I didn't want to leave Brooklyn, but ever since the shooting in the alley—and the miraculous rescue by Dominic's friend, Manny—the whispers in the department had grown stronger than ever. Even after the "hero cop," Frankie Donovan, cleared my name.

And it wasn't like I didn't appreciate Dominic's protection. I did, but I couldn't take it. The whole mess was yet another reason why I couldn't consult a shrink. How the hell could a shrink understand what I was going through? I was a damn cop, and a mob boss had raised me.

I put on my jogging suit, grabbed my iPod and headphones, and headed to the park for a quick run. Running was my therapy. Sometimes I ran to relieve stress or get rid of anxiety about Uncle Dominic. At other times, like today, it was to clear my mind and help me think.

It didn't take more than a mile to confirm my feelings about going back, and once that was done I began making lists of things I had to do. I had to make arrangements for the apartment. I thought about writing Bon Jovi another letter. Yes, *another letter;* I wrote him once as a teenager. He probably had that letter tucked in the top drawer of his dresser, next to his underwear, waiting for his wife to leave him. I let that fantasy play out in my mind for about a mile, and then I returned to reality and headed for home. I had work to do.

I said goodbye to Uncle Dominic and Zeppe. It was more painful than I thought it would be, and more scary. The closer it got to me leaving, the more I realized I *was* afraid to go back. Dominic assured me that I needed to do this, but I could tell he was worried, too. He asked far too many questions—where I'd be staying, who I'd be partnered with, and what kind of neighborhood I'd be living in. I told him Houston was different than New York, but he didn't understand. He had lived here since he was a young boy; it was all he knew.

That night I arranged for Tariq and Marley to sublet my place. It was far better than the apartment they had, and I gave them a great deal on the rent. Besides, Tariq would take the fish, which solved another problem. I intended to leave Hotshot with Tariq but at the last minute I decided to take the cat. I figured as big as Texas was, it had room for a three-legged cat.

Before going to bed I packed a couple of suitcases, made yet another list for Tariq on how to feed the fish, and then called Tip to remind him what time to pick me up. He reminded me of how warm it still was down there—in the 70s, he said—and I shoved a few more summer clothes in the least-packed suitcase. I finally crawled into bed at 1:00.

***

I was waiting outside of the baggage area when Tip's SUV pulled up. He got out and gave me a big squeeze, damn near crushing me. This crazy Texan had no gentle side.

"Good to see you, partner."

"Same here," I said. "You find a place for me to stay?"

"I did, and it's nicer than what you had before, except it's not free."

"I didn't expect free. I'm just glad you found something because I brought my cat." I pointed to the carrier next to my bags. "Hotshot's his name."

Tip smiled. "I like that. It means you're planning on staying." He grabbed my bags and tossed them in the back of the car. "Put the cat in the back seat."

I climbed in and we headed out. "Where to?"

"Drop off your bags and the cat, and then we'll get you set up."

"I need to rent a car."

"No need to. You impressed John the last time you were here. He not only approved your duty, he got you a car."

"I assume you mean John Renkin, the new Chief of Police, the one who was our boss?"

"Yes, smart ass, *that* John Renkin, but that's a few too many names for me. I just call him John."

A warm feeling rushed through my veins and put a smile on my face. It was good to be back in Texas.

The *apartment* turned out to be a house that a friend of Tip's owned. The previous renters had moved out a few weeks before. It was a lot like Julie's house, a three-bedroom ranch with a fenced-in yard, and it sat near the front of a nice neighborhood with quick access to the main road. And all of this for less than half of what I was paying in Brooklyn.

It took us a couple of hours to get me settled—at least the basics—and then we were on the freeway heading downtown. "Do we have anything to work on?" I asked.

"We've got that brutal case I told you about."

"You mean the one that looks like a heart attack?"

Tip laughed. "That's the one. All we have to do now is find that serial-killer prostitute. At least until something better turns up. We'll check you in first, though. And introduce you to Captain Cooper and the rest of the crew."

"I heard Julie's with you."

"Fat Charlie, too. John brought us all over."

We arrived at the station in record time, even considering it was Tip driving. "This is a lot bigger," I said when he pulled up to the station.

"It's a whole lot bigger," Tip said. "I think we have 60-70 people in homicide."

I got the jitters as we walked in the station. This reminded me of Brooklyn, and anytime I thought of that I expected someone to question my loyalty to the badge, all because of Uncle Dominic. I shook my head. Had to get that out of my mind. This was Texas. Half the damn people here didn't know what the Mafia was unless they'd watched the Sopranos.

As I climbed the stairs a familiar voice greeted me. "Connie! So good to see you."

I looked up to see Julie. She was the same as she was when I left—purple stripe in her hair and iridescent nails. I half expected to hear *Mr. Tambourine Man* playing in the background.

I took the rest of the stairs two at a time and gave her a big hug. "It's great to see you. How are the kids?"

She stepped back and smiled. "They're fine. The question is how are *you*."

"Now that I'm back in Texas, I'm doing great."

A voice behind me said, "You got any hugs for a fat man?"

I turned to see "Fat Charlie" only he wasn't fat. "I would hug you but nothing's there. Good God you look great."

"Yeah, he went and screwed things up," Tip said. "Now I can't call him Fat Charlie anymore."

I hugged Charlie. "I missed you guys. It's good to be back."

Tip grabbed my arm. "Come on. You can catch up later; we've got to see the sweetheart."

"I assume you mean the captain?"

"None other," Tip said.

Tip introduced me to Cindy, and she escorted us into the captain's office. Captain Cooper was sitting behind her desk. She was short and thick like the stump of an old oak.

"Captain Cooper, this is my partner, Connie Gianelli."

Coop stood and reached to shake hands. "Now I see why Tip's been whining and crying to get you down here. You're gorgeous."

"I should let you know, Connie, that the captain's first name is Gladys."

Coop smiled. "Pay no attention to him, that's just his pitiful attempt to shut me up."

"He does have a way of getting under a person's skin," I said.

"That he does," Coop said. "Did you get in today, Connie?"

"A few hours ago."

"And you're ready to go already?"

"As soon as I get the paperwork done, Captain. I've been sitting still for too long."

Tip got up, fidgeting. "I've been sitting still too long myself. We better get going."

Coop shot him a look. "Give us a minute, Tip."

"What, you gonna tell her lies about me?"

"I couldn't make up anything worse than the truth. Now get out of here and give us a minute."

When the door closed, Coop looked at me with a fake smile. "I know you're a professional. And I've heard nothing but good reports from Tip and the Chief, who pushed hard to get you down here."

I nodded, waiting for the "but," that I knew was coming.

"But I'm responsible for you now, and I need to know if you're ready."

"I'm ready, Captain. You don't have to worry about that."

"It's my job to worry. I won't pretend I know what you went through or how you feel, but I *do* know it has to hurt. And it's got to bother you." Coop reached up and removed her glasses. She set them on a stack of papers to her left.

"Did you see a shrink?"

"I received plenty of counseling, if that's what you're worried about."

She opened a folder and flipped through until she found what she wanted. "Not according to your lieutenant. He said you went twice, and, according to the psychologist, 'neither visit was productive.'" Coop leaned forward a little and squinted. "Seeing a psychologist twice might be good for some things, but it usually doesn't fix the problems that come with being beaten half to death and raped."

I looked off to the left. A picture of an old hardware store in a small town hung on her wall next to a portrait of an older couple. There was enough resemblance to the woman to make me believe it was Coop's mother. I looked around some more. The captain was waiting for my answer and I didn't know what to say. I didn't want to start off this relationship with a lie, but could I tell her my counseling consisted of extended talks with my Uncle Dominic, head of one of New York's Five Families.

I took a deep breath and stared. "I opted for private counseling instead of the department shrink. We didn't click." There. I'd done it, and hadn't lied. Uncle Dominic could certainly be considered private counseling.

Coop squinted tighter. "Private counseling?"

"Yes."

She leafed through the papers in the folder again. "I don't see any insurance reports. Did you pay for this yourself?"

"This was more like family counseling."

One of her eyebrows raised, and she went back to that damn folder. After scanning half a dozen papers, she leaned back in the chair. "I don't see a mention of any living relatives in the files."

Here we go.

I didn't know how much was in that folder, or how much Lieutenant Morreau had told her about my past in Brooklyn. She might have everything in there. Might have the dossier on Uncle Dominic, complete with his picture, maybe even one of him holding me as a little girl. I'd seen that one in the shrink's file. The only thing I did know was that I couldn't start off this relationship with a lie. That wasn't going to work. I closed my eyes, lifted my head and wished I had stayed in Brooklyn with the fish. I'd tried the "almost a lie" cover up, and it hadn't worked.

I gathered my thoughts and tried to spit it all out with one breath. "I have no living relatives, but the guy who raised me after my mother died is Dominic Mangini. He's known by a lot of aliases, too, but the bottom line is he heads up one of the Five Families in New York."

Coop's eyes grew wide and big. "Why is it always me?" she mumbled. She fiddled with a pencil, twisting it in her hands and staring at it, then she slid her top drawer open and dropped it in. "And you think advice from a mobster is better than a psychologist?"

I suddenly wished I asked Tip a lot more about Captain Cooper. What kind of person she was. What answers she would expect. Since I didn't have that information, I opted for the truth. Again. "I don't know. I know that when I talk with him, he makes sense. And he makes me feel better about myself. And I know that shrink and I didn't click." I leaned back and shook my head. "Besides, what the hell does a doctor from the Upper East Side know about getting raped?" I crossed my legs and sneered. "If you don't count the silver spoon that's been stuck up his ass all his life."

Coop burst into laughter. She tried stopping twice, and after a few seconds she finally succeeded. She looked at me with warmth in her eyes. "Tell me, Connie, what would your Uncle Dominic say? Are you ready to be back on the job?"

I smiled at her. "He's the one who told me to come back to Texas."

Cooper walked out from behind her desk and extended her hand. "That's good enough for me. But you have to promise me you'll take care of that troublemaking partner."

I cocked my head to the left and gave her a crooked smile. "The Tipster? He's a big pussycat."

"I know he is," Coop said, "but someone needs to remind him of that. Daily."

"Count on it," I said.

"I will." Coop patted me on the shoulder. "See Cindy to get all your paperwork. There are more forms to sign than a medical-release statement."

"Captain...thanks for..."

Coop shook her head. "No thanks necessary. I like the truth. I can work through a lot of problems if I know the truth."

***

Coop watched Connie walk down the hallway, waving to her as she turned the corner.

"She's a sweetie," Cindy said.

"She'll be perfect as Denton's partner," Coop said, and smiled.

She went back in her office, closing the door behind her. When she got situated at her desk, she opened the file for Connie Gianelli, picked up the phone and dialed the number from her file.

"Brooklyn Homicide."

"Lieutenant Morreau, please. This is Captain Gladys Cooper from the Houston Police Department."

I need to find out how much she didn't tell.

Chapter 8

LOOKING FOR TIFFANY

Twenty minutes after I left Coop's office, Tip and I headed out. I told him we needed to stop for coffee, but he ignored me. "Next time I'm driving," I said.

"You don't like my driving?"

"You know I don't like your driving, but even more important is I want to be the one in charge of when and where we get coffee."

"We'll get some at the hotel," he said. "We'll be there in a few minutes."

I didn't relish the thought of hotel coffee, but it was better than nothing, and I couldn't crank up all cylinders until I had at least a few espressos. Tip could get by on hot tea, iced tea, or any kind of coffee. I'd even seen him substitute a Coke and be fine with it.

"You still think this is a case?" I asked.

"I don't know. But we'll act like it is unless Ben rules it accidental."

"Where do we start? I'm not familiar with the districts in Houston."

"We're gonna start by interviewing the hotel employees again. If she's a pro and works that area, somebody knows her."

We pulled up to the Four Seasons hotel a few minutes later. "Must have been a high-end hooker," I said.

"That's what you get when you're a lawyer."

We walked inside and Tip pointed to one of the bellhops. "Didn't I see you yesterday?"

"I was talking to the other officer," the bellhop said.

Tip handed him a card. "Tip Denton. This is my partner, Connie Gianelli. We've got a few more questions."

"I'm supposed to take these to a room," he said, gesturing to a cart loaded with luggage.

"Go on. We'll wait."

When the bellhop returned Tip handed him the picture we had from the security cameras. "Have you seen her before?" Tip asked.

He nodded. "A few times, and usually with different guys. Middle-aged guys."

"Any special day or time?" I asked.

He shook his head. "Not that I can think of. She was here more than most of them. Maybe once a week."

Tip squeezed in close and gestured toward the concierge. "Does he know her?"

"Oh, he knows her," the kid said, and he smiled.

"*Knows* her?" I asked.

He flashed big white teeth. "I'm talkin' *knows* her, like intimate. Carnal type knowledge."

Tip reached into his pocket and came out with a fifty-dollar bill. He waved it in front of the bellhop and then wrapped the bill around one of his contact cards. "If you remember anything else, there might be another Grant for you."

I smiled. The kid probably didn't know what a Grant was, but he definitely recognized the big 50 on the bill. Tip referred to all bills by name—Jacksons, Grants, and Franklins were his favorites when he was dealing with informants.

We talked to a few more employees, mostly bellhops, and we drilled the desk clerk again but he gave us nothing new. "Time we got intimate with the concierge," I said.

"Shoot, I bet he tells us what we need right off," Tip said, and he didn't even laugh.

I showed the concierge my badge. "Detectives Gianelli and Denton. We have questions about the incident in room #614."

He moved to the side and his eyes darted around the room. "I told the other policeman everything I know."

I moved to the left, planting myself in front of him. Then I leaned on his desk. "That was one of the uniformed officers, and I understand you've talked to him, but my partner and I are stuck with this case so you'll have to tell it again."

"If you insist," he said, as if we were asking him to do taxes.

"Let's start out with your name," I said. "And how long you've been working here."

"My name is Sebastian Dubois." He shot Tip a look and then puffed himself up. "And as I told the other officer, this...*incident*...didn't happen on my shift." The way he said it implied it wouldn't have happened if he'd been working.

"Are you saying you wouldn't have let her check in with Mr. Lipscomb?"

He blushed. "I didn't say that. It's simply..."

I waited.

After a few seconds I said, "How much did she give you?"

The skin on his forehead bunched into wrinkles. "What?"

Tip stepped forward, getting close to Sebastian. "We don't have time for your shit. Give us her name and everything you know or we'll take you downtown and arrest you for aiding and abetting prostitution."

Sebastian maintained his indignant look. It was a damn good look. He must have practiced that since he was a kid. It was so good it probably worked on most people. "I'm not some pimp on the corner that you can frighten. I've been—"

Tip grabbed Sebastian by the arm and spun him out from behind the desk. He slapped the cuffs on Sebastian's left wrist and then pulled his right arm back and closed the second cuff on that wrist. Panicked, Sebastian offered up the girl before Tip got done reading the first part of his rights.

"Tiffany," Sebastian said. "Her name is Tiffany—as far as I know. She comes here quite often."

Tip turned him to face us. "What's she do here?"

Sebastian cast worried looks around the lobby. "Can't we take these cuffs off? It's embarrassing."

"But pimping a young girl isn't embarrassing?" I said.

Sebastian, for all his pomp, was like most people. Embarrassment was a public thing. He wouldn't get embarrassed if he did something wrong, only if he got caught. Uncle Dominic raised me to believe that embarrassment was a personal thing. *You are the only one who can embarrass yourself,* he said.

I crowded Sebastian's space. "How do we find her?"

"I can reach her," he said.

"You have a phone number?"

Sebastian shook his head. "She uses a pager. A lot of the girls do."

"How do you reach her?" Tip asked.

"If I have someone…interested, I page her and she calls back."

"Do it," I said, and I removed the cuffs.

"She'll suspect something if I call this early."

"Do it," Tip said.

Tip's command must have carried more weight. Sebastian began dialing. The fact that he didn't have to look up her number told me he'd done this more than a few times.

We waited twenty minutes. "How long does it take?" I asked.

"She normally calls me back in a few minutes."

"Try her again," Tip said.

After fifteen more minutes, Tip pulled out a card and gave it to Sebastian. "Call if you hear anything."

The muscles in his face relaxed. "I will."

"You know where we can find her?" I asked.

He seemed to think for a few seconds, then, "There's an old house converted to boarding rooms down by the bus station. A few of the girls stay there."

"You have an address?"

"No, but if you ask around someone's bound to know."

Before we left I pulled him aside. "If we find even a little lie in what you told us, we'll make sure you lose this cushy job. I'm certain the Four Seasons doesn't want a pimp working for them."

He reached down and straightened his collar. "I told you everything."

It took us five minutes to get to the bus station, and about half an hour to locate the house. Tip parked behind an old Ford pickup loaded with what looked like junk from a garage sale. A black girl who looked to be no more than 18, sat on the front porch wearing cut-off shorts and a top that looked like a bra.

She shot us a look, then pulled out a cigarette and lit it. "Who you lookin' for?"

Tip flashed her a smile. "Who said we're looking."

"Only reason cops come here is to bust somebody or get some action." She glanced my way and said, "Since she's with you, I figure you're here to bust somebody."

"We're looking for Tiffany," I said, "but not to bust her."

She laughed, the cynical laugh of the street people. "Just want to talk, huh?" She looked straight at me. "Don't know no Tiffany."

"She lives here," Tip said.

"Big house," the girl said.

I heard footsteps behind me and turned to see a young girl carrying a sack of groceries. She looked bad, like she'd been knocked around a bit.

"They giving you trouble, Teesh?"

"Askin' about somebody named Tiffany," Teesh said.

The new girl was even skinnier than the one on the porch. I pulled out my badge. "Connie Gianelli," I said. "This is my partner, Tip Denton."

She handed the bag to Teesh. "Take these up. I'll talk to them."

"You know Tiffany?" I asked.

"What'd she do?"

"Don't know that she did anything, but we found a body in a hotel, and Tiffany was the last one seen with him."

The girl shook her head. "Tiffany wouldn't do that."

"I understand, but we still need to talk with her."

"Ain't seen her in two days," the girl said.

"We just need to talk," Tip said. "What's your name anyway? I don't like talking to someone I don't know."

The girl pulled a mint from her pocket, unwrapped it, and popped it in her mouth. "Not that we'll be doin' a lot of talkin' but I'm called

LaDonna." She stared at Tip. "You got a card? If not, write down your number and I'll tell Tiff if I see her."

I moved a step closer to her. "Look, we've got a dead man, and I need to know what happened. As long as Tiffany didn't do it, we're good. She could have fucked him to death, and I'm okay with that. We've got a case to close and I need a reason why this guy died. If Tiffany didn't do it, she doesn't need to worry. And she doesn't need to run."

"She might not need to run, but she ran."

"When? Do you know where?"

She shook her head. "I came home to find her gone. And she must've been in a hurry, 'cause she only took half her clothes."

"When was this?" Tip asked.

"Night before last."

"We need to check her room," I said.

The girl cocked her head and looked at me. "You carrying a warrant or are you just crazy? Tiffany lives with me, and I ain't letting you in."

"We can get a warrant," Tip said, "but it'd be a lot easier if you invited us in for coffee and maybe let us look around."

She cocked her head to the side and gave Tip a look. "Coffee? That's all? Sure you don't want to leave your partner out here?"

"No, but I'll make you a deal. I'll donate $50 to your favorite charity if you invite us up for coffee or tea."

"Charity? Now I know you're crazy. You think I got a charity?"

"I'm guessing you might. I had one guy who said his favorite charity was himself, so when I gave him $50 that's who he donated to."

She narrowed her eyes and stared at Tip. I did the same.

"To *himself?*" she said. "You're gonna give me $50?"

"Or I can get a warrant."

She cracked a big smile. "Would you detectives like to come up for tea?"

As we followed LaDonna in, Tip whispered, "You do the talking, Gianelli."

The "apartment" was one big room that had been converted into two bedrooms and a tiny kitchen and bathroom. Tiffany's room had a stand-up closet—the kind you'd buy at Ikea—and it had a dresser, a bed, and a few bare walls. A few clothes hung in the closet, and a few pair of panties and socks lay in the top drawer of the dresser. The rest of the drawers were empty.

"You don't know where she might be?" I asked.

"No idea. I didn't see her before she left."

"When was the last time you *did* see her?"

"Day of her big deal. She cleaned out that night."

I looked over at her. "What big deal?"

"Tiffany had a big client that night."

"How do you know?"

"She told me."

"And Tiffany wouldn't lie?" I said.

"Not to me she wouldn't. Besides, I had a guy who wanted two girls, and this dude was payin' $200 each. Tiff said that'd be nothin' compared to what her client was paying."

"What time did she tell you this?"

"Early. I'm talkin' right after lunch. I remember because I only got up about an hour before."

"And you haven't seen her since?" I said.

She shook her head. "I got home about 5:00 in the morning, and her shit was gone."

"Tiffany have any relatives you know of? Other friends?"

"Nobody but us, far as I know."

"You know where she was from?"

"I don't know where she was from, but she lived in Nashville for a while."

That piqued my interest. I moved closer. "What makes you say that?"

"She was always talkin' 'bout how her father dragged her whole family down there lookin' for a country music career, and all he found was the bottle." LaDonna shook her head. "Could've found that anywhere."

"You know when that was? Or where she came from before?"

She shoved another mint in her mouth and shook her head again. "Nashville's all I know. She never said much more than that."

I looked at the girl. She was junkie thin and had the track marks to prove it. Her left eye was half closed, probably from a John who got too rough. "What's your name?"

"Here it comes," she said.

"Just asking your name."

"Already told you. It's LaDonna."

"I know what you told us. I'm talking your real name."

She looked at the floor. "Real names don't matter."

"But they do," I said. "Your name is who you are." I turned to Tip. "Give me one of your cards."

"I already gave her one," he said.

"Give me a card, Tip."

He handed me one and I wrote my name and number on it. "LaDonna, call me if you ever need something. I owe you one." Then I said, "Let's go, Tip."

LaDonna got a look on her face as if I shocked her. "You ain't like them others. Most of the bitch cops look down on us, and the men want tricks for free."

"I definitely don't want the tricks. As to the other, I've got an uncle who once told me never to judge another person. He said anybody could end up a king or a pauper, alive or dead, depending on which path they choose. And you choose paths *every* day."

"Damn, girl. Gonna have to light one up to digest that."

"Wait till I leave, okay?"

LaDonna laughed. "Deal."

"And just so you know, we'll be sending a tech down here to dust for Tiffany's prints. That okay?"

"Make sure they don't come before noon."

As Tip and I walked down the steps, I thought about LaDonna. Not for the first time, I wondered if Uncle Dominic knew what he was doing. He might not run prostitutes but everything he did supported it.

Does he know what he's doing to little girls?

We got in the car, Tip driving again. "You talk to the lawyer's partners yet?"

"Not yet. I wasn't in a rush because it looked like a heart attack. It still does, but now we have a missing prostitute to go with it."

"She might have simply gotten spooked and took off," I said. "Maybe went back to Nashville or wherever she came from."

"Maybe," Tip said, "but I still want to talk to the partners. It's time we found out how well Mr. Lipscomb knew Tiffany."

I looked at my watch. "That'll have to wait until tomorrow. It's been a long day."

"Sissy," Tip said.

"Pussy," I said back.

He laughed.

A couple of minutes later, he laughed more.

Chapter 9

DEAD FOR SURE

*E*l *Terrible* woke at 4:00 AM, made the bed, and arranged clothes for the day. Dressing came first, and then packing what was needed into a small bag—nurse uniform, name badge and hospital ID, and *nurse* shoes. Coffee was next, followed by two thin-bladed knives. *El Terrible* walked to her car and then drove to the hospital, parking two blocks away, far from the prying eyes of surveillance cameras or inquisitive guards.

Fifteen minutes later, when the morning traffic was heaviest, *Nurse Terrible* joined a small group entering the hospital. *Nurse Terrible* walked down the long, sanitary hall, keeping perfect stride, blending in with the traffic. It was the six o'clock shift on Friday, and everyone seemed to be in a rush. *Nurse Terrible* suspected the rush had more to do with anticipation of the weekend than it did with administering care to the sick.

Nurse Terrible turned right, passed the cafeteria, made a stop at the restroom to change clothes, took an elevator to the fourth floor, and then completed the short walk to the ICU. The nurse pushed open the double doors, careful not to leave fingerprints. It only took a few seconds to locate Martin's room. After checking to make sure no one was looking, the nurse entered. Martin lay on the bed asleep. It would be easy to inject something into the IV bag and leave before he woke, but that wouldn't send the right message. Besides, *Nurse Terrible* hadn't gotten into this business for the security; risks came with the job.

Nurse Terrible put on gloves, prepared a syringe, and then covered Martin's mouth with duct tape. *Nurse Terrible* also taped Martin's hands and legs to the bed rails. He stirred, fear in his eyes.

Nurse Terrible leaned close and whispered, "You should have listened."

Martin squirmed, tried to get up, but *Nurse Terrible's* arms lay across Martin's throat. Next the nurse located a good vein in Martin's neck and injected a few milliliters of ketamine. Martin would be out in seconds and feel no pain.

Once Martin succumbed, the nurse took a knife from the pocket in the front of the uniform, opened it to reveal a four-inch blade, and jammed it into Martin's left eye, but not far enough to kill him. Then the nurse opened another blade and shoved it into his right eye. Señor Martin had learned his lesson, and *El Terrible* had earned a small fortune.

Nurse Terrible exited the hospital the same way, making sure to avoid the only two cameras that might reveal a face. After getting into the car, *Nurse Terrible* headed toward the house. There was still a lot of work to do.

***

Rosalee pulled the pillow off her head, and reached to shake her husband. "Phone, Ribs. Get up."

Ribs ran his hand over the nightstand until he found his phone. He hated the sound of a phone in the morning. "Delgado."

"Go to the hospital," Coop said. "Your suspect's dead."

Ribs got up quickly and sat on the edge of the bed. "What!"

"Somebody killed Martin. Call me when you get there."

"Did you call Cruz?"

"That's your job. I was still asleep."

"I was asleep, too," Ribs said.

"You're not a captain," Coop said, and she didn't laugh.

Ribs leaned over and kissed Rosalee on the cheek. "Body at the hospital. Gotta go."

"Who is it?"

"That guy from yesterday." He dressed quickly and called Cruz before leaving. It took 45 minutes to drive to the hospital. Cruz was waiting.

"Have you been in there?" Ribs asked.

"You're not gonna believe it," Cruz said.

"Tell me."

"It would be better if you see it yourself."

A small group of hospital staff had gathered nearby even though Martin's room was sealed off. Two uniformed officers guarded the door. One of the officers nodded to Ribs as he approached. "They already processed it," he said. "It's all yours."

Ribs stared at the onlookers, mostly nurses and techs, but he noticed one doctor. "Everybody loves a dead body."

"Especially one like this," Cruz said, and led the way into Martin's room. Ribs followed.

"*Dios mío.*"

Blood covered the sheets, and the floor, and a knife was stabbed into each of Martin's eyes. "*Dios mío,*" Ribs said again.

"Somebody wanted him dead for sure," Cruz said.

"The question is, why?" Ribs asked. "It couldn't have been the stickers. For that they could have waited until he got out."

"How about that *terrible* guy?" Cruz said.

"Julie said he was a professional killer. What the hell did Martin do to warrant that?"

"I guess we better take a look at the apartment," Cruz said. "There must be more to Señor Martin than we suspected."

"We'll go in a minute," Ribs said, and dialed Coop.

"What's going on, Delgado?"

"He's dead all right. Big ass knife jammed in each of his eyes."

"I heard. What's it look like down there?"

"Captain, I need help on this. Cruz and I are going to Martin's place to see what we can find, but I need some uniforms down here to question people. Somebody *had* to see something in a damn hospital."

"I'll get a few people down there. I hope the hospital has video, and that we got a good picture of whoever did this. I don't need the chief all over my ass about this."

"Okay, we're off. I'll call you later."

Martin's apartment was on the ground floor. A patrolman met them at the front entrance.

"Good afternoon, Detectives."

"Jakes, how's it going?" Ribs said.

"Quiet. I hope I can get out of here soon."

"Did anybody come by?"

"A lot of people came by, but nobody that looked out of place, and nobody tried going in. Millner's inside."

Ribs and Cruz entered Martin's apartment, both wearing gloves. A couch sat against the outside wall and a chair was on the adjacent wall, facing a big-screen TV. The rest of the room was bare. Officer Millner sat at a table in the eating area, munching on a burger.

"I hope you didn't touch anything," Ribs said.

"Do I look like a fuckin' rookie?"

"You look like a fuckin' pig," Cruz said. "Are you eating this man's food?"

Millner wiped his mouth and stared at Cruz. "Do you think I'd eat something that was in *this* place? Give me a break, Cruz. Besides, it's not like he's coming back for dinner."

"I'll check the bedroom," Cruz said.

"I've seen a lot worse than this," Ribs said to Millner. "This place is clean."

"Except for these naked girl pics on the bedroom wall," Cruz said as he came back down the hall. "You need to come see this. The whole damn wall is covered in naked women."

"Same one?" Ribs asked.

"All different," Millner said. "And some of them look damn sweet."

Ribs shot him a sideways look. "Goddamn pervert."

Cruz was checking under the bed when Delgado walked in. "Damn, Cruz, I think Señor Martin has a problem."

"*Had* a problem," Cruz said. "And I don't think he was gay."

"They look like working girls."

"That's my guess. Do you recognize any?" Cruz said, and then he pulled a small box from under the bed and set it on the nightstand.

"Let's see what's inside," Ribs said.

Cruz opened the box and started pulling things out. "St. Anthony medal, rosary, a picture of an old woman—probably his mother, a money clip with nothing in it, and a pair of dice." He shut the box. "Not much to take through the gate."

"Not much? What do you think the rosary and medal are for? That's for St. Peter to let him pass."

"And the old woman's picture?" Cruz asked.

"To show St. Peter his mother is there waiting for him," Ribs said.

"What about the dice?"

"In case St. Peter doesn't believe him. That's when he brings the dice out to gamble."

"In other words more of your Catholic bullshit and no clues."

Ribs shook his head. "I don't know. That St. Anthony guy might have done it."

"Or the old woman," Cruz said.

"We better keep looking," Ribs said.

Ribs and Cruz went through the bathroom, the closet, and the only dresser in the room, but they found nothing other than a couple of days worth of clothes and an empty wallet. The kitchen only took five minutes to search, and then they checked under the cushions of the couch and chair. Cruz walked to a waste can next to the table where Millner sat.

"Did you look through here? Or throw anything in it?"

"I didn't touch it," Millner said.

Cruz knelt and searched the can, bringing out a few crumpled pieces of paper, some of them stained with ketchup. Ribs set them on the table and unfolded them. "Receipt from grocery store, and one from Wendy's."

"Couple of lotto tickets here," Cruz said.

"Hey, Cruz, this note has 'Mandy' written on it, with a phone number next to her name."

Cruz looked down at the paper he held. "Got a phone number here, too, but no name. Just says, 'lawyer.'"

Ribs took the note from him. "Lawyer? Didn't Martin ask for a lawyer?"

"Sure as hell did," Cruz said. "Why would he ask for one if he had one?"

"Let's see who owns this number." Ribs took out his phone and dialed.

A receptionist answered on the third ring. "Barnes, Griffin, and Lipscomb."

Ribs paused. Lipscomb was the dead guy's name. "Is Mr. Lipscomb in?"

A long hesitation, then, "Who may I say is calling?"

"Oscar Salinas."

"And what is the nature of the call, Mr. Salinas?"

"What are all the questions about? Is Mr. Lipscomb in or not?"

An even longer hesitation followed, then, "I'm sorry, Mr. Salinas, but Mr. Lipscomb has passed away. May I connect you to Mr. Barnes, our senior partner?"

"No thanks," Ribs said, and hung up.

Cruz looked at him. "What the hell was that all about?"

"That body we found in the Four Seasons, the lawyer. It was no other than Mr. Lipscomb, the guy who used to be at the other end of this number."

Cruz narrowed his eyes. "Something doesn't sound right about that."

"What are the chances that a guy like Martin even knows a high-priced lawyer? And how do they both end up dead a few days apart?" Ribs started to dial another number.

"Who are you calling?"

"Gotta call Tip. He's not gonna believe this shit."

Chapter 10

JUST LIKE OLD TIMES

We stopped at the station so I could get my car, and then I headed out. Tip said he had work to catch up on. "I'll come by later," I said. "I have to feed Hotshot, and I could use a shower."

"You could always shower—"

"With you?" I said, and laughed. "I see nothing's changed in Tip's world."

"See you tonight," Tip said. "I'll cook something."

It felt strange going to a house instead of an apartment, but strange in a nice way. I liked the privacy and the space, and I felt sure Hotshot was going to love being able to go outside more often. After I got Hotshot introduced to the yard, I began the arduous task of cleaning a new house. It wasn't dirty, not by any means, but it wasn't *mine*. I didn't feel like a place was mine until I'd cleaned it and fixed it up.

I scrubbed the cabinets, did a quick dust job, and then an even quicker vacuum run. Then I unpacked a few things and placed my pictures of Dominic and Zeppe and his family on a shelf in the living room. After that I tackled the bathrooms. No way I was showering without a thorough scrubbing. After cleaning tile for almost an hour, I took a shower, fed the cat, and decided I'd better call Uncle Dominic. He answered on the second ring.

"Pronto."

"It's me," I said. "I wanted to let you know I'm in Houston, and I'm safe."

"I would have heard if you weren't," Dominic said.

"*Zio!*"

"No reason for concern, Concetta. You know I have no connections in Houston."

"I don't know *anything* about your business, and that's the way I want to keep it." I laughed, and he did too. It felt good. "How are Zeppe and the kids?"

"You know Zeppe. He has never seen a cloudy sky." He paused for a moment, then said, "Sometimes I wish our roles were reversed, that Zeppe and I could have traded places."

I had never heard Dominic like this. It seemed strange. "Maybe you should come visit me, Uncle Dominic. Take a vacation, ditch the FBI, and we'll go to a nice restaurant and eat Mexican food."

"Don't be surprised if I knock on your door one night."

"I'll be waiting," I said, and then, "I need to get going. I—"

"No need to explain. I'll say hello to Zeppe. Call when you can. And be safe."

"*Ciao, Zio Domenico. Ti voglio bene.*"

"*Ciao, Concetta.*"

I pulled up Tip's address on the map and routed it on my phone, then headed out. I thought back on my conversation with Dominic and realized it was the first time I'd talked to him in many years that I didn't get stressed, or have the feeling that someone was watching me. I looked forward to more of that, especially at work. I could do without other cops second guessing my motives or my loyalty to the department.

Before I knew it, my exit came up on the freeway. I was tempted to check the map, but waited to see if I'd remember. Within minutes I was close, and as I got close it all came back to me. When I crossed through Tip's "private property" gate and headed down that old gravel drive, fond memories returned—deer, coyotes, the sounds of the woods. A far cry from Brooklyn. I'd have to go to the zoo to see as much wildlife as Tip had on his few acres.

The car in the driveway wasn't Tip's, and it sure as hell didn't look like it would be something Elena would drive. As I wondered whose car it could be, it hit me—Mollie. Tip hadn't mentioned Mollie since I'd been back, but I'd bet the few bucks I had she was still cleaning his house and sticking her nose into his investigations.

I walked toward his back porch. The barking started before I got within twenty feet. A light went on in the family room, then the door opened and Mollie poked her head out. She stepped onto the porch. Inside, the dogs still barked.

"Could've told a damn person you were coming," she said. "That would've been the civil thing to do."

Same old Mollie. It was good to be back in Texas. "I didn't know you'd be here."

"Tip knows you're comin'?"

"He told me to meet him here."

She opened the door and shook her head. "Should've known. Damn inconsiderate man is what he is. But there I go wastin' words again. 'Man' would've been enough to say."

I hid my laugh as I greeted the dogs. "Flash, how are you, girl?"

She gave me one of her crazy snarls and jumped on me. Then I was drawn to the quietness of the other dog. "Come here, boy. Who are you?"

"That's Sacco," Mollie said. "Damn dog acts like he's royalty. Don't even bother to say hello."

I reached over and brushed my hand across Sacco's head, but that's all I could do because Flash was up to her old jealous ways, squeezing in and demanding attention. "I see it's gonna take a lot more than a bullet to slow Flash down."

"Come in the kitchen," Mollie said. "You want coffee?"

"I remember Tip's coffee. I'll take a beer."

"Smart girl," she said, and grabbed two beers from the fridge then sat in the chair next to me. "What brought you back?"

I didn't know how to answer that. After a brief pause, I said, "Things weren't the same back home."

"They never are," Mollie said, and then she looked me up and down. "You look good, considering."

"It took a while." I said. "And for a long time I never thought I'd be the same."

She nodded. "I reckon that's what brought you back. Had to come back to where you were done wrong so you could face your demons. My husband had to do that when he quit the bottle."

As I gave thought to what Mollie said, a car pulled into the driveway. Flash barked. Sacco stayed where he was.

Tip walked in a half a minute later, gave Flash the mandatory greetings, waved to Sacco, and then came into the kitchen. "I see ya'll started without me."

"I'd have been just as happy to have finished without you, too," Mollie said. "Don't even have the courtesy to tell me Connie was coming."

"You weren't supposed to be here, so why should I tell you."

Mollie got up from the chair and got a beer. "Not supposed to be here? You tell me how one person's gonna clean this house the way you keep it."

Tip gritted his teeth. "Mollie—"

"Don't go cursing me. Sit down and drink your beer and tell me what case we're working. I'll cook something up for us."

"Get it straight that *we* are not working any case. But you can cook something if you want."

Mollie tapped me on the shoulder. "You need to thank me. If it wasn't for me he might never have solved that case. Got you hurt as it was 'cause he wouldn't listen. Too damn hardheaded."

"Bullshit," Tip said. "I had that case solved six ways from Sunday."

"Six ways from Sunday? What the *hell* is that supposed to mean?" She walked off mumbling. "Man walks around spitting out shit that don't make sense."

"It was just as much my fault," I said. "I missed the same clues Tip did. Maybe you and Tip should partner up."

"Don't even say that as a joke," Tip said. "God might punish me in my next life and stick me with her."

"You could do worse," Mollie said.

Tip gulped the rest of his beer. "We don't even have a case, Mollie. Not a real one."

"I wouldn't worry too much about that. Won't be long before some crazy starts killing people." Mollie went to the fridge and pulled out a few containers. "Who wants leftovers? We've got BBQ and some damn good potato salad."

"Count me in," I said.

Tip and I ate dinner while Mollie talked, or at least it seemed that way. Not only could she talk almost non-stop, but she jumped topics without any transition. Tip finished his plate then started on the dishes in the sink.

"I'll get them," Mollie said. "You talk with Connie."

We went on the side porch, and for a while just sat there listening to the night and rocking in the chair. A few minutes passed, and then Tip said, "You ready for this?"

"Of course I am."

After another minute or so, I looked at him. "Truth is, Tip, I don't know if I'm ready."

He nodded. "I know."

"Have you ever…"

"Been afraid?" he said, and then he nodded again. "Too many times to count."

I stopped rocking and leaned forward as I turned to face him. "It's not like this is the first time I've been scared…but up North I had family. Even during the time I didn't associate with them, they were there. I know that sounds crazy, but it's how I felt."

"Don't worry about it; you've got family here, too. You got me. And you've got Mollie."

I almost choked on the beer I'd just sipped. And then I laughed. Hard. Tip joined in. "On that note, I'm getting another beer," I said.

"Time to go in anyway," Tip said, and as we walked into the kitchen his phone rang. He pressed the speaker button and answered.

"Tip Denton, best damn detective in Texas."

"You better put your detective hat on."

"Why's that, Delgado? You need help already?"

"We have a guy in the hospital on this sticker case, or I should say we *had* a guy in the hospital. Somebody walked in this morning and stuck a blade in each of his eyes."

"What the hell? Did this guy kill somebody's mother or something?"

"I don't know, but Cruz and I went to his apartment afterward and we found a piece of paper with 'lawyer,' written on it and a phone number. Guess who the lawyer was?"

"Don't tell me it's our guy."

"None other."

"What the hell's that all about?"

"You tell me," Ribs said. "How about you and your new partner check out the law firm. Cruz and I will do the hard work and figure out who killed Señor Martin."

"That sounds good. We'll catch up afterward."

Tip hung up and looked at me. "Looks like we got a case now," he said.

"We sure do," Mollie said, and shook her head. "A knife in each eye. Told you it wouldn't be long before the crazies struck."

"Mollie's right. Why would you stab someone in the eyes? What the hell is with that?"

"My guess is somebody's sending a signal," Tip said.

"But what signal? And who is it intended for?"

"That's Delgado's job. We need to figure out who killed this lawyer, and why, and what he has to do with the dead guy in the hospital."

"Since we've got a real case now, I think I better get sleep." I finished off my beer and dumped the empty in the trash can. "I'm heading out, Tip. See you tomorrow. And thanks for dinner, Mollie. It was good."

"You take your time and get settled in your new house," Mollie said. "We'll have this solved before tomorrow."

I laughed as I walked out the door, certain that Tip was cursing me under his breath.

Chapter 11

Legalese

Tip picked me up and we drove straight to Lipscomb's office, which was downtown. It was in one of the tall buildings, at least forty stories. I hadn't been here long enough to know which one, but it was shiny and new, like all of downtown Houston.

We parked in a garage half a block away and walked to the lobby. Their main office was on the 25th floor. The receptionist was young and pretty— no surprise—and after we explained what we wanted she said we'd have to talk to Mr. Griffin or Mr. Barnes, the two senior partners. Griffin wasn't in and Barnes was in a meeting for the next half hour. We opted to talk to Lipscomb's secretary. The receptionist didn't like us doing that, but she was naive enough to be afraid of a couple of homicide cops, especially Tip; he wore his mean look.

We met the secretary in a conference room.

"Do you know what he was doing in town, at the hotel?" I asked.

"He must have worked late and didn't want to make the drive," she said.

"Didn't he have an apartment or condo down here?"

She nodded. "A condo."

"If he had a condo, why would he go to the hotel?" Tip asked.

Hesitation, then, "He sometimes did this when he was…entertaining someone."

"You mean a woman?" I said.

"Someone not his wife, yes."

"And usually a young someone, I'm guessing."

The secretary fidgeted for a moment. "How can I say this...Mr. Lipscomb would have considered me ancient."

I looked her over; she was no older than I was. "Ancient?"

She nodded, and by the look she gave me I could tell she was warming up to us.

"Any place in particular he liked to meet these women?"

"Any of the clubs downtown. He seldom strayed far from his turf. You might try the jazz club on Texas Avenue. And there's one in Montrose he went to sometimes. He liked busy places where the young crowd hung out."

"What else can you tell us?"

"Nothing to speak of."

"What about his wife?" Tip asked. "Did they get along?"

She looked at Tip with eyebrows raised. It was obvious she was restraining a laugh. "I'm not speaking out of turn to say this, but Mr. Lipscomb's wife hated him as much as he hated her, and she was never shy about letting people know it. If she's not a suspect, I imagine it's because she has a strong alibi."

"Seems like Lipscomb was loved by all," I said.

"Maybe his mother," she said, "but I'm glad he's gone."

"I guess you've got an alibi?" Tip said.

She smiled. "Three kids and a mother-in-law."

We finished with the secretary and waited a few minutes for Barnes, the senior partner. He met us in the same room, rushing in as if he were late for an appointment. "I don't have a lot of time," he said, before the door closed.

"Tell us what we need and it won't take long," Tip said.

"Was Mr. Lipscomb seeing anyone special?" I asked.

"You mean a client?"

Tip leaned close to him. "If you stick to answers like that it's going to take a *real* long time."

Barnes nodded. "If you mean women, no one special that I know of."

"But he did see women other than his wife?" I said.

He looked to me. "Yes. Quite often."

"Did you know any of them?" I asked.

He shook his head. "They weren't the kind of women he would introduce to people at the firm. Besides, most of them were young from what I heard."

"Any idea where he met them?" Tip asked.

Barnes thought a moment, then reached for the phone on the desk and dialed an internal number, keeping it on speaker. "Bruce, I'm here with two detectives about Forrest. What was the name of the club Forrest took us to that night?"

"I don't remember the name, but it's the one on Texas Avenue. He always went there."

"Okay, thanks," Barnes said and then looked at us. "That's all I know, detectives."

"You don't sound like you miss him much?" Tip said.

Barnes looked at Tip and then me. "Forrest Lipscomb was a partner in our firm, but I never liked him and I don't know of anyone who did. I'll miss the business he brought in and the hours he billed. Aside from that, his passing won't cross my mind." Barnes extended his hand to shake. "If you'll excuse me, I have another meeting. Call me if you need anything else."

We spoke to a group supervisor in the research department on the way out, a lady named Gretchen. "Did Mr. Lipscomb have a client named Martin?" I asked. "Edward Martin?"

She looked around, then back to me. "I'm not supposed to do this, but I guess confirming a client list won't hurt." She searched the computer and came up empty. "No Edward Martin. I have a Martin listed but it's a woman, and she's been a client for many years."

"How about the other lawyers?" I asked.

"I searched all client files. Edward Martin isn't in the system."

I made a note to check back with Delgado on that, and then we asked Gretchen more questions. She had even less flattering things to say about Lipscomb than his partner or secretary, but we found out that Lipscomb quit work Tuesday night around 8:30, and we managed to get a good picture of Lipscomb from a Christmas party album. It would be better than the shot we had. After that Tip and I got in the elevator and headed back to the car.

"What do you think?" I asked. "Even if it wasn't a heart attack, this guy was an ass."

"You're saying he deserved it?"

"I'm not saying I'd have killed him myself, but from what we've learned so far, I'm not losing sleep about him being gone. Hell, neither are his partner or his wife."

"I can't argue that," Tip said, "but I'd still like to find that prostitute."

"We've got nothing else to do," I said. "Let's go."

"The clubs will be closed," Tip said. "Let's ask around a bit while we wait."

We cruised the streets looking for some of Tip's *eyes* and *ears,* as he liked to call them. The *eyes* were street people who always kept watch on things, and they had a knack for remembering details on anything that looked suspicious. The *ears* were also street people, but they were good for *hearing* things on the street. A lot of their information wasn't first-hand knowledge; it was a conversation they overheard, or a persistent rumor. Technically information like that wasn't any good, but a cop like Tip knew how to work that kind of lead.

I lowered the window and enjoyed the cool breeze. "Who are we looking for?"

"A guy named Buster. He walks hunched over, and he's usually pushing a shopping cart or pulling a wagon."

"White? Black?"

"Black," Tip said. "With a shiny gold tooth on the bottom left."

A few blocks later he pulled to the side and leaned out the window. "Ricky, you seen Buster?"

Ricky squinted and moved closer. "That you, Tip?"

"It was me when I got up this morning."

Ricky laughed. "Same old fuckin' Tipster. Always full of shit."

"That's me," Tip said. "So what is it? Have you seen Buster?"

Ricky leaned down, resting his elbows on Tip's door and bringing his head level with Tip's. "See you're wearin' a new suit."

"I moved back with HPD when John got his new job."

"John? You talkin' about Renkin?"

"That's him. He's the chief now."

Ricky cocked his head and squinted. "The chief? That slipped by me. Need to pay more attention." He looked at me and smiled, then back at Tip. "What'cha need Buster for? Maybe I got what you need."

"You know a working girl named Tiffany?"

"Tiffany? I might. What's she look like?"

"Young, skinny, blonde. She lives down by the bus station, and she might work the hotels."

"Tiffany…" Ricky looked desperate to come up with an answer but it wasn't happening. "I guess you're gonna have to find Buster after all. Can't help you this time. But I seen the *B* this morning, pullin' a wagon down by the Center. He's been workin' the line lately."

"If you were looking for Buster right now, where would you start?"

"Maybe halfway 'tween here and the zoo."

Tip pulled out a twenty and handed it to Ricky.

"Well *hello*, Mr. Jackson," Ricky said. "Ain't seen you in a long time."

Tip laughed. "Keep your ears open. You hear the right thing and you might earn yourself a Grant."

Ricky tapped the top of the car. "Come back and see me, Tip. I'll have somethin' for you."

Ten minutes later we found Buster right where Ricky said we would, making a slow march up Main Street, and tugging a wagon loaded with junk. Tip turned on a side street, pulled to the curb, and got out. I followed.

Buster stopped and looked at Tip, and then he smiled. "It's been a long time."

Tip shook Buster's hand. "I'm looking for a working girl named Tiffany."

"I know her. But I ain't seen her since…" Buster raised his head and closed one eye. "Must've been last Saturday when I saw her last."

"Last Saturday? You're sure about that?"

"Why you askin'?"

"She took a high-priced lawyer to a hotel. The next day we found the lawyer dead, but no sign of Tiffany. I doubt it's her fault, but I've got to cover bases."

Buster nodded. "You figure Tiff was too much for him, huh?"

"Something like that," Tip said, and then, "Are you sure it was last Saturday?"

"Sure as I can be. I was workin' the bus station and saw her on the way out. I always work the station on Saturdays."

"Do you have any idea where she'd go?" Tip asked.

"I'm sure you asked the girls in the house. If they didn't know, I don't."

"Okay, thanks," Tip said. He handed Buster a twenty and started for the car.

"Don't go runnin' off," Buster said. "I got some more for you."

Tip turned around. "What?"

Buster looked down the street, then up the other way, and then he stared at me. "Somebody's been movin' a lot of ice in town," he said to Tip.

"You're talking about meth?"

"Almost givin' it away."

"Who's behind it?"

Buster shook his head. "Somebody new. That's all I know."

"New? So he's trying to carve out a territory?"

"Don't know about territory. But dealin' ice is like printing money, Tip. Who can afford to give that away?"

Tip peeled a fifty from his roll and handed it to Buster. "If you hear anything about Tiffany call me, but I might be more interested in who's giving out ice."

"You're still the man," Buster said, and began his slow walk down the street.

We got in the car and Tip started it up. "I need to call Bobby. If anyone's moving that quantity of meth, he'll know."

"Is that the guy who helped us with Tony's case last time?"

"That's him," Tip said. "He's been working Narcotics a long time."

As we drove, Tip dialed a number on his phone and put it on speaker. A guy answered right away.

"Denton? Is that you?"

"Sure as hell is, Bobby. How are you?"

"It's been a while, Tip. What can I do for you?"

"Have you heard anything about a new player in town pushing meth?"

Bobby laughed. "Somebody's always pushing it, and there are plenty of crazy fucks lining up to get it."

"I know that, but I heard a new guy is moving lots of it and almost giving it away."

A pause followed, then, "I haven't heard anything, but I'll keep an eye out."

"Okay, Bobby, you do that. And say hi to Janet."

"Will do, Tip. Take care."

Tip hung up and put the phone in his pocket.

"That was bullshit," I said.

"He never asked who I heard it from," Tip said.

"A good cop would have had a lot of questions."

Tip turned right, heading back toward the station. "An honest cop would," he said.

"Don't forget we're working Homicide, not Narcotics or IA."

Tip gave me one of his sly looks. "Nothing saying we can't poke around a bit; besides, it's still too early to go to the club. Let's see what we can find out about this meth."

While Tip drove, I thought about how to say what I wanted to say. Finally I opted for blurting it out. "Tip, there are a couple of things you need to know since we're permanent partners now."

"I'm guessing that now you're gonna tell me you love me."

I laughed. "Not hardly, but please shut the hell up and let me talk." I half expected another smart-ass comment, but none came, so I continued. "First thing is, I'm Catholic. If anything happens to me, call a priest. And after you call the priest…" I took a deep breath before saying this, not knowing how Tip would react.

"I'm waiting," Tip said.

"After the priest, call my Uncle Dominic. His number is on my phone."

"Are you talking about your mobster uncle?"

"I don't think of him that way."

Tip shot me one of his crooked-eye looks. "It doesn't matter how you think of him, he's a mobster. Admit it."

I knew this shit would happen. "Never mind. I shouldn't have said anything."

"I didn't say I wouldn't call him, but I like to get the facts straight." Tip shook his head. "And I still can't believe you associate with him."

I didn't want to respond. Didn't want to start off our relationship this way. "Forget about it, Tip. Just forget it."

"I can't forget it. And besides, you brought it up."

"Never mind. You wouldn't understand. It's about family. It's..." I suddenly realized what I'd said, and wished I could take it back. Tip was silent. I was afraid to look at him. "I'm sorry about that. I didn't mean—"

"You're right. I wouldn't understand. But don't worry, if something happens, I'll call him."

"Tip, I'm sorry."

"Don't worry about it. We've got a case to solve."

Chapter 12

A Couple Of Questions

Julie was at her desk when we got in.

"Connie, when do you want to come for dinner?"

"Let me get settled in and get a jump on this case. Maybe next week."

"Anytime is good for me, just let me know."

"If you ladies are done," Tip said, "I've got work to discuss."

"What do you need?" Julie asked.

Tip leaned closer. "I know this is stretching the boundaries, but can you pull me up the file on Bobby Stenson?"

Julie looked around, then back at Tip. "I don't mind stretching boundaries, but you know I can't do that."

"I wouldn't ask if I didn't need it," Tip said.

She shook her head. "I can't do it, Tip. I'm sorry."

"Can't do it, my ass," he said, and walked away.

Julie's face drooped. She looked as if she would cry.

"Don't worry about it," I said. "You did right, and he'll get over it."

Tip passed Charlie without a word. "What's wrong, Tip? Did I do something?"

I followed close behind. "Nothing, Charlie. He's just pissed off."

"Hey, partner," I said. "You want to slow down?"

He stopped. "I don't want to hear it, Gianelli."

"You're going to hear it. You were out of line with Julie, and you're pissed off because you know you were."

"She could've looked it up. She's done worse."

I poked my finger in his chest and stared up at him. "We have no business messing with Narcotics. If you're concerned Bobby's crooked, report it to IA or tell Coop. Don't take it out on Julie."

He looked as if he'd get pissed at me, but then he smiled. "You're a feisty little thing, aren't you?"

"That's why you love me."

"I guess so," he said. "Let's get coffee."

We took it slow drinking the coffee and then settled in at our desks, killing time until the after-work crowd showed up at the clubs. Tip approached Julie right about quitting time. "I'm sorry about earlier. I was out of line."

"Don't worry," she said.

He handed her a slip of paper with Forrest Lipscomb's name on it, and the name of his firm. "This is the lawyer we found—"

"I know who he is, and I've already run everything on him. He's clean. Two parking tickets in seven years. Other than that, nothing. We've run all the phone logs, too. Nothing but business and the occasional call to his wife and a sister in Dallas."

"I knew that much. What I want you to run is his firm. See if there's anything that raises questions. Suspicious lawsuits or any complaints that stand out."

"I'm about to go home, but I'll get on it," she said, and then, "Thanks for understanding."

"You know I can be an ass sometimes," Tip said.

"We all do," I said, from behind him.

We worked for a couple of hours, and then Tip looked at his watch and stood. "Gianelli, let's go find us a whore."

I grabbed my phone from the desk and followed. "That's why I like you, Denton. You've got such a classy vocabulary."

We headed down to Texas Avenue fighting traffic all the way. It was nothing like Brooklyn, but bad enough to put a person on edge. Tip pulled up to valet parking and we got out. A young guy who looked to be in his twenties greeted us with a big smile.

"Here for the night?" he asked.

I flashed my badge. "We won't be long, so keep the car handy." I then showed him the picture of Lipscomb. "Do you know this guy? He might have been here Tuesday night."

"Not me, but I only work two nights a week." He turned toward another guy, older, maybe early forties. "Greg, did you work Tuesday?"

Greg came over to us. "I was working. Why?"

Tip gave the kid a ten dollar bill and he took the car. I showed Greg the picture. "Did you see this guy?"

He stepped toward the door so he had better light. "He was here. He came in around nine if I remember and left not long after, maybe ten or ten-thirty."

"Did he leave alone?" Tip asked.

Greg smiled. "Mr. Lipscomb almost never left alone."

"So who was the lucky girl Tuesday night?"

"I never saw her before, but she was young and pretty."

"Blonde hair, about twenty-five or so?" I asked.

Greg thought for a few seconds and said, "The age is about right, but she wasn't blonde. I think she had brown hair, dark brown."

"You're sure about that? She wasn't blonde?"

"I can't swear to the hair color, but she wore a really short skirt, and she had great legs."

"What you're saying is you never looked at her hair," Tip said.

"I only saw her for a second," Greg said. "It was busy."

"Okay, thanks," Tip said and handed him ten dollars and a card. "Call me if you think of something else."

"So much for witnesses," I said.

We went inside and waited for the bartender to catch a break. Tip showed him the badge and the picture of Lipscomb. "He was in here Tuesday night. Do you remember him?"

It didn't take the guy two seconds to respond. "Mr. Pinot Noir. He sat right next to where you are now and he spent most of his time trying to hit on a woman sitting next to him—strawberry daiquiri."

"You remember what time he got here?" I asked.

He seemed to struggle with that. "I tend to lose track of time when I'm working. If I had to guess, maybe halfway through the shift. No later."

"What's your shift?" Tip asked.

"I come on at 6:00 and get off at 2:00."

"What about the girl?" I asked. "Was she a blonde, early twenties?"

He was shaking his head before I finished. "Definitely not a blonde and early thirties is more like it. She looked great though. Sexy as hell."

"Describe her," Tip said.

"Short dark hair, knockout body, short skirt. Business-woman look. You know, a professional. Like I said, sexy."

I looked at Tip and then back to the bartender. "You're saying professional as in *business*, not working girl."

He laughed. "Working girl? No way. She looked like a salesperson or somebody in marketing, a job like that."

Tip said, "And you're sure she wasn't a blonde? Maybe she wore a brown wig."

"This lady wasn't a blonde. She didn't have blonde *skin*. She had darker skin and a hint of a Mexican accent. And like I said, she definitely wasn't early twenties. I can tell by the eyes."

The bartender waited for Tip to finish writing notes, then he said, "What's up with the questions? What did this guy do? Did he hurt her?"

"He got himself killed," I said.

The bartender cocked his head and looked at me. "No shit? I'd have thought the other way."

"Why do you say that?"

"The guy's a creep. He was always trying to pick up young women. He tried hiding it the other night, but he stalked that woman. Watched everything she did, almost drooling over her when she wasn't looking."

"Did she leave with him?" I asked.

He shook his head. "She was waiting for somebody, but the guy never showed. She asked me to call her a cab. When the creep heard that, he offered her a ride, but then she got a call from her guy just before leaving."

"How do you know?" I asked.

"I heard her. I think she called him 'Andy.' Something like that."

"Andy?" I said. "Are you sure?"

He seemed to consider it, and then, "I can't swear to it. It could have been Mandy or Randy, but it was something similar."

"With all the people in here, why'd you take interest in them?"

"Like I said, she was sexy as hell and I was dying to see that fool make an ass of himself."

I handed him a card and asked him to call if he remembered anything else. He said he would, and I believed him.

We left the bar, questioned the valet-parking guy again before leaving. He stuck with his story that Lipscomb left about 10 or 10:30 with a woman in a short skirt with brown hair, and great legs.

Tip got on the freeway and started for home. "Let's go over what we've got," I said.

- Lipscomb left the bar around 10 or 10:30.
- According to the cameras at the hotel, he got there about 10:35.
- The bartender said she left without Lipscomb.
- The parking attendant said Lipscomb left with a brown-haired woman.
- Lipscomb checked into the hotel with a blonde.

"And it's not more than ten minutes from the bar to the hotel, even with traffic," Tip said.

"What the hell went on here? Lipscomb left the bar with a woman he just met. A few minutes later, or even half an hour later, he checked into the hotel with a different woman. Did he drop the dark-haired woman off somewhere?"

"But the bartender said she got a call from the guy she was supposed to meet—Andy or something."

I thought about this for a moment. "Where did *she* go? And how did Lipscomb hook up with Tiffany?"

"He could have dropped the girl from the bar off somewhere and then called Tiffany," Tip said.

"That might work, but there weren't any calls on his phone after he called his wife."

Tip switched to the right lane and slowed down to almost the speed limit. "We have to assume he had this set up beforehand."

"He had to," I said. "Remember, LaDonna told us Tiffany said she had a big-money client."

Tip looked over at me, and said, "So if he had it set up with Tiffany, what was he doing trying to get lucky with the woman at the bar? It doesn't add up."

We rode in silence for a half mile or so. What LaDonna said was bugging me, about how Tiffany turned down $200. "Lipscomb didn't line this up out of the blue," I said. "If he was willing to pay a lot more than $200, he must have spent time with her before."

"If he did, there'd be a record of him calling her," Tip said. "Either he did it from work or on somebody else's phone. Julie said his cell was barely used."

We drove another couple of miles, and I said, "Nothing works, Tip. Even if we assume he had things set up with Tiffany ahead of time through someone else, that still leaves us with the God-awful coincidence that the woman at the bar *happened* to be leaving at just the time Lipscomb would have to leave to get to the hotel to meet Tiffany. And it doesn't answer the question of why she got in the car with him."

"You're right," Tip said. "That dog just don't hunt."

"I wondered how long it would be before you brought out one of your sayings."

"I guess now you know."

"Maybe someone else made the arrangements," I said.

"Like the concierge," Tip said. "Let's have another go at him. He might be more of a pimp than he's letting on."

We dropped in on Sebastian while the place was swamped. He was less than excited to see us, probably recalling how Tip embarrassed him earlier with the cuffs.

"What is it you want?" Sebastian said. "As you can see we are very busy."

"I need to know about Tiffany," I said. "How often she came here, where else she plied her trade, and who set up her appointment that night."

Sebastian's head was shaking before I finished. "She had one or two appointments a week here," he said. "As to where else she worked, I have no idea, and as I told you before, I have *no* idea who set up her appointment the night in question."

"Did you get your cut on this one?" Tip asked.

"I don't *ever* get a cut from the ladies. They keep everything."

"Who pays you?" I asked.

He smiled at a patron passing by, and waved to another, and then he looked at me and whispered. "Occasionally a gentleman might see it fit to leave me a tip. But I never ask for anything," he was quick to add.

"Weren't you concerned when Forrest didn't leave you a *tip?*"

"For the last time," he said. "I wasn't here that night, and I had nothing to do with them getting together. Now, do what you will, but I have customers."

"Go on," Tip said, and we headed back to the car.

Chapter 13

A Friendly Conversation

"Where are we headed?" I asked.

"We've still got to find Tiffany, but first I need to have a chat with someone."

"Who?"

"Bobby."

It took him three calls to find out where Bobby was. It turned out to be a bar with a not-so-good reputation. Tip parked across the street, checked his gun, and got out. "Stay here," he said. "I won't be long."

"I'm coming with you."

"It'll go better if you don't."

Against better judgment, I let him go in alone.

Bobby was sitting at the end of the bar with another cop. Both had been undercover longer than they should have been, and they looked the part. Two black guys occupied stools a few seats away from them, and a couple of Mexicans sat in a booth near the back. Other than that, the place was empty. The bartender, rail thin, greeted Tip.

"What'll it be?"

Tip never took his eyes from Bobby. "Nothing for me," he said, and moved toward the back. His holster was unbuckled and he had a backup gun in his waistband. Bobby looked his way.

"Denton! What the fuck are you doing here?"

"Came to see an old friend," Tip said.

Bobby looked around, a surprised expression on his face. "Where is he?"

The guy with Bobby laughed. Tip looked to the blacks and Mexicans, but they hadn't moved. "You didn't tell me he was back in town, Bobby."

Bobby set his drink down, a scowl forming on his face. "I don't know who *he* is, but it don't matter much, 'cause it's none of your business."

Tip gave him one of his hard-eyed glares, the kind where his eye twitched and the scar on his face twisted. "How much is he paying you?"

"That's a dangerous question to ask, considering where you are."

"I'm still asking."

Bobby and the cop with him stood. The two Mexicans stood also and moved slowly toward Tip.

Connie walked in the door. "No need to get up for me, boys. I just came to take my partner home for dinner."

They kept moving. Connie came alongside Tip, her hand rested on her gun. "I think *everyone* better sit."

Bobby glanced at the Mexicans, then back to Connie.

Tip stepped away from the bar. "Better do what she says. She's crazy enough to shoot you."

Bobby and his men sat, staring as Tip and Connie backed out of the bar. "Ya'll enjoy it while it lasts," Tip said. "I'll get to the bottom of it."

"You better have a plan for when you get there, Denton."

"Don't worry, Stenson. I've always got a plan."

Tip got in the car and started it. Connie climbed in the passenger seat. "You want to tell me what good you did coming down here?"

"I let that son of a bitch know I was onto him," Tip said.

"You could have done that with a phone call."

"But then I wouldn't have been able to see his eyes. I needed to see how he reacted."

"And did that do you any good?"

"He didn't react like I thought he would," Tip said. "But I don't know what it means yet."

Tip put the car in gear and made a u-turn. "I know we don't always agree, but sometimes I like to do things my way."

"Just sometimes?"

Tip laughed. "Have I told you I like you as a partner."

"Just drive, asshole. We've got a case to solve."

Chapter 14

OLD ENEMIES

Carlos pushed his plate to the side and wiped his mouth with a napkin. Manuelo brought a fresh carafe of coffee, poured a cup for Carlos, and placed it on the table.

"Thank you," Carlos said. "Tico and I have business to discuss."

"Si, señor," Manuelo said, and left the room.

Tico took the seat across from Carlos. "You wanted to talk, señor?"

"Updates, Tico. What have you discovered since we've been in Houston?"

"After talking to our men on the streets, I have a better picture. In six months we should control the market in Houston. We increased distribution by 250% since you lowered the price four months ago. Every dealer not with us is suffering. We have regained almost all of our territory, and we have moved into new operations."

Carlos sucked on a piece of hard lemon candy. "And the police?"

"We have made inroads. Enough to give us information, and *some* protection."

"We need more."

"It is early," Tico said. "We have things working."

"We need it to happen sooner. It won't take long to control the market in Texas, and once we own the distribution we can raise the price. The demand will be there." Carlos picked another candy from the bowl. "I have been looking into things myself. That unfortunate event in Wilmington cost us more than a few men. Now the police are poking into our affairs."

"That will settle down. The cop who did that is gone, and—"

"Tico, sometimes you're so smart, and at other times…" Carlos finished his cup of coffee and lit a cigarette, a Fortuna. "A policeman in the United States is not going to kill 11 men and then disappear. And the police don't burn down houses."

"But, señor."

"Someone else did this, and we need to find out who. Have our men look around Wilmington and see who benefitted the most from our misfortune."

"It was the black gang, the one run by the man called Monroe."

"Now you're thinking, Tico, and while we're on the subject of thinking, what are we doing with our money?"

"Señor Snider has resisted all attempts, and the man we used before is under investigation."

"It seems as if we will have to convince Señor Snider. Leave that to me. I already have things working."

The phone rang. Tico pushed the speaker button and answered. "Your line is secure?"

"I wouldn't call if it wasn't. We have problems."

"Describe them."

"Tip Denton is asking questions. He's *not* the kind of cop you want to mess with."

Tico looked at Carlos and then asked, "Who is he working with?"

"His old partner from New York. She just came back."

"Keep me informed," Tico said, and hung up.

Carlos crushed his cigarette in the ashtray, grinding it until it was flat. "I thought she was half dead. That's what you told me."

Tico sighed. "Don't get ideas, señor. You can't kill cops in this country. Forget about her."

"Who said anything about killing? She's a dirty cop associated with the mob. All we have to do is expose her."

"We have no proof of her being dirty."

"But Mangini helped her in Brooklyn. And a mystery person killed two men in the hospital in Houston. Someone is her guardian angel. We need to find out why. Have one of our men in New York look into this. I want everything he can find on the detective, her mother, and the man who *supposedly* is her father."

Tico got up to leave. "Si, señor. I will have it done."

Chapter 15

SURVEILLANCE

The man handling the surveillance on Patrick Snider brought the pictures to Carlos. "These are good. He won't be able to explain them away."

"Let me see," Carlos said, and thumbed through the photos—explicit pictures of Snider and his lover in compromising situations, and his lover was a former employee of the bank. "Good work, my friend. Now tell me about the routine."

"She checks into the hotel and within a couple of hours he shows up and goes to her room. She gets the same suite every time, so he must have it reserved. Sometimes she comes down afterward and has a drink at the bar, but only after he's gone."

"And you found all of this out in just a few weeks?"

"He's a horny gringo."

Carlos looked at the pictures again, taking time to examine each one. "How did we get the pictures from inside his room?"

"Consuela's sister knows one of the maids at the hotel. She let us in to plant the mic and camera."

Carlos nodded as he paced. "This is good. Give Consuela and her sister a bonus and send them home. They are to tell no one about this."

"Si, señor. And do I continue with the surveillance?"

"No need. Now we will teach our friend a lesson."

Patrick Snider gave a rousing speech detailing his investment plan for the Latino community. It incited the people to a thunderous applause and a standing ovation. New money for the community meant cleaning up the streets, getting rid of drug dealers, and bringing prosperity to the deteriorating Mexican district. It was a long-standing platform for politicians attempting to secure the Latino votes, but this was a first for the banking community. Snider was a clever man. He knew how to grease the wheels, and this move would put him in a position of power.

Carlos waited for Snider to leave the stage, then he dialed the number.

"Hello."

"Excellent speech, Señor Snider. You sounded like you really meant all of those things. Were those emotions real?"

"Who is this? How did you get this number?"

"Does it matter?"

"I'm hanging up," Snider said.

"Before you do, I have something to say about your girlfriend."

There was a long pause. "What do you want?"

"Ah, now there's a question that *does* matter." Carlos let his pause equal Snider's, then said, "We should find a place to meet."

"About what?"

"About the pictures I have of you and…let me see…Sharon, I believe her name is. They are nice pictures. She has an attractive figure and she looks especially good in that picture where you have her bent over the table at your suite in the hotel."

"You fucker. What do you want?"

"All in good time. I will see you soon."

"Wait—" There was a short pause, then, "I won't be blackmailed. Not even if it means the end of my career."

"And what about your marriage?"

"Fuck you. Print the pictures, tell the press, tell my wife if you want. I won't be subject to blackmail. I'd rather resign my job or get divorced."

Carlos fidgeted while he talked. "A bold stance to take, señor, but I should remind you that there are things worse than resigning. Even worse than divorce."

"I don't know who you think you are, but you're not dealing with some two-bit crook. I'm not afraid to admit my affair. I don't want to, but it's not the worst that can happen."

Carlos laughed. "Señor, you are right. I apologize for not understanding you. Perhaps we'll talk another time."

"I don't think so. Do what you want with your pictures and any other evidence you have. I have a company to run."

"Good luck," Carlos said, and hung up.

Carlos turned to Tico, standing rigid, awaiting orders. "I am going to work out, but afterward…I think I'll need companionship."

"Si, señor."

"She must be beautiful. Sexy. Seductive." Carlos smiled, the kind of smile that made Tico shiver. "She must be fit. And this time I would prefer a dark-skinned girl with smooth skin."

Tico waited but when it appeared as if Carlos had finished, he started to leave. "I will see it is done."

"One who speaks Spanish would be nice."

"Si, señor," Tico said, then left the room.

Chapter 16

GIRLFRIENDS

Sahrina finished her coffee, set the cup in the sink, and then walked down the hall and banged on the bedroom door. "Get up, Andrea. It's almost noon."

Andrea's voice was groggy. "I usually sleep later."

"Not if you're staying here."

A few minutes later Andrea came out of the bedroom wearing pajamas and a pair of heavy wool socks. "You keep it cold in here."

"It's November. It's supposed to be cold."

Andrea rubbed her eyes. "Do you have any coffee made?"

Sahrina gestured to her left. "A few hours ago I did. But you can make your own. It's in the counter next to the refrigerator."

"I'll get you some money for food as soon as—"

"Don't worry about that. And our boss won't want you working for anyone else as long as he has things for us to do."

"Yeah, well that thing we did the other night didn't go so well. Do you think he'll give us more work?"

"I'm sure," Sahrina said. "Make your coffee and come outside. It's a nice day."

After the coffee brewed, Andrea grabbed a cup from the cabinet and took the pot with her. It was going to take more than one cup to get her started today. She opened the sliding door, walked outside and sat next to Sahrina by the pool.

"I could get used to this."

"No reason why you can't have it," Sahrina said.

Andrea laughed. "Me? I'm lucky to afford the room I share with LaDonna. Damn junkie whore."

"Remember I told you we'd be paid well for the other night?"

Andrea nodded. "You said $500, but I figured we're screwed since he died."

Sahrina smiled. "The man we work for is fair. And generous. He knows we didn't do anything wrong. After all, how could we know he'd have a heart attack?"

"You mean we're still getting paid?"

Sahrina walked to the kitchen, pulled an envelope from behind a few plates in the cabinet, and handed it to Andrea. "Not just paid. Paid extra."

Andrea ripped open the envelope. It was stuffed with hundreds. "Damn! There must be—"

"Two thousand dollars," Sahrina said. "For each of us."

Andrea continued counting, and then looked up at Sahrina. Her face lit up. "And you said there might be more work?"

"Plenty more," Sahrina said. "As long as we do our job, we'll both get rich."

"What about the guy who died? Suppose they try to pin that on us?"

"That should blow over soon. They're not going to spend a lot of time on a guy who died of a heart attack. Besides, that's why you're staying with me. Nobody will find you here."

"How long do you think I have to stay?"

"Until our boss says it's clear. And remember, don't go back home, don't talk to anybody, don't go anywhere you'll be recognized. Not until we get the okay."

"You don't have to worry about that. I can hang out here a while."

The phone rang. Sahrina went to get it. She talked for a few minutes then returned wearing a big smile. "Things are looking good. We have a new client."

Chapter 17

A Dangerous Workout

B rent Davids locked his briefcase, tucked it under the seat, and closed the car door. He clicked the remote twice to make sure the doors were locked. He felt good today—filled with excess energy. It was a good thing because today was leg day.

He entered the gym, signed in, hung his keys on the rack, and made his way to the back room. Squats came first. He loaded two 45-pound plates and two 10-pounders on the bar. With the bar weighing 45, that got him to 155 pounds—up almost 11% from last month. Progress. That's what mattered. If he could show returns like that at work, he'd be CEO within a year.

The first two sets came easy; the last set he struggled with. After finishing, he wiped his forehead and leaned on the bar to rest. A young woman with a knockout body walked by, her sweats so tight Brent thought her ass might pop out. She had an iPod hooked to an almost-see-through top, with headphones stuffed in her ears. A great set of tits pushed hard on the front of her shirt. *What a fantastic ass!*

She stumbled on the protruding edge of a rowing machine, almost caught herself, then fell. Hard. Brent rushed over to her. "Are you all right?"

She pushed up on her elbows, started to stand, and almost fell again. "Oh God, that was embarrassing."

Brent smiled. She had a strong Texas twang. It sounded sexy. "Are you okay?"

She nodded. "I'll be fine. But thanks." She took two steps and faltered, grabbing hold of Brent's arm for support. "Damn!"

"What's wrong?"

Her face scrunched up. "It's my ankle. I must have twisted it."

"You better sit. I'll get some ice."

"That's all right," she said. "If you can just help me to my car."

"Are you sure?" Brent said, and wondered if his disappointment was evident in his voice.

"I'm sure, but thanks again. I really appreciate it."

"What about your clothes? Didn't you bring something?"

"Everything's in the locker. I'll get it tomorrow." She took another step, grimaced, and held out her hand to him. "If you can help me to the car, I'll make it home from there."

Brent walked slowly toward the front door of the gym, enjoying her firm grip on his arm. Her hair had the scent of…strawberries. Mixed with the smell of sweat from her workout, it was almost too much. He felt himself grow excited.

They weren't twenty steps into the parking lot when she pointed to an Accura near the front row. "Right there," she said. "The silver one."

Brent opened the door and helped her into the car. "I can drive you home if you want."

She laughed. "And how would you get home?"

"No, I meant I could drive you home in my car. You can get yours later."

"You're sweet, but I can make it." She reached up and pecked him on the cheek. "Thanks for the offer," she said, and drove off.

Brent watched her drive away, but thoughts of her stayed with him through the night. That peck on the cheek, combined with the smell of her, and the image of that fantastic ass pushing against her sweats was enough for several weeks of dreaming, but Brent packed them all into one restless night. He barely slept.

The next night he stopped for a drink on the way home. A young woman was limping across the floor from the bar with what looked like a strawberry daiquiri in her hand. When he got closer he saw she was the girl from the gym. He walked up to her, a smile on his face. "How's the ankle?"

She looked up at Brent, squinted her eyes, then said, "Oh my God—the gym." She laughed. "I didn't recognize you in the suit."

"Today is my day of rest," he said. "But it's back to the grind tomorrow."

She took a seat at a small table. "I've got a week or two of rest left. It's not what I wanted but…"

Brent fidgeted. "Well, good seeing you. I'm going to get a drink."

"Are you here with someone?" she asked.

"No. I just stopped on my way home."

She gestured to the chair opposite her. "Nobody's sitting here," she said, then, "By the way, I'm Sahrina."

He reached his hand out. "Brent Davids. Nice to formally meet," he said. "I'm getting a drink. Be right back."

"Take your time," Sahrina said. "I need to send a text anyway."

Brent returned a few minutes later with a beer.

"Beer?" Sahrina said.

Brent proudly held up the mug. "Not beer—Guinness."

"I didn't figure you for the beer type."

"That's me," Brent said. "Full of surprises."

She smiled and looked up at him over the rim of her glass. "I *like* surprises."

"Do you come here often?" Brent asked.

"I don't know the answer to that yet," she said. "I just moved here from San Antonio." She pronounced it the way Texans do, without the "i" or "o" sound at the end of the word.

"San Antonio, huh. I love that city. Austin, too."

"So what're you doing in Houston?"

Brent sighed. "Business. I was transferred here about five years ago. I'm not complaining; I like Houston, but someday I'd love to get back to Austin." He took a sip of beer and then said, "How about you? What brought you to Houston?"

"I was with a small software company and they went under. I tried finding another job there and one in Austin, but Houston won out."

"Lucky us," Brent said, and he felt himself blush.

"What do you have planned tonight?" Sahrina asked.

"I guess dancing's out of the question," he said.

"More surprises," She said, and laughed. "Dancing would be out of the question if I *wasn't* hurt. I'm a terrible dancer."

Brent shot her an I-don't-believe-it look. "Now *I'm* surprised. I figured you for the kind to tear up the dance floor."

Sahrina seemed to ignore his comment, then she stretched to the side looking past Brent's shoulder. A smile lit her face and she stood and waved her hands. "Andy! Over here."

Brent's heart sank, until he turned to see 'Andy' was a nice-looking young blonde in a dress cut shorter than Sahrina's hair.

Andy and Sahrina hugged. "Take a seat," Sahrina said, and gestured toward Brent. "This is Brent, a friend of mine."

The friend part sounded nice. "What are you drinking?" Brent asked.

"White wine. Whatever you pick is fine with me."

***

When Brent was out of earshot, Sahrina turned to Andy. "Remember, you're supposed to be a waitress. You moved here from Nashville, and you're living with me until you find a place."

"I know how to handle myself," Andrea said.

Sahrina lost her sweet tone. She stared at Andrea and gritted her teeth. "I'm only going to say it once. You're a *waitress* not a hooker. You're an innocent young woman who is about to be enamored by this handsome young businessman, who likes to dance by the way. If you screw up…there are plenty more like you I can find."

Andrea gulped and nodded. "I can do innocent. Most of my clients want innocent or dirty. I can do either."

"Good. Be ready, he's coming."

Brent set the glass of wine in front of Andrea. "I hope you like it."

She smiled. "I'm sure I will."

The three of them chatted for a while, and then a Taylor Swift song started playing, filling the dance floor with people. Andrea grabbed Brent's hand. "Come on, let's dance."

Brent looked at Sahrina. "Go on," she said. "You know I can't."

Andrea and Brent danced to Taylor Swift, and Beyonce, and then Lady GaGa. In between, Brent gulped down the Guinness and Andrea slowly sipped her wine. And while they danced, Sahrina prepared her syringe. She didn't want to use it, but it was better to be prepared.

After a few more dances, Sahrina yawned and said, "I'm getting tired, Andy. We should be going."

Brent appeared to panic. "It's early," he said, and his words slurred a little. "How about coming back to my place?"

"Sounds fun," Andrea said, the excitement showing in her voice and her eyes.

"I don't know," Sahrina said.

Andy grabbed her hand. "Come on, Rina. The night's young."

Sahrina looked at Brent. "How far is it?"

Brent perked up. "Not far. Maybe twenty minutes."

Sahrina shook her head and laughed. "All right. Let's go. We'll follow you."

Brent tossed a twenty on the table for a tip, and then grabbed hold of Sahrina's arm to help her out. "I hope you like swimming."

"Swimming? It's November, for God's sake."

"Don't worry, the pool's heated and I have a huge hot tub."

As they drove up the freeway, following Brent, Sahrina said, "Follow my lead. Question nothing."

"I'm good," Andrea said.

Chapter 18

A NIGHT TO ANALYZE

I spent most of the day Saturday getting the house in order. Tip said he was going to talk to a few informants and insisted he didn't need me. I fought him about it, but by noon I was glad I didn't go. I forgot how much work it took to get settled into a new place. One good thing about being here was I was able to keep the sliding door open all day allowing Hotshot free rein in the back yard. He had a ball chasing bugs and moths, and despite missing a leg, he managed to catch a few of them.

Late in the afternoon, about the time I was thinking of what to do for dinner, Tip called.

"Did you do any good?" I asked.

"It depends on how you look at it," Tip said. "I found three concierges who swore they never laid eyes on her. I figured they were lying so I checked with the bellhops, desk clerks, and even valet attendants. Unless it was a damn big conspiracy, she didn't ply her trade at those hotels."

"Maybe she only worked the Four Seasons, which wouldn't be bad if she was getting enough business," I said. "But from what we saw of her room it didn't look like it."

"Keep your thinking hat on and drive up to my place. I'll cook dinner."

"Partner, you've got a deal. I'm hungry."

The drive to Tip's place was now familiar, and that turned out to be a problem. Every landmark and every road reminded me of that sick pervert who had beaten me half to death. *And raped me,* I thought, as I drove past the apartment complex where he attacked me. I turned my head but it was like the image of his sick, disgustingly handsome face had found a permanent place in my mind. Like a picture that wouldn't burn.

I shook my head and slowed the car. If I didn't watch out I'd be approaching Tip Denton speed. I got off the next exit and made my way to Tip's driveway. It was the second time I'd been here, but I still half expected Kassie and Kelly to greet me…but that was before I remembered helping Tip bury them, compliments of another sick son of a bitch—Carlos Cortes.

Tip's car was parked in front of the garage. I pulled in next to it and got out. Halfway to the side porch, Flash ran to greet me. I got on my knees to give her a hug. She smiled and jumped on me. "It's good to see you again," I said, and rubbed my face in her fur.

"I wouldn't do that," Tip hollered from the porch. "You never know what she's been rolling in."

"I need a man who greets me as enthusiastically as Flash."

"Good luck with that," Tip said, and opened the door.

I followed him inside. Sacco was on the floor by the kitchen. "Hey, Sacco," I said, and got one wag of the tail in response. I reached to pet him. "He's quiet."

"At least somebody's quiet around here," Mollie said. "Anything new on our case?"

"How many times do I have to tell you?" Tip said, "*We* aren't working any case."

"Don't fret none. I heard you." A timer sounded in the kitchen. "That's dinner," Mollie said. "Tip, get some plates. Connie, beer's in the fridge."

Mollie placed ribs, coleslaw, and baked beans on the table and then she took a seat next to me. "I made pecan pie for dessert, so don't fill up."

"Pecan pie?" I said. "Life doesn't get much better than this. Good food. Good beer. All we need is a few Bon Jovi songs and we'll be set."

Mollie looked at me, squinted and said, "Who? Bon Javi?"

"No. Jon Bon Jovi. He's a musician."

"He a foreigner?"

"Sort of, he's from New Jersey."

"Sounds like a damn foreigner to me. Gettin' to be all there is anymore is foreigners."

I had to cover my mouth to keep from laughing. "We were all foreigners once," I said.

She looked at me with one eye half closed. "Yeah, yeah, yeah. Heard that before."

Mollie made tea for Tip and coffee for us. Tip got the files and laid them out on the table in the other room.

"What have we got so far?" I asked.

"Don't go startin' without me," Mollie said.

Tip was about to say something but I shook my head. "Not worth it," I whispered.

A minute later Mollie brought in coffee and tea—and pecan pie for each of us. "What have we got?" she said.

Tip pointed to a couple of charts. "This is what we have so far."

Dead lawyer. Possibly a heart attack.
Lawyer was with a prostitute—Tiffany.
Meeting seems to have been planned. (According to LaDonna)
Tiffany is missing. On the run?

- **Bartender described her as:**
- ✓ Dark hair.
- ✓ Dark complexion.
- ✓ Not blonde.
- ✓ 30 ish, professional.
- ✓ Mexican accent.
- ✓ Probably didn't leave with Lipscomb.
- ✓ Was waiting for a guy named Andy.
- ✓ Said Lipscomb was waiting for someone, too, but might have been lying.

- ✓ Hotel said our girl had blonde hair.

- ✓ Tiffany had blonde hair.
- ✓ Valet parking guy said she went with Lipscomb.
- ✓ Where did he meet Tiffany, and how?
- ✓ If Tiffany said she had a big client, how did she know in advance?
- ✓ If Lipscomb planned it, why would he be trying to pick up the other woman?

I looked at what Tip had on the chart and shook my head. "So we've got a dead lawyer, who might or might not have had a heart attack, but who was with a prostitute who has since disappeared."

"Let's not forget the mysterious dark-haired woman at the bar who either left with Lipscomb, or, left with Andy, depending on who you ask."

"And that brings up another question," I said. "Who the hell is Andy?"

Tip scribbled a question mark on the bottom of the chart. "The bigger question is how did Lipscomb meet Tiffany?"

The phone rang and Tip reached for it. "I have you on speaker, Delgado, and ladies are present."

"No need to worry about me. I don't curse."

"Have you solved that sticker case yet?" Tip asked.

"You mean the fake inspection-sticker case, that turned into a homicide, that is now a drug case too? If you mean that one, the answer is no."

"How'd it get to be a drug case?"

"Cruz and I went *cruisin'* today. We rousted a bunch of low-life scum until we found a few who talked. It seems like our victim, Señor Martin, was dealing meth along with the stickers."

"Meth?"

"Yeah. *Ice is nice,* as they say on the streets. He was dealing a lot of it, too. The crime scene unit found 20 grand in spendable denominations in his apartment. It was stuffed in envelopes and stapled to the underside of cabinets in the kitchen. If it hadn't been for the drug dog we might have missed it, but the money had traces of meth and cocaine on it."

"Did you find the meth?" Tip asked.

"Not yet."

"Ribs, this is getting stranger by the minute."

"Why's that?"

"Are you by yourself?" Tip asked.

"Just me and Rosalee."

"Yesterday, when Connie and I were tracking down our prostitute, I got a lead from one of my informants. He said somebody new in town has been dealing meth and selling it cheap."

Delgado whistled. "Amigo, this *is* getting strange. Martin had the number for the stiff at the hotel, and now we both get leads on meth."

"You know what's even worse?" Tip said. "I called Bobby Stenson to ask him about it and he said he didn't know anything about a new player."

"Nothing?"

"That's what he said."

"If Bobby hasn't heard anything, and both of us have, that kind of makes me wonder what streets Bobby's been working."

"Yeah, and I went to see Bobby at his favorite watering hole. Let's say he wasn't happy to see me. In fact, if it wasn't for Connie walking in I might have had to fight my way out of there."

"I can't believe Stenson would turn," Delgado said, "but you never know. Drug money buys a lot of things."

"And a lot of people," Tip said. "So let's keep this between us."

"You got it. I'll keep you up to date."

Tip looked at me. "I think it's time we had another talk with Bobby."

"That's not our business," I said. "Give it to IA or Coop. We've got our own case to solve."

Mollie moved next to Tip. "Speaking of your case, I see what's wrong with your thinking."

"Don't start," Tip said.

Mollie grabbed a pen and pointed to where Tip had written Andy's name on the chart. "Instead of Andy," she said, "Suppose the bartender got it wrong? What if it's *Annie?*"

"Son of a bitch!" I said. "I wasn't thinking of a woman. But the bartender might still have it right. What if it's *Andie*, as in short for Andrea?"

Tip gave Mollie a kiss on the cheek. "Be careful or I might kiss you again," he said.

Mollie narrowed her eyes. "I shot the last man who kissed me," she said, but then she smiled.

I ran through what we had, considering this new possibility. "If we assume 'Andie' was Tiffany, that solves all of our problems as far as how Lipscomb met up with her."

Tip nodded. "So Tiffany called the dark-haired woman in the bar, and they arranged to meet at the hotel."

"Exactly," I said, "And then Lipscomb left with the mystery woman, went to the hotel, and Tiffany was already there."

"I like it," Tip said, "But where did the mystery woman go? We didn't see her on the surveillance tape."

I thought for a few seconds, and then said, "Maybe she didn't go in. Or maybe she went to somebody else's room. There are a lot of reasons that could explain why we didn't see her on tape. But…"

"What?" Tip said.

"No matter what reason we come up with, it still doesn't explain how Tiffany knew beforehand that she'd be getting a big payday. LaDonna told us that Tiffany turned down $200 because she had a better deal that night. By all accounts Lipscomb meeting the mystery woman in the bar was by chance."

"That does knock the wind out of us," Tip said.

I took a few sips of beer and then said, "Unless we look at it from a different angle. Suppose Lipscomb wasn't the one paying Tiffany?"

"The mystery woman?" Tip said.

"And if she was the one paying, it makes a heart attack look a lot less likely."

"Ya'll can thank me anytime you want," Mollie said.

I laughed. "Mollie, I might have to rethink who my partner is."

"Partner?" she said with more than a hint of sarcasm, "That man can't think his way out of the bathroom."

Tip cracked a smile. "Be careful, old girl, or I'll kiss you again."

"You better practice that, too," she said, and then went to get more coffee.

"I'm beginning to think somebody wanted Lipscomb dead," Tip said. "We need to talk to his partners again."

"Looks like we got a case after all," I said.

Chapter 19

A MIDNIGHT SWIM

Sahrina kept a safe distance behind Brent as he drove west on I-10. He took the Gessner exit and headed south. Within minutes he pulled into the driveway of a large two-story French Colonial. A balcony wrapped the second floor of the house.

"I'm liking this," Andy said.

"Don't forget the plan. We're here to get pictures. When I tell you it's time, get naked and get close."

"Suppose we can't get the pictures?"

"If we don't get the pictures, we don't get paid."

Brent got out of his car and waited for Sahrina and Andy to join him. Brent opened the front door and they followed him in.

"This is beautiful," Andy said.

Brent took them on a quick tour of the first floor, ending up in the kitchen. Andy went to the sliding door and looked at the patio. "I love the patio. And the pool."

"I don't mean to be rude," Sahrina said, "But do you have anything to drink? My throat is dry."

Brent rushed over. "My apologies. I don't know where my manners are tonight."

Sahrina looked at him and smiled. "What would your mother think?"

He laughed. "She'd be appalled that I'm about to get naked with two beautiful women."

Sahrina raised her eyebrows. "Who said anything about naked?"

"We talked about going swimming, remember? Unless you brought bathing suits…"

Andy laughed. "I don't care about naked, but I would like some wine if you have any."

Brent opened a bottle of Chardonnay. "How about you ladies pouring wine while I get towels."

"I'm not swimming," Sahrina said, as he left the room.

"I've got a hot tub. Maybe you'll feel like taking a dip later."

Andy reached for the bottle, but Sahrina stopped her. "Wait and let the gentleman pour. We're ladies, remember?"

Andy smiled. "Sorry."

Brent turned out to be quite a conversationalist, showing off a broad-based knowledge of music, books, movies, and business. He also seemed to have a particular interest in the "unclothed" female body. After almost an hour of talking, and another bottle of wine, he started his spiel again. "I know you've got to be ready for a dip in the hot tub. Come on. It'll feel great."

Andy looked at Sahrina and shrugged. "I'm game if you are."

Brent smiled. "Well?"

Sahrina pursed her lips and shook her head slowly. "I'm not sure, Brent. I—"

"What's it going to take?" Brent asked.

Sahrina put her finger to her lips, and said, "Get the tequila, salt, and lime. We'll see what kind of man you really are."

Brent almost jumped from his seat. "Hot damn," he said, and went to the liquor cabinet. He returned holding a bottle of tequila. "If one of you gets the salt and lime, we're set."

"Get three shot glasses," Sahrina said to Andy. "I'll get the salt and lime."

Brent grabbed a towel, opened the sliding door, and walked out to the patio. "Don't forget the towels," he said.

"Andy, grab the towels. I'll get the door," Sahrina said.

As Andy stepped onto the patio, Sahrina grabbed a couple of pills from her purse and followed Andy out. She used her elbow to slide the door closed.

Sahrina set the salt and lime on a table next to the tequila. Brent had the hot tub running. He reached for his pants.

"Easy mister," Sahrina said. "I don't get naked with just any old man. Here are the rules. After the first shot my top goes off. Second shot and the bottoms come off. Third..." A seductive smile popped onto her face. "We'll have to see about that."

Brent poured the tequila and then downed the first shooter.

Sahrina removed her top, leaned toward him and gave him a short kiss.

Brent never took his eyes from her. He poured another shot and downed it as quickly as he had the first, his gaze shifting to below her stomach. She stepped out of her pants and removed her panties, revealing a taste of heaven. He moved forward and pulled her to him, kissing her. She pushed him back.

"Easy stud. You haven't finished drinking. Pour another one."

He fumbled for the bottle and poured another. Sahrina grabbed him, turned him around and locked lips, her tongue exploring his mouth. While he held her, she dumped 2 milligrams of alprazolam into his tequila and stirred it with her finger. She continued kissing for a short while, then broke the embrace. "Whew, cowboy. I think it's time for you to finish."

He reached for the glass and gulped it down. "Damn that one tasted bad," he said, but a smile lit his face. He took Sahrina's hand and said, "Shall we?"

Sahrina moved her hand down and rubbed him. She smiled. "I think you're ready, big boy. But let's take a dip in the hot tub first. That way we don't have to shower." She stepped into the tub and sat near the edge.

Brent stumbled over, almost falling twice.

Sahrina said, "Help him, Andy."

Brent stood in the middle of the hot tub on shaky legs. "Close your eyes while Andy gets naked," Sahrina said.

He covered his eyes while Andy stripped. He could barely maintain balance. *It's time,* Sahrina thought.

"Your turn," Sahrina said. "We'll close our eyes."

"No need to," he said, but Sahrina insisted.

"Okay, you can take off your pants now," she said.

Brent reached for his pants. Sahrina grabbed hold of his ankles and yanked backward. He fell face-first, his head smashing against the concrete edge. "Oh my God!" Sahrina screamed, and when she did Andy opened her eyes.

"Brent!" Blood poured from his forehead, tainting the water red. Andy reached for him.

"Don't touch him," Sahrina shouted. "Get a towel."

"I'm calling 9-1-1," Andy said.

"Not yet. Let me check him."

Sahrina knelt beside Brent, lifted his head from the water and felt for a pulse. She looked at Andy and shook her head. "He's gone."

"I'm calling 9-1-1," Andy said again.

"No. They'll think we did it. Especially after what happened at the hotel." Sahrina looked around. "I've got to think."

Andy stood on the patio, shivering. "What are we going to do?"

"Get dressed. We need to clean up so no one knows we were here."

Andy started for the house. Sahrina yelled to her, "Take the glasses with you, all but his. Put them in the sink. But don't touch the door handle," she said.

As Andy walked away, Sahrina added, "And don't wipe anything down. We don't want them thinking someone cleaned prints."

When Andy's back was turned, Sahrina pushed Brent's head underwater. She held it there for a full two minutes, making sure he was gone, then she got out, grabbed a towel and headed inside.

Andy stood in the kitchen crying. "I can't believe this happened again. My God. What are we going to do?"

"Did you touch anything?"

Andy looked around. "No. Wait. Yes, the glasses, and…nothing else."

"Wash all the glasses except his and put them away without leaving prints on the glasses or the cabinets. Leave one wine bottle on the table.

We'll take the other one with us. Put the towels in a plastic garbage bag. We'll dump them on the way home."

"I can't believe it," Andy said.

"Hurry up. We can't stay here forever."

Sahrina finished cleaning up, checked to make sure nothing would point to them having been there, and then she and Andy left, careful not to touch the door handles on the way out.

Chapter 20

WHAT ARE YOU AFRAID OF?

S unday mornings were never my favorites. When I was young they held promise of fun times with Mom, and family dinners with Uncle Dominic and Zeppe's family. But along with that was the mandatory attendance at church. I never felt comfortable sitting there listening to a priest give sermons that I didn't believe in, and even worse, being forced to sit next to all the fakes who pretended they were good people. It wasn't until later in life that I understood why Uncle Dominic never went to church. He never was one to pretend.

I sipped my coffee and wondered what I'd do for the day, then I remembered Julie had invited me to her house. I dialed her number. "Hey, Jules. What are you doing today?"

"Nothing much, except cleaning a sink full of dishes, helping my son fix his bike, and trying to find an electrician for a bad outlet."

"This is your lucky day," I said. "I'll trade my awesome electrical skills for lunch and some of your good coffee."

"You have a deal. I'll start on the dishes so we have a mug to drink from. And plan on staying for dinner."

I pulled into Julie's driveway a couple of hours later. The unmistakable gravelly voice of Janis Joplin blasted me when Julie opened the door. Then she led me through a doorway covered with long strings of beads. I felt as if I were going back in time and would emerge on a field in Woodstock. Her kids, Zach and Kirsten greeted me with a big hug.

"What's in the bag?" Zach asked.

"I brought tools to help your mom fix the electric."

"What about my bike?"

"We'll fix that too, if we can."

It only took half an hour to fix the electric, and then I moved on to Zach's bike. That was just a loose chain, a five-minute job to fix it, and ten minutes to wash the grease from my hands.

"Where did you learn to do all that?" Julie asked.

"The benefits of growing up in New York," I said. "No one can afford to hire an electrician, and if you wait for a super to fix something you might be waiting a month, so you learn to do it yourself."

"We're going out riding," Zach said, as he and Kirsten raced for the door.

"Be home in an hour," Julie said.

"Two," Kirsten hollered, and laughed as the door closed.

"Great kids."

"They *are* good kids," Julie said, and then, "Do you want coffee, or something to drink?"

"Coffee's fine for now, as long as it's that good stuff you gave me last time."

"You mean the Turtle Creek? I'm still using it," she said, and started grinding beans.

After the coffee was made, we sat on her back patio chatting and enjoying the sunshine. After a few minutes, Julie said, "How are you doing, Connie?"

"I'm great."

She smiled. "I mean how are you dealing with what happened?"

I set my mug on the table and looked up at the sky, not wanting to look at her; she had a hypnotist's gaze. "I know what you meant. I'm doing okay."

"From *great* to *okay* in just a few seconds. What's it going to be if I ask again?"

She had gotten me to laugh, which is what Julie was best at. "Some days I'm great. Some days I'm just okay. And some days…not very good." I turned to look at her. "But I'm not ready to talk about it."

She didn't give me a chance to breathe, before asking, "What are you afraid of?"

I thought about what she asked—what am I afraid of? My hands were shaking.

"If you mean, am I scared? Yeah, Julie, I am. I'm scared I'll never have a man to share my bed two nights in a row. Scared I'll never wake up to a warm kiss instead of a goodbye peck on the cheek." I looked away again. "And I guess I'm scared I'll never have someone that understands me. *Really* understands me."

"Now you're treading dangerous ground. When you start wishing for a man to understand you, that's crossing the line into a fantasy realm. I don't know if it exists."

She made me laugh again. "I'll take that drink now if you don't mind."

"Sure, what do you want?"

"Wine, beer, anything."

"How about a beer," she said, and bounced off the couch like she had springs. I don't know where she got all the energy.

She brought two beers back in bottles, handed me one and set hers on the table. "You know, Connie, there's no reason you can't have all those things. And you're smart enough to know that, so that means something else is bothering you." She grabbed her bottle, clanked it against mine, and took a sip. Then she leaned back against the sofa and hit me hard. "What are you *really* afraid of?"

I laughed. "Julie, we did pretty good today. We fixed the electric and we fixed Zach's bike. Fixing me will have to wait for another day."

"All right. I know when to quit," she said.

The rest of the day went great. We had tacos for dinner and then we played games with the kids. Around 7:00 I told her I had to get going. "Tip and I have a lot to do this week, and I'm still trying to get settled in."

"Say goodbye to Connie," Julie said, and Zach and Kirsten rushed over to give me a hug.

"Thanks for fixing my bike," Zach said.

"And for playing games with us," Kirsten said.

Julie walked me to the door. "I'll see you tomorrow."

"Yeah, see ya'. Dinner was great."

I got in the car and headed for home. I thought about a lot of things on the way, but mostly I thought about what Julie asked me. *What are you afraid of?*

I dodged her question, like I dodged everything I didn't want to face. But I knew damn well what I was afraid of. I was afraid to fall in love. Afraid because the people I was attracted to were criminals. An image of Frankie Donovan came to mind. He wasn't a criminal, although my gut told me he wasn't far from it.

But Frankie "Bugs" Donovan wasn't the kind that worried me. He had his primal urges, if that's what they were, under control. The ones that worried me. *The one* that worried me, was Fabrizio. The first time I saw him, my body tensed, a combination of fear and lust. And every time I'd seen him since then I had to stop myself from dragging him to bed at gunpoint.

I had dated *honest* men. Men with good jobs and rigid morals. Hell, I'd almost married one. At the last minute something inside me roared denial. At that moment I *knew*, beyond any doubt, that I'd never be happy with an *honest* man.

So there, Julie, there's your answer. The one you'll never hear me say. I'm not just afraid, I'm terrified *of falling in love, because I know what kind of man he'll be.*

Chapter 21

An Accidental Death

Tip and I shoved our weight around at the law offices of Barnes and Griffin, formerly Barnes, Griffin, and Lipscomb, but we didn't do any good. It's tough to bluff your way through a law firm. What little cooperation we got didn't help or add anything new to the case file. We spoke to Barnes again, but Griffin was out of town. We talked to several lawyers and a few admins. No matter who we talked to, no one could think of anyone who'd want to kill Lipscomb unless it was his wife or a jealous husband, and we didn't see either one of those as the motive.

A few minutes before noon, the phone rang. "Gianelli."

"Connie, it's Captain Cooper. We've got a dead body west of town. It might be nothing more than an accident but we need to check it out. Can you and Tip get there this afternoon?"

"We just finished at the law office. Yeah, we can get there."

"I'm sending you the address."

"Did I hear Gladys on the phone?" Tip asked.

"We have a possible case out west," I said.

Julie called while we drove and filled us in on a few details. The body belonged to the former Brent Davids, a senior vice president at one of the banks in the Galleria area. He was a bachelor, and was as clean as Lipscomb had been, with no apparent financial problems.

The house was a large French Colonial with a gorgeous front yard and a balcony to die for. Ben Marsh was at the scene when we arrived. We walked in and were directed out back by the officer at the front door. Ben was standing by a hot tub which sat next to a large pool. The stiff was in the tub.

"You saved me a phone call, Tip. I know you don't want to hear this, but I'm fairly certain the lawyer at the hotel died of a heart attack brought on by shock. It's most likely a result of the amount of Viagra he took. I'm ruling it an accident."

"I think you better get your *fairly certain* hat off. Somebody killed him as sure as I'm standing here."

"I see you standing there," Ben said, "but I'm ruling it an accident."

"Even though you know it's not an accident?" Tip said.

Ben's voice raised. "I know of no such thing. And I'm not changing my opinion because you need a case to keep busy. Wait a day or two, I'm sure somebody else will get killed."

After Ben calmed down, he nodded to me. "Connie, it's good to see you." He turned to Tip. "As far as your *opinion*, when did you get your medical degree?"

"The week before you got your detective badge."

Ben laughed. "Okay, I'll admit I'm no sleuth. Now why don't you tell me what you have that makes you so sure he was murdered."

Tip filled him in on what we had, which was mostly a handful of suspicions and a few things that didn't add up. Ben made a note on a pad he had on a table by the hot tub. "I'll run some more tests and go back over everything. It shouldn't take long."

"What have we got with the new guy?" I asked.

"He's a bigwig with one of the banks. When he didn't show up this morning they sent someone to check. They found him like this."

"Was the door open?" I asked.

Ben nodded. "According to the woman who found him."

"You have a TOD?" Tip asked.

"I have a guess right now. I'll narrow it down when I get him back to the office. The hot tub, water, and cool air might throw this off, but if I had to guess, I'd say late Saturday night or early Sunday morning."

"What's it look like?" I asked.

"If you mean was this an accident?" Ben shook his head. "I don't know. It *looks* like an accident."

"Tell me why," Tip said.

"No prints wiped off door handles or the liquor bottles," he said, and gestured to the empty tequila bottle. "And I have to tell you, if he drank a lot and then got in that hot tub, it could easily have made him fall."

"And that's what it looks like? Like he fell?"

Ben rubbed the back of his head. "So far it does."

Tip looked around. A towel lay on a chair beside the tub, and an empty tequila bottle and shot glass sat on the table, along with a salt shaker and a few lime slices. "I don't like the looks of it," Tip said. "People don't do shooters alone. I've known a few who did, but not many."

"And the door being unlocked," I said. "Unless he was expecting someone, why leave the front door unlocked?"

"I hear you," Ben said. "I'll get back with you as soon as possible."

"And don't forget to check Lipscomb again," Tip said.

We spent time going through the house but found nothing out of place. No drugs, nothing looked as if it had been searched, just an ordinary, immaculate bachelor's house.

"I wish we'd get some hard-core criminals to investigate," Tip said. "At least that gives us a place to start."

On the way back to the station, Delgado called. "I have you on speaker, Ribs. Connie's with me."

"Gianelli, one of these days you'll realize your mistake and ask to be transferred so you can work with a good detective."

"I'm already thinking that, Ribs. What's new on your case?"

"Remember how I told you that somebody got into ICU and put a four-inch blade in our lowly victim's left eye, and then for grins, they shoved another one in his right eye?"

"I remember. Those details tend to take root."

"Here's the best part," Ribs said. "He got away clean. *Nobody* saw him and it was in ICU. What the hell kind of shit is that?"

"Have you got any leads?" Tip asked.

"Nothing yet. The knife came from Academy. We checked and they sold almost 200 of them in the past month in Houston, and most of those were cash transactions."

This didn't sound right for a guy who wasn't on the radar two weeks ago. I leaned toward the speaker and said, "Who wanted him so dead they'd risk sneaking into ICU to kill him?"

"I don't know," Delgado said. "Like you said, our guy was a small player. I'm guessing whoever he took those stickers from got a little pissed off and they wanted to use him as an example."

"Or it might have something to do with the meth," I said.

"You might be right. It's more logical that this is about the meth," Delgado said.

"We're going to have to talk with Stenson," Tip said.

"Talkin' to Stenson could be dangerous, amigo."

"That's the way I see it, too. We'll call you when we're ready."

Chapter 22

BLOOD DOESN'T LIE

The Bronx, New York

Janice Quintana got off the subway and walked the six blocks to the hospital where she worked for the past 22 years. Today would be different though. Today she would be breaking the law. If not for her brother and his drug problems she wouldn't be involved in this. She didn't like breaking the law for anything, but what she was doing didn't seem so bad. Accessing a few old hospital records. *What could it hurt?*

By mid morning Janice had gotten the birth record for Maria Gianelli's husband. The hospital had no record for Maria, as she had been born in Italy. At lunchtime she gained access to the birth record for Concetta Gianelli, as well as the death certificate for both of her parents. She thought it odd that someone would want this information. *Perhaps it's for insurance purposes.*

When Janice got home that night she downloaded the information onto her computer and sent it to the address they had given her. She went to the kitchen and boiled water for tea. Now her brother was safe. *Damn him.*

***

Anna Santiago finished vacuuming the carpet and then wrapped the cord around the holder on the upright handle. She placed the vacuum in the closet, grabbed a clean cloth and began dusting from the back side of the room. Father Benjamin Rosario shut off his laptop, changed into his jogging pants, and headed for the stairs.

"Are you ready, Anna?"

"You go, Padre. I have much cleaning to do."

"It's late. You should go home to your children."

Anna smiled. "It won't take me long, Padre. You run. It's good for your heart."

"If you finish before I return, lock the door. I have a key."

"Good night," Anna said.

She pulled the curtain back and watched from the window, waiting until Padre Rosario was halfway up the block. Then she sat in front of his computer and turned it on. It took no time to get into the baptismal records, and then into the matrimonial records. Gianelli was not a rare name, but it wasn't that common a name either, not even at Our Lady of Mount Carmel.

She blessed herself before downloading the information, and then she tucked the flash drive into her purse, turned off the computer, and went home to her little ones. This information would give her enough money to pay bills for the next six months. She hoped God would understand.

***

The phone rang three times. Dominic pulled the disposable phone from his pocket. "Pronto."

"I was told to call this number if anyone ever accessed certain records at the hospital."

"What is your name?"

"Henry Barnes. I work in IT."

"Which record was accessed?"

"Just a minute, sir…There were several. Maria Gianelli, Tommy Gianelli, and Concetta Gianelli."

After a few seconds of silence, Dominic said, "Let me know if there is any more activity. I also want to know who accessed the files. You can do this?"

"I can narrow it down to a few who have that access."

"Send the list to your contact," Dominic said, and then he hung up and dialed another number. It was picked up on the second ring. "What exposure do we have on the Gianelli hospital records?"

"Let me think," a man said, then, "Dates of birth for the man and Concetta. Death certificates for the parents. Nothing else."

"Suppose they had information from other sources?"

"The father is the weak link."

"What conclusions could be drawn?"

"That he is not Concetta's father would be a logical one, but there would be no proof of that."

Dominic thought for a moment. "But nothing about Maria?"

"Not without DNA. Blood type alone won't do it."

"Henry Barnes will get you the name of the person who did this. I want to know who the information was given to."

"I will see it's done."

"And make sure to reward Barnes."

Before Dominic could even think, the phone rang again. "Pronto."

"This is Mazza."

"What troubles do I have today?" Dominic said.

"Somebody's been asking a lot of questions about you."

"What kind of questions?"

"About the old days. About you and Maria." Mazza swallowed hard. "And Connie."

"Do you know who is asking?"

Mazza's tone seemed to lighten. "I have a lead on him. It won't be long."

"When you find him, keep him. You'll hear from me."

"Yes, sir," Mazza said.

Dominic hung up the phone, and sat in his chair by the back patio. He lit his pipe and stared out the window. Just stared. Setbacks in his business he could tolerate. Problems with the police he could tolerate. He *could not* tolerate problems with his family. He tapped the bowl of the pipe on a cork buffer at the side of his ashtray, set the pipe in its holder, and reached for his phone.

"Si, signore."

"Fabrizio, call The Doctor. Tell him to be prepared. We will want him to see Mazza at the warehouse."

"Si, signore."

Dominic didn't like using The Doctor, but he was a firm believer in using the best tool available. If he needed information from a computer, he would get a hacker. If he needed to extract a bullet from next to the spine, he would get a special surgeon. But when information had to be extracted from a human being, The Doctor had no equal.

Chapter 23

A Few More Questions

We pressed Brent Davids' co-workers and the people who worked for him, but nobody had anything bad to say. About the only thing we discovered was that Davids worked out three times a week at a local gym, and he frequented a bar on the nights he didn't work out.

"I bet it's a gay bar," Tip said.

"And you think that because he's single?"

"No, because we need a lead on the case."

We drove to the bar in heavy traffic. While waiting for a light to change, Tip looked at me. "You know I don't ask about what happened because I figured you'd say something if you wanted to talk."

I laughed. "I know, Tip. And nothing pleases me more."

"Really?"

"Really," I said. "If I need to talk, I'll tell you."

"Damn, that worked good. I never get it right with Elena."

"Where is Elena, by the way? I thought she was coming back yesterday."

"She decided to stay another week, something about a fashion show in Paris that she just *had to* attend."

"What's up with you two? Is it getting serious?"

"Gianelli, mind your own business."

"I guess I'll have to ask Mollie," I said.

Tip laughed so hard I thought he might crash the car.

The club was on Richmond Avenue, near the *district*. The area had been a favorite for nightlife back in the 90s but then crime chased the scene inside the Loop. Now it was making a small comeback. Tip parked and we went inside. I had called beforehand to make sure the bartender who worked Saturday night would be there. They told us his name was Don. When we arrived, a young woman greeted us at the door.

"Can I help you?"

I showed her my badge. "Here to see Don. They told us he was working tonight."

She pointed toward the side. "He's the guy cleaning the tables."

We showed Don the badge and asked if there was a place we could talk.

He pulled out a chair and sat. "Right here's as good as any."

"You worked Saturday night?" Tip asked.

"All night. I started at 6:00 and closed at 2:00."

I showed him a picture of Brent Davids. "Do you remember seeing this guy in here?"

Don took the picture, adjusted for the light, and said, "Brent Davids. Yeah, he was here." He looked around and said, "He sat at that table over there with two women."

Tip perked up. "Two women? You're sure?"

"I remember," Don said. "One of them, I think it was the one he was with, had blonde hair. She was maybe in her mid twenties."

"If you knew Brent by name, he must have been a regular," I said.

"He came in about twice a week. Sometimes just once. Nice guy."

"Did he bring a partner or a friend?" Tip asked.

Don smiled. "If you mean was he gay? I don't think so. Before the night was over he was usually talking it up with a woman, and if it was a weekend he often left with one."

I shot Tip a glance. So much for his gay theory. "You said earlier that Brent was *with* the blonde. Why did you say that? Did they come in together?"

Don looked at me. "I can't swear he was with her, but it seemed like it. He danced with her two or three times. And he bought her a couple of drinks."

"He paid for the drinks?" Tip asked.

"He put it on his tab every time. She drank white wine. He had Guinness."

"What about the other one?" I asked.

Don shook his head and whistled. "Sexy," he said.

"That's a great description, but perhaps you could be more specific," I said.

"She had a killer body, with light brown hair, and blue eyes. And she had a deep Texas drawl."

I looked at Tip, confused. This didn't sound like our mystery woman. "What was she wearing?"

Don closed one eye and cocked his head to the side. "Tight skirt. I remember that."

I waited him out while he squinted and frowned. "Beige," he said. "I'm pretty sure her blouse was beige and the skirt was black."

"And tight?" I said.

He blushed a little. "Yes, ma'am. It was tight."

"I don't suppose you got her name, or a credit card?" Tip asked.

"She paid cash for her drink—a strawberry daiquiri—and I tried getting her number. Believe me, I did, but no luck."

"Blue eyes?" I said. "You're sure about that?"

Don nodded. "I'm sure. I remember thinking it was strange that she had such a great, natural-looking tan with those bright blue eyes."

"It sounds like she made quite an impression on you," Tip said.

Don took a long swig from a bottle of water, and said, "I see a lot of women in here. This one made me look twice. I'm telling you, she was sexy as hell."

"What time did Davids leave?" I asked.

"I can't swear to it, but if you forced me to say, I'd put it around 10:00."

"The women left with him?"

"Both of them," Don said. "They weren't here that long. Maybe two hours."

Tip pulled out a picture of Tiffany. "Is this the blonde?"

"No doubt about it," Don said. "That's her."

"Anything else you can tell us?" I asked.

He thought for a few seconds and then said, "The other one had a limp."

"A limp?"

"Yeah, I believe it was her right leg."

"That's good," Tip said. "You've got a good eye for detail. Which is why I'm gonna ask you to get with a sketch artist."

"No problem," Don said. "I can do it tomorrow before I come to work if that's good."

"That would be great," I said, and gave him the address for the station. "We'll have the artist call you to set up a time."

"I'll be here all night," Don said.

"Thanks again for the help," Tip said, and handed him a card. "If you think of anything else in the meantime, call me."

"And if you find her, get me her number."

We walked out of there feeling a little confused. "What do you think? Was it the same woman?"

"There's no question in my mind," Tip said. "But to be safe, we need to have that other bartender give a sketch also. We should have done that to begin with."

I got in the car. Tip slid behind the wheel. "Tell me why you think it's the same woman."

"It's not that hard to figure," Tip said. "You can change hair color. You can change eye color using contacts. You can *even* change beautiful. But you can't change sexy."

I looked over at him. "That's it? That's your theory—that you can't change sexy?"

"You heard it here first," he said.

"God help the state of Texas."

Chapter 24

18 Wheels

Victoria, Texas

Joel Ford mopped up the egg yolk with the last bite of toast and stuffed it in his mouth. He chased it down with a half a strip of bacon and a swig of lukewarm watered-down coffee. As he wiped his mouth with a napkin he signaled his waitress, Barbara Jean, for the check.

"You goin' home this early, Joel? The night's just gettin' started."

"The night's almost over for me," Joel said.

Barbara Jean wrote him out a check and said, "Come on, I'll walk you to your truck so you don't get mugged."

"I thought you said the night was just starting?"

"It is. I'm off and now I'm ready to have fun," Barbara Jean said.

Joel laughed. "Must be nice being young. I can't remember if I ever was or not."

Joel paid the cashier and then Barbara Jean walked with him to his truck. "Take care, big boy. See you next week."

"Have a little fun for me," Joel said and climbed into the cab.

Houston was almost three hours away and he was tired. *Dog tired.* If he was lucky he'd be home before midnight. Might give him time enough for a little lovin' with his honey. He pulled out of the diner and headed north on US 59, toward Houston. It wasn't the best ride, but on a chilly November night in Texas, it would do. Except for the bumps. He kept the speed within reason; they loved nabbing truckers down in this neck of the woods. Speeding tickets brought good money for the locals.

There wasn't much traffic on 59 tonight. The little town of Edna was dead, looking more like a ghost town than ever. He passed Ganado without even knowing he did, and as he approached El Campo, he spotted a car on the side of the road. A woman stood outside of it, waving him down.

Joel downshifted, hit the brakes, and brought the big rig to a crawl, stopping behind the car on the shoulder. He activated the flashers and climbed down from the cab. As he walked toward the car, he could see the woman was young. She had a good look about her.

"Car trouble?" he asked when he got within shouting distance.

"It just stopped on me," she said.

"Stopped?"

"Flat out died," she said, and then held her hand out. "My name's Andy."

"Andy?" he said, and laughed. "You don't look like no Andy."

When she didn't say anything, he said, "What do you mean it just died?"

"My friend said it ran out of gas. She went to try and find a station."

A few seconds later, a car coming from the other direction stopped in the road. Sahrina got out carrying a can of gas. She waved to the driver and said bye.

Joel looked at her strangely and then at Andy. "I assume this is your friend."

"That's her," Andy said.

"I told her she ran out of gas but she didn't believe me. That man had to take me all the way to El Campo to get this."

Joel looked at Sahrina and smiled. She had an accent that pegged her as coming from deep in the woods of East Texas.

He poured gas in the tank, saving a little in case he needed to prime it. After a few dry pumps on the gas pedal, the car started right up. "I guess you're all set," Joel said to the girls, and then he headed toward his truck.

"Aren't you going to thank the man?" Sahrina to Andy.

Joel got in his truck, but before he could fasten his seat belt, the passenger door opened and Andy climbed in. She was naked. "What the hell are you doing?"

"I wanted to thank you proper."

He shook his head. "It's not that I don't appreciate a good-looking woman, but I'm married. And I guess I'm one of those few that are happy about it. Now go on and get your clothes back on before you catch a deathly cold."

Andy lifted her legs up on the seat and put her feet on his lap. "It won't take long. I really do want to thank you."

"Whether you really want to doesn't matter. I'm tired and need to get home."

The passenger door opened again. Sahrina pointed a gun at him. "I admire your morals, but I'm afraid you'll have to be unfaithful tonight. You see, we're playing a game and for us to win she has to fuck a trucker on the front seat of his cab."

Joel narrowed his eyes and stared. "That's disgusting. Both of you, get the hell out of my truck."

Sahrina held the gun with both hands. "I'm afraid it's not just about you, Joel."

His eyes went wide at the mention of his name.

"Yes, I know who you are. Listen closely. I'm going to tell you something, and it will make you want to kill me. If you try anything, I'll kill you first. Do you understand?"

"My ears still work."

"Good. Now listen. I have someone watching your house right now. If you don't do everything I say, he's going to enter your house and rape Nora, and then he'll shoot your son."

Joel started to go for Sahrina, but he controlled himself. He gripped the steering wheel and squeezed. The vein in his forehead tightened. "If you—"

"I've heard every threat imaginable so please don't waste them on me. We don't have much time. I suggest you take your clothes off and move over on top of Andy."

Andy's eyes darted back and forth from Joel to Sahrina.

"Spread your legs, Andy. It won't take him long."

Joel got on top of her. He hesitated and looked at Andy, but she shook her head. "You better do what she says."

He had trouble getting ready. "I can't do it," he said. "I can't get hard."

"That's all right. Kiss her neck."

When Joel started kissing her neck, Sahrina grabbed Andy's hand, and placed her finger on the trigger. She pushed the gun against the back of Joel's head and pulled the trigger twice. Andy screamed. Sahrina put the gun against Andy's head and pulled the trigger again.

Sahrina got in the car and drove to a remote spot north of El Campo where she met the guy who dropped her off earlier with the gas can. "We need to get rid of this evidence," she said, and dumped gas all over the back seat. "Get the front," Sahrina said. "Make sure you soak it."

He opened the door, put his knee on the seat and emptied the gas can. Sahrina placed her foot on his back and kicked him into the car. Then she slammed the door, tossed a match inside, and stepped back quickly. The car erupted in flames, the man inside screaming. Sahrina stepped further back and waited until he no longer moved. Then she got in his car and headed north toward Houston.

Chapter 25

CONNECTING THE DOTS

I was sitting at my desk in the station when the phone rang. Caller ID showed it was from the Medical Examiner's office. "Gianelli."

"Connie, it's Ben."

"Have you got results already?"

"I don't have everything on Davids, but after your partner ranted on and on about Lipscomb, I went back over his results." A long silence followed, then, "As much as I hate to admit this, that damn clown might be right."

"You mean about it being a murder instead of a heart attack?"

"Lipscomb had taken a heavy dose of Viagra. We already knew that. But Lipscomb didn't have a history of heart trouble, so I did a few more tests, specifically for nitrates. I found small traces of amyl nitrate."

I took notes while he talked. "Ben, you're going to have to explain that to me. What would that do? And why does that change your mind?"

"Amyl nitrate has been used for a long time in the gay community, inhaled by using *poppers*. So this could have been nothing more than a man living on the edge and he went too far."

"Or?"

"Or, someone who knew what they were doing could have given him too much Viagra. Combined with the nitrates, it could easily have sent him into shock. Blood pressure would have crashed."

I thought for a minute. "So what you're saying is that someone *might* have murdered him?"

"*Might have,*" Ben said. "But that's the problem. I can't prove anything."

"Okay, thanks," I said, and then, "How about Davids? You said you didn't have everything. What have you got?"

"Davids drowned, which is no surprise, but I have no way of telling if it was an accident or if he had help. There were *very* high levels of blood alcohol, and he also had alprazolam in his system. When you combine those two, along with the effects of a hot tub…I can easily see him falling and hitting his head."

"And time of death still looks good for Saturday night?"

"I'd say between 10:00 PM and 1:00 AM."

"Thanks, Ben. I'll tell Tip."

"What're you gonna tell Tip?" Charlie asked as he made his way to the coffee room.

"That was Ben. He was giving us the preliminary results on that banker."

"Ya'll got a case?"

"I'm not sure, Charlie. But we definitely have a case with the lawyer."

"You mean that one in the hotel?"

I nodded. "That's him."

"Damn," he said, and then, "You want coffee, Connie?"

"I'm good, but if you see Tip tell him Ben called. He'll want to know."

"I doubt if I'll see him. I'm getting coffee and then going outside for a smoke. You want to join me?"

"Thanks anyway. I have too much to do." I turned and looked at Charlie. "When did you start smoking?"

"When I went on this diet. I gained most of the weight when I quit, so I thought I'd try losing it the same way."

"Good luck with that," I said.

Tip came back a few minutes later. "I ran into Charlie and Herb. Charlie said Ben called."

"He called me because he didn't want to talk to you."

"What did he find?"

"After you bullied him into believing this might be a homicide, he found evidence that might support that theory."

"I knew it," Tip said.

"Don't get excited. He can't prove anything, but it looks more and more like somebody wanted Lipscomb dead."

Just then Tip's phone rang.

"Hang on, Connie. This is Buster."

Tip stepped to the side and said, "Buster, what've you got for me?"

"No shit? When?"

"You're sure it was her? What time of night was this?"

"Did you get a plate? What kind of car is it?"

"So was that *before* or *after* you had a bottle?"

Tip laughed and then he said, "All right. I hope you're dreaming of a big steak, 'cause that's what I'm buying you.

"No, not tonight, but I'll be down soon. Thanks, Buster."

Tip hung up. He was all smiles.

"Sounds like Buster has a lead," I said.

"Tiffany came and got her car. Buster even got us a partial, if we can believe him."

"Can we trust what he says?" I asked.

"He usually gets things half right. Good enough to check out since we don't have anything else."

Charlie was just coming back from his smoke. Tip grabbed him and said, "Take this to Julie and tell her to get it out on the radio. Green Nissan, and a partial on the plate is T32. Don't know the year. And tell her not to be too sure on the make either. This came from a mediocre source. But she can check all green Nissan's with T32 in the plate and see what we come up with."

"I'll take care of it," Charlie said.

Tip turned to me and said, "Now you can fill me in on Davids."

I had already started listing things, which I laid out on the table between us. "Ben's report said Davids drank too much alcohol. Combined with a hot tub and alprazolam it could easily have been an accident."

"I think Ben's on an accident binge," Tip said. "Let's look at what we have."

I pulled out the file.

- No prints except the victim.
- Front door wasn't locked, but he seemed to be a security type of guy, plus he worked at a bank. His car was locked. Windows were locked. Computer was locked.
- Nothing was wiped down, so either there really wasn't anyone else with him, or they planned it well and didn't touch anything.
- And he had no prescription for alprazolam. I had Julie check with his doctor and the pharmacy.
- No empty bottle of alprazolam.

Tip chewed on the end of a pencil and kicked his feet up on an empty chair. "If we look at the evidence, we've got nothing. But we know he left with Tiffany. And we know she was with Lipscomb when he died."

"And then there's the mystery of the alprazolam," I said. "If he didn't have a prescription, and we found no bottle, that means he got the pill from someone."

"Or someone slipped it in his drink," Tip said.

"But wouldn't he taste it?"

"Not if he was doing shooters," Tip said. "At least not until he'd already taken it. And like I said before, nobody does shooters alone."

I thought about what we had. "But this time they didn't mess up. They didn't leave us any prints. We've got nothing on camera."

Tip sat up straight, a strange look on his face. "Hang on a minute. I need to see Julie."

I followed him to Julie's office. As soon as Tip walked in, she reacted.

"No, I don't have an answer for you yet, Tip."

"I'm not concerned about that, but what I am wondering is why we didn't get a hit earlier?"

"What do you mean? A hit on what?"

"That car and plate Charlie just gave you to run—it belonged to Tiffany, our suspect."

A short silence followed, and then Julie said, "I ran those prints, Tip."

"Then tell me how her prints didn't come up if she has a car. Everyone gets printed for a driver's license."

"We need a thumb print to match with a license. We had several sets of prints from that hotel room, but if her thumb wasn't there we wouldn't get her car."

"What about the prints from her room? Didn't we get anything there?"

Julie shook her head. "We didn't get prints. LaDonna is the legal resident, and she wouldn't let the tech inside."

"Son of a bitch," I said. "After we helped her."

"All right. Forget that for now. Get that car out on the radio and make sure they call it in to you."

"Charlie's already taken care of it."

"And one more thing," Tip said. "Look for any suspicious deaths in the past few weeks. Go back a month if you have to."

"I'm kind of busy here, Tip."

"Find time."

Julie looked to the side and took a deep breath. "What are you calling suspicious deaths?"

"I'm talking heart attacks where the victim didn't have a record of heart trouble, *accidental* deaths, anything outside the normal realm."

"That's going to be a lot of—"

"If that's too much, start with the past couple of weeks," Tip said, and started back down the hall.

He turned to me. "We've got no prints on record for Tiffany, and she disappeared after Lipscomb's death. I'm not so sure whoever did this messed up like we think they did. Maybe they left the prints at the hotel on purpose. Or maybe Julie's right and they aren't her prints. Or maybe we've got her prints, but no thumb print."

"Why would they do that?"

"I don't know yet. But so far they haven't made any mistakes. We have no clue who the other woman is, and she's managed to avoid all cameras.

She's been described with dark hair, light-brown hair, blue eyes, and brown eyes, a deep Texas drawl and a Spanish accent."

I nodded. "You're right. Something doesn't add up."

I pulled out the crime scene report and went over it again, bit by bit, digging into each detail. Two hours later, about the third time I went through it, something caught my attention. "Take a look at this."

He rolled his chair beside mine. "What?"

"Remember the towel Davids had by the hot tub?"

"What about it?"

"He had three more in the bathroom just like it. But get this—he had six washcloths and hand towels that matched."

Tip looked at me and then nodded. "We're missing two. And that's about the same number of women we think he was with."

I looked at my notes again, then, "Let's assume for a minute that Tiffany and the mystery woman were at his house. If they were all in the hot tub, they would have had towels. So what did they do, take the towels with them?"

"That's a good way to get rid of evidence," Tip said.

"Okay, if we figure that much, then what else did they have that they might have taken?"

Tip thought for a minute and said, "I already said he wouldn't be drinking shooters alone, but there was also a bottle of wine. If they were with him, they'd be drinking wine."

"Don, the bartender, said Tiffany drank wine." I scribbled a few notes on a paper tablet and then checked the sheet. "But all the wine glasses are accounted for, assuming he had the same number of each kind."

Tip picked up the phone and dialed.

"Who are you calling?"

"Sarah. We need to ask about prints."

The phone rang a few times before she answered. "Tip, is that you?"

"I know your heart's probably beating mighty fast right now, darlin' but try to control yourself."

She laughed. "Will you shut the hell up and tell me what you want."

"We're trying to figure out what went on at Brent Davids' house. Ben is leaning toward an accident, but Connie and I don't think so."

"We didn't find anything. You've got the report. No prints, no DNA on him. Of course the hot tub and chlorine would have ruined that anyway."

"How about prints on the wine glasses?"

"Nothing," Sarah said.

"Did you check the stems?"

"Of course. We dusted everything you told us and more besides. We had his prints on some of the glasses but not others."

"And I'll bet two of those glasses didn't have prints. Not even on the stems."

"Are you going to make me check this?" Sarah asked.

"I'll wait while you look it up."

Sarah came back on in a couple of minutes. "Maybe you *are* the best damn detective in Texas. Two glasses were clean as a baby's bottom. No prints anywhere."

"I'm gonna ignore that baby's bottom remark since it makes no sense, but I owe you one for the prints. Thanks."

"You bet. Tell Connie I said hi."

Tip hung up and looked at me. "I'm gonna shove this so far up Ben Marsh's ass, he's gonna choke on it."

"I'll ignore that and focus on the case. As I see it, Tiffany and the other one finished with Davids, cleaned up, washed and dried the glasses and everything else, and then took the towels with them."

Tip kicked his feet up and tapped a pencil on the desktop. "We know we've got a couple of women killing people. All we have to do now is figure out *why*."

Chapter 26

What The Street Knows

Tip and I went downtown to pay Buster for the lead, but also to pay a visit to LaDonna, Tiffany's roommate. We pulled to the curb in front of Tiffany's place and started up the walk. LaDonna poked her head out the window.

"She ain't here."

"And I suppose she ain't been back since we left?" Tip said.

LaDonna shook her head. "Not a peep."

"So I don't guess you'd mind if we take a look in her car?" Tip said.

The window closed. A minute later LaDonna opened the front door. "I shoulda known," she said.

"What you should have done is call me," I said. "We did right by you, damn it."

LaDonna leaned against the wall, her hands folded in front of her. "She came and got it while I was workin'. I swear I didn't see her. Hell, I didn't even know it was gone till the next day."

"What else did she take?" Tip asked.

LaDonna squeezed her lips together and shook her head again. "All her goddamn clothes. I was countin' on them for myself. Shit."

"She took them all?" I asked.

"Every damn piece down to her underwear. Didn't even leave me a pair of socks."

"You know where she went?" Tip said.

"I already told you. She came while I was working."

"How come you didn't let the tech in?" I asked.

LaDonna's face twisted into a sneer. "It's my damn room. Ain't lettin' nobody in there."

"That didn't stop you when Tip donated to your charity."

"Money makes a difference, girl. You ought to know that."

I felt like smacking her in the head; instead, I handed her another card. "If you see her again—"

"I know. Call you," she said, and went back inside.

"Seems like everybody is always one step ahead of us, Tip."

"I know, and it's pissing me off."

As we drove toward the station, Julie called. "We have a report from an officer on the west side who said he might have seen the car."

"Might have?" I said. "How come he's not sure?"

"He saw it Sunday, before we put the description out."

"And he remembers it?" I said.

"That's what he claims," Julie said.

We got the officer's number and called. "Officer Dewey, this is Detective Gianelli. They said you might have seen a vehicle we're looking for."

"I'm not positive, but I think so."

"How is it you remember a partial from two days ago?" I asked.

"I was taking some kid to his parents after catching him with a joint, and the car in front of me was going slow. I noticed the plate had T32 in the middle. I only remembered it because I had a plate with T32 on it."

"Did the car fit? Was it a green Nissan?"

Dewey laughed. "You're gonna think I'm dizzy, but I have no idea. I couldn't swear to anything else on the plate or the make of the car, or even the color, but I *think* it was green, or maybe gray. The bottom line, detective, is it might have been the car, but it might not."

"Where did you see it?"

"On Shadow Lake Drive, off Memorial by Dairy Ashford."

"Okay, thanks. We'll check it out."

"That's mostly a residential area," Tip said. "Expensive houses. Quiet. I wonder what she was doing out there?"

"You want to check it out?"

"We might as well," Tip said.

While Tip drove, I called Julie and told her to alert patrols in that area.

Tip's phone rang. "What's up Delgado?"

"I'm heading over to see Chicky, and I figure I might need some juice."

"Tell him if he doesn't treat you right, I'm through paying his way."

Delgado laughed. "Thanks, Tip."

Ribs headed west, toward the Galleria.

"Where are we going?" Cruz asked.

"Going to see a guy named Chicky Ramirez. He's the best informant in town. If he's not on your list you're missing out."

"He's on my list now," Cruz said, and jotted down the name in his notepad.

Ribs pulled into the parking lot of a strip mall and honked the horn at a guy standing about thirty feet away, looking into the back of a pickup. The guy jumped and turned.

"I hope you weren't thinking of doing any early Christmas shopping, Chick."

Chicky squinted, then moved quickly toward Ribs' car. "If it ain't Hector Delgado. My favorite detective."

"Cut the shit. I know you for the two-timing fucker that you are."

Laughter poured out of Chicky. "I meant my favorite *after* the Tipster and Gino."

Ribs and Cruz got out of the car. "This is my partner Cruz. I expect you to treat him same as you do me."

Chicky reached out and smacked Cruz's hand. "Goes without saying. Now what can I do for you?"

"We've got a dead guy named Martin who was dealing ice. And we found a stash of illegal inspection stickers in his crib. You know anything about that?"

"I know the ice is heating up this town. I'm surprised you boys haven't been down here sooner. I mean, I don't mind a little nose candy, but that shit...uh uh. Not for this dude. Fuck you up is what it does."

"I know what it does, Chick. I need to know who's moving it."

"Shit! Who ain't moving it. You're better off askin' that."

"Who's giving the orders?" Ribs asked.

Chicky looked to his left, and then behind him. "Can't be certain about that."

"I think you can," Ribs said.

"Okay, so maybe I *can* but I *won't*. A man's got to protect himself. You know what I mean?"

"I hear you," Ribs said, "But all I'm asking for is a name. Nobody's going to know it came from you."

"I can't do it."

Ribs moved closer to Chicky. "I know you heard what happened to Martin."

Chicky nodded.

"A knife in each eye. *Dios mío,* Chick. They took a knife and stabbed him in each fuckin' eye." Ribs let him think on that for a few seconds, and then, "You want that shit to happen to you?"

"That's why I ain't saying nothing. These fuckin' people are nuts."

"Which fuckin' people would that be?"

"Aw fuck." Chicky thought for a moment, then he said, "You'll keep this quiet? And tell Tip I helped out, right?"

"I'll tell Tip. And we'll keep it quiet from everybody else."

Chicky nodded. "Remember that dude Carlos? The cartel guy? It's him. He's back in town and his men are pressing hard."

"That's who did Martin?"

"Word on the street is he wanted to use Martin as an example."

Ribs pulled out a twenty and handed it to Chicky. "I'm not flush like Tip. You'll have to wait for him to get a payday."

"Not worried about it," Chicky said. "Unless you're taking a lot more than your paycheck, I know a man with six kids got no extra green."

Ribs laughed. "You got that right, my friend. And thanks for the help."

"Be careful," Chicky said. "Bad dudes you're messing with. Bad!"

"That didn't sound like good news," Cruz said, as Ribs started the car.

"Not good at all. Carlos was the one who had Tony killed, and he tried killing Tip's partner Connie."

"No shit?"

"No shit," Ribs said. At the first break in traffic he pulled onto Westheimer, then took a left and went down to Richmond and then another left on Fondren. A couple of hundred feet further, he turned into an almost-vacant strip mall and parked in the back where a guy was selling tacos and burritos from a trailer. Rolando had been operating there and a few other places for the past couple of years.

"Are you hungry?" Cruz asked.

"Not me," Ribs said. "And I don't recommend eating here."

"Why are we stopping?"

"I see you're not up on the street scene, partner. Rolando, known as 'Ro' to his friends, always has information."

"For a price, I presume?"

"A price or the right kind of threat."

Ribs and Cruz got out of the car and walked toward the trailer. Rolando poked his head out the window. "Hector, it's good to see you."

"How's it going, Ro?"

"If I could sell more tacos, I'd be happy."

"Sorry to disappoint," Ribs said, "But we're not hungry, and besides, I don't eat goats."

"That's all right, I'm almost out of tacos anyway. What else can I sell you?"

"You can *tell* me what you know about who's moving a shitload of ice in town. And while you're at it, throw in some information on the fake inspection stickers."

Rolando looked at Cruz, and then back to Ribs. "Ice? That's dangerous shit, amigo. I might have to hide for a while if I told you about that. And hiding takes money."

Ribs laughed and slapped the side of the trailer with his palm. "Ro, you're a funny guy. But I know about hiding. For example, I'd bet if I were to come inside that trailer and check the spices you have, I might find illegal substances hiding in a lot of places."

Rolando lost his happy face. "You got a search warrant? Because if you don't have a warrant—"

"I don't need a warrant," Ribs said. "Not when I can smell drugs."

"Smell drugs? You can't smell no drugs. Get the fuck outta here before I call a *real* cop." Rolando reached below the counter.

Ribs pulled his gun and pointed it at Ro. "Stay still. It wouldn't be good if you moved. Detective Cruz is coming inside to search the place."

Cruz moved for the door to the trailer. He opened it and stepped inside.

"Hey partner, take a look under the counter and see what my man Ro was reaching for."

It only took Cruz a few seconds to spot a .38 stuffed inside a half-empty box of taco shells. Cruz slipped his finger inside the trigger guard and lifted it. "Take a look at this. I think old Rolando here planned on shooting you."

"Okay," Ro said. "Fuck man, can't you take a joke?"

Ribs took hold of Ro's shirt and pulled him closer. "I don't joke when it comes to drugs, amigo. And I don't *ever* joke when it comes to guns."

"Got something else," Cruz said.

Ro's eyes opened wide. "Okay listen. Forget you found that and forget about the gun, and maybe I got something for you."

"Found what?" Ribs said. It brought a smile to Ro's face.

Ro poked his head out the window and looked around the parking lot. "All I know is there's a new player, and he's selling ice for 20% of street value."

"How much is he moving?" Cruz asked.

"As much as you want. And he's cutting the dealers in for 75%."

"I can't imagine the old guard is taking this lying down?" Ribs said.

Ro shook his head. "They fought back at first, but after a few of them disappeared, the others fell in line. Besides, this new guy's got protection."

Cruz perked up. "What kind of protection?"

"The kind only you can offer," Ro said. "Midnight blue protection."

"You're saying cops are giving this meth dealer free rein?"

Ro nodded. "That's what I hear."

"Do you know a guy named Martin, or Martinez?" Ribs asked. "He was selling ice and stickers both."

"I *used* to know him, but I heard he lost his sight."

"You hear a lot from way down here in this pissy trailer," Ribs said.

Ro shrugged.

"Who did Martin piss off?"

"From what I hear he got the idea to sell the ice for more than the 20%. He got greedy."

"What about the stickers?" Cruz asked.

Ro shook his head. "I don't know nothin' about stickers. I already told you that."

"Who did the job on Martin?" Ribs asked.

"I don't know."

Ribs grabbed his shirt again.

"Do what you want, but I still don't know."

"All right, Ro. But you better call when you hear something. Don't make me come back here." Ribs handed him a card before leaving.

"You just make sure you forget you *were* here," Ro said. "I don't want to end up like Martin."

Ribs pulled out of the lot and onto Fondren, heading north. "What do you think?"

Cruz shook his head. "It's hard to say, but if you pressed me I'd say the guy was telling the truth."

"Or at least the truth as he knows it," Ribs said. "And how about that cop shit he spit out?"

"I don't like thinking about it, but let's face it, if somebody's moving that much ice and we haven't heard about it, they've got protection. And remember what Tip told us?"

"It fits," Ribs said. "Goddamnit, it fits."

As he turned left onto Westheimer his phone rang. It was Rosalee. "I'm sorry, Rosalee, I can't come home and make love to you."

"I think I'm being followed," Rosalee said. There was panic in her voice.

Chapter 27

A Few More Bodies

Tip and I were at our desks when Julie came by. "Was somebody looking for Andrea Marsh?"

"If Andrea Marsh is Tiffany, we're looking for her." Tip leaned toward Julie. "Do you have *two* purple stripes in your hair now?"

"I'm trying to decide which side I like it on. What do you think?"

Tip shook his head. "I don't think you want to know what I think. But let's get back to this Marsh lady."

"Back in the decade that mattered, they would have called Andrea Marsh a free spirit. I believe you tagged her as a prostitute."

I sat up straight. "You found Tiffany?"

Julie smiled. "Print match just came in. But don't get too excited. She's dead."

"Dead?" Tip reached for the report Julie had in her hand. "What happened?"

"She was found in a trucker's cab north of Victoria. They were both shot in the head. She was naked. He had his pants down."

"Shot in the head as in murdered?" I asked.

"The initial report lists it as possibly a murder/suicide," Julie said.

"Bullshit," Tip said. "Plain bullshit."

"Where's Victoria?" I asked.

"It's a few hours south of here," Julie said. "Down 59 toward Corpus Christi."

"What the hell was she doing down there?" I said.

"And with a trucker," Tip said. "A trucker isn't exactly the kind of client she's been with lately."

"The trucker was from Houston. Maybe there's a connection," Julie said.

"Did I hear you say you got more bodies?" That came from Herb.

"*We* don't have them," I said, "but at least one of the them ties to our case—the prostitute we've been looking for."

"So you found Tiffany?" Charlie walked up with a cup of steaming coffee. "Fresh pot made if anyone's interested."

I started to get up, but Julie stopped me. "I'll get it, Connie."

"Thanks, Jules."

"How about you, Tip? Do you want coffee?"

"I think I will, darlin'. Thanks."

Tip turned to Charlie. "This happened close to El Campo. Why don't you call down there and see if Buck Murdock is still sheriff. If he is, get me his phone number."

"Are we going down there?" I asked.

"I don't think we need to go down, but I'd like to get the skinny from Buck. He's pretty sharp."

"That's good. In the meantime, let's see what we can find out about the guy who was in the truck with her." I turned to Jules, who was returning with coffee. "See what you can do on that, okay?"

"I'm all over it," she said.

"And don't forget about Tiffany, or Andrea. Now that we know who she is, maybe we'll get something."

"I'll get it," Julie said.

I took a big sip of coffee. I hated to admit it, but my blood raced when we got a lead, even if the lead was dead bodies. I downed the rest of the cup and headed out for more. I passed Charlie in the hall and he gave me the number for the sheriff. "Tip's wondering what took you so long," I said.

"Herb and I went to catch a smoke. I hate going outside, but it's gotten to be where you can't smoke anywhere."

Tip called his friend on the phone as soon as I returned.

"Buck, it's Tip Denton. I'm gonna put you on speaker so my partner can hear."

"I'm guessing you're calling about the trucker."

"The woman's prints came up regarding a case we're working. What can you tell me about what went on down there?"

"I know it wasn't a suicide," Buck said. "Even though somebody tried to make it look like one."

"What makes you so sure?"

"Because I know Joel Ford. He's been running his route from the Valley up to Houston for twenty years. He usually stops in Victoria or El Campo for breakfast, day or night. We've gotten to know him. He's not the kind of man who'd be in his truck with another woman."

Tip jotted a note on the paper in front of him.

Talk to wife.

"You're sure about that?"

"I'm sure, Tip. But there's a lot more. I talked to Barbara Jean, the waitress at the diner in Victoria. Joel ate there just before this happened, and there wasn't no woman with him."

"So you're saying he picked up this woman somewhere between Victoria and El Campo?"

"That's what I'm saying. And as you know, there's not a damn thing out there except a few dead armadillos."

"And you didn't find any cars on the road, or anything like that?"

"No, but I'll tell you what we did find. I've been saving this for last. We found a car outside of El Campo in a deserted stretch of grassland. Somebody set that car on fire and burned it up. Whoever did it poured accelerants all over it. And there was a body inside. Male."

"How far was it from where the truck was found?"

"Not more than seven or eight miles. And here's the best part, the car was registered to the dead girl. We found a suitcase stuffed with clothes in the trunk."

"Okay, Buck, you sold me. This has been helpful. Can I get you to send the file up here so we can take a look?"

"Be up there tomorrow. I'll call you with anything new I get."

"Anybody notify the wife yet?"

"Harris County did."

"Thanks, Buck. I'll call over there and tell them we plan on talking to the widow. And tell Jean I said hi."

Tip hung up and looked at me. "Well, there you have it."

"What's that supposed to mean? Are you saying he wasn't with Tiffany because Buck said so?"

Tip laughed. "Hell no. It was what he said about the girl not being with him at the diner that convinced me. And of course the bit about the other car."

"Tell me what makes you so sure," I said.

"You'd have to know the area. Buck said he makes runs to the Valley. That's at the border with Mexico. That means he's driving 300 miles or so on a road with not much besides 18 wheelers. And you got the King Ranch in between, which is bigger than the state of Delaware. They even have a sign when you approach that says 'Entering the King Ranch. No gas for 53 miles.'"

"So you're saying there wasn't any place to pick her up?"

"I'm saying if she wasn't with him at the diner, then there's not a damn place he could have picked Tiffany up between there and El Campo."

I thought about what he said, and what we had. "Besides all that," I said. "What was Tiffany doing that far out of Houston, and with a trucker?"

"And how did she get there?" Tip said. "And what's that shit about her car being found seven or eight miles away, burned up, and with a body in it?"

Tip scribbled some notes on his pad. "One week ago she was with a high-priced lawyer at a fancy hotel."

"And he ends up dead," I said.

"A few days after that, she was with a wealthy banker."

"And he ends up dead."

"And now she's with a trucker down by Victoria?"

I nodded. "The only thing in common is he ended up dead also."

Tip didn't say anything for a moment, and his eyes were all scrunched up like he did when he was thinking hard. "Something else is bothering me, Connie. Don't you think it's an awful coincidence that Tiffany ends up dead the day after we found out about the car?"

"I was already thinking the same thing," I said. "They knew we were onto them. That's why they burned the car. And I'm guessing it's why they killed Tiffany."

Tip tapped the pencil on the desk. "Somebody planned these murders and used Tiffany to do them. I'm guessing either they're done killing or they're done needing her. Either way, we have to find out who was behind this."

"If we're going to do that much thinking, Tip. I need a few beers."

"Maybe we should talk to the wife first."

Chapter 28

AN AWKWARD CONVERSATION

We got the address for Joel Ford. He lived on the west side, near Bear Creek, about half an hour drive. I asked Julie to get us as much information as she could. "Text it to us," I said. "We're going to talk to his wife."

Dunnethead Road sat in a big neighborhood off Highway 6. Ford's house was a small, indistinguishable ranch house in the middle of a block full of them. Tip parked on the street and we walked up to the door and knocked. A middle-aged woman answered the door. Her brown hair was peppered with gray, and she looked…worn out.

Tip showed his badge. "Ma'am, I'm Detective Tip Denton and this is my partner, Detective Connie Gianelli."

She nodded and opened the door wider, stepping back to let us enter. "I guess you're here about Joel."

"Yes, ma'am," Tip said. "We're very sorry about your loss."

We followed her into a small living room. Tip and I sat on the sofa; she took a seat in a chair next to us. "I know this is a terrible time," Tip said, "But it's important for us to get as much information as we can."

"I understand," she said. "I've barely been able to function since they told me. I just…" She reached for a box of tissues sitting on the table. "I still can't believe it."

"Did your husband make this same run all the time? Has there been anything different in the past few weeks or months?"

"Nothing different," she said. "He's been running the Valley route for 20 years, and he was normally home before midnight unless weather slowed him down."

I waited for Tip to write his notes, then I addressed her. "Mrs. Ford, can you think of anyone who would want to hurt your husband? Did he have financial troubles? Or was he involved with gambling or drugs?"

She seemed surprised by the question. "Hurt Joel? Good Lord no. Who would want to hurt him?" She squinted and her forehead wrinkled. "Why would you ask a question like that?" Anger tainted those words.

I'm sure *my* expression registered surprise now. I looked to Tip, but when he didn't say anything I answered. "Mrs. Ford, didn't the deputy tell you? Your husband was murdered."

She bolted up out of the chair. "Murdered! Joel?"

I got a sick, nasty feeling in my gut. I wasn't used to dealing with grieving family members. "Mrs. Ford, I'm sorry. I thought they would have told you." I stood and held her hand. "Are you all right? Would you like me to get you something? Tea or coffee? Or a glass of water?"

She cried. "How could he be murdered? What happened?"

Tip leaned forward and took her other hand. "Mrs. Ford, I know this is going to be a shock, but they found your husband in the cab of his truck, shot in the head."

Her hands flew to her face. "Oh my Lord. Who would do that? Why?"

Tip grabbed her hand again and held it. "Ma'am, that's not all. There was a woman with him. And—"

"A woman!" She sat straight in the chair, her back as stiff as a board. "Detective, that's impossible. My husband would never be with another woman."

I tapped Tip's arm. "Do you think you can make a few cups of tea?"

He took the hint and went to the kitchen.

Mrs. Ford looked at me after he left. Tears were in her eyes. "You're a woman. I'm sure you'll understand. I've been married to Joel for 26 years, ever since we were 19. We have…" she stopped, closed her eyes for a second, and then continued, "*Had* a good marriage." She wiped her eyes and leaned forward. "I would have *known* if Joel was fooling around. A woman knows these things." She shook her head. "Out of all the nonsense you told me tonight, there is one thing I'm positive of—Joel *wasn't* with that woman, whoever she was." She pointed her finger at Tip, who was just returning, and then at me. "*Somebody* killed my husband. I don't know why, but somebody did and it wasn't about any woman."

I decided to go out on a limb. If we were wrong I'd fix it later. "I believe you, Mrs. Ford. I think someone set him up to look bad. What we have to determine is who would want to do that, and why?"

She relaxed a little. "What do you need to know?"

"Did Joel gamble? Even if it seemed innocent, like on sports?"

She shook her head. "He barely even watched sports. He loved fiddling with engines and mechanical things. He had very little time for sports, or for that matter for television at all. As to drugs, he was cautious about anything. He didn't even like taking his prescriptions. And he never took pills to stay awake like a lot of drivers do."

"What did he like?" Tip asked.

She seemed to think for a moment, and then said, "He and his brother have been truckers all their lives, and he never seemed to want anything else. He sometimes complained about his back hurting, or being tired, but no more than any other person."

"Was he happy?" I asked.

She sniffed a few tears and smiled. "Yes, detective, he *was* happy. Of that I'm sure."

She looked at her watch and stood. "If you'll excuse me, detectives, I have to get ready for my son. He was with his cousin up in Dallas when I heard about this. They're bringing him home."

Tip stood and said, "Of course, ma'am."

I placed a business card on the table. I was going to shake her hand, but she looked as if she could use a hug. I let her head rest on my shoulder and then said, "Please call if you need anything."

"I will," she said. "Thank you."

Tip was on the phone before we reached the car. "Buck, who the fuck did you send to the Ford's house for notification?"

I could hear even though he didn't have it on speaker.

"I told you, Harris County did it."

"Well they fucked up. Goddamnit, I just came from there and the wife didn't even know it was a murder. She didn't know there was a goddamn woman in the car with him either. And she still doesn't know that woman was naked. What the fuck is wrong—"

"Hold up, Denton. I'm sorry somebody got your ass in a bind but it wasn't me. Somebody in Harris County fucked up. Not us."

Tip kicked at the grass a few times, and then he said, "All right, goddamnit."

"All right my ass," Buck said. "You better think before you bitch at someone."

"I'm hanging up."

Buck laughed. "Since I know that's as close as I'm getting to an apology, I'll say goodnight."

"Sounds like Buck knows you pretty well," I said.

Tip opened the door and got in the driver's seat. I climbed in the passenger side. "That pissed me off. They made us look like asses."

"It won't be the last time," I said, "Besides, we learned something."

"What?"

"We know that Tiffany didn't kill these people. We don't have proof yet, but we *know* it. There's no way she was smart enough or experienced enough to plan those murders and clean up like they did. If she was smart enough to do that she sure as shit wouldn't kill herself."

"That leaves us the mystery woman," Tip said.

As Tip pulled out onto Highway 6, I said, "Are we looking at a woman serial killer? You know there aren't many of them."

"I don't know about a serial killer," Tip said. "But we might be looking at a woman hit man."

Hit man. Every time I heard the words I thought of Dominic. "Tip, drop me off at my house. I've got a lot to do, and we need to get an early start on this."

Chapter 29

FAMILY IS EVERYTHING

Brooklyn, New York

Dominic's private cell number rang. "Pronto."

"It's Mazza."

"What have you found?"

"We have the man who's been asking questions. And we know who accessed the records from the hospital."

"Has the man talked?"

"Nothing," Mazza said. "Should I—"

"I'll send someone," Dominic said, and then, "Who was responsible for the hospital records?"

"Her name is Janice Quintana."

Dominic remained silent.

"Do you want me to bring her to the warehouse?" Mazza asked.

"Blindfold her, and don't let her see anyone. Call me when she arrives."

A few hours later Mazza called. "She's here."

"I'll be there soon," Dominic said. "Has the Doctor arrived?"

"He's with the other man."

"Keep him alive. And find out what the woman knows."

Dominic grabbed his coat from the closet, and then put on his gloves and hat. He seldom left the house without his hat. He arrived at the warehouse 30 minutes later.

Mazza greeted him. "He talked. It only took twenty minutes."

"And what did we learn?" Dominic asked.

"As you assumed, the orders came from Mexico. He said from a man named Tico, but Tico works for Carlos Cortes."

Dominic nodded. "And what were the questions he asked?"

Mazza took a big sip of water. "He was asking about you and Maria. About the old days."

"What else?"

"He asked if anyone ever saw Maria with Tommy Gianelli. Or even knew of Tommy Gianelli."

"And what report did he send?"

Mazza took a deep breath. "That no one from the neighborhood had ever heard of Tommy Gianelli, and that you and Maria were *very good* friends."

Dominic closed his eyes and clenched his fists. "Tell the Doctor he can do what he wants with him."

"And the woman?"

"Take me to see her."

Mazza led the way to the back of the warehouse. A metal door opened into a small rectangular room with three folding chairs and a small table. The floor and walls were concrete. Janice Quintana sat in one of the chairs, blindfolded, with her hands bound by rope.

"She refuses to talk," Mazza said.

Dominic moved a chair next to hers and sat. He motioned for Mazza to leave him alone. When the door closed, Dominic patted her leg gently. She jumped. And shivered.

"I don't know anything," she said.

"I don't want to hurt anyone," Dominic said. His voice was calm.

Janice shook. "I really don't know anything. They told me to get those files. That's *all* I know. I swear."

"Who told you?" Dominic asked.

"I don't know who they are."

"Why would you do something illegal and risk losing your job for someone you don't know?"

"They paid me a lot of money," she said. "I know I shouldn't have done it, but—"

Dominic stood and paced, the sound of his leather heels clicking on the concrete floor echoing. "I don't like being lied to."

"I'm not lying. I swear."

"You shouldn't swear, Ms. Quintana."

She tensed up when he said her name. "How do you…"

"Know your name?" Dominic laughed. "We know *everything* about you. We know about your children, your debts, and your no-good brother who deals drugs. I suspect the reason you did this was because of him." Dominic moved closer and whispered. "Tell me I'm wrong."

Janice trembled. "Don't hurt my children. Please?"

Dominic kept his voice low. "I would never hurt a woman or a child. I won't even threaten to hurt your children. But I need this information because this concerns *my* family, and I would do *anything* for my family. Give me what I need or I will make sure you lose your job. And I will make sure you never get another job in New York." Dominic paused, and then said, "In case you're wondering, yes, I can do that."

Janice shook her head and sighed. "It wasn't the money. I would have never done this for money. They threatened my brother if I didn't help. They said they'd kill him."

"What did they ask you to do?"

"They wanted the records for three people. Maria, Tommy, and Concetta Gianelli. That's it. After I got the records I was supposed to email the information to an address they gave me."

Dominic reached down and untied her hands, and then he helped her stand. "I'll have someone take you home. Please accept my apologies for putting you through this, but I had to know."

"You're letting me go?"

"You're free to go. Give my friend the email address you sent the information to, and you'll never hear from us again."

Janice rubbed her wrists where the rope had been. "Thank you," she said.

Dominic walked her to the door and signaled Mazza. "Make sure she gets home safely. And get the email address from her and then call me."

"Did you find out what you needed?" Mazza asked.

"I'm certain that when we trace this email, we'll find Carlos Cortes at the other end of it."

"What are we going to do?"

"I'm not sure yet," Dominic said. "But we *will* do something."

Chapter 30

FOLLOWED

Ribs tried digesting what Rosalee said. "Followed? What do you mean?"

"I mean *followed*. I drove Sandra to pick up her car, and I noticed a black pickup following me. Now I'm on my way to the mall and it's there again, about three cars behind me."

"There are a *lot* of black pickups in Houston. Are you sure—"

"Get out of cop mode, Ribs. I'm not an idiot. It's a Chevy and the last three numbers on the plate are 472."

Son of a bitch. "Where are you now?"

"On 1960 heading East from 290. And I just looked in the mirror. He's still there, two cars behind me in the other lane."

"Can you describe him?"

"There are two of them. I'm pretty sure they're Latinos, but that's as much as I can make out. They haven't gotten up close."

"Let me think," he said.

"Do you want me to go home?" Rosalee asked. "Or over to Sissy's house?"

"No. If somebody's following you, I don't want them going there. We want it where we control the situation."

A short pause, and then Rosalee said, "There is no *if*. I told you, they're following me."

"You're right. I'm sorry. I'm still 30 minutes away, so go to the Willowbrook Mall and park by the Sears' entrance. Get as close as you can to the entrance, check to make sure they aren't close by, and then go inside. *Stay* inside near people. Find a security guard, but don't tell them the situation unless you have to. Give the guard my phone number in case he wants to call."

"Why don't you call another officer to come by?"

"Rosalee, listen to me. This is important. If we report this and the cops come out, all they'll do is ask the driver if he was following you. He'll deny it and go on his way. And the next time, he'll be more careful. We'll do this my way, *amorcita*. Trust me."

"I do trust you, but hurry up. I'm only 10 minutes from the mall."

"Don't worry. I'll call when we get there. *Te amo.*"

"I love you too," Rosalee said.

"What the hell was that all about?" Cruz asked.

Ribs put the siren on and hit the gas. On the way, he filled Cruz in on what Rosalee said.

"Son of a bitch! Do you think this has anything to do with the case?"

"I'm not thinking about it yet," Ribs said. "Let's wait until we get there."

Twenty-five minutes later Ribs pulled into the parking lot at the back of Sears, the side opposite of where Rosalee went in. He called her cell.

"Where are you?" Rosalee asked.

"At the back of Sears. Where are you?"

"I'm by the perfume."

"Have you seen them?" Ribs asked.

"Not since I came in here."

"Stay inside until I call. I'll check the parking lot. You said the last three numbers are 472?"

"Yes. A black pickup and the plate ends in 472. Be careful."

Ribs drove around the lot slowly, as if he was looking for a spot to park.

Cruz sat low in the passenger seat. "Do you see anything?"

"Not yet."

Ribs reached the end of an aisle, and turned right, going back down the other side.

"Don't look now," Cruz said, "but there's a black Chevy truck near the end, sitting off by itself."

"I see it. Get down so they can't see you. I'll drive by and verify the plate."

Ribs swung around the corner quickly, glancing at the plate when he checked for oncoming traffic in the next lane. "It's them," he said. "Two of them just like Rosalee said."

"You're going to owe Rosalee an apology for doubting her," Cruz said.

"She's gonna want a lot more than an apology," Ribs said, "But I can't worry about that now."

"What do you think?" Cruz said, "Take them fast or sneak up? I say we take 'em fast."

"You got it," Ribs said. "Duck down and be ready. I'll swing around again."

Cruz got low in the front seat and drew his gun. Ribs drove toward the truck, slowing as he got in front of it. "Now!" he said, and got out with his gun drawn, pointed at the driver. Cruz got out the other side, his gun pointed at the passenger in the truck. The passenger made a quick move. Cruz fired into the windshield.

"Police," Ribs said. "Don't move. You move and I'll fuckin' kill you."

Cruz took the passenger, Ribs the driver. "Get out. Hands on the hood of the truck. Now."

Ribs found a gun on each of them and enough ice in the truck to keep a meth head high for a year. Cruz handcuffed them. "Why were you following my wife?"

The driver said, "*No hablo ingles.*"

"That's all right, we speak Spanish, so pick your language and answer the question."

"Lawyer," the driver said. "Is that clear enough for you?"

"Plenty clear," Cruz said. "The way I figure it is we've got you for illegal firearms, and we've got enough ice here to charge you with intent to sell. That should put you away for a *long* time."

The driver smirked. "We'll be out by tomorrow."

Ribs put his gun to the driver's head. His hand was on the trigger.

"Not if you die tonight," Cruz said. "My partner is a little nervous."

Chapter 31

A Talk With Dominic

Brooklyn, New York

Dominic walked into his house, removed his gloves, and tossed them onto a chair in the foyer. He lay his coat over the arm of the chair and set his hat on top of the coat. The espresso pot called to him, but he poured a grappa instead. And then he poured another.

Despite all that he'd done in his life, he raised Concetta the best way he knew how. And now…this. If she found out what he'd done…who her father really was…He couldn't let it happen. No matter what, he *had* to stop that.

He called Zeppe but no one answered. After downing another grappa he decided to call Concetta. Depending on what Carlos did with this information, it might be the last time she spoke to Dominic. He used a disposable cell and dialed her number.

Tip had dropped me off at the house. I put water on for coffee and had just gotten Hotshot into the back yard when I heard the phone ring. I cautioned the cat to stay put and went for the phone.

"Hello?"

"Concetta, I was almost ready to hang up."

"Uncle Dominic? What are *you* doing calling here?" I'm sure my voice changed from surprise to panic as a thousand thoughts raced through my mind. *Is Zeppe okay? Is Dominic hurt? Is he locked up?* "Is everything okay?"

"I'm fine," Dominic said. "I thought I'd call my favorite person in the world and chat. How is your weather?"

"My weather? Uncle Dominic, are you sure everything's okay? I've *never* heard you ask about the weather. Not once."

"Someone…I think someone famous, said, 'There is a first time for everything.'"

I laughed. "I'm glad you called. I missed you."

"Already? I think you miss the food more. Or my espresso."

"You might be right about that. How are Zeppe and the family?"

"You know Zeppe. He is *always* all right. But enough news of here, tell me how Texas is treating you. What interesting cases are you working?"

A cold shiver ran up my spine. Instinct had me wondering, *why is he asking that?* But then I remembered I was in Texas now, away from the suspicion in the department, and away from his influence and the taint of his reputation.

I almost overcame my reluctance but decided to test it. "Why the sudden interest in my work, Uncle Dominic?"

He laughed. "Concetta, put your mind at ease. I have always been interested in your work, but while you were in New York I couldn't ask. Now that you're in Texas, it presents no problem. So tell your uncle what you're working on."

Hearing that made me relax, and made me happy. It was the first time in my life he'd ever shown an interest. "We caught a tough one, Uncle Dominic. It started out with a lawyer that we thought had a heart attack, and then a banker who drowned in his own hot tub, and now a murder/suicide of a trucker. We're convinced they're murders, and that they're connected, but we haven't put it together yet. I'm going up to Tip's house tonight to go over it with him."

"This is the partner you had last time?"

I knew Dominic blamed Tip for what happened to me last time I was in Texas. "Yes, and he's a damn good cop. Stop worrying."

"That's an odd combination of occupations to be connected," Dominic said.

"The banker and lawyer certainly might run in the same circles, but the trucker throws a wrench into our theories."

"I can see why," Dominic said, and then, "But enough talk of murders and police work. If you keep that up you'll make me nervous."

He laughed after he said that, and I joined him. "I really miss you guys."

"How about you? I mean yourself. How are you feeling?"

Uncle Dominic was perhaps the worst person in the world to ask about personal feelings. He lived his life with the belief that you handled your own problems and never discussed problems with others. I guess that's why I had such a difficult time with it. I was raised by him since I was twelve. "I'm doing better. Thanks for asking."

"Do you have someone to talk to? A friend?"

"I have a good friend, Uncle Dominic. She works at the station and she's great."

He seemed to perk up. "Good. But if you ever need to talk, you know you can call me."

"You should retire down here, then we could talk all the time. Besides, the weather's nice."

"There is more to life than nice weather. And I have coats for when it isn't so nice."

"Uncle Dominic, I have to get ready, but maybe we can talk next week."

"I would love to. I'll call again when Zeppe is here. Goodbye, Concetta. *Ti voglio bene.*"

"*Ti voglio bene.*"

I hung up the phone, called Hotshot into the house and put his food down, and then I took a quick shower and headed out. We had to figure something out about these cases and we had to do it quickly. As I drove to Tip's I realized how great I felt. Relaxed. Maybe even relieved. Uncle Dominic and I had a great conversation and I never once felt threatened, or scared. I never worried that I'd have to report something he said and I didn't have to watch what I said. *I even discussed a case with him.* A warm feeling rushed through me. This was the first time I had ever talked shop with Uncle Dominic, and it felt good. *Damn good.*

Dominic hung up the phone, took another shot of grappa, and then put the top on the bottle. If he didn't put it away now he might finish it, and that much grappa wasn't good for thinking. And he had a *lot* to think about. The problem with the information from the hospital was one thing—and it worried him greatly—but what she told him about her cases worried him even more. He recognized the connection as soon as she told him, and it wouldn't be long before Connie and her partner put the pieces together. They were busy trying to connect the people. They should have been connecting the occupations. A lawyer, a banker, and a trucker. Legal representation, money laundering, and drug distribution. Carlos Cortes was back in Texas, and Connie was on a collision course with him.

As Dominic saw it, there was only one thing to do. He dialed a number on his disposable phone. It was answered right away.

"Si, signore."

"Pack your bags. You are going to Houston."

"For how long?"

"I don't know yet."

Dominic got up and started the process for making espresso. He would need it tonight. If Connie found out he sent someone to watch over her she would be furious. But Dominic would rather her be furious than dead.

Chapter 32

CONNECTING THE DOTS

Tip's car was in the driveway, parked next to Mollie's. I pulled onto the grass, got out of the car, and walked in the back door. Sacco was in his spot by the kitchen doorway. His tail barely wagged. "Hi, Sacco. I see you're excited about me being here."

"He's about as excited as any man gets," Mollie said. "Unless he wants something besides dinner."

"I'm with you on that," I said. "Where's Tip?"

"He's taking a shower or doing some other private business in his bedroom. But before he gets out here how about you telling me what we're working on."

"That depends on what we're eating," Tip said as he walked into the kitchen.

"Fajitas, corn, and refried beans. And I'm making my homemade guacamole."

"Sounds delicious," I said. "I'm hungry as hell."

"I don't know how hungry hell is," Mollie said, "But I'll take that to mean you want more than a couple of fajitas, so I'll cook extra."

"I'll have five," Tip said. "One for each murder we have to solve."

Mollie scooped the guacamole into a small bowl and looked at Tip. "Five? You got five bodies now?"

I grabbed a few beers from the fridge, popped one open for Mollie and me, and handed the other to Tip. "We've got five bodies, Mollie. And one of them is a prostitute who used to be our prime suspect."

Tip went to the table in what used to be his living room and started a chart.

Lawyer	Banker	Trucker	Prostitute
Heart attack	Accident	Murder	Suicide

"Only four people on that list," Mollie said.

"We haven't identified the other body," Tip said. "He was burned up in the car."

"The world is full of crazies," Mollie said.

I took a swig of beer and grabbed a marker. "Here's what we know so far."

'Lawyer who runs around with young women, dies of heart attack.

Banker who owns a pool, falls in hot tub and hits head.

Trucker who appears faithful to wife, is killed while with prostitute.

Prostitute, who was seen with all of them, kills self for no apparent reason.'

"And all of them were clean. Good credit, no arrests. Nothing." Tip downed his beer and got another one. "Something ain't right in San Antone."

"Where's the connection?" I said. "The only lead we have is the mystery woman. What connects the victims?"

Tip made more notes. "Let's look at what we have again. The lawyer met the mystery woman at the bar. She got a call from Tiffany, and he ends up at the hotel with Tiffany a few minutes later."

"And we know that Tiffany expected a high-dollar client that night because she told LaDonna."

Tip made a new line. "The hotel room was clean, except for a few partial prints belonging to Tiffany. But she wasn't in the database, and we only matched the prints when the trucker died."

I thought about what Tip said, and it suddenly hit me. "You know what? We wouldn't have known anything about Tiffany if it wasn't for the prints in the hotel. We wouldn't have matched her to the trucker, which means we would have never connected the trucker's death to the others."

Tip scratched out a new chart and we took a look.

Lawyer	Banker	Trucker
Met mystery woman at bar Was with Tiffany at hotel	Met mystery woman at bar Tiffany was there also	Was killed with Tiffany
Tiffany's prints at scene	No evidence	Staged like murder/suicide

"Time to eat," Mollie said, and plopped a few plates on the table.

I took a seat next to Mollie and Tip sat on the other side of her. "Think about it, Tip. The mystery woman had this planned from the beginning. I think she left those prints in the hotel on purpose."

Tip nodded. "She's never been seen by the cameras, which can't be a coincidence. The bartender who saw her with Lipscomb said she had a Mexican accent, and the other bartender said she had an East Texas accent."

"And the valet attendant said she had no accent," I said.

"And she looked different," Tip said. "Dark brown hair, light brown hair, blue eyes, brown eyes."

"That doesn't explain *why*," I said. "Even if we assume she's behind all the killings, unless these are random victims we still have no connection or explanation for *why* they've been killed."

"Who wants them dead?" Mollie asked. "If they're dead, somebody's got to want them dead."

"I agree, Mollie, but we can't figure out who. None of them had records. None of them were in debt. And they didn't seem to have any enemies. At least not obvious ones."

I finished my first fajita, and said to Mollie. "These are damn good. I think they're better than what I've had in the restaurants."

Mollie cocked her head and stared. "Of course they're better. That guacamole recipe's been in my family for a long time. And those fajitas have been sittin' in my special marinating sauce since early this morning." She shook her head as if disgusted. "Ain't no damn restaurant doin' that for a meal."

"Why did she need Tiffany?" Tip asked. "And for someone who seems like a professional, why use a prostitute?"

I thought for a moment. "The obvious answer was to use her as a scapegoat. Blame everything on her and the cases are solved with the death of the trucker and her lying underneath him."

Tip polished off his third fajita and opened another beer. "I don't think we're going to find anything on the woman. We need to figure out the connection between the victims. First thing tomorrow we'll visit the lawyer's office again. After that, we'll go see the banker, and if we have to, we'll have another talk with Mrs. Ford."

"Somebody's got to know something," I said.

Chapter 33

WHERE'S THE CONNECTION

Tip picked me up and we headed into the station to get an early start. Lipscomb's office was first on our list, but we had an hour or so to kill before the partners got in. I checked my email and then headed to the coffee room. Detective Ramirez stood behind Herb and Julie. Charlie was holding up the line.

"Charlie, get your ass moving," Ramirez said.

"I'm stirring the creamer in," Charlie said. "It gets lumpy sometimes."

"Stir it someplace else," Herb said. "I'd like to get my coffee while it's hot."

Charlie looked as if he was about to say something but then Tip walked in. Charlie grabbed a napkin and hustled out of the way. For some reason Tip terrified him. I fixed my coffee and took a seat next to Julie. Tip sat next to Ramirez. A couple of minutes later, Delgado and Cruz walked in.

"How's it going, Ribs?"

He looked over at me. "Guess you haven't heard," he said, and pulled up a chair.

"I'll get coffee," Cruz said from behind him.

"What happened?" I said.

"Cruz and I were working our case yesterday and I got a call from Rosalee. She said two guys were following her. At first I thought she might be imagining it, but she convinced me it was real so I told her to go to the mall. Cruz and I went up there, and sure enough she was being followed. Two guys. They were carrying, and they had a shitload of ice in their truck."

"Son of a bitch," Tip said. "Did you get anything out of them?"

Ribs shook his head. "Nothing. They screamed *lawyer* as soon as we busted them."

Cruz set a cup of coffee in front of Ribs and stood behind him. Ribs took a sip and looked at me, then Tip. "Guess who they called for a lawyer?"

Tip sat up straight. "Don't tell me it was Lipscomb's office."

"None other," Ribs said. "And they asked for Griffin, one of the partners."

"What the hell is going on here?" Tip said. "What kind of low-life scum threatens a man's family?"

As soon as Tip said that, it hit me. Uncle Dominic always said the Mexican drug lords didn't play fair. He said they went after families and friends instead of the person they wanted. "Carlos!" I said. "Goddamnit, it's Carlos."

I pounded my fist on the table, furious at myself for not seeing it earlier. "That's why all the dead people are clean. The lawyer, the banker, the trucker. It wasn't them Carlos was after. He killed them to scare someone."

"How did you know?" Ribs said.

Tip shot me a look and then grabbed Delgado's arm. "Are you saying Carlos was behind what happened with Rosalee?"

"I can't swear to it, but he's the one moving the meth, and we're convinced he's the one who had Martin killed."

I dunked my empty coffee cup in the trash. "And he's behind these killings, too. I guarantee you."

Delgado looked at me and nodded. "She's right. After the two we busted called Griffin we had him checked out. He represented Cortes last year."

Tip stood and kicked his chair. "Julie, why *the hell* didn't we know about this? I told you to check out that law firm."

Julie's face turned red. "I'm sorry, Tip. It must have slipped by me."

"Slipped by you? Shit like that can't afford to *slip by you*."

"It's my fault." That came from Charlie. His head was lowered and he wouldn't look at Tip.

"What?" Tip yelled.

"I said, it's my fault." It sounded like Charlie barely managed to get it out. "Julie asked me to check that out, and I guess I misunderstood. I thought she meant just check out Lipscomb. I never checked out the rest of the firm."

It looked as if Tip was going to yell again. I tapped his arm, and when he turned to me I shook my head.

Charlie stood and headed for the door.

Delgado went to get more coffee. "No question these cases are connected."

"We need to follow up on a few leads," I said. "Now that we know what to look for it puts things in a new light."

Tip said, "Ribs, you and Cruz get your shit together. Connie and I will get with you after we're done questioning the banker's people and the trucker's wife."

"What about the lawyer?" Ribs asked.

"No need in going there," Tip said. "We know Griffin's involved. What we've got to figure out is who Carlos targeted with the banker and the trucker."

I was at the doorway, one foot in the hall. "Let's go, partner. We're wasting time."

We decided to see Mrs. Ford first, thinking we'd get the most honest answers from her. Depending on what she told us, we might ask different questions at the bank. As we drove west on I-10, I read through the notes from when we interviewed her. "Tip, we might be able to shortcut this visit."

"What do you mean?"

"She told us her husband's brother was a trucker also. That might be who Carlos is trying to intimidate. A phone call might determine that."

"Call her," Tip said.

I had her number in the file. She answered right away. "Mrs. Ford, this is Detective Gianelli."

"Hello, Detective. Is there any news?"

"No, ma'am. I'm afraid there isn't yet, but I did have a question. You said your husband's brother was a truck driver. Do you have his number? We'd like to ask him a few questions."

She gave me his phone number, but then said, "I doubt if you'll get him until tomorrow or the next day. He's on a run and when he's in Mexico he usually turns his phone off."

I looked to Tip and tapped his arm. "You say he's in Mexico? Do you know where he goes on his deliveries?"

"I believe he goes to Monterrey," she said. "I'm sure he makes other stops, but that's the main destination."

"Okay, thank you, ma'am. I appreciate your help. And we'll call when we have news on your husband."

I made sure the line disconnected, and then I looked over at Tip. "Joel's brother makes runs to Monterrey."

"Son of a bitch," Tip said. "You were right. Sure as shit stinks, it's Carlos behind this." Tip moved to the right lane of the freeway. "Where's the brother live? We need to pay him a visit."

"She said he's in Mexico now and he doesn't answer his phone. We'll try that later, but for now let's talk to a few bankers."

It didn't take us long to get to the bank where Davids worked. We talked to a few of the employees who weren't in the last time we were there, but we didn't learn anything new. Davids' admin was a big help, though. She walked us through his emails—after making sure there was no sensitive material—and she gave us a few contacts that we didn't have before, contacts that weren't on his personal computer.

"You mentioned that he went to the gym and to that one bar a few nights a week. What else did Mr. Davids do? What did he do on the weekends?"

"I know he sometimes played poker on Friday nights, and if the weather was nice he golfed on Sundays."

"He wasn't a church-going man?" Tip asked.

She shook her head. "I don't think Mr. Davids attended church. But he *did* enjoy golf."

"Was there a regular group he played with?" I asked.

"Every Sunday that weather permitted," she said. "Mr. Parker and Mr. Masterson, two of our biggest customers, and Mr. Snider."

"What do Parker and Masterson do?" I asked.

"Mr. Parker owns a real-estate development company, and Mr. Masterson owns a furniture company."

"And what about Snider?" Tip asked.

She smiled. "Mr. Snider is president of one of our competitors. First Banc of Texas."

"We'll need his number," I said.

"Why don't you get us all of their numbers," Tip said.

She typed a few commands on the computer and said, "They're printing now, detectives. Is there anything else I can get for you?"

"No, this has been helpful," I said. "Thanks."

She handed me the printout of the contact information and then said, "Has there been any news on Mr. Davids? I mean…was it an accident?"

"We're not sure yet," I said. "Why? Is there a reason why you asked?"

"No. It's just…well, Mr. Davids wasn't the kind of man to have accidents. He was meticulous about everything he did. It just seems strange."

"We think so too," Tip said. "Let us know if you think of anything else."

As we got in the car, Tip said. "We might have hit the mother lode. Any one of those guys he plays golf with could be a target."

"Yeah, but Snider looks prime. He's the one dealing with money, and drug lords need money laundered."

"Then I guess we talk to him first," Tip said.

Chapter 34

A Convincing Argument

Patrick Snider finished with his tie, making sure that the knot was perfect. He adjusted the collar stays and fit the tie snugly into place. Then he grabbed his coat and went downstairs. Marissa and Trish were seated at the table, waiting on him.

"Good morning, girls. Were you waiting for me?"

Marissa smiled, baring a few missing teeth. "You're always late, Daddy."

"That's because Mommy doesn't help me get dressed," he said. "Besides, little girls are *never* late."

"Trish is late all the time," Marissa said.

Patrick leaned down, kissed her on the head, and whispered. "But she's older. Pre-K girls are the ones on time."

Marissa stuck her tongue out at Trish, and then smiled.

Patrick walked to the counter and kissed his wife, Cathy, and then he poured a cup of coffee and returned to the table. He positioned his iPad in a holder and flipped to his favorite news app.

"Patrick, put that away. The news isn't going anywhere."

Marissa took a bite of toast and then a big sip of milk. "Is there anything in the news, Daddy?"

"The only thing that looked important was an article that said milk mustaches can make little girls laugh." And then he reached over and tickled her.

Trish shook her head. "Are you ever going to quit doing that?"

"You liked it when you were her age."

"I don't know how," she said, but she hid a smile.

Cathy grabbed her coat and car keys. "Hurry up, girls. I'm driving you today, and it's almost time to go."

"I'm ready," Marissa said.

Trish wiped her mouth and took her dishes to the sink. Marissa did the same, and then stopped to kiss her father. "Bye, Dad. Love you."

"Love you too," Trish said.

"Bye, girls. See you tonight," Patrick said, and kissed Cathy on the cheek.

After they left, he drained the coffee cup, grabbed his coat and briefcase, and headed out. He had a big day planned.

It was almost noon before Patrick finished addressing the board regarding his investment plans for the Second Ward. He'd done a good job of allaying their concerns about the rise in crime statistics and he assured them that would not interfere with the bank's plans to invest in the community. He also addressed the rumored budget cuts for road improvements. Nothing got investors in an uproar quicker than rumors. For all of that, though, the Second Ward was making headway. Young people were moving into old warehouses converted into lofts, and businesses were springing up to support the new crowd. That's what was needed to get money flowing into the area again, and Snider was making certain his bank was positioned to profit from the influx of money.

As the last board member left, he shoved his hand into his pocket and retrieved his cell phone. It had been on vibrate but the damn thing rang four times while he was talking. He looked at the caller ID—*unknown*. Who the hell was calling him, and so often? He checked voicemail but no one had left a message. He pressed the speed dial button for his secretary. She answered on the second ring.

"Mr. Snider's office."

"Janet, did my wife call?"

"No, the only call you had was from a Mrs. Mercer, something about a leak in her apartment building. For some reason she thought you could help her."

"If she calls again, tell her to call a plumber. And I'll be going out for lunch. Don't call me unless it's an emergency."

"Yes, sir."

The Mrs. Mercer nonsense had to be Sharon's way of telling him to meet her at the hotel. Damn, she was horny, but he loved every minute of it. And that was going to make it all the more difficult to do what he had to do. Snider switched the phone to *ring* and headed out the door.

It only took fifteen minutes to get to the hotel. He parked in the garage, then went straight to the room where Sharon was waiting. She was so hot he could barely control himself, but it didn't matter today; he hadn't come for that. After receiving the call from that blackmailer, Patrick decided to stop seeing her. It would be one major step toward cleaning up his act should those photos leak, and besides, Sharon had begun asking questions about marriage and divorce. Stupid bitch didn't realize there would be no divorce. For God's sake, he wasn't going to marry someone like her. Fuck her—hell yes. Marry her—not a chance.

Using his key he let himself in. "Sharon?"

"Right here."

He turned to the sound of her voice and found her lying naked on the sofa with her legs crossed.

"Are you ready for a gourmet lunch?" she said.

He sat on the sofa next to her, trying to muster the nerve to tell her. Then his cell phone rang.

"Don't answer it," she said, and wrapped her legs around him.

He tried getting up, but she began unbuttoning his shirt. The phone rang two more times, then the phone in the room rang. Sharon tried to hold onto him, but Snider pulled away. "Does anyone know you're here?" A hint of panic clung to his words.

"Nobody," she said, her own tone defensive. "Come back here."

Patrick hovered above her, torn between her luscious body and the urgency of a ringing phone. "Get the phone," he said. "It might be important."

She lifted herself off the sofa and moved to the bureau. "Hello."

"Mr. Snider, please."

Sharon held her hand out to him. "For you," she said.

A suspicious, yet concerned look came over Snider. "Yes, this is Patrick."

"Señor Snider, how are you today?" The voice was smooth and polite, almost like a news announcer.

"Do I know you? Who is this?"

"How soon we forget. We talked a short while ago, after your last speech. Remember, I told you about the pictures of Sharon."

Sharon wrapped her arms around Patrick, fondling him. He shoved her away. "Listen, I don't know who you are, but I told you before what you could do with those pictures."

"Yes, I know, but that was before I had Cathy. Now you must meet me or I will not only show her the pictures, I will kill her."

"You wouldn't *dare*."

"Goodbye, señor."

"Wait," Snider screamed, but the line went dead.

"What's wrong?" Sharon asked.

"Nothing. I don't know. Some lunatic is trying to blackmail me." Patrick dialed Cathy's number, pacing as he waited for her to answer.

After five rings it picked up.

"Hello, Mr. Snider."

Patrick's heart raced. His chest tightened. It was the same man he had been talking to. "Where is she?"

"All in good time," the man on the phone said. "Go outside and wait at the corner for someone to pick you up. They will arrive in less than ten minutes. And don't worry about our business. It won't take long. Perhaps an hour or two."

Patrick turned to Sharon. "I've got to go. You need to get out of here, too."

"What do you mean? What's going—"

"Never mind," he shouted. "Just get out of here. I'll call you when I want you."

She grabbed her clothes and started dressing. "I won't be waiting," she said.

Snider buttoned his shirt and raced to the elevator. Ten minutes left him barely enough time. While he waited he thought about what this man wanted, and how he could keep from making himself dirty. The man had a Spanish accent. In this part of the country that usually meant Mexican, and that usually meant drugs. Snider shook his head. *I won't get involved in drugs.*

Two minutes after he got to the corner, a blue Honda van pulled to the curb. The back door slid open. "Get in," a voice called from inside.

Snider climbed in the back seat, the door closing automatically. Two men sat in the front and another sat alongside Snider in the back. "Where are we going?"

"You'll see when we get there," the one next to him said, his accent confirming him as Mexican.

"You're not blindfolding me?"

The driver laughed. "This isn't the movies, señor."

The man in the passenger seat said, "If we don't want you telling anyone we'll kill you."

Within fifteen minutes they pulled up to an old warehouse being renovated into new condominiums. It was in the Second Ward, where Snider's investments would take place. "What are we doing here?"

"Perhaps we would like to buy some condos, señor." The doors opened and everyone got out. "Follow me," the driver said. He walked into the building and headed for the construction elevator.

"Are you the one who called me? You don't sound like him."

"Not me."

"Where's my wife?"

"Everything will be answered in time."

The elevator took them to the third floor, gutted of old walls and with signs of new construction everywhere. New plumbing, wiring, all new metal studs. Patrick looked around as he exited, searching for his wife. Halfway across the room, a man greeted him with a warm embrace, as if they were old friends.

"Welcome, Señor Snider. I am sorry we had to meet under such circumstances."

"You're the one I spoke with?"

Carlos bowed. "Forgive my rudeness. I am Carlos Cortes, and these are my associates." His hand swept to encompass them. "The one who drove you is Tico, and this is Roberto to my right. Behind you is Chaparrito."

"I don't care who your men are. I just want to know where my wife is and what you want."

Carlos walked toward a table in the center of the room. "I like a man who gets to the point. I am that way myself. Now, as to your wife—in good time. As to what I want…" Carlos pulled out a chair and offered it to Snider. "Please, señor, make yourself comfortable."

Patrick sat, then Carlos pulled his chair next to him and leaned forward, facing him. "You have done a good job of bringing new investments into this…how do you say it…ward?"

Patrick nodded.

"Yes, well, I have made major investments into this area." Carlos spread his arms wide. "This warehouse is mine, as is the one next to it. And soon, there will be luxury apartments here. I like that."

Snider stared, his expression prompting Carlos to continue.

"But I also have other businesses that bring in a lot of cash." Carlos shook his head. "And that, my friend, is where you can help." He leaned in until he was inches from Patrick's face. "I'm sure you understand my dilemma."

"You're talking about cleaning money?"

"I see you are an intelligent man." Carlos smiled and lit a cigarette. "This is not something I ask as a favor, but as a business proposition. Your cut will be lucrative."

Patrick jumped from his chair. "Forget it. I'm not getting involved in drugs."

"Your friend, Señor Davids felt the same way. I believe he was about to change his mind when he had his…accident." Carlos stared at Snider. "But enough of this talk of death. Besides, you are already involved in drugs. Doesn't Sharon use drugs before she has sex with you?" Carlos wagged his finger to drive the point home. "Yes, I believe she does, and perhaps you do, too, maybe to make the sex just a little better?"

"That's nothing. And it's over with." Snider said it was nothing, but that was his weak attempt at a bluff. The news about Davids shocked him. He never imagined it was murder. He hadn't been too concerned about the affair, but this man was a lunatic. There was no telling what he might do.

Carlos' face lost all of it's humor. "You say it's over? And I believe you, but it doesn't matter because I *do* need this favor."

Snider stood and walked around. If he believed what the man said, he'd already killed Davids. God only knows what he was capable of. He had to think of something to stall this maniac. "I have no problem with an occasional deposit, but I can't do this on a regular basis."

Carlos slapped Tico on the back. "You see, Tico. I told you we could count on him."

Patrick was the one wagging his finger now. "I said an *occasional* deposit. I'm not getting into bed with you, and I can't get involved with drugs. Not only can't but *won't*."

Carlos' face wrinkled into a concerned look. "I am sorry to hear that, señor. Truly, I am." He glanced at Chaparrito and nodded.

Chaparrito picked up a two pound rubber mallet from the table and slammed it into Snider's thigh.

Snider reeled, then his knees gave out and he crumbled to the concrete floor. He tried to stand, supporting himself with one arm, but Chaparrito grasped the mallet with both hands and swung, bringing it down onto Snider's left kidney. A low-moaned cry took the wind out of Patrick as well as his consciousness. He fell onto his back.

"Tie him up," Carlos said. "When he wakes we'll see if he is more amenable."

Snider came to a few minutes later, tied to the chair, hands bound behind his back. "I don't care what you do to me."

Carlos nodded to Roberto, who walked over and stood in front of Patrick.

"Take your pants off, Roberto. Señor Snider is going to suck your dick."

Patrick tried to stand but the ropes held him. "You're crazy! I'm warning you, you better let me go."

Carlos looked to Tico. "If he doesn't do it, blow his head off."

Patrick shook his head. "Kill me if you want but I'll never do that. And if you try to force me, I'll bite it off."

A smile came quickly to Carlos' face. Too quickly. "I see I have underestimated you. My apologies, and, my respect. But this forces me to resort to other measures." He turned to Tico and nodded.

Tico left the room returning in a moment with Patrick's wife.

"What is she doing here? Let her go." He tried his best to stand and hop forward in the chair but he couldn't. "I'll kill you. Do you understand? I'll kill you."

"Yes, I understand," Carlos said, then turned to the wife, smiling. "I did not want to resort to this, señora. It is not my style to involve ladies, but your husband left me no choice. If you do not do everything I say, the moment I say it, I am going to kill your husband. Do you understand?"

Cathy cried. "Why are you doing this? What have we done?"

Carlos grabbed her by the cheeks, eyes glaring. "Do you understand me, señora?"

She sobbed more. "Yes. Yes, but why—"

"Good. Now, my friend is going to pull his pants down. When he does you will suck his dick."

She screamed. "No! I'm not—"

"Kill him," Carlos said.

She ran to Patrick, arms outstretched. "No. No. I'll do it. Just don't hurt him."

"No!" Patrick screamed. "Don't you dare. I'll do it. Make me do it."

Carlos smiled. "That's better, I like cooperation, but I think Roberto would rather have your wife do it." He nodded to Roberto, who pulled his pants down.

Patrick fought to get free, but the ropes held him. He tried standing, but the one called Tico shoved him back. Finally, he gave up and looked away.

Carlos would have nothing of it. "Tico, make him watch. And take pictures, too."

When Roberto was finished, Carlos let her go to Patrick. He stood above them, staring down. "If you tell anyone, or if you decide at any time that you no longer need to help us, then I will take Marissa, your daughter, and make her do the same thing. Only I will make her do it with all of my men, and then I will let them do whatever else they want with her."

Patrick's eyes nearly bulged from his head. He tried kicking and even biting at Carlos. His wife jumped up and scratched at him, but Tico caught her in time.

Carlos' smile did not disappear. "Yes, señor. I know about Marissa. I know the security code to your home. I know her teacher, Ms. Christie, and I know the secret word for her school—alligator."

Patrick's tears were drowned by his wife's screams. "What do you want? Haven't you done enough?"

"All I want is your husband's cooperation. Will you guarantee that?"

"Yes," she screamed. "Anything. Just leave us alone."

"Good. He knows what I want. Are we clear on this, señor?"

There was a pause, then his wife nudged him. "Patrick!"

He looked up at Carlos, venom in his glare. "I'll get it done."

Carlos clapped his hands. "Excellent! Then everything is settled." He turned to Tico. "Untie him and help Señora Snider clean up." Carlos seemed lost in thought for a minute. "You know there is a very good restaurant a few blocks from here where they serve the best fajitas. Would you like to join me for lunch?"

Patrick lunged for Carlos, but Cathy stopped him. "Not today," she said. "We need to get home."

Carlos nodded. "I understand. I'll have Tico drive you to your car. Please have a safe journey, and I hope we do not have to meet again. Truly, I do."

Chapter 35

Interview With Snider

Patrick gripped the steering wheel with both hands. Despite that, he occasionally strayed into the other lanes.

"Watch where you're going, Patrick. Do you want me to drive?"

"I'm fine. I just…"

"Just *what*?" Cathy screamed. "Did you do something to bring this on? How did that man get your name?" She burst into tears. "What have you gotten us into?"

Snider hit the steering wheel several times with the palm of his hand. "I didn't do *anything*, goddamnit. I already told you that."

"What are we going to do?"

"We have no choice." Patrick said.

"No choice? We have to call the police. You can't deal drugs for that man."

Patrick looked at Cathy as if she were nuts. "Are you crazy? We can't call the police. You don't know who you're dealing with. These people are lunatics."

"I *know* what they're like, Patrick. I was the one who paid the price back there. Or did you forget?"

"Look Cathy, this isn't like Pittsburgh, where the mob might threaten you, maybe even burn down your building or break a few bones. These goddamn people are nuts. They'll do things to our children. You heard what that man said. For God's sake, I'm not risking our kids."

"But I'm okay to sacrifice? Is that it?" Venom filled her words.

"That's bullshit, and you know it. I tried stopping them. I—"

Cathy started crying again. She reached over and touched Patrick's hand. "I know. I'm sorry I said that."

Patrick turned into the right lane and took the next exit. "Where are you going?" she asked.

"To pick up the girls," he said. "I'm not leaving them in school."

"You don't think—"

"I have no idea what to think," he said. "Until we figure this out, the girls will be safer with us."

"We should leave them in school," Cathy said. "Those men won't do anything today, and the girls would wonder why we're bringing them home. Let's wait until we figure something out."

"Maybe you're right," he said, and then called his office. "Janet, I'm not feeling well. I'm going home for the day. If anything urgent comes up, call my cell; otherwise, I'll see you tomorrow."

After he hung up, Cathy said, "What about the FBI? Can't we call them? Don't they have witness protection or something like that?"

Snider beeped the horn at a car in front of him and then stepped hard on the gas, running a yellow light. "They'd probably find us in witness protection. But even if they didn't, what kind of life would it be? We'd be living in a small hick town in Iowa or some place like that, and I'd be selling farm implements."

The rest of the ride home was in silence. When she got to the house, Cathy raced to the bathroom. She brushed her teeth half a dozen times, and then she took two showers, scrubbing the filth of that man from her body. She wrapped herself in the thickest robe she had and tied the sash tight. Then she put on her slippers and went downstairs. Patrick had tea brewing when she walked into the kitchen.

"I thought you might like a cup of tea," he said.

She closed her eyes and sighed. "Thanks. It might help me relax."

Patrick paced the kitchen floor. After a moment, Cathy said, "I know I've asked this before, but what are we going to do?"

"We're going to act as if nothing happened. We'll get up tomorrow and take the girls to school. I'll go to work. You will do whatever you have planned on your calendar…"

"And?"

"And I will do what that man wants, including laundering his money. And *someday* this nightmare will end."

"Will it?" Cathy said.

The doorbell rang. Cathy jumped. "Oh my God! Who is it?"

Patrick headed for the foyer. "Shut up. Do you hear me? Act as if nothing happened."

Tip pulled to the curb in front of the Sniders' house and we got out of the car. The sidewalk meandered through a garden filled with native Texas plants, and an artificial stream circulated from a small pond off to the side. It was a nice effect. The house was a two-story English Tudor boasting a huge double door with etched glass.

"I guess banking pays off," Tip said, and pressed his finger on the doorbell.

A few seconds later the door opened and a man in a suit greeted us. "What can I do for you?" he said.

I showed my badge. "I'm Detective Gianelli. This is Detective Denton. Are you Patrick Snider?"

"What's this about?" he asked.

"Are you Mr. Snider?" Tip asked.

The suspicion on his face turned to a smile. "I'm sorry. Yes, I'm Patrick Snider. May I ask what this is about?"

"May we come in?" I said.

"Certainly," he said and stepped aside.

Just then a woman came into the foyer. She was thin, with blonde hair. "Patrick, who is it?"

"It's the police," he said.

She extended her hand and said, "I'm Cathy Snider. Is something wrong? Has there been a break in?"

"Nothing like that, ma'am," I said. "But we'd like to talk with you and your husband for a moment. Is there someplace we can sit?"

"Of course," she said, and led the way to a small room off the foyer with a sofa and several chairs.

Her husband took a seat on the sofa, and she sat next to him and held his hand. She sat very close. Tip and I took seats in the chairs.

"We've been investigating a few homicides," Tip said, "The case has drug connections. In fact, one of your colleagues has turned up as a victim—Brent Davids."

"Brent Davids?" Cathy said. "I thought that was an accident."

"It was made to look like an accident," I said, "But we're pretty sure he was murdered, although we haven't released that to the public yet, so we don't want it known."

She seemed genuinely shocked by the news, but Snider wasn't. He pretended to be, but it was obvious he knew, which meant Carlos had already made contact. It was time to find out for sure. I tapped Tip on the arm.

"I'm sure you're wondering why we're here," Tip said. "We have reason to believe that the same man who had Mr. Davids killed will be contacting you. His name is Carlos Cortes."

Cathy Snider tensed. She squeezed her husband's hand.

"Why would he contact me?" Snider said.

"Has he made contact?" Tip asked.

Snider looked away, then turned quickly back to Tip. "What? No, I haven't heard from anyone named Carlos."

Mrs. Snider stood. "Would anyone like a drink?"

"Tea," Tip said.

"Nothing for me," I said.

She left the room as if she were in a hurry. "I'll be right back," she said.

I waited for a minute, and while Tip was engaged with Snider, I went to the kitchen. She stood by the refrigerator, leaning on the counter. She was trembling. "Is everything okay?" I asked.

She spun toward me. "Yes. I'm fine. I just got a little chill, that's all. The news about Brent shook me up."

I walked over and stood close to her. She didn't seem to be able to control her shaking. "Did you know Mr. Davids well?"

She nodded. "He played golf with my husband almost every weekend. And sometimes they played poker together. I felt so bad when I heard of his accident, but now…to hear this…" She shook her head a few times. "It's hard to believe he was involved in something like drugs."

"Mrs. Snider, we don't know if Mr. Davids was involved with drugs. All we know is that the man selling these drugs needs someone to launder his money, and we know he'll stop at nothing until he gets someone to cooperate."

She lifted the teapot to pour, but her hand shook so much I thought she'd spill the tea. I reached for the pot. "Let me get that, Mrs. Snider. And if you don't mind, I think I will have some tea."

"Certainly," she said, and went to a cabinet for a teacup and saucer.

When we returned to the front room, Tip was questioning Mr. Snider. Cathy handed Tip the tea.

"Thank you, ma'am," he said, and then to her husband, "How well did you know Mr. Davids?"

"I knew Brent for more than twelve years. We played golf almost every weekend, and we got together for social events."

"Did he seem different in the last few weeks? Or did he mention anything about problems he was having?"

Snider shook his head. "We played golf the week before he died. Brent acted as he always did. Happy, easy going. He didn't seem to have a care in the world." Snider looked to his wife and smiled. "With all apologies to my wife, Brent said he was so happy because he was single."

"And he never said anything about being approached by anyone to launder money?"

"Not a word, Detective. And I believe he'd have told me. We were good friends."

I watched both Snider and his wife as I sipped my tea. He had control of himself; she didn't. "Has anyone approached you, Mr. Snider?"

He turned toward me. "Me? No. No one."

"And you've never heard of Carlos Cortes?" Tip asked.

He shook his head again. "Never."

I noticed his wife tense when Tip mentioned Carlos' name. I was convinced she'd heard his name before, and *not* from Brent Davids. I looked at my watch and stood. "I guess we better get going."

Tip handed a card to Snider. "Call me if you think of anything."

"I will," Snider said. "Thank you for stopping by."

As we walked to the car, Tip said, "I guess you thought we weren't making progress."

"I didn't think we'd get anything from him, if that's what you mean."

"But she's a different story," Tip said. "That woman looked like she was coming apart."

"You should have seen her in the kitchen. She was shaking so badly I thought she'd spill the tea."

Tip opened the car door and got in. I climbed in the passenger side. "They're not telling us something," I said.

"That ain't no shit," Tip said. "I guess you're going back?"

I nodded. "I've got to wait and get her alone. She's not talking with him there."

"I agree," Tip said. "In the meantime, let's find out what the hell is going on with Delgado's case. I don't like that they were following Rosalee."

Chapter 36

CLOSING IN

On the way back to the station, Tip called Delgado. "I have it on speaker, Ribs, and Connie's with me. Where are you?"

"I'm on my way in. I just got Rosalee and the kids settled in with friends."

"I'm glad you did that. You can't trust these people."

"I don't think Carlos would be crazy enough to go after a cop's family," Ribs said, "But it's better to be safe."

I leaned close to the phone. "Don't forget, this is the guy who killed Tony."

"I'm glad you said that, Connie. I forgot. And by the way, Coop's looking for both of you. She said she called."

"She called a few times," Tip said, "But I was busy."

"Where'd you put the kids?" I asked.

"With one of the cousins."

Tip laughed. "That's the safest place for them. It would take Carlos a month to get through the Delgado family tree."

"Sometimes it pays to have a lot of relatives," Ribs said. "I'll see you when you get in."

Twenty minutes later, Tip and I walked into the station. The desk sergeant shook his head at us as soon as we got in the door.

"What's wrong?" Tip asked.

"Coop is looking for you two. The first few requests were polite. The last one mentioned shoot on sight."

"I guess you should have answered those calls," I said to Tip.

We made our way to Coop's office, where Cindy greeted us with a warning look.

"You might need a vest," she said. I worried a little because she didn't bother to open the door for us.

Tip walked in first. "Gladys, how's my favorite captain?"

"Close the goddamn door," Coop said.

I pushed it shut and made sure the latch clicked.

Tip sat in a big chair across from her. I sat next to him. "Who's got you pissed off?" Tip said.

"Would it mean anything to you if I mentioned the name 'Stenson'?"

Tip sat straight in the chair. "Bobby Stenson?"

Coop removed her glasses and set them on the desk. I'd only been here a couple of weeks but I knew that was a sure sign she was pissed.

"You know goddamn well who I mean. It's come to my attention that you two think he *might* be a candidate for an IA investigation. That he *might* have something to do with drug distribution. And that those ties just *might* mean he could be implicated in a murder investigation." Coop stood, planted the palms of both her hands on the desk, and leaned toward Tip. "When the hell were you going to tell me?"

"I was trying to save the department the embarrassment in case he wasn't dirty."

"In other words, you were going to look into this yourself?"

"Kind of, yeah."

Coop didn't relax her stance. "Kind of? What the hell does 'kind of' mean?"

Tip leaned in closer to her. "*Kind of* means if I found out he was dirty and involved with Cortes, I'd have dragged him behind the car for a couple of hundred yards, then I'd have gagged him and tied him in a dumpster and let the rats eat his ass."

"Don't even joke about things like that," Coop said.

"I'm not joking," Tip said. "That son of a bitch is wearing a badge."

Coop looked over at me. "Connie, I expected more out of you. Keep a rein on this man or you'll find yourself in as much trouble as him." She sat and put her glasses on. "Now one of you better fill me in on what's going on with your case."

"Lipscomb and Davids were definitely murders," Tip said. "And we've connected them to a couple of bodies in Victoria that were set up to look like a murder/suicide."

"Victoria?"

I leaned forward and said, "It all looks drug related, Captain. And we think it ties into Delgado's case, too."

"The guy at the hospital? When was I going to hear about that?"

"We didn't tell you because we're not sure yet, but we're getting with Delgado as soon as we leave."

"All right, damn it. Keep me posted."

As we walked out the door, Coop yelled, "And stay away from Stenson. That's an order."

I was almost out the door when Coop called me back. "Gianelli, I need to see you."

I shot Tip a what-the-hell-is-this-about look. He shrugged, and said, "I'll get Herb and Charlie. We'll be at Julie's desk."

"Shut the door," Coop said.

She waited for me to sit, and then said, "I spoke to Lieutenant Morreau."

I didn't like hearing that, but I wouldn't have thought Morreau would do me wrong. "Yeah?"

"He backed up what you told me, and he said you could be trusted."

Some of the lump that had been building in my throat disappeared. "I like to think so, Captain."

"The trusted part was the most important thing for me to hear."

I leaned forward. "Go on."

"You need to keep Denton away from Bobby Stenson. That's all I can tell you, so don't ask questions."

I didn't know what the hell was going on, but the message was clear. "Will do, Captain. You can count on it."

She stood and let the tiniest crack of a smile show. "I *am* counting on it."

I took note of the tone in her voice. This was a warning. "Yes, sir," I said, and headed out the door.

Captain Cooper waited a moment before picking up the phone and dialing.

"Is that you, Cap?"

"You know who it is. And you won't have any more trouble."

"How's that? Denton doesn't get off a scent, and sure as hell he thinks he's got one."

"I know all about Tip Denton, but he's got a new partner who's almost as tough as him, and she and I have an agreement. She'll keep him in line."

"I'm trusting you on this."

"Hang up, Stenson. You've wasted enough of my time already."

I called Delgado on the way to the coffee room. "I'm on my way. Anybody need anything."

"Just you," Ribs said.

By the time I reached Julie's desk she had a video loaded on the screen.

"We're assuming for right now that Carlos Cortes is behind everything," Tip said, "which means that whoever killed our stiffs might have done Martin. And we're pretty sure a woman is involved. She might not have done the killing, but she planned it or put it into action."

"Do you know what she looks like?" Ribs asked.

"This is who we're looking for," Tip said, and gave everyone a copy of the sketch we had drawn of the mystery woman. "If you see anything else suspicious let us know, but focus on this face. We think she might be the killer."

"We're going to be seeing tapes from the hospital," Ribs said. "Cruz and I went through them earlier but we were focused on the killer being male. Let's focus on the killer being female, specifically the one in that sketch."

"What do the cameras cover?" I asked.

"Unfortunately all we have are the entrances," Cruz said, and moved closer to the screen. "The first one you'll see is the side entrance. It's used primarily by hospital employees."

Julie had the video paused.

"What time is this?" Tip asked.

"I've got it set to an hour before the first shift in the morning," Julie said. "And it runs up to approximate TOD."

"Suppose she came in earlier?" I said.

"Then we've got more tape to look at," Ribs said. "But Cruz and I checked the night before. There wasn't much activity until early morning."

Julie hit *play* and the video started.

"We watched as dozens of employees came through the doors—guards, techs, orderlies, cafeteria workers, nurses, even a few doctors—but none that looked remotely like our suspect. When we got to the end of the tape, Julie popped in another one.

"This is the front entrance," she said. "It's the busiest one."

We watched for almost an hour and we must have slowed or paused the video ten times, but we got nothing. After that we looked at the video for the back entrance, and then we ran through all three of them again. Everyone was tired and more than a little frustrated.

"What the hell are we missing?" Tip said. "I know the son of a bitch did it."

"It might not be her," Cruz said. "Or, she could be smarter than us."

I reminded Tip that she seemed to be adept at disguising herself, affecting limps, using different color hair, and even changing her eye color with contacts. "If she tossed on a blonde wig, put glasses on, and dressed conservatively, we'd never recognize her."

Tip's face lit up. "What about red hair, a frumpy hat, and dirty clothes?"

"What?"

"Julie, go back to the front entrance video about halfway through."

As Julie advanced the video, Tip said, "We're looking for a woman with red hair, wearing a weird hat and clothes you'd see on a homeless person."

A few seconds later, I spotted her. "That's her. Pause it, Jules."

Julie stopped the video and focused in on the redhead. She looked as Tip described her, red hair, definitely a frumpy hat, dirty clothes, and she also wore big, thick-rimmed glasses. Delgado stared at the video then at the sketch.

"It's her," he said. Everyone agreed.

If I'd had any doubts about the mystery woman being the person who killed Lipscomb and Davids, those doubts were gone. I also pegged her for pulling the trigger on Tiffany and Joel Ford. "We've got us a damn female hit man," I said.

Tip nodded. "Damned if we don't."

Ribs looked at Tip and then me. "Our vic, Martin, was terrified of *El Terrible.* I figured him for a man this whole time, but suppose *El Terrible* is a woman."

Julie moved to another computer and pulled up a file. "The reports we have on him—or in this case, possibly her—never mention gender. In fact, the report says no one has ever seen *El Terrible.*"

"I think we're looking at her," Tip said.

"That means we need to be *real* careful," Ribs said. "I saw what she did to Martin."

Chapter 37

LOOKING FOR A KILLER

Ribs paced the room. "If we look at it from the angle of drug distribution, it all fits. Everything that's happened is connected with a drug operation, and that means Carlos Cortes."

Cruz took a big sip from a bottle of water. "Carlos lost control to the Dominicans and rogue bands of Mexicans. He had to get it back or risk losing the city."

Delgado nodded. "So he built a network of distributors using the counterfeit stickers, and then he converted them to pushing meth. And he's selling the meth so cheap he'll control the market in no time."

"It makes sense," I said. "And once he has the distribution locked up, the rest of the drug market falls in line."

"More than makes sense," Tip said. "I don't know why we didn't see it before. Carlos needs the lawyer for representing his people who get in trouble. Griffin's a big-name, high-priced lawyer which makes Carlos' people feel safe. He's got the trucker to move his goods, and we know Joel Ford's brother has been making runs to Monterrey for a long time. Ford's wife told us. We'll assume he's been smuggling drugs for a good part of that time."

"Why kill his brother?" Cruz asked. "And if he's been doing it for long, how is it he hasn't been caught at the border?"

I shook my head. "Maybe he wanted out. Maybe the pressure was getting to him. I don't know what prompted him, but something did, and Carlos killed his brother to send a message."

Charlie had been taking notes the whole time. "As far as the border goes, and not getting caught, I'd bet a box of popcorn that Carlos bribes half the border patrol in Laredo. With all the money he has, it wouldn't take much to buy safe passage."

"A box of popcorn?" I said.

"I was just thinking about popcorn and that saying kind of jumped out of my mouth."

"I liked you better when you were fat," Tip said.

I looked at what Charlie had written down. "Okay, we've got Ford's brother, and probably others, moving the goods into Texas. We've got an army of distributors on the streets. And we've got Griffin and his law firm for legal protection. What's that leave us?"

"Laundering," Delgado said. "Which I'm sure is where your banker comes in."

"And storage," Tip said. "He's not bringing an 18-wheeler into town and unloading it on Westheimer."

Ribs slapped the back of Cruz's head. "The Second Ward," he said. "We know Carlos has been buying property down there."

"Navigation Boulevard would work," Tip said. "All he'd have to do is buy a warehouse or old business and he'd have a front for drugs. And from what we've heard, he's bought plenty."

Cruz got up for coffee. "And let's not forget protection. We've had two snitches tell us Carlos is protected by men in blue. Ribs and I figure that has to be Stenson, especially after hearing what Tip said about Bobby not knowing about the meth."

"We need to put that to rest," Tip said. "I'll be goddamned if I'm gonna have that fucker out there ruining our reputation."

"Coop will bury your ass if you try," I said. "I wouldn't ordinarily mind that, but my ass is tied to yours, so don't try it."

"Speaking of your ass…"

I shot him a look, Cruz and Herb laughed, and Ribs said, "Don't worry, Connie. He talks about my ass, too."

"You men are disgusting," Julie said, and I high-fived her.

"I'm serious," Tip said. "You didn't let me finish."

"Go on," I said.

"When we were at Snider's house, if you'd have seen the way he looked at your ass when you went to the kitchen. He almost broke his neck turning to stare."

"What's that got to do with anything?" Ribs said.

"It wasn't a normal, 'look at that ass' type of stare. This was a look that a guy who runs around gives."

I looked at Tip and said, "What difference does it make if Snider runs around?"

"If there's another woman, maybe she knows something. Guys like Snider tell things to the women they run around with."

"I hate to admit it, but Tip's right." I turned to Julie. "We need everything we can get on the Sniders: financials, phone logs, arrest records, IRS troubles, bank audits. And while we're checking on Snider, let's look at unusual purchases, hotel charges, anything that might point to a woman on the side." I turned to Charlie. "That means look real close at the phone logs, and see if he has a private cell phone that his wife might not know about."

"What do we know about the Sniders now?" Ribs asked.

"They're hiding something," I said.

Tip nodded. "He was definitely holding back, but he was good at it. The wife looked ready to crack."

"She's ready," I said. "I'm going back tomorrow, but I'm waiting until after her husband leaves for work." I looked at Julie. "Do you think you can have any of this ready for me tomorrow?"

"What time?"

"As early as you can. I plan on being at Snider's house as soon as he leaves for work."

"I'll get it for you tonight," Julie said.

"Let's not forget about finding that woman," Cruz said. "Remember? The one who is killing everyone?"

Tip stood. "Charlie, you and Herb are good with computers. I want ya'll to help Julie. Go through that video and get the best picture we have of the mystery woman. Run it through the FBI's face recognition database and see if we get any hits. Send it to Harris County and the Constable's office. If we're lucky somebody will recognize her."

"How about Narcotics?" Herb asked.

"No, keep them out of it," Tip said.

"Why's that? They might—"

Tip glared at him. "I said 'no.'"

"What about the news?" I said. "We could splatter her image and that sketch on the news."

Tip looked at Ribs and Cruz, then back to me. "What's everyone think?"

"By now she's got to know we're onto her," I said. "I don't see the harm in running pics. You never know, somebody might actually call in a lead."

"Go for it," Ribs said, and Cruz agreed.

"I'll call Roberts," Tip said.

Herb stood and stretched. "Charlie, it looks like it's going to be a long night. I'm catching a smoke. You comin'?"

"Right behind you," Charlie said, and followed him out.

"I'd love to be able to subpoena the books to Snider's bank," I said. "And we need to find out if there's anything we can do with Griffin."

"You can't go poking around a lawyer's files," Ribs said.

"I'd like to put Griffin where a few big rednecks can poke his ass," Tip said.

"There he goes again," Ribs said. "Talkin' about asses."

I stood. "That's my cue. I'm heading out."

"Not without me," Tip said. "I drove."

"I'll cover this," Ribs said. "See you tomorrow."

As Tip drove, I thought about what I'd say to Mrs. Snider. It was critical to get her cooperation. She was the key to this case, but she wasn't just going to open up for nothing. I had to find a way to make her.

Chapter 38

WOMAN TO WOMAN

I got up early, made coffee, and checked email. I had no message from Julie, which was unlike her. I checked voice mail—nothing. It was only 6:00 AM, so I didn't call. I figured I'd wait at least half an hour. Coffee was brewing when the phone rang. Caller ID showed it was Julie.

"Hey, Jules. How's it going?"

"Sorry about last night. Zach had a school play and I promised I'd be there. And when we got home I found out both kids had homework."

"I wouldn't have wanted you to miss that for the world," I said. Memories of Uncle Dominic and Zeppe flooded my mind. They came to every event I ever had at school, as if I was an up-and-coming star.

"What did you find for me?"

"I'm not finished," she said, "but from what I found so far, he's clean. His financials are good. No arrests. Very little debt, with great credit. Nothing jumps out as suspicious."

"I hate to hear that," I said. "It doesn't give me much to go on."

"I'm not through," Julie said, "but don't get your hopes up."

"Thanks, Jules. I really appreciate it. Tell Tip I'll call him after I leave Snider's house."

I got to Snider's house a little before 7:30, but I passed it by when I saw his car was still there. I circled the neighborhood and parked half a block away behind a large SUV. The position left me a clear view of their house, but it would have been difficult for them to see me. Mr. Snider exited the house at 7:45. I waited a couple of minutes and then called her home phone.

"Hello?"

"Mrs. Snider, this is Detective Gianelli. We met yesterday."

"Oh yes, Detective. What can I do for you?" Her voice was more relaxed

"I wondered if I could come by and chat for a few minutes?"

"About what?"

"I had a few follow-up questions. Nothing important," I said.

For a few seconds she said nothing, and then, "I have to drive the children to school. Perhaps when Patrick gets home."

"I can stop by after you drop the kids off. This won't take long."

More silence followed before she said, "All right. I guess that would work. I'll be home in about forty-five minutes."

"Great. I'll see you then."

I watched as she escorted the kids to her car, buckled in the younger one, and then drove off. I leaned back in the seat and closed my eyes. Something was bothering this woman and I intended to find out what. If her husband was involved in money laundering—and she knew about it—that might explain things, but that explanation didn't seem to fit. The way she acted was different, and yet it seemed familiar.

Fear was a strange beast and it came in different forms. I'd been in a car accident, I'd been beaten up by criminals, I'd even been shot in a drug bust. But none of those affected me the way the *incident* had. When that lunatic raped me it took everything away from me. All of my pride, all of my confidence. I felt as if I had no control. Felt *helpless*.

I had long ago healed physically, but I was far from healed mentally. During the first six months I don't think I had five nights of *honest* sleep. Honest, as in, sleeping without telling myself I would be okay. That, soon it would be in the past.

I'd been scared for so long that it hurt. And I didn't know if it would ever get better. I think that's what bothered me the most, the not knowing. It wasn't until I talked to Uncle Dominic about it that anything changed. I asked him how he dealt with fear.

He looked at me and said, "I don't let it win."

"What the hell is that supposed to mean?"

He said, "Every day I go out that door knowing someone might shoot me. I accept that. I could hire an army of bodyguards. I could wear a Kevlar vest. I could put bulletproof glass in my car. But I don't. If someone wants to shoot me, they will. Even the president can't be protected. So instead of worrying about being shot, I go about my business. I refuse to allow my enemies to win with fear."

I made headway after my talk with him. I practiced on the shooting range. I trained harder physically. I kept alert. But I also told myself I was vulnerable. That at any moment I might be beaten, or killed—or raped. I was surprised to learn that Uncle Dominic was right. After I admitted my vulnerabilities, I started healing. I started feeling *free* again. I wasn't *fixed* yet, but things were improving.

A car passed by, bringing me out of my ruminations. It was Mrs. Snider.

I waited for her to enter the house, and then pulled my car into her driveway and got out. She answered right away.

"Good morning, Detective. This was good timing, or were you waiting?"

"I arrived early and parked up the street," I said.

"You mentioned you had a few questions," Mrs. Snider said. "And please, have a seat."

She led me to the same room as yesterday, the small sitting room off the foyer, and she did her best to avoid looking at me. "Would you care for tea or coffee?"

Her eyes were red, like she'd been crying, and she looked as if she hadn't slept. "I'd love coffee if it's not too much trouble."

I followed her into the kitchen. Dishes were stacked on the counter by the sink and two half-eaten bowls of cereal sat on the table. She fumbled with the coffee pot, and almost dropped it. "Mrs. Snider, are you okay?"

"I'm fine," she said.

"You don't seem fine."

She was facing away from me, filling the pot with water. She rested her palms on the counter and lowered her head. "I'm tired, that's all."

"I don't think so, Mrs. Snider. I've seen that look before."

"What do you mean by that?"

"I mean you're afraid of something. If you and your husband are in some kind of trouble, we can help. We can—"

"You can't do *anything*." She screamed when she said it, as if frustration had reached deep inside her and yanked that scream out.

She put the coffee on and turned to me. "I'm sorry."

I cleaned the table and set the dishes on the counter. "Why don't you tell me what the trouble is," I said. "It can't be that bad."

She gave a small, sarcastic chuckle. "Trust me, Detective. It's worse."

I knew I had to push her if I was going to get any information. I waited until she poured the coffee and sat. "Mrs. Snider, I saw the way you reacted when we mentioned Carlos Cortes yesterday."

She tensed. "I don't recall."

"If your husband is involved with Cortes…if he's laundering money for him, we can help."

She put her cup down and stared. "Detective, my husband would *never* be involved with a man like that. Patrick is an honest man. He doesn't deal in drugs."

"What kind of man is that, Mrs. Snider? I never said what Carlos did."

She got flustered. "I believe you did yesterday. I remember."

I waited until she looked at me again. "Mrs. Snider, they'll never stop. They'll use your husband until he's caught, and then they'll kill him. Or, they'll kill you and the kids."

She had picked up her coffee cup, but her hand shook so badly some of it spilled. "That's nonsense," she said. "If this is what you came to ask me, I think we're done."

It was now or never for me. I lowered my voice and leaned toward her. "Mrs. Snider, they will *never* let him go. That's how they work. More than 70,000 people have been killed since this drug war started in Mexico. And it's not going to stop. It certainly won't stop by helping them get their money."

When she didn't answer, I stood. "If this is what you want. If you want your husband in prison, or dead. And your kids without a father—or dead—then keep doing what you are. If not, I'm your last chance to set it straight."

She sat at the table, shaking. And crying. I recognized something in her face. I leaned down and rested my hand on her shoulder. "Mrs. Snider, what's wrong? What happened?"

She grabbed a Kleenex and wiped her eyes, and her nose. And she kept shaking her head, as if in denial.

"Why don't you tell me," I said.

"There's nothing to tell," she managed to get out.

"That look on your face says differently. You can't lie to me because I've seen that look before."

"What *look* are you talking about?" She was taking an aggressive, defiant stance now.

I opted to take a chance. "The look that tells me someone did something to you. The look that comes from inside of you. From your soul."

She looked at me, but said nothing. I took hold of her hands and looked into her eyes. "I *know*, Mrs. Snider. I see it *every single day* when I look in the mirror." It was difficult for me to say that, and I had to fight to keep from shedding tears, but it felt good to get it out.

She sat straighter in the chair, and she squeezed my hands. "You know?"

I hesitated before saying anything. I almost didn't, but I figured this might be the only way to get through to her. "I was raped six months ago. I was almost killed."

"Oh my God! What happened?"

"It happened on the job. A serial killer—"

She gasped. "The one here in Houston? The one with the lips?"

I nodded. "If it wasn't for my partner, I'd be dead." A few tears escaped and for the millionth time I silently thanked Tip. "The truth is, Mrs. Snider, there have been *so many* days since then that I wished I were dead. Every morning for months I looked in the mirror and said, 'Why me, God? Why did this happen to me?'"

"Does it get better?" she asked.

"With help, it does. With the right kind of help."

We talked for hours after that, and she told me what happened at the warehouse, and what Carlos said about their daughters. It was all I could do to keep from rushing out and shooting Carlos, but I was determined to do this the right way. I would never resort to doing things like Uncle Dominic.

"Patrick and I have fought about this," she said. "He's convinced we have to do what that man said."

I took hold of her hand and squeezed. "Listen closely. I'm not going to tell you this is easy. I'm not going to tell you we can protect you and everything will be fine. It won't be. The truth is something shitty happened to you, like catching cancer or having a car accident. It's not nice. It's not fair. But that's the way it is. And there's only one way out of this."

She seemed to be listening, so I continued. "We can get you protection, but it's not fun. It sucks. They'll make it seem good for a while, but you have to make a new life and you can't do the same things you used to do. Your names will change, even your first names. And your husband can't be a banker, so he has to learn new skills. And you won't be making nearly as much money."

"Oh God. Why did this happen to us?"

"That's what I'm trying to tell you. You can't ask that question because there is no answer. It's no different than saying 'Why did God give me cancer?'"

She broke into tears again. "I'm scared," she said. "Scared for my girls."

I ached for this woman. She had been through so much, and now I saw it was nothing compared to the primal fear for her daughters. I didn't have kids. I couldn't *know* that feeling but I understood it on a different level.

I hugged her, and then I said, "I'm going to help you get through this. You'll be all right."

She gave me a squeeze, and then stood tall. "What do we have to do?"

"You have to press charges against Carlos Cortes. We can't arrest him unless you do that."

She remained silent for a moment, but then she nodded. "I'll do it."

When I looked into her eyes, I saw determination. This was a strong woman, and she was ready to fight.

Chapter 39

A SAFE HOUSE

I stood in the foyer reminding Cathy Snider of what she *had to* do, and what she *absolutely couldn't do*. On the *had to* side, was pack clothes and necessities for her and the kids. I told her to plan on a minimum of 3-4 nights. *Necessities* meant things like toothbrushes and prescription medications. It didn't mean video games or a coffee maker. She also had the onerous task of instructing her husband to do the same—*after* she explained to him what was going on. Cathy said he'd fight the decision tooth and nail, but she had made up her mind, and she promised me they'd go through with it. I believed her.

On the *absolutely couldn't do* side, were the taboo items of all witness protection work, even the very early stages. Once the process started she couldn't call *anyone*. Not her mother, or sisters, or best friends. And she couldn't tell the neighbors she'd be gone, let alone where she was going. The same rules applied to the kids. No friends were to know. No cell phones allowed. No computers to check email or surf the internet. When the time came we'd get them disposable phones to make a few calls. And when that time came, the FBI would take over and slap a whole new set of rules on the them.

I didn't like thinking of what they'd go through in the witness protection program, but I felt good that I'd done my best to explain it to her. I certainly didn't paint a rosy picture.

"What's the procedure?" she asked.

"Like I said, we'll get the forms for you to press charges. We'll put you and Mr. Snider and the kids in a safe house, and then we'll arrest him."

"You'll arrest all of them?"

"We can certainly get Carlos and Roberto. We might need a lineup though."

"It doesn't matter," Cathy said. "I'll recognize them. There's no way I'd forget."

I knew exactly what she meant. I still had the image of that maniac who attacked me burned into my memory. His face, his smile, and especially his eyes.

"It will take us a day or so to get the safe house approved and set up. In the meantime you can prepare. Do everything I told you. Think positive. And call me if you need to. Any time of the day or night. I sleep with that damn phone on my nightstand."

She laughed and gave me a hug. "I think I've got it, Connie. Everything as normal until we hear from you."

"That's right," I said. "Send the kids to school. Make sure Patrick goes to work as usual and does nothing differently. Do whatever you normally do. I'll get the house set up, and, once you're safe, we'll arrest that son of a bitch."

"I hope so," she said.

We covered everything one more time, and then I said goodbye. "Are you sure you're okay?" I asked.

"As good as can be expected," she said. "All except for the girls. I'm so worried about them."

I gave her a hug, and said, "They'll be okay. I promise."

She smiled, and then I walked to my car.

It had been a good visit, a productive one. Not only did I convince Snider to cooperate, I think I helped her get on the road to recovering from her own *incident*. On top of it all, I felt as if I helped myself. It was the first time I'd opened up to a stranger about what happened, and it had the surprising benefit of making me feel better. The only thing that still worried me was the same thing that worried Cathy Snider—her girls. If something happened to them, I'd die.

I started the car and drove off, waving bye as I pulled onto the street. I thought about Uncle Dominic and how he must have been scared for me *so* many times. When he was arrested, and he worried over what would happen to me if he went to prison. Or when he was shot during the war with the other families, and he worried about leaving me alone in the world. I never thought about life from his end, only that he was a disgrace, a mobster, a killer. I never thought about him being a loving uncle or someone who cared for me, and loved me.

If I was certain of anything in life it was that. For all of his faults, Dominic Mangini surely loved me more than anything in the world. I could feel it when he kissed my cheek. Hear it in his words, and the way his voice changed when he said *ti voglio bene*. And most of all, I could see it in his eyes, the way they sparkled when he looked at me. He had always been so proud of everything I did.

I shook my head to clear the thoughts. If I didn't watch out, I'd be an emotional mess, and I couldn't afford a chink in my Brooklyn armor.

I got back to thinking about Cathy Snider. I empathized with her on several fronts, and that empathy put a fire in my soul. I made a vow to uphold the law when I took the oath and got this badge, despite that, I wanted nothing more than to kill Carlos Cortes. To walk right up to him, stick my gun in his face, and pull the trigger. Some people didn't deserve to live. Uncle Dominic taught me that years ago. I never believed him until today. *"People don't have a* right *to live,"* he said. *"They have to* earn *that* right.*"

Uncle Dominic and the Constitution didn't see eye to eye on that issue. In the past, I sided with the Founding Fathers but now I wasn't sure. I felt I could justify making an exception in Carlos' case. *No way he has a right to live.*

As I waited at the traffic signal a few blocks from the Sniders' house, I happened to glance to the side. A man driving a blue Hyundai Sonata sped off through the parking lot. I shook my head to clear it. The driver looked like Fabrizio.

Mother of God! What the hell is wrong with me?

It wasn't bad enough I dreamt about him, now I was seeing him during the day. *I need to find a lover.*

It was a 20 minute drive back to the station, and by the time I was halfway there I convinced myself a dozen times that the guy in the Sonata couldn't have been Fabrizio. But I dreamt it *was* him a couple of dozen more. Either way, I now knew that somewhere in Texas there was a drop-dead gorgeous man-tiger who was probably prowling the streets after dark looking for me. And Bon Jovi was likely with him. Fortunately, the phone rang and brought me to my senses.

"What's up, Tip?"

"Did you do any good?"

"I hope so. I convinced Mrs. Snider to press charges. Whether that's good or not remains to be seen," I said, and then I filled him in on what happened to her at Carlos' warehouse.

"That motherfucker," Tip said. He didn't often say the "f" word in front of me, but when he got pissed he did. And when someone hurt a woman, child, or animal, Tip got *really* pissed.

"I feel the same way, Tip."

"Are you on your way in?" he asked.

"Yeah, I should be there in ten minutes."

"I'll see you when you get here, and we'll figure out what to do."

I arrived a few minutes late. Tip was waiting with coffee. I could have kissed him—if he wasn't Tip.

"Let's see Coop," he said. "She'll have to approve everything, and we're probably going to need help from the FBI with witness protection."

"I agree. If anybody needs witness protection it's the Sniders. Even after Carlos is in prison, I don't think they'll be safe."

We got in to see Coop right away. I filled her in on what happened this morning with Mrs. Snider, and Tip reminded her that we still had suspicions of a leak somewhere, but we didn't know where.

"What kind of *leak*?" she asked.

"We've had too many instances of this mystery woman, who we now believe to be *El Terrible,* being one step ahead of us. And we know that Carlos has a lot of connections." Tip paused before adding, "And you know about Stenson."

Coop's glare focused on Tip. "As far as the department is concerned, we know *nothing* about Stenson."

I thought I better interrupt before Tip pissed her off. "Captain, we're concerned about Carlos. He's got powerful connections and unlimited money. We'd like to get the Sniders into a safe house as soon as possible, and then execute an arrest warrant for Cortes and the other men at the warehouse."

"Where are you thinking of putting them?" Coop asked.

"None of the new sites," Tip said. "Do we still have some old houses that we haven't used in a while?"

Coop leaned back in her chair and unwrapped a mint to chew on. "I'm not sure. I can't think of any, but there must be some." She leaned forward and hit the intercom.

"Yes, Captain."

"See if Delgado's in the house. Tell him I want him here now."

"What's Delgado got to do with it?" I asked.

"He's been here longer than any of us," Coop said. "If anybody knows the old safe houses, it'll be him."

For a few minutes we discussed the FBI and what their role would be in this. Coop wanted to keep it to a minimum, but once you called for federal help you usually had to take the baggage that came with it.

Ribs walked in a few minutes later. "You wanted me, Coop?"

"Have a seat," Coop said. "We were discussing Tip and Connie's case with the Sniders. They need a safe house and we're reluctant to use any of the well-known ones."

It didn't take Ribs long to come up with a solution. "I know the perfect spot," he said. "Remember that place we used in Jersey Village?"

Tip sat up straight. "Yeah. The one by Jones Road. I'd forgotten about that."

Delgado snapped his fingers. "That's the one."

Tip hit the desk. "It's perfect, Coop. We haven't used it in years. And it's a decent house with good access to major roads."

"Let's wrap it up," Coop said. "I'll get approval from the Chief. Have Julie dig out the paperwork. It will need to be cleaned and prepared, and we need it done fast. I want them in by tomorrow night."

"Shouldn't be a problem," Tip said. "If we're lucky."

I left Coop's office in a good frame of mind. Things were moving and I felt we were getting closer to putting that prick Carlos behind bars. We filled Julie in on what needed to be done. She asked Herb to set up a cleaning operation; Charlie was responsible for the keys; Julie would handle the mounds of paperwork and make sure it never entered the system—a near-impossible task.

I didn't get home until almost 11:00, which left me enough time to take a hot bath, eat a frozen pizza, and say a prayer before I crawled into bed. I seldom prayed, but I found that since my *incident* I had taken to it more. This time it wasn't for me, though; it was for the Sniders. I hated what I was doing to them, but I knew it was the right thing.

I hope.

Chapter 40

ALLIGATOR

The alarm went off at 7:00. I wasn't ready for it, but I hopped out of bed and into the kitchen, eager for morning coffee but anxious about what lay ahead. While waiting for the water to boil, I emptied the dishwasher and checked off my to-do list on a mental calendar.

We needed a warrant, but Coop was taking care of that. Julie and her crew were handling the safe house, and the Chief and Coop were going to contact the FBI. As I sipped life's liquid, also known as espresso, I realized I had nothing to do myself. That revelation made my day brighter, so I decided to call Cathy Snider.

"Hello?" Her voice sounded tense.

"Cathy, it's Connie Gianelli. Everything okay?"

She sighed. "As good as it can be. The girls are getting ready for school and Patrick already left for work."

"You're not driving them?"

"Not today," she said.

"How are you holding up?"

"I'm better. Patrick and I talked last night. He didn't want to go through with this, but after I told him all the things you said, he agreed we had to."

"You're doing the right thing," I said.

"I hope so," she said. "Patrick is sacrificing a lot. We're *all* sacrificing a lot. I can't imagine what the girls will do when they find out. Especially Trish."

"It's always tougher on the older ones," I said. "The funny thing is I don't know if it ever gets easier. When I moved here from Brooklyn…well, let's say I almost didn't move here."

"The Lord will provide," she said, as if in prayer, and then, "Detective, I need to help the girls get ready. I'm sure we'll talk later."

"You bet we will. We should have things ready today. After your husband gets off work, we'll eat a nice dinner somewhere and get you settled into the new place."

"Is it nice?" Cathy asked. "The place we'll be staying, I mean."

I wanted to tell her yes, even though I hadn't seen it. Instead, I told her the truth. "I doubt it's anything like you're accustomed to. But it's only temporary."

"All right, Detective. I'll see you tonight."

"I'll call when we're ready," I said, and hung up the phone. For a minute I sat and did nothing. I felt sorry for her, not only for what Carlos did to her, but for what I was about to do to her and her family. Their lives would never be the same.

El Terrible was up before dawn. She put on her jogging suit, and then headed out for a 2k run. The house she used was in the type of neighborhood where men left for work dressed in suits and carried their laptops or tablets in a leather briefcase. The type of neighborhood where the men leered at her, and would do unspeakable things to her—if they thought they could get away with it. If there was one thing *El Terrible* was certain of, it was that none of these men could get away with it.

It didn't take her long to crank out the 2k, and afterward she returned to the house, showered, opted for orange juice instead of coffee, and then made a hearty breakfast—eggs with peppers and onions, and bacon with toast. *El Terrible* was never one to shy away from good food. When she ate well she had to work harder to maintain her figure, and that meant she stayed in better shape. At least on the outside. What it was doing to her insides she didn't know. But she didn't worry about her insides; she never figured she'd live long enough for that to matter.

She set the dishes on the counter, made tea for herself, and opened her laptop. She checked the map for the third time, confirmed the other vehicle was ready, and then kicked her bare feet up on the seat of the chair next to her. The money she would make today was more than Patrick Snider earned in a year, but money was not a consideration for Señor Cortes. She could have charged him twice as much, even three times as much. But if she had done that, she would have to watch her back.

The tea relaxed Sahrina, calmed her and kept her focused. When she finished, she set the cup next to the other dishes and went to the bedroom. She pulled on a pair of dark blue jogging pants and a loose-fitting top that matched. Then she slipped her feet into a pair of size 6 running shoes purchased at Walmart. With her hair tied in a ponytail, a pair of dark green shades covering her eyes, and a bandana wrapped around her forehead, no one was going to pick her out of a lineup—if it came to that. It would only come to that if she made a mistake, and *El Terrible* didn't make mistakes.

She drove to Hermann Memorial Hospital, in Memorial City, and parked near the back of the lot. Less than a hundred yards away, a Honda minivan waited for her, the keys in a magnetic holder under the rear bumper. She climbed into the van, started the engine, and drove to where she would meet Marissa's bus. She turned onto Gessner Road, headed south, and then turned right onto Memorial Drive. The original plan had been to nab the young girl from the day-care center, but after close surveillance Sahrina determined it might be easier to kill the president than to snatch a kid from day care. Hijacking a bus, however, was another story.

A few miles later she caught up with the bus. It was a mini-bus, not much more than an oversized van. She turned her blinker signal on and moved into the left lane. A car in the right lane moved ahead and in front of the bus. The passenger signaled Sahrina as they passed. After a few stops to pick up kids, the bus turned left onto Dairy Ashford. Sahrina followed it for half a mile and waited for it to come to a halt at a four-way stop sign on a street with little traffic. The man in the other car pulled into the intersection, blocking it. She got out of the car, stepped quickly to the left side of the bus and shoved a gun against the window, by the driver's head.

"Don't move. Open the door."

The driver looked at her, eyes wide, brow furrowed. "What do you want?"

"No one will get hurt if you follow instructions. If you don't, I start killing kids. Understand?"

"Yes."

"Good, now open the door and let the man in."

The driver looked to the side, where Sahrina's partner stood. She opened the bus door and let him in. He held a gun pointed at the driver.

"Marissa Snider," he said. "Bring her up here."

The driver was a large woman, and past the age of motherhood, but all women seem to have nurturing in them, no matter the age. "What do you want her for?"

"Get her up here, or a bullet goes into the kid closest to me." He put the gun into his left pocket, but the barrel pressing against the fabric was visible. "And give me your phone."

The driver eyed him, but she gave him the phone, and then turned toward the back of the bus. "Marissa, come here, darlin'. This man would like to speak with you."

A small, thin child with curly brown hair stood and walked to the front of the bus. She stared at the man. "Who are you?"

"I'm here to take you to see your father," he said. "He's been hurt."

"Daddy? What happened?"

"He'll be all right, but he wants to see you."

"Why didn't Mommy come?" she asked.

"Your mother went to pick up Trish," the man said. "She's going to meet us."

Marissa reached out and took hold of his hand. "Let's hurry. I don't want anything happening to Daddy."

He took her off the bus, handed her over to Sahrina, and signaled to the other man in the car, who then drove off. The man got back on the bus and instructed the driver where to go. Twenty minutes later the bus pulled into a hospital parking lot and came to a stop near the back, under a string of old oak trees.

The driver turned toward the man with the gun. "What do we do now?"

"Wait for instructions," he said. "In a few hours I'll let you leave. No one will be hurt."

***

Sahrina put Marissa in the back seat, buckled her in, and drove back to Memorial City, where her other car was parked. She switched cars, and drove to her house.

"Where are we going?" Marissa asked. "I thought we were going to see Daddy."

"You'll be able to see Daddy soon."

"I'm scared. What if something happens to him?"

"Don't worry, dear. As long as your daddy does what we say, everything will be fine."

Chapter 41

ANOTHER DAY AT SCHOOL

I drove into the station feeling upbeat. Tip planned on stopping by the safe house in Jersey Village on his way in, partly to get a feel for the neighborhood but also to map out the route we'd take when we transported the Sniders. I dialed Julie's number.

"I hope you're having a great day, Connie."

Julie was always in a good mood. I wondered how she did it, especially with two kids and no husband. "I'm having a fantastic day. What's up?"

"Everything's a go for the house. We've got two officers reporting for duty this afternoon. They'll stay until relief arrives."

"Where did we get the uniforms?"

"Captain Cooper assigned them from another division."

"Good. I don't want anybody knowing about this."

"You might want to call the captain," Julie said. "I heard she's having a tough time with the FBI."

"Shit! Okay, thanks, Jules. I'll give her a shout."

I decided to wait and see Coop in person since I only had about five miles to go, and besides that, a Bruno Mars song that I loved was playing on the radio.

In less than ten minutes I was walking in to see the captain. She was planted behind her desk, wearing a scowl.

"I hope you're better than me this morning," Coop said.

"Julie said the Feds were giving you trouble."

"Sons of bitches. It's all politics with them."

"What's the problem?"

"They won't approve *anything* until they talk to Snider, and I don't mean *Mrs.* Snider."

I shook my head. "I assume you told them what Carlos and his men did to her."

"They don't care one bit about that. All they want is to nail Cortes on money laundering. If Patrick Snider can't hand them Cortes wrapped up pretty for that, it's a no go."

I plopped down in the chair across from her desk. "If that's the way it's going down, we need to tell the Sniders. Unless we can assure them they'll get in Witness Protection, there's no way I'm letting her press charges. Carlos will kill them."

"I doubt she'd even consider pressing charges if we can't protect them," Coop said. "And I can't say I'd blame her. But don't give up yet. Renkin is putting pressure on the Feds. He's even got the mayor helping."

Coop's phone rang. She punched the button and put it on speaker. "Chief, we were just talking about you. I've got Detective Gianelli in my office. Did you hear anything?"

"Is anyone else is with you?"

Coop's eyebrows raised. "No, just the two of us."

"We've got a problem, Captain. A school bus is missing out on the west side."

When I heard *west side*, I tensed. "Where?" I asked. "Where on the west side?"

"It's a day care off Memorial," he said. "By Dairy Ashford."

Dairy Ashford? My body shook and my heart felt as if it would stop. I'm sure there are a lot of day cares in that area…*but what are the chances a bus from one goes missing today?*

"What school?" Coop asked.

"Oakwood," the chief said.

"I'm going to check on the Sniders," I said. "It might be her kid."

Coop slammed her hand on the desk. "Damn! I didn't think of that. Hold on a minute, Chief." Coop looked up at me. "See what you can find out and get back to me."

I rushed out while she was still talking to Renkin.

Herb was staring at a spreadsheet when I rounded the corner. "Herb, find out what school the young Snider girl attends."

"What?"

"Never mind, goddamnit." My voice packed more impatience than I wanted it to, but right now I didn't care.

"What's the matter?" Julie asked.

"I'm not sure yet, Jules. Maybe everything." I thought it through and knew I couldn't call Cathy Snider without answers. "Julie, get the number for Oakwood pre-school and day care on Dairy Ashford. See if Marissa Snider was on that missing bus."

"A bus is missing?"

I nodded. "I'm afraid it's her," I said, but the voice in my head said, *I know it is.*

I was on the phone with Tip when Julie got back to me, confirming my worst fears. "Goddamnit!"

"Tell me," Tip said.

"That fucking Carlos. He did it, Tip. He took the girl."

"I thought she drove the kids to school," Tip said.

"Only sometimes. This is a fancy day care; they have buses for pre-k students."

Tip was silent for a moment. "Cortes is gonna pay this time. I promise you. He's gonna pay."

"I have to call Cathy," I said.

Tip said, "I'll be in shortly," and hung up.

I stared at the phone for what seemed like hours, afraid to pick it up, knowing what I'd hear.

Cathy Snider emptied the dishwasher, folded the laundry, and dusted the furniture in the dining room. She didn't know why she bothered since they'd be leaving in a matter of hours. Maybe it was her way of hanging on, hoping—or pretending—that she'd be back some day.

"Fat damn chance of that," she said, and grabbed another dust cloth before heading to the living room. Fifteen minutes later, Cathy finished dusting and went upstairs. It was time to tackle Trish's *cave*. She opened the door, spent five minutes picking up clothes from the floor and under the bed, and then set about straightening drawers. As messy and disorganized as this room was, it was Trish's, and she loved it. This move was going to break her heart.

A phone rang, and Cathy realized she had left her cell downstairs. A tinge of panic set in, and she rushed down the steps. She grabbed it on the fifth ring. "Hello?"

"Cathy, it's Detective Gianelli."

I heard the panic in her voice. My instinct was to hang up the phone. Run. Hide from her. Because I *knew* what was coming. "Cathy, I don't want you to panic, but something happened."

"Is it Patrick? Is he all right?"

"It's not Patrick. We don't know if anything's happened, but Marissa's bus never got to school this morning."

"What! Oh my God. Oh my God." Her pain came through the phone. I could almost feel it.

"Did they hurt her? Is she—"

"Mrs. Snider, that's all we know for now. We have every available unit searching. We'll find them soon. I promise."

"You promise? You *promised* me things would be all right. You said we had nothing to worry about."

It didn't matter that I'd never said those words. Whatever I did say must have implied that. That was my job—to make her feel safe so she would testify. *What a piece of shit I am.*

"I understand how you feel, but right now we have to stay calm."

"Stay calm? My daughter is missing. How the *hell* do I stay calm?"

I didn't want to raise my voice, but I had to get her attention. "Cathy, listen to me. Where is Trisha?"

"School. God, she's at school. I'm going to get her."

"No. Give me the phone number and name of the school. We'll send officers to get her. And call Patrick. Tell him not to leave the office, or talk to anyone. We'll send officers for him as well."

She was crying nonstop. "Cathy. Cathy, listen. The same goes for you. Don't call anyone but Patrick, and don't leave the house. I'll send a patrol car to get you."

All that came through the phone was sobbing. She sounded like a broken woman. *And it's all because of me.*

I wanted to scream. To cry. To kill Carlos. But most of all I wanted to know *how* they knew to take the Snider girl. How did they know the Sniders were turning on them?

Somebody leaked it. It had to be.

Chapter 42

IN THE DARK OF NIGHT

I was sitting at the desk when Delgado walked in. He grabbed the chair from Tip's desk and pulled it close to mine.

"I hope you did some good with *El Terrible*. We didn't."

I shook my head. "It's like this woman disappeared. I know Houston's a big city, but Roberts has had her face plastered on the news and in the paper. And every cop in the city has her photo."

Cruz walked in while we chatted. "What about the FBI? Did we run the picture through face recognition?"

I nodded. "Nothing. And Tip circulated it through Harris County and the Constable's office. No one ever saw her."

"It makes sense," Ribs said. "If she is *El Terrible*, even if she's been operating here before, I doubt anyone would know."

I looked up at Cruz. "I'm assuming you struck out at the hospital?"

"We questioned everybody again, and this time we had the photo to show them. Nobody remembered seeing that woman." He took a sip from a bottle of water and said, "How can she walk into the hospital, sneak into the ICU, and stab a patient—and then walk out without being seen?"

"What's going on with the Sniders?" Ribs asked.

"I've got officers picking up the older daughter and Mrs. Snider. And I just got word that the father is on his way in."

Charlie signaled me from his desk across the room.

"What's up, Charlie? You got something?"

He stood and walked toward me. "The bus came in. Everyone's safe."

"Yes!" I pounded my fist into the other palm.

"Not so fast," Charlie said. "The Snider girl's missing."

"Son of a bitch." It was all I could think of to say, so I said it again. "Son of a *goddamn* bitch."

"The driver said three people intercepted the bus, two guys and a woman. The only thing they wanted was the Snider girl."

"Where has the bus been?"

"They made them stay in a parking lot until just a few minutes ago."

"Okay, get all the details. And get someone down there to talk to that driver. We need descriptions of the people and any cars they had. Anything."

Delgado grabbed his keys off the desk and stood. "Charlie, give me the address. Cruz and I will take the driver."

Tip came charging in as Delgado and Cruz were leaving. I heard the conversation from the hall. "Anything?" Tip asked.

"Kids are safe, but the Snider girl's gone. Connie will fill you in."

"Where you going?"

"Interview the bus driver," Ribs said.

A few seconds later Tip walked in. "I just saw Ribs."

"I heard. What he didn't tell you is that the rest of the Snider family will be here any minute. And I'm sure they'll want blood."

"I'm sure they will."

I looked around, made sure no one could hear, and then whispered to Tip. "We need to talk. Somebody leaked this. Nothing else explains it."

Tip nodded. "I was thinking the same thing."

Patrick Snider arrived at the station first. I wanted to hide, but I found the courage to face him head on. "Mr. Snider, I can't tell you how sorry I am about this."

He stared, eyes narrowed and full of disgust. "How sorry you are? That's all you've got to say?"

I led him to my desk. Tip sat close by. "We'll find her," I said.

Snider shook his head, as if in denial. "I didn't want to do this. I told Cathy not to do this, but *you* convinced her." He pointed his finger at me, reminding me it was my fault. "You *assured* her it would be all right. Now look," he said. His voice cracked and he lowered his head.

His words hurt, and they should. He was right. Even if I didn't say it in so many words, I did *assure* Cathy that things would be all right. *And now look what's happened.*

A uniformed officer brought Mrs. Snider and her daughter to us a few minutes later. *Hysterical* wouldn't begin to describe her and, even though I wasn't a mother, a small part of me understood. Carlos Cortes had already taken too much from this woman. For him to do this was something God should forbid.

Tip gathered the family and took them to a vacant interview room. When he returned, we went to see Coop. Julie was keeping her up to speed, so she knew where we stood on things; in fact, she was on the phone with the FBI when Tip and I walked in.

"Agent Nash, ya'll don't know me—yet. But I don't give a rat's ass what hoops you have to jump through. I have half a dozen dead bodies, and now a young girl's been kidnapped. I know that doesn't mean much to you, but let's not forget that we're dealing with a major drug dealer, so unless you want the Houston Chronicle and every major paper in the country wondering why the FBI would be protecting the leader of a drug cartel, I suggest you find a way to get this family into the program."

Coop's face scrunched up and her eyes narrowed to tiny slits. I had only known her a short time, but Tip had warned me that if Coop lapsed into her East Texas drawl, it meant *somebody* was pissing her off. FBI or not, I wouldn't want to be Agent Nash right now.

"Yes, Agent Nash, that *is* a threat. And yes, I *do* know who I'm talking to. Furthermore, if you check around you'll discover that Gladys Cooper just doesn't give a fuck, so find somebody with authority and get back to me. Quickly." She slammed the phone onto the receiver.

"Sounded like fun," Tip said.

"Cut the shit, Denton."

I moved toward Coop's desk. "Captain, we've got the Sniders in an interview room, but still no word on the daughter. Delgado and Cruz are interviewing the bus driver, and we've got every available officer looking for the woman."

"The house is ready?" Coop asked.

"I checked it on my way in," Tip said. "Everything looks good."

Coop leveled her gaze at Tip, then me. "What's the plan?"

I took a deep breath before answering. "Delgado and Cruz are moving the Sniders tonight. We decided to wait until after dark. Tip's got two deputies from County who volunteered for duty at the safe house."

"And Cortes?" Coop asked.

"We're going to get him as soon as we get the warrant," Tip said.

"Good," Coop said. "I want that son of a bitch to rot in prison."

We left Coop's office and made the long walk to see the Sniders. I felt as if I were headed to the gallows, and wondered if facing the hangman's noose wouldn't be easier.

"You want me to do this?" Tip asked, before we walked in.

"Yeah, I *want* you to do it, but this is on me." I reached to grab the door handle, and turned toward Tip. "Thanks for offering though. I appreciate it."

Cathy Snider sat on the edge of her seat, her hands folded on the edge of the table. Her face had the look of a recently widowed woman, and her eyes told the same tale. Patrick sat beside her, his left hand resting across her shoulder, a futile attempt at comfort. And Trisha sat on the floor, slouched against the wall by the corner.

Patrick came to attention when I walked in. "Any news, Detective?"

"Nothing yet," I said. "But we've got everyone on this. I mean *everyone.*"

I expected Cathy to jump up, scream, claw at me. Something. But she did nothing. I'd been prepping myself for a lot of possible reactions. *Nothing* had not entered my mind. I think *nothing* was worse.

I started to reach for her, but Tip tapped my arm and shook his head.

"We'll be moving you to a safe house after dark," he said. "We'll have two officers with you the whole time. You'll be safe."

"We're arresting Carlos tonight," I said. "He's not getting away with any of this."

Patrick Snider jumped up from the chair. "No!"

Cathy reached for him but he yanked free. "I don't want him arrested," Patrick said. "He won't hurt Marissa if we don't press charges."

Tip pulled a chair next to Snider. When he spoke it was almost a whisper. "Mr. Snider, I know you probably think that, and it even seems logical to think he'd keep her safe as long as your wife doesn't testify, but that's not the way he works."

"How do you know how he works?" Snider said. "You didn't count on him taking Marissa."

I didn't know how to answer Mr. Snider's statement. I couldn't tell him that Carlos killed a cop last year, or that he killed Tip's dogs, or that he tried killing me. But I had to respond. "Something triggered him to do that. He must have suspected you were cooperating."

Snider shot me a look filled with disgust. "If he suspected something, Detective, it came from here. Cathy and I told no one."

Tip stepped close and addressed Mrs. Snider. "You'll have to trust us on this. I know how Carlos thinks. He'll keep her safe as long as there's a chance you'll change your mind about testifying. If he thinks he has something to negotiate, some bargaining chip, he'll keep her alive—and unharmed. If you drop the charges, you have nothing."

Mr. Snider was about to say something when Tip stopped him. "The money laundering is dead. You're useless to him. You're all useless. The only reason your daughter is alive right now is because your wife can put him in prison."

"Bullshit," Snider said, but then Cathy stood and grabbed his arm.

"Patrick, they're right. I saw the look in that man's eyes when they..." She turned and looked at her daughter, and then back to Tip and I. "I know what I saw. He'll never let her go if we give in."

Patrick hugged her for a few seconds and then he looked at Tip. "Promise me you'll find her?"

"We're gonna find her," Tip said. "And he's going to pay."

I didn't gasp, but I almost did. Tip never promised victims or families of victims resolution. Smart cops never did.

"We have to go," I said, "But Detective Delgado will let you know when it's time to move."

"You'll keep us informed?" Cathy asked.

"Every step of the way," I said, and then Tip and I left.

"Not very smart," I said to Tip.

"You mean promising them we'd get the girl?"

"That's exactly what I mean."

"We're gonna get her," Tip said. "End of discussion."

Chapter 43

You Have The Right To Remain Silent

Tip drove, and for the first time since I'd known him, it wasn't fast enough. "Hurry up," I told him for the second time.

"We'll get there. Don't forget we've got two units following us. Besides, it looks like you might need time to cool off."

"Bullshit," I said, but he was right. We had to play this by the book. No way I was letting this arrest get tossed on a technicality.

"About the leak," Tip said. "Who knew that Snider was cooperating?"

I thought for a moment. "Besides us—Delgado and Cruz. Coop. Julie, Herb, Charlie, Renkin."

"Didn't Coop send a couple of uniforms to the house?"

"Yeah. I forgot about them. That makes far too many. When we add in Cindy, Renkin's admin, and God knows who else from the other division."

"We need to figure this out," Tip said. "We can't afford more mistakes."

We arrived at Carlos' house a few minutes later. The place looked the same as it had the last time we were there, which seemed like years ago, but it had only been seven months. Tip parked across the street, and the backup units pulled in behind us. Two officers got out of each car.

"Keep your eyes open," Tip said. "We're damn sure this guy killed one of our own last year. And he tried killing Connie."

"We're ready, Tip," the senior officer said.

I rang the bell. It barely had time to chime before the door opened. "I'm guessing we were expected," I said to Tip.

He nodded and showed his badge to the guy who opened the door. "We have a warrant for Carlos Cortes."

The man stepped back, allowing us entry. The foyer was even bigger than I remembered. A sofa and three waiting chairs sat along the side walls and the door to an elevator at the rear. The marble floor looked as if it had been laid yesterday.

I turned to the officers who arrived in the second unit. "Wait here while we go up. Detain anyone you see."

Tip and I, and the other two officers, walked to the elevator. When the door opened, the young cop with us jumped a little, his hand moving toward his gun. I grabbed his arm. "Easy," I said, but I was glad to see him ready.

The elevator stopped on the fourth floor, where another man greeted us, again without a word, and led us across another foyer and into a room that resembled a library. Carlos sat in a stiff-backed chair next to a small table. A cigarette burned in an ashtray. A second man sat in a chair opposite him. Neither stood.

I glanced around the room, checking to make sure no one else was there. "Keep your eyes open," I whispered to the young cop.

"What do you want?" Carlos asked.

Tip held out the paper. "We have a warrant for your arrest," he said. "And the arrest of three of your men: Roberto, Tico, and Chaparrito."

"On what charge?"

I stepped forward. "Sexual assault and rape."

"Rape? Is she now saying she didn't *want* to do that? I have witnesses that say otherwise."

"We have our own witnesses," Tip said.

"Witnesses or not, you must understand that Señor Snider *wanted* this. He is a man with a strange sexual appetite."

"You expect me to believe—"

"I expect nothing. I have pictures of him and other women. Naked pictures."

"I don't care about pictures of him and other women," Tip said. "But you *will* pay for what you did to Mrs. Snider."

"I did nothing," Carlos said.

My body tensed, but I fought for control. "Stand up," I said, and held out the handcuffs.

Carlos turned and reached toward the table.

"Gun!" I shouted, and drew my weapon.

Carlos froze and slowly raised his hands above his head. "I have no gun. I am not armed." He turned, a smirk on his face. "You won't get to kill me so easily, Detective."

I gripped my gun with both hands. It was pointed at his head. My hands were shaking, and I felt my finger pressuring the trigger. It was a surreal moment, not unlike the thousand times I'd shot him in my dreams. A voice inside me told me to stop, but something stronger fought that voice.

Carlos lost his smirk. His eyes opened wide, and he slowly shook his head.

From the corner of my eye I saw Tip moving toward me, his hand reaching for the gun. "Gianelli."

I didn't move.

"Gianelli!" he yelled louder.

I closed my eyes, just for an instant, and then I let my finger off the trigger. And then I lowered the gun. "Cuff him," I said to the young cop. *Put 'em on tight.*

Tip looked to the man with Carlos. "What's your name?"

"Roberto Vasquez."

"Cuff him," Tip said to the senior officer, and then he faced Carlos and read him his rights.

"Where are the others?" Tip asked.

Carlos glared at me. "I believe I have the right to remain silent."

"Search the house," Tip said. "Make sure you don't break anything. Don't even ruffle the sheets."

"What if we don't find them?" the senior officer said.

"Stay here. They'll be back," Tip said, and then, "Maybe you better call for another unit."

We headed across the upstairs foyer. As the elevator door opened, Carlos said to his man, "Call Señor Griffin. Tell him what happened."

"Good old Señor Griffin," Tip said. "I guess you've got him shook up pretty good after killing his partner."

"I have no idea what you're talking about."

"I'm sure you don't," Tip said. "But that's all right, because we *do* know what we're talking about."

I wanted to get this son of a bitch into a lineup so the Sniders' could ID him, but I knew that wouldn't happen until morning. On second thought, it might be better to let him sit in jail all night. That would piss him off. Tip put Carlos and Roberto in the back of the second unit's car, and then we followed them back to the station.

The first few minutes of the drive were silent, unless you count the screaming going on inside my head. I had almost blown it. If I had... I turned to Tip and said, "Thanks."

"What's that?"

"Thanks," I said again.

"Say it again. I can't hear you."

"You son of a bitch." Tip had done it again. Made me laugh.

"I almost lost it, Tip."

"I didn't notice," he said. "But I bet Carlos has shit in his pants right now."

I was still shaking, afraid of what I almost did. I turned toward him. "Have you ever—"

"Wanted to blow somebody's head off?" He nodded. "*Way* too many times."

"How do you control it?"

He didn't say anything. I let it go for a few seconds and then asked again. "What stops you?"

"I still need to find out who killed my mother," he said. "And I can't do that if I'm not a cop."

That surprised the hell out of me. I knew he wanted to find her killer, but I had no idea the feelings ran that deep. "She must have been a good woman."

"Unfortunately I can't say that she was. Fact is, she was a son of a bitch."

I almost said something, but then he continued.

"But she was the son of a bitch that raised me. And she was the only person who gave a shit about me. I owe her for that."

I didn't know how to respond to that, so I said the first thing that came to mind. "Now you have one more person who gives a shit. You saved my career tonight."

He turned onto the North Loop and headed west toward the station. "You can pay me back when I find the one who killed her, 'cause if you're not there, I intend to pull the trigger."

I looked at him, at his pursed lips, narrowed eyes, and the twitch on the side of his face. That only happened when he got pissed off in a dangerous way. I made a promise to myself that I *would* be there. I owed him that.

Chapter 44

Information From The Enemy

When we arrived at the station, Tip went with the two officers to process Carlos and Roberto. I wanted his ass in a jail cell long enough to make him squirm. While Tip took care of the processing, I went to see the Sniders.

Delgado and Cruz were with them. I walked in, and Mrs. Snider almost sprung from her chair. "Any news?"

I shook my head. "Not yet, Cathy. But we've got people everywhere. We'll find her."

"When?" Her voice broke on that one word, and she fell into my arms. "Is she going to be all right? Have they hurt my baby?"

I held her, but there wasn't much to do except let her cry. I had nothing to tell her. Now I wished I could replay that scene at Carlos' house. I might have pulled the trigger this time.

After a few seconds she lifted her head. "Did you arrest him?"

"We just brought him in. Carlos and Roberto. The other two weren't there, but we'll find them. I've got officers waiting at his house."

Mr. Snider stepped forward. "Did he say anything…about Marissa?"

Something in his voice told me he was wondering about more than Marissa. Maybe what Carlos said about Patrick Snider and another woman was true. I *knew* the rest of what he said was a lie, but the *other woman* part might have been on target.

I looked at him and shook my head. "He said nothing about Marissa."

Cruz stepped in close and said, "Mr. Snider, we're ready to move."

Trisha stood and Delgado took hold of her hand. "You want to ride with me?"

"No need for you to go," Cruz said. "We've got two deputies, and I plan on staying."

Delgado cocked his head and looked at Cruz. "Are you sure? I can do this."

"No way," Cruz said. "Go home with Rosalee and the kids. They'll need you."

I had forgotten Delgado moved Rosalee to another house because of those men following her. "I can join you, Cruz."

"I got it covered," he said. "I don't think we can squeeze any more cops into that house."

"I'll go with you to the house," Ribs said. "You can take it from there."

I said goodbye to the Sniders and moved toward the door. "Ribs, you got a minute?"

He stepped into the hall and we walked to the coffee room. "Did you get anything from the driver?" I asked.

"Not much. She confirmed what we knew—that it was a woman and two men, and the woman took Marissa. Ordinarily that would make me feel better, knowing a woman has the kid, but if it's the same woman that we're after…"

"I hear you. Judging by what we've seen of her work, she's one cold son of a bitch."

"I can't figure out what they plan to do," Ribs said. "This is a sexual assault charge. Assuming she's working for Carlos, why would he risk kidnapping charges?"

I had to agree with Delgado. It seemed crazy for Carlos to order Marissa kidnapped when his high-priced lawyer would probably get him off anyway. "I think it's ego. This guy is a real nutbag. Don't forget, we're positive he's the one who killed Tony, and Tip's dogs."

"And tried killing you," Delgado said.

"Exactly. I'm not about to forget that."

My phone rang. "Tip, what's up?"

"We're about through processing him, and then we're taking him downtown."

"Okay. See you in a minute." I looked at Delgado. "Gotta go, but keep us up to speed," I said, and then, "When are you leaving?"

"In about an hour, which reminds me. I've got to get the keys from Julie."

"She left early," I said. "I think her son was sick. But she put the keys in her desk drawer."

"Okay, Connie. See you later."

I met Tip and we followed the other officers to the jail. After they logged Carlos and Roberto in, Tip and I took Carlos to a room to talk.

Carlos sat at the end of a small rectangular table. Tip sat to his right and I took the seat on Carlos' left. "It will go a lot easier on you if you tell us where the girl is," Tip said.

"I have no idea what you are talking about," Carlos said.

I wanted to beat that smug look off his face, but I kept my cool. "We know all about *El Terrible,*" I said. "And we know she took Marissa. If you know where she is, and we get her back safely…let's say I'm confident that the Sniders might reconsider their charges." I was lying through my teeth and I'm sure he knew it, but it was worth a shot.

Carlos turned his head slowly. When he was facing me, he smiled. "I believe in this country I am allowed legal representation, am I not? I would like to invoke those rights now."

I thought I had myself under control, but the look on his face…I balled my right hand into a fist and clenched my teeth. I wanted to hit this man, to hurt him.

He leaned toward me, his smile replaced by a smirk. "You want to kill me, don't you?"

"You're damn right I want to kill you, but I'll be satisfied with putting you in prison—for a *long* time."

He wagged his finger at me, as if I were a child. "Detective, of all people, you should know I won't be here for long."

"What are you talking about?"

"Ask your father. He'll tell you how it works."

"What the hell do you mean, ask my father? You never knew my father."

When I didn't say anything, Carlos said, "I see the blood runs strong in your family. You are just like him."

"My father?" What he said set me back. I wasn't about to let him know he was getting to me, but I did wonder what the hell he was talking about. "Ramble on all you want, Cortes."

The smirk on Carlos' face begged to be smacked off. "I would have thought he taught you his business. It doesn't matter, soon you'll find out you don't know Dominic Mangini like you think you do. He is no different than I am."

"Dominic Mangini has nothing to do with me, and besides, he might have broken a few laws in his life but he's a good man."

Carlos laughed. "Yes, I'm sure he is. My children think that, too."

"Your *children*? I'm not his daughter."

Carlos cocked his head to the side. "Really?"

I was getting pissed now. "Yeah, *really*. Mr. Mangini happened to be a friend of my mother's and he helped raise me when she died. I call him uncle but he's no relation." I shook my head. "I don't even know why I'm telling you this."

"Perhaps to try and convince yourself."

Tip reached over and grabbed my arm. "Forget this, Connie."

I shook him off, and glared at Carlos. "Listen, asshole. Who Dominic Mangini *is* or *isn't* doesn't matter. What matters is what you did to that woman, and what matters more is where you're hiding that little girl."

"Aren't you going to ask me about him?"

I scoffed. "Dominic Mangini *is not* my father."

"Ask him," Carlos said. "If he isn't, *someone* went to great lengths to cover up who your father was. It certainly wasn't Tommy Gianelli."

I leaned back in my chair. "You don't know what you're talking about."

"Your father had a birth record," Carlos said. "He had a marriage license. He had a death certificate. He had a credit card and a driver's license. What he *didn't* have, though, were church records. He was never baptized. Or confirmed. Or married. Not in a Catholic church." Carlos waited a few seconds and then said, "Don't you think a good Italian couple would have been blessed by the church?"

I stood and leaned toward Carlos. "In a few minutes, I'll be going home, and tonight I'll pray that someone in here has the balls to kill you."

"Don't waste your prayers on such foolishness, Detective. In here I am a king."

I walked to the door and opened it. "Tip, I'm going down the hall. I won't mind if you kill him."

"Don't leave angry, Detective. I will tell my men to look out for the girl. After all, she has such beautiful lips—like her mother."

I started after him, but Tip stepped between me and Carlos, and then he shoved me out the door. "Get out of here. I've got this."

Tip put the cuffs on Carlos and yanked him toward the door. "Time to go."

They walked down the hall, past the coffee room and the bathrooms on the way to the lockup.

"Your partner gets upset easily, Detective. Just like a woman."

Tip stopped, turned and headed back the way they had come. "I need to use the bathroom," he said, and dragged Carlos with him. Once inside, Tip checked the stalls and then slammed Carlos against the wall. The first punch went to Carlos' right kidney, dropping him to the floor. "That was for Kassie," Tip said. "She was a damn good dog."

He hit Carlos again, this one in the left kidney. "That was for Kelly."

Carlos lay on the floor gasping for breath. Tip kicked him in the balls. "That's for what you're doing to the Sniders."

Carlos screamed, and he squirmed away. Tip reached down and grabbed him by the hair, yanking him to his feet. "If that girl dies, or if anything happens to her, I'll make sure you suffer."

"Señor, you are the one who will suffer. Trust me. You will suffer like no other."

Chapter 45

In The Dark of Night

Delgado grabbed the keys from Julie's desk and walked to the coffee room, surprised to find Herb and Charlie still there. "Coop have you working late?"

"Everybody's working late," Herb said. "I think Coop called in every off-duty officer, and the chief has a dozen deputies from County on it too."

"We need to find her," Delgado said. "And quick." He poured a coffee and grabbed a pack of cheese crackers from the table.

Charlie said, "Ya'll heading out?"

"As soon as I finish this coffee and bleed the lizard."

"Bleed the lizard?" Herb said.

Charlie laughed. "He means take a piss. Don't tell me you never heard that?"

Ribs gulped down the last sip of coffee and tossed the cup in the trash. "Time for me to go."

"I'll walk with you," Charlie said. "I'm going outside to catch a smoke anyway."

"Wait up," Herb said. "I need a smoke myself."

Ribs gathered up Cruz and the Sniders. He held his hand out to Trisha. "You want to ride with me?"

She shook her head and grabbed her mother's hand.

Ribs laughed. "I don't blame you. I'd ride with your mom if I were you." He turned to Mr. Snider. "We're ready."

"What's the plan?" Snider asked. "Where is this place?"

"I'll be driving the lead car. Your family will be in the second car with two deputies, and Detective Cruz will follow them. It's not far from here, but we'll be taking a lot of detours and roundabout ways to get there. Don't worry. No one will be able to follow us."

Snider nodded, and then he whispered, "I want to get them someplace so they can sleep."

"I understand," Delgado said, and he headed for the door. "Let's move."

The trip from the station to the safe house was only about 12 miles, but Ribs and Cruz had planned a route designed to lose a tail. That turned a 15-minute drive into almost an hour, but it ensured a safe arrival. Ribs parked on the street in front of a ranch house, with a two-car garage facing the street. After scanning the area, he opened the door and stepped out of the car. Cruz signaled to the deputies to stay put and then followed Ribs inside.

Delgado unlocked the door and he and Cruz entered, weapons drawn. The door opened into a small entry hall. A few short strides led them to a hall branching off to the left. "Three bedrooms down there," Ribs said. "Stay here while I clear the kitchen and garage."

The living room lay open straight ahead, with a sliding door that led to the back patio and yard. To the right of the living room was a large kitchen with a table big enough to seat eight. "Kitchen clear," Ribs said, and walked slowly toward the laundry room. "Clear," he said, after opening the door leading to the garage. He then joined Cruz and they checked the bedrooms. After 10 minutes they came out of the house and gave the okay sign. The deputies pulled into the driveway and escorted the Sniders into the house.

"Is *this* where we're gonna live?" Trisha asked.

"Only for a little while," her mother said. "Just until Marissa comes home."

Ribs waited to catch their attention. "Remember the rules. No calls to anyone. Not friends, or relatives. Not even your mother. No leaving the house." He knelt next to Trisha and pinched her cheeks. "And no worrying."

She smiled. "I won't."

"Good girl," he said, and rubbed her head.

Before leaving he took Cruz aside. "A relief watch will be here in the morning. The password is 'mansion.' If they don't have the password, shoot them."

"We're good," Cruz said. "And tell Rosalee she owes me for this. I canceled a date."

"I think it's your date who owes *me*," Ribs said. "See you tomorrow."

***

Cruz shut the door and locked it before joining the Sniders in the kitchen. "In case you haven't been introduced," he said to the Sniders, "These fine deputies are Justin and Daniel."

"We met in the car," Cathy said. She fidgeted in the chair as she glanced around the room. "Will we be safe here?"

"We've got three officers, and we'll be with you the entire time," Cruz said, and then he turned to one of the deputies. "Justin, why don't you show Trisha to her room and find something on TV for her."

"She's going to sleep with us," Cathy Snider said. "At least for tonight."

"Of course," Cruz said, and then to Justin. "The Sniders have the master bedroom at the end of the hall on the right."

"Come on, Trish," Justin said. "I'll get you settled in."

When she was gone, Cruz sat with the Sniders. "Do you have any questions? Is there anything you need?"

Cathy Snider's hands gripped the seat of the chair. She was shaking. "I'm worried about tomorrow."

"About the lineup?"

She nodded.

"Don't be afraid. You'll be in a separate room, behind a one-way glass. He won't be able to see you. And you will never have to see him until the trial, if there even is one."

"I know," she said. "But I'm still frightened. That man terrifies me."

Patrick wrapped his arms around her and stroked her hair. "It's all right. This will be over soon. We'll get Marissa back and be a family again."

"Your husband is right about that, ma'am. We *will* get her back."

"You should take a shower and get into something comfortable," Patrick said. "After tomorrow, things will be better."

"Your husband is right again, ma'am. We'll get you through tomorrow, and then things will look up."

"Have you ever done this before?" Cathy asked.

"You mean sat all night at a safe house?" Cruz laughed. "Detective Delgado and I spent three nights one time with a family, and the house was much smaller than this. I might add you should be thankful, Delgado isn't here. He snores louder than anyone I know."

Cathy Snider cracked a smile. "He seems like a nice man."

"He is a good friend, and an excellent detective. And more importantly, he is a wonderful husband and father. If I get married…I should say *when* I get married, I intend to learn from Delgado." Cruz walked to the refrigerator and poured a glass of iced tea. As he returned to the table, he said, "But don't dare tell him I said that."

Mrs. Snider smiled again. "Your secret is safe with me," she said, and then reached her hand to cover a yawn. "Patrick, if you don't mind, I think I will take that shower you suggested. Good night, Detective Cruz. You've been helpful."

"Good night, ma'am."

***

Tico's phone rang as he was driving back to Carlos' house. Chappo was in the passenger seat. "Hello?" It was unnatural for him to answer in English, but Carlos insisted on them perfecting the language, and Carlos was not a man to disobey.

"Don't go home," the voice on the phone said in a thick Mexican accent. "Carlos has been arrested, and cops are at the house."

"Thank you for the call."

"That's not all. I have an address."

"Wait," Tico said, and he pulled to the side of the road. He opened the console and found a pen and a pad of paper. "What is it?"

The voice gave him an address, which Tico scribbled on the notepad. He confirmed the address, and then hung up the phone.

"Who was that?" Chappo asked.

"A voice on the telephone," Tico said, and he turned at the next intersection.

"Where are we going?"

"To the warehouse. Police have Carlos and they are waiting at the house."

At the next traffic signal, Tico turned on the overhead light and looked up a number. He dialed the phone. A woman's voice answered.

"I have an address for you," Tico said.

Chapter 46

WHO IS MY FATHER?

I drove home at slower than normal speed, afraid I'd fall asleep and kill myself, or worse, someone else. My head throbbed and I didn't know if it was the muggy weather or the stress of this case. None of it was helped by what Carlos said. No matter how much I tried dismissing it as him trying to get under my skin, the fact was, what he said carried the ring of truth. If there really weren't any church records—why?

I never knew my father, but if I knew anything, it was that my mother would have never been married outside the church. *If Carlos is telling the truth, why aren't there church records?*

Other things came to mind. *Like how Dominic took care of Mom, the way he read to her when she was bed-ridden, and how he took her to church every Sunday, no matter what he had to do. Why did he do that? And why didn't Mom get married again?* I stopped, dumbstruck. For the first time in my stupid life I realized that Dominic was in love with her.

And then I wondered if Carlos was right.

I resisted the urge to dial Dominic's number. In ten minutes I'd be home; I could call him from there. Hotshot greeted me with a swat when I walked in the front door. I scooped him up and gave him a hug. He must have been in a good mood because he let me. After a few minutes of pampering the silly cat, I took a deep breath and got down to business. This was not going to be a pleasant call.

Dominic answered on the third ring. He seldom let it go longer. "Pronto."

"Uncle Dominic, it's me."

"Concetta, what did I do to deserve a call from you?"

I thought of how to answer that, and decided for the truth. "That's what I'm calling to find out."

"What does that mean?"

Uncle Dominic appreciated directness in others. I hope he didn't mind it from me. "What you told me about my father, was it the truth?"

"About your father? Why do you ask?"

"You taught me too well, Uncle Dominic. That sounds like a question to avoid an answer."

"I told you before. Your father died when you were young. No more than a few months old."

"You told me my father was a drug addict."

"He was, and he died because of drugs."

I didn't like hearing what Dominic said. Despite that, I wanted to believe him. "Uncle Dominic, I have trusted you, and I have loved you all of my life, *please* tell me the truth. Are *you* my father?"

A moment of silence followed. When he spoke I thought for sure I'd be hearing a lie. "My dear, Concetta. Nothing in the world would make me prouder, or happier, than if I were your true father. I'm not. What I told you is true. Your father died when you were young. If you don't believe me, do one of those tests with DNA."

"And my mother?"

He was silent for what seemed like an hour, and when he spoke his pain came through the phone. "Maria was the only woman I have ever loved. I would have done anything for her, but she wouldn't marry me because of who I was. My biggest regret in life is that I didn't marry her."

I heard familiar sounds through the phone—the dull thud of Uncle Dominic's pipe as he tapped it against the cork surrounding his ashtray; the click of his lighter, followed by the intake of short, rapid breaths, as he brought life to the tobacco; and the subtle hiss of air being sucked through the twisted stem. I could almost see the billows of smoke, smell the pungent aroma. *God I missed my family.*

"I would have," he said.

"Would have what, Uncle Dominic?"

"I would have married her."

Tears ran down the side of my face. "I'm sorry I asked. It's just…"

"That's all right. I understand. *Ti voglio bene.*"

I wiped my eyes, and said, "I love you, too, Uncle Dominic."

"Now that we have that nonsense settled, you better get to bed. It's late."

I laughed. Uncle Dominic was forever telling me to get sleep, but he seldom heeded his own advice. "I will. Goodnight."

"*Buonanotte.*"

I felt better after talking to Uncle Dominic. I hated to admit it, but I usually did. He had a way of making me see things in a different light. I should have known Carlos was full of shit, but…something in the way he said it made me believe him.

After taking a quick shower, I got dressed in pajamas and crawled under the covers. As I lay there, staring at the ceiling, I decided I needed to say a prayer. I folded my hands and closed my eyes.

"God, I know you don't hear much from me, but I guess you know that when I do ask a favor it's real, and it's not for me. I know you're supposed to see everything, but in case you haven't been paying close attention, we've got a family suffering down here. Their little girl has been taken by horrible people. You've *got* to help me find her, God. *Please?* I'll owe you one if you do."

I made the sign of the cross, and lay my head on the pillow sideways. Then I reverted to the folded-hands position. "One more thing, God. Try to help Uncle Dominic. I know he's done a lot of wrong, but he's a good man. He just needs guidance."

I had a smile on my face as I drifted off to sleep.

Dominic hung up the phone and drew heavily on his pipe. After a few moments he poured a glass of brandy, and took a seat in his favorite chair, overlooking the patio. He didn't stir when Zeppe walked in.

"Dom, what are you doing in here?"

"Smoking my pipe."

"I can see that," Zeppe said, "but you never smoke in here. Something happen?"

Dominic swirled the brandy in the glass and took a sip. "Concetta called."

"No shit. I wish I'd been here. How's she doin' in Texas?"

"She wanted to know about her father. She wanted to know if *I* was her father."

Zeppe shook his head and took a seat in another chair. "What did you tell her?"

"I told her I wasn't, and that her father died when she was young."

"So you told her nothing."

Dominic blew smoke from the side of his mouth. "I almost did. I wanted to…"

"It would have been the perfect time to tell her. If she called, she was prepared to hear something she didn't know. She would have been forgiving."

"We're a family, Giuseppe. We will stay a family."

Zeppe stood and paced. "I know what you sacrificed for me. I know how much it hurt you not to be with Maria. All I'm saying is don't let Connie slip away. Don't risk it."

Dominic stared out the window. "I never imagined I could love that little girl. The night I killed her father, she was just a baby—a gift for Maria."

"What are you gonna do, Dom?"

"I don't know, but I can't lose another family."

Chapter 47

ASSAULT

Sahrina woke early, dressed in her sweats, walked down the hall, and then unlocked the door to the girl's room. She was sitting on the bed.

"Where's my mom? Why am I still here? You said I'd be going home."

"It won't be long," Sahrina said.

"When? I want to go now."

"Marissa! If you don't listen to me I will have to make you go to sleep again. You didn't like that, remember?"

Marissa lowered her head and pouted. "I'll be good."

"Excellent. I'm going for a run but I won't be long. Stay in the room until I get back, and don't make noise. I'll know if you do."

"All right."

Sahrina locked the door and headed to the kitchen. She grabbed a bottle of water and then dialed a number on her cell. A man answered.

"Are you dressed properly?" she asked.

"In my best Sunday suit," the man said.

"Don't play games with me. Yes or no is what I like to hear."

Silence followed. Sahrina almost felt the defiance she knew was there. These men didn't like that she was in control, but they'd get used to it. It was that or die. She waited him out. Finally, he said, "Yes."

"Good. Be ready in forty-five minutes. I'll meet you in the parking lot. You know which one?"

"Yes."

"Perfect," she said, and hung up. Afterward, she exited the front door and started her run. It would be a short run today; she needed to be back by 6:00.

When Sahrina returned, she went to see the girl.

"I'm hungry," Marissa said.

"Close your eyes, and I'll give you a surprise," Sahrina said.

When Marissa closed her eyes, Sahrina covered her mouth with tape and blindfolded her, and then she tied her to the bed. Marissa thrashed about. Sahrina watched for a moment, making sure the girl couldn't escape, and then she left. It wouldn't do for a neighbor to hear the girl squealing.

She packed a gym bag with a nylon stocking to cover her face, gloves to hide fingerprints, and a 9mm, 15-round Beretta 92FS with suppressor, along with two extra clips. Next, she went to the garage and loaded a few other items into the car. Now it was time to go.

Sahrina pulled into the back side of Cypress Fairbanks Hospital. From there it was a little more than a mile to their destination. A few minutes later the SUV pulled alongside of her. The passenger window rolled down and a man peered out.

"Are you riding with us?"

"No. At your signal, I'll be coming in from the street behind them. You remember the signal?"

The man narrowed his eyes and he looked as if he might argue, but he nodded and said, "Yes."

"And your friend?" she asked. "Everything is good?"

"Yes," came the voice from the driver.

Sahrina looked at her watch. "Relax. We have four minutes before we leave."

He started to roll up the window, and Sahrina said, "You know where to go afterward?"

"Yes," he said.

Four minutes later, Sahrina started the car and lowered her window. The man in the SUV looked out. "It's time," she said, and pulled out.

***

Cruz woke early and checked the perimeter of the house while he waited for Justin to make coffee. He heard the shower running from the master bedroom and presumed the Sniders were awake and preparing for their long day. *Long ordeal is more like it.*

Mrs. Snider was a wreck, and he couldn't blame her. It was bad enough pressing charges against a normal criminal—when that criminal was someone like Carlos Cortes it was something else altogether. Patrick Snider walked into the kitchen with his daughter.

"Any news on Marissa?"

"I haven't spoken to anyone yet, sir. I'll be calling them in a minute."

"Is there coffee?" Snider asked.

Cruz pointed to the counter by the sink. "Justin is making some. It should be ready in a few minutes."

"I'm hungry," Trisha said to her father.

"Food is in the refrigerator," Cruz said, "But if you want to wait until the relief arrives, I'll make a run and get you something else."

That seemed to perk her up. "How about a taquito from Whataburger?"

Cruz laughed. "That sounds good. I could go for a couple myself."

"When are they coming?" Trish asked.

"The relief team should be here by 8:00. We don't have long to wait."

"Coffee's ready," Justin hollered from the kitchen.

"Pour me a cup, will you?" Cruz said.

Daniel, the other deputy, walked in. "Save enough for me, partner. I'm gonna need a few cups this morning."

"Not used to staying up late?" Cruz asked.

"Not this late," Daniel said.

The sound of footsteps coming down the hall made Cruz turn his head. It was Mrs. Snider, and she looked as if she hadn't slept all night. "Good morning, ma'am. Justin has coffee made if you'd like some."

"I think I would, please. It's going to be a long day."

"Yes, ma'am. But you'll have support all the way. Detectives Gianelli and Denton will be with you. They'll take good care of you."

She nodded her head, but she didn't seem any more relieved. "Is there any—"

Patrick hugged her and rubbed her back. "Nothing yet, dear. But the detective hasn't spoken to the people at the station yet."

She looked at her watch. "Can you call now?"

Cruz smiled. "Sure thing, ma'am. I'll see who's in."

He walked out a sliding door onto the patio in the back yard. A six-foot fence separated this house from the neighbors on both sides and the back. Half a dozen trees shaded the main part of the lot. Cruz walked out a few feet and dialed Ribs.

"What's up, Cruz? Everything okay?"

"We're good. The Sniders are asking about the girl. Do we have any word?"

"I haven't heard anything. Did you call Tip or Coop?"

"No way I'm calling Coop this early," Cruz said.

"Check with Julie. She'll be in."

"Okay, good idea." Cruz hung up and dialed Julie.

"Good morning, Detective Cruz."

"Julie, I'm with the Sniders and they—"

"Want to know about their daughter? We don't have anything. It's like that woman disappeared."

"Okay. Call me if you hear anything different."

"I will. See you later."

Cruz hung up the phone, but he didn't go in right away. He didn't want to walk in there and face the Sniders and take their hope away. Things were *not* looking good. As he pondered what he'd say, the door opened and Patrick Snider poked his head out.

"Anything?"

Cruz turned and walked toward Snider. "Not yet, sir." He tried to keep the hopelessness from his voice, but from the look on Snider's face, Cruz didn't think he'd been successful.

"Try to give my wife some hope, Detective. She needs it."

"I understand, sir. I will."

They walked in together and Cruz got his coffee. He put as much enthusiasm as he could into his voice. "Mrs. Snider, Detective Gianelli isn't in yet, but I spoke with Julie and she said everyone's out working on it. They're following some good leads they picked up on during the night."

Cathy's face sunk. "But we don't have her."

"No, ma'am. Not yet."

Mrs. Snider nodded and took a seat at the table. "Thank you."

"When will the other cops be here?" Trisha asked.

"It won't be long," Cruz said. "About an hour if they're on time, but they might be early."

Patrick finished his coffee and took his cup to the sink. "I think I'll take a shower, Cathy. I won't be long."

She got up from the table and started for the hall. "I'll come with you. I need to dress in something else anyway." She turned to her daughter. "Trish, are you coming? You need to change clothes."

"Not yet, Mom. I'm going to ride to Whataburger with Detective Cruz."

Cruz raised his eyebrows. "I don't think that's a good idea. I'd love to take you, but you should stay here."

"I'm tired of staying here."

"No arguing," Cathy said, and she walked with Patrick.

"Relief coming in," Justin said from the foyer.

"Woo hoo," Daniel said.

Cruz looked at his watch—7:00. Not that he wasn't grateful, but he never knew a relief team to be *this* early. "Don't open the door," he said.

Justin shot Cruz a look. "This ain't my first rodeo, Detective."

The two deputies walked toward the door. One of them stopped to talk on the radio before joining the other. Justin watched from the glass side panel on the front door. The bigger deputy knocked twice.

"What's the color of the day?" Justin said from inside.

"We don't have a *color*, but the password is 'mansion.'"

Justin reached for the door handle. "Mansion it is," he said, and opened the door.

The first shot wasn't much louder than a balloon pop. It hit Justin in the chest, near the center. His eyes went wide, and his mouth opened. He fell backward and reached for his gun. The second shot sounded louder, like cap gun going off. This bullet caught him in the throat. Blood gurgled out. Justin's arms flailed and he lost control of his legs. He landed flat on his back in the foyer.

The two men dressed as deputies burst into the house, guns raised, and firing. Cruz had been moving through the living room. He squeezed Trish's hand tightly and dragged her as he ran down the hall, screaming. "Snider, open the door. Call 9-1-1."

He busted through the bedroom door. Mrs. Snider was in the midst of dressing. Snider was still in the shower. He shoved Trish at her. "Put her in the closet! Get in there with her."

Snider came out, a towel around him. Cathy was crying. Cruz got on the radio. "Officer down at the safe house. Officers under fire. Repeat. Officer down."

"What can I do?" Snider asked.

"Stay away from the door," Cruz said, and then he grabbed hold of a corner of the mattress and yanked it off the bed. "Help me with this. Put it against the door."

Snider slid the nightstand behind the mattress to support it. Cathy and Trisha were huddled in the closet. Cruz called in on the radio again, repeating the distress call. This time he added something. "Tell Delgado they knew the password. Repeat, they knew the password."

***

Daniel ducked into the kitchen when the first shot hit Justin. A three-foot wall separated the eating area from the living room. Daniel crouched behind it and peered over the top. He fired as the two men entered the house. The return fire came rapidly, peppering the wall in front of him, bullets whizzing past his head. He ducked, moved to the right and took a shot from a position near the floor. His hands shook. He missed.

The men rushed him, taking turns firing. Daniel retreated toward the garage. As he made a move from the kitchen to the laundry room, he caught a shot in the right leg. He fell to his knees, rolled left, and fired, getting off three rounds—all misses. Daniel braced his left foot against the door jamb and pushed himself into the laundry room. Before he could close the door, they rushed him. The first shot hit him in the back, just above the kidney. Two more followed quickly. Daniel fell to the floor, and this time he didn't get up.

***

Sahrina walked quickly through the back yard of the house behind the safe house. She tossed her gym bag over the fence, and then tossed another bag. Inside were two small cans of gasoline and a Molotov cocktail. She then climbed the fence and moved swiftly toward the safe house. Shots were coming from the bedroom—the loud ones were the cops. A window faced the back yard, with shades drawn.

Drawing her gun, Sahrina entered the house through the sliding door and walked to the kitchen. She grabbed a frying pan from the cabinet and went back outside to the bedroom window. Using the pan, she broke the glass, unscrewed the top on one of the gas cans and threw it into the room. Shots came from the room in a spread pattern. The cop was hoping to hit her, or at least hold her off. She unscrewed the top of the other can and tossed it into the room. More shots came, but only a few. She felt certain he wanted to conserve ammunition.

From inside the room she heard a man yell, "Take them into the bathroom. Lock the door and don't come out."

Sahrina lit one of the kerosene-soaked rags on the end of a bottle and tossed it gently into the room. A huge whoosh sounded as flames consumed the room. A man screamed. Sahrina darted for the back door and into the house. She approached the hallway and shouted. "Time to go."

Her accomplices ran toward her. When they were a few feet away, she fired two shots into each of their heads, and then she lit the other two Molotov cocktails, tossing one into the hallway and the other into the kitchen. Afterward, she exited through the back door and climbed over the fence. Less than a minute later she was in her car and driving home.

Only one more loose end.

Chapter 48

A Leak

The alarm went off *way* before I was ready. I was half-tempted to push the snooze button, but we had too much planned today, and at the top of the list was bringing Cathy and Patrick in for the lineup. I couldn't wait to see Carlos get his due.

I went to the kitchen, put water on for espresso, popped a bagel in the toaster, and then back to the bedroom to dress. I was tying my shoes when the phone rang. I looked at the caller ID. "Good morning, Tip."

"Morning yourself, darlin'. I hope you're ready."

I looked at the clock. "It's only 6:30."

"I'm on my way," Tip said. "We need an early start."

"Shit. All right, but we'll have to stop for coffee on the way in."

"I'll be there in ten minutes," Tip said.

"Have you talked to anybody this morning?" I asked.

"Ribs called a few minutes ago. He talked to Cruz. Everything's fine, and they plan on bringing the Sniders in by 9:00."

"Okay. See you in a few."

I was waiting outside when Tip pulled up. I climbed in the car and said, "First stop is coffee."

"Starbucks?"

"I don't care where, as long as it's not corner-store coffee."

Forty minutes later we turned onto the North Loop heading west. That's when my phone rang. It was Coop. "What's up, Captain?"

"They hit the safe house! Officers down!"

"What? Who's down? What about the Sniders?"

"We don't know anything else. I've got units on the way. Cruz called it in."

"We're on it," I said, and then told Tip.

Tip put the lights on and punched the gas. We hit 90 within seconds. "Call Ribs. See if he knows anything."

Tip's phone rang before I dialed. It was Ribs, so I answered.

"You hear?" he asked.

"We're on the way. Almost to #290 now."

"I'm coming in from Highway 6," he said. "I'll be there in five."

"Son of a bitch!" I said. "How the hell did they find them?"

"There's a leak," Tip said. "We've got a fuckin' rat in the house."

I tried thinking of who it could be as we drove. "Who knew?"

Fortunately we were going against traffic on #290, but there was still plenty of traffic. The siren helped. Cars moved out of our way, but some not fast enough. Tip laid on the horn as we passed a car that had been slow to react. "Get the fuck out of the way, asshole. I'll shoot you next time."

I don't know if the guy heard him, but he might have. We passed cars so quickly, it was almost like a blur. I didn't want to but I glanced at the speedometer. We were doing 100. *God help us.*

Tip exited at Jersey Village and took the first turn so fast I thought we'd flip. We were only blocks away. He made the turn into the subdivision falling in behind a Harris County cop car and an ambulance ahead of him. Smoke filled the air. "The house is on fire," I said.

When we turned the corner, my heart sank. The house was engulfed in flames. Two fire engines were working the blaze and a couple of ambulances were parked near the house. Ribs was standing on the side of the road. He rushed over.

Tip and I got out of the car. "What have we got?" I said, but I took one look at his face and knew. He was crying.

"They killed everybody. The deputies, the Sniders…" He took a breath, like he was trying to control himself. "And Cruz is gone," he said, and then he lost it.

Tip held Ribs up. He didn't say anything, just held him.

I gave Ribs a hug. "How do you know Cruz is gone?"

For a few seconds he didn't say anything, then he straightened and wiped his eyes. "When Cruz made the call he said an officer was down and he was under fire." Ribs pointed toward the house. "Look at it. Nobody came out of that alive."

What Ribs said started sinking in. The deputies dead. Cruz dead. And the Sniders..." *Mother of God. This wasn't right.*

"That was supposed to be me," Ribs said. "Cruz took my watch so I could be with Rosalee."

Tip patted his arm. "Don't worry. We're gonna get the fuckers who did this."

I didn't say anything, but I nodded my head. Tip was right about that. If nothing else, we'd get them.

More cops arrived at the scene, and a huge crowd gathered. Tip approached two officers from HPD and two more from County. "Take as many men as you need and canvas the area. Talk to everyone who's here. I want *every* damn house accounted for. Somebody had to see something. We need to know what that is."

Sahrina made sure to stay under the speed limit. The last thing she wanted was a cop pulling her over. She took back roads from #290 down to I-10. From there it was a short drive with little exposure. In ten minutes she would be *home*. At least that's how she referred to it for now. She had planned on taking the girl with her to Mexico, a sweet thing like her would fetch a good price from the right people. For one as sweet as Marissa, *El Terrible* might even get an auction going. But considering the heat this morning's incident would generate, she decided the girl had to be killed; smuggling her over the border would be too risky.

She turned left into the subdivision on Rolling Sands Drive and followed it south. About one block from where she would turn to go to her house, she reached for the blinker signal, but stopped herself before turning it on. A cop car was parked beside the curb on the street where her house was. *Do they know? Did they get a description of the car?*

Sahrina had considered dumping this car, but that would have meant stealing a replacement, which she didn't want to risk. She glanced at the cop car again. Only one officer, and he appeared bored. *Maybe it's nothing.*

As she approached the corner, she flipped the right turn signal, came to a full stop, and then turned right. Just in case, she unzipped the bag lying on the seat next to her, providing easy access to the gun. After driving three blocks, she took another right turn. A quarter mile from here was a small shopping center with a coffee shop—a good place to wait this out.

Tip must have given orders to half a dozen officers before he returned, and he looked to be in a hurry. "We need to get to the station and figure out how to find that little girl."

"And whoever did this," I said.

Tip looked at Delgado. "You want to ride in with us?"

Delgado shook his head. "No sense in it. I could use the time to myself."

"All right. See you there," Tip said, and headed for the car.

On our way into the station, one of the officers called. Tip put it on speaker.

"A neighbor saw a young woman, early thirties maybe, and carrying a gym bag. He said she drove off in a blue Honda Accord."

"Plates?" Tip asked.

"He made out a partial. The middle of the plate read 'V-E-2' but he didn't get the rest."

"That's good," Tip said. "Call it in and tell them to put it out on all channels. And send it to County, too."

"You got it, Tip."

After Tip hung up, I said, "That partial is something at least. More than we've ever had on this woman."

"If she hasn't ditched the car, we might even get lucky," Tip said.

We were at the station in twenty minutes. Delgado arrived five minutes later and found us in the coffee room. I had asked Julie for the recording on the radio call and she brought it in.

"There are two separate calls," she said. "The second one was about one minute after the first."

Tip and Delgado sat at the table, and I hit the play button.

Officer down at the safe house. Officers under fire. Repeat. Officer down.

The second call followed after a quick pause.

Tell Delgado they knew the password. Repeat, they knew the password.

Delgado balled his fist, but before he could say anything, Tip slammed the table.

"It's one of our own. It's a goddamn cop," he said.

It didn't seem possible that a cop had done this. I felt like screaming, *no way,* but then I remembered how my own partners had betrayed me for a drug deal. How my own boss had set me up to die. "We've got to figure out who," I said.

Delgado stood. "Nobody wants to find out who it is more than me," he said, "but we have to find Marissa. With the Sniders dead, *El Terrible* has no reason to keep the girl alive."

Chapter 49

WHERE'S THE GIRL

Every available officer was looking for *El Terrible,* but so far no luck. We figured the best way to find Marissa was to locate the leak, so we retreated to a private room where no one could hear what we discussed. Julie brought us the case files from both investigations—Delgado and Cruz's, and the one Tip and I had been working on. We laid the files out on the table and started going through the notes.

I separated the notes so we could look at them side by side in chronological order. "What we need is anything that points to a *possible* leak. No matter how simple it seems."

I moved the file on Lipscomb, the first body we found, to the top left. "What do we have on this one?" I said. "Anything suspicious as far as leaks go?"

"Not much, unless we count Tiffany disappearing from her apartment."

I shook my head. "She might have been spooked. We can't swear that was a leak."

"How about Martin getting killed in the hospital?" Delgado said. "Cruz and I questioned him one day, and the next morning they killed him. Seems like more than coincidence now that we know about *El Terrible.* Martin was talking about her."

I moved the file on Martin to the top right. "Who knew about *El Terrible?*"

Ribs thought for a moment and then said, "When we heard the name *El Terrible,* I called it in to Julie. She checked it out for us."

"And?" Tip said.

"And the next morning Martin was dead," Ribs said.

I saw the look on Tip's face. "Don't even think that. There's no goddamn way Julie is the leak."

"We don't get answers by assuming everyone is innocent," Tip said, and then he moved some papers to a spot underneath Lipscomb's file. "Remember when we asked Julie to process the prints from the hotel room?"

"They didn't come up on the system," I said.

"Exactly," Tip said. "But now we know Tiffany had a car, and a driver's license. That means her prints *were* in the system. Why didn't they show up?"

Delgado shook his head. "That doesn't mean anything, Tip. If we didn't have a thumb print it wouldn't show up. They only take full prints for a criminal offense."

Tip moved another file underneath the one he had just placed. "When Dewey reported spotting Tiffany's car it disappeared. And the next day they found Tiffany dead and her car burned up in El Campo."

"Too many people had access to that information," I said. "Same with the warrant we were getting on Cortes."

"How about the biggest leak of all," Delgado said. "The safe house. Nobody knew where that was."

Tip moved that file to the top, above the others. "And they had the password. They probably weren't counting on Cruz being able to tell us about that, but having the password is the clincher. It *has* to be an insider."

El Terrible sat at an outside table sipping on a cappuccino. Every now and then she took a bite from a cinnamon stick. This was the third cappuccino she'd had, and still no word from her contact. If she didn't hear soon she would have to improvise. Five minutes later a call came in. It was Tico.

"Yes?"

"Ditch the car. It's no good."

"Anything else?"

"Everything else is the same. Finish up and go home," Tico said.

"And the girl?"

"Leave her. We'll clean up later."

El Terrible hung up the phone. She looked around, hoping to spot an easy target. It didn't take long. With her gun tucked into the back of her pants, she followed a middle-aged man to his car. As he opened the door to get in, she approached him.

"Excuse me, sir. I was wondering if you could give me a ride. It's not far."

He looked at her, a combination of suspicion and lust in his eyes. "Where do you need to go?"

"I'm supposed to be at a doctor's appointment in ten minutes, and my car broke down. It's only about three miles from here, but I'll never make it walking."

The man looked her up and down, smiled, and said, "Sure, I'll take you. Get in."

He started the car as she climbed into the passenger seat. She pointed a gun at him and said, "Do exactly what I say and you'll live."

Julie called as we were arguing over whether she was the leak or not.

"Connie, we just had a call from an officer about the car."

"Who called it in?" Tip said.

"Officer Briggs," Julie said.

"I know him. Patch me through."

"Briggs, it's Tip Denton."

"Tip, how are you? It's been a long time."

"Yeah it has, but we'll have to catch up later. Tell me what you can about that car."

Tip put the call on speaker.

"I can't swear it was the car you're after. But when the call came in, it reminded me of a vehicle that passed by me not twenty minutes before."

"Where are you?" Tip asked.

"On Shadow Lake Drive, over by Memorial."

Tip said, "Briggs, here's what you do. If you see that car again, call it in and request backup. Don't try to take this woman by yourself."

"A woman? Come on."

"I'm not blowing smoke up your ass. If it's who we think it is, she's killed 8 or 10 people in the past few days. And she's probably killed a lot more than that before."

"No shit?"

"No shit, Briggs. Call it in."

Tip hung up and said, "Maybe we're catching a break."

"Now if we can find this leak…" Delgado said.

I was thinking the whole time Tip was on the phone. Something Briggs said…It hit me just as Tip hung up. "Forget the leak. What was Tiffany's car doing down by Memorial Drive?"

"What?" Tip asked.

I looked at him and then Delgado. "Let's assume the report from Briggs is accurate, that he really did see her car. What is *El Terrible* doing on Shadow Lake Drive?"

"How the hell do I know?" Tip said.

"Remember that cop Dewey? The one who said he saw Tiffany's car?"

Recognition started to show in Tip's eyes.

"Dewey said it was on Shadow Lake Drive. So what was Tiffany, a prostitute, doing in that part of Memorial Drive, with all those expensive houses?"

"And on the same street that our shooter's car might have been spotted," Ribs said.

"Son of a bitch!" Tip said. "She's hiding out. *El Terrible* has a house there."

"Let's go," I said. "And we're *not* calling it in. Nobody but us three will know."

It took us twenty minutes to drive to Shadow Lake. Briggs stepped out of the car when we arrived. He reached out to shake Tip's hand, and nodded to us. "Tip, it's been a while."

"Briggs, this is my partner, Connie Gianelli. I think you know Delgado."

"Where did you spot the car?" I asked.

He pointed to an intersection not fifty yards away. "She was coming south and turned right on Shadow Lake. After I received the call, I checked to the end of the street but there was no sign of the car. Two other units showed up since I called it in and they haven't seen anything yet."

Tip looked down the street both ways.

"It goes about 8 blocks east," Briggs said, "And maybe 10 to the west."

"We can't knock on every door," Tip said.

"Where did Dewey spot Tiffany's car?" Ribs asked.

"Good question," Tip said.

I looked up Dewey's number on my phone. "Dewey, this is Connie Gianelli. Where did you spot that car we asked you about? The one on Shadow Lake."

"Hang on a minute." He came back on about thirty seconds later. "The kid I was taking home lived at 13115. The car in front of me was heading east."

"Thanks, Dewey. That helps."

"East of here," I said, and pointed to the left, the opposite of where she'd turned.

Tip looked both ways and said, "What do you think?"

"If she was coming back to her house and saw Briggs sitting there, what's she going to do?" Ribs asked.

"Turn right," Tip said.

"No sense in sitting around guessing," I said. "Let's start to the left and see what we find."

"I agree," Ribs said, "But in the meantime, we should get Julie to check who owns any house where we don't get an answer."

"What's that going to do for us?" I asked.

"Maybe nothing," Ribs said. "But if we figured this right, and *El Terrible* is working for Carlos, just maybe one of these houses will have a suspicious owner."

"I don't want Julie doing it," Tip said.

"That's bull," I said. "It's time we trusted Julie. If you don't call it in, I will."

Delgado nodded. "I'm with Connie on this one. I don't give a shit what it looks like, there's no way Julie's the leak."

"Let's do it," Tip said, "but we're pairing up for this. We don't know what we'll find, and I don't want any more dead cops."

"I'll go with Delgado," I said. "You take Briggs."

"Sounds good," Tip said. "Time to go to work, Briggs."

Tip and Briggs took the north side of the street. Delgado and I, the south. The first four houses were a bust and the people didn't know anything about a woman and daughter new to the neighborhood. I began to wonder how much people paid attention to their neighbors. Where I came from people knew when you had *visitors*. New neighbors were greeted and grilled.

The next house brought no answer. I called Julie with the address, and she said she'd check it out. By the time we hit the end of the first block, Ribs and I had two that didn't answer. Tip and Briggs had one. The second block brought more of the same, as did the third. We had twelve houses that brought no answer, but so far Julie hadn't found anything that looked suspicious from the property records. We hit payday on the next block.

It was a two-story house with a detached garage and a fenced-in back yard. Curtains covered all the windows. When we didn't get an answer, I called Julie with the address. We were two houses further down when she called back.

"Something fishy about that last one, Connie."

"Tell me about it," I said.

"It was foreclosed on two years ago, and bought at auction by Sentinel Properties."

"What's fishy?"

"Sentinel Properties owns several warehouses and businesses on Navigation Boulevard and quite a few houses on the East Side."

I wasn't familiar with Houston yet, but when Delgado heard, he said, "That's it."

"What's it?" I asked.

"Those other places are all in the Mexican district," he said. "I'd bet money it's Carlos."

I called Tip, and he and Briggs came over. "Let's go in," I said.

"We need a warrant," Tip said. "I don't want anything screwing this up."

"I'm not waiting, Tip. I'm going in."

"Gianelli—"

"No way I'm letting that little girl sit in there one more minute. She could be dying."

Ribs looked at Tip and said, "I'm with her, amigo. It's a kid."

We rang the bell a few more times, and knocked as loud as we could on the door, but when that brought no answer, we went around the back, where Tip broke a window to get us in.

Ribs climbed in first, gun drawn. Tip and I followed. Briggs stayed out front to guard the door.

I called her name as we cleared each room. There was no reason to be quiet. If anyone else was here, they knew we were inside. "Marissa!"

Tip led the way, clearing the kitchen, living room, dining room, and a sitting area. After that, we started up the stairs. We found her in the third bedroom, tied to the bed, blindfolded, and with tape covering her mouth. She was shaking.

I moved quickly to her side, undoing the blindfold first. "Marissa, it's all right. We're the police." When I showed her my badge, she seemed to relax a little.

I reached for the tape covering her mouth. "This is going to hurt a little when I take it off. Is that okay?"

She nodded, and I quickly peeled the tape back. Tip untied her, and I picked Marissa up in my arms. Her pants were soaking wet, and she was crying.

"That mean lady tied me up," she said.

I hugged her to my chest, and almost cried myself. "I know, baby. Don't worry. Nobody's going to hurt you now. We've got you."

"Where's my mom? Where's Daddy? That lady said Daddy was hurt." Marissa cried more, and said, "Is he all right?"

I wanted to lie to her, to tell her things would be okay…but I couldn't. Right then I couldn't even talk without fear of crying. Instead of answering her, I patted her back.

Fortunately, Delgado was there. He leaned in and kissed the top of her head. "I'm sure wherever your daddy is, he's all right. Don't worry right now. I'm calling some people to help you."

Delgado stepped away and then got on the phone with Julie. "We need child services over here. As soon as they can, yeah."

I had piss all over my top, and my heart was breaking for this little girl, but I made a vow right then and there. *El Terrible*, whoever the hell she was, would pay for what she did.

Chapter 50

Aftermath

We waited for child services to show up. Marissa wanted to stay with us, and my heart broke again when they took her. I promised her I'd visit, but I worried about her reaction when she found out what happened to her parents.

"She'll be okay," Delgado said. "Kids are resilient."

I knew as well as anyone how resilient a kid can be, but vivid images of finding my mother lying at the bottom of the stairs still haunted me on too many nights, and it had been 20 years since that happened. I was 12 at the time. Marissa was five. I couldn't imagine facing what she was in for. Seeing her face and hearing her cry and ask for her mother had changed me. Perhaps forever.

Since we'd found Marissa, Tip hadn't been himself either. He wasn't the type to let it show that things bothered him, but inside he hurt. I could tell.

We drove back to the station to pick up where we left off. "We still need to find the leak," I said. "It might be the only way to get *El Terrible*."

Tip got onto the West Loop, heading north. "I'll be the one to say it. I was wrong about Julie. She came through for us back there."

"Did you really think it was her?" I asked.

"I didn't want to, but I tried to look at the facts, and they pointed to her."

"Too many people could have known," Delgado said. "She wasn't the only one with access to the information."

"Let's talk about that," I said. "Who else knew about all the leaks—not just one or two, but all of them?"

"Herb and Charlie," Tip said. "And Coop."

"Rodriguez was there once or twice," Delgado added, "And Vasquez."

"I don't know how this is going to work," I said. "We had people from County. From different departments at the station. And we have no way of knowing if the chief or Coop told anyone."

"But only one of the leaks matters," Ribs said. "The safe house. How many people knew about the safe house *and* the password?"

Tip said, "You're right about that. Not many of us were around then. You, me, Cruz."

"And there's no way anybody followed us," Ribs said. "We took the most evasive route I could think of, with plenty of backup for spotting tails."

"It doesn't matter how many knew about the safe house before," I said. "Too many people were exposed to it while we were setting it up—Julie, Charlie, Herb, Coop, Renkin, whoever was in on it from Harris County. When we're done adding up people, it could be 20 or more."

We were almost at the station when Coop called. "Where are you?" she asked.

"About to pull in," Tip said. "Why?"

"Is Delgado with you?"

"Him and Gianelli," Tip said. "Why? What's up?"

"Come to my office when you get here."

Tip hung up and looked at me. "You have any idea what this is about?"

I shook my head. So did Delgado.

Ten minutes later we walked into Coop's office, surprised to see Renkin standing behind her desk, but Bobby Stenson's presence explained it.

Tip said, "What's he doing here?"

Bobby stepped forward. He looked a lot better than he did that day in the bar. "I'm here to tell you and your partner to stay the hell away from my case. And my men."

Before Tip could react, Chief Renkin stepped between them. "Bobby has men in *deep* undercover. They've been working on this meth deal for months. And all of it with my approval."

Tip's brow wrinkled up. He relaxed and looked at Bobby. "Why the hell didn't you tell me?"

Bobby got close to Tip. "Because I've got men whose lives depend on me. I didn't know who I could trust."

"What the hell are you talking about?"

"There's a leak," Coop said. "You and Connie were right about that. But the leak started long before your case. Or Delgado's." Coop pointed to a file on her desk. "Somebody's been getting information to these dealers. Every time that Stenson thought he had them trapped, they changed course."

"But your men never got caught?"

"That's because only two people knew who they were—besides me— Chief Renkin and Captain Cooper. Nobody else." Bobby shook his head. "That's why I couldn't tell you, Tip. It wasn't that I didn't think I could trust you, it was because I *had to know* the leak wasn't us, and the only way to do that was to contain it."

I looked to Coop and then Renkin. I now knew why she had told me to keep Tip in line, but judging by their looks, they were holding back something. "Why are we hearing about it now?"

Renkin stepped forward. "On my orders, Captain Cooper let certain people in on the investigation. We've narrowed it down to three or four people."

"Who?" Tip asked.

Coop removed her glasses and rubbed her eyes. "Vasquez, Julie, Herb, and Charlie." She shook her head several times. "I hate to say it, but as far as we can tell it has to be one of them."

"We've got our list down to almost the same people," I said. "I was going to see Julie when you called."

"I don't think that's a good idea," Renkin said. "We don't want to tip our hand."

I looked Renkin in the eyes. "Chief, I know I haven't been here long, but you've got to trust me on this."

He stared at me, then turned to Coop. She looked to Stenson. "Bobby?"

"One of you needs to tell me what the hell is going on," Tip said.

The Chief nodded to Stenson.

"We have information on two of Carlos' men, the two you were after—Tico and Chappo."

"Why are we just getting this now?" Delgado asked.

"Because if we can get them on the drug charges it will put them away for a lot longer than a sexual assault charge, that might or might not have stuck."

"I'm guessing you're telling us this for a reason," I said.

Bobby nodded. "As far as we can tell, they've got the meth in a warehouse on Navigation. The problem is we can't get a warrant. We need a way to make them move the drugs."

Tip smiled. "So if the leak sends a message that we're onto them…"

"Exactly," Stenson said. "We can both get what we want."

Chief Renkin said, "Gianelli, if you're positive Julie is clean, and that she can help, do it. But keep us posted. Everything will be coordinated with Captain Cooper."

I walked over and shook Bobby's hand. "Sorry about the other day."

He smiled. "I thought you were going to shoot me."

"I was," I said. "Can't let my partner get hurt."

Tip smacked Bobby on the back and laughed. "She's a crazy son of a bitch isn't she? That's why I love her."

"Your partner's all right, but you're still the same asshole you've always been."

Tip said, "Thanks, Bobby. I try"

When we left Coop's office, I went to see Julie. This wasn't going to be a pleasant conversation, but Uncle Dominic had taught me to be direct with people. Sometimes it pissed people off, but most of the time they appreciated it.

She was at her desk when I walked in. "Hey, Jules. How's it going?"

"These past few days have been crazy," she said. "I don't know how you're holding up."

"Have you got a minute?"

She looked up at me and said, "Sure. What do you need?"

I checked to make sure we were alone, then I pulled a chair over and sat beside her. "Julie, I don't know how to say this, so I'm asking straight out. We've been going over this case, and all the trouble with information leaking, and there's one thing we can't figure out—how did *El Terrible* get the password?"

Julie looked up at me. "You think *I* did it?"

I saw the hurt in her expression—brow furrowed, skin around her eyes bunched up, tears welling. Sometimes I hated my job. "No, Jules. I *don't* think you did it, but I have to ask."

"What about Tip? Does he think that?"

I sat next to her and grabbed her hand. "Look at me. None of us want to believe you did it. Hell, we don't want to believe *any of us* did it, but the fact remains that somebody did. Somebody from this department." I took a deep breath and said, "I know you're upset. I'm sure you're pissed off that I asked, but I don't have time to worry about that. So, did you tell *anyone* about the password. Did you mention it in front of anybody?"

She was shaking her head before I finished. "Nothing, Connie. I swear."

The look she gave convinced me. I sat up straight and made sure I had her attention. "Cruz is dead. Two deputies are dead. The Sniders are dead, and we've got other dead bodies. We've got to find a way to catch this person, and we need your help."

Julie took a deep breath and sighed. "Tell me what to do."

"Can you access phone records of employees?"

"Depending on who it is, yes."

"Herb and Charlie. Let's start with them. I want all calls made for the last two weeks." I gave Jules a hug. "And don't say *anything* about this."

"I won't, but you don't think Herb or Charlie are involved." She stared for a few seconds, and then said, "Do you? For real?"

"I don't know what to think yet. That's why we need to keep it quiet. So when I say don't say *anything*, I mean it."

"You can count on that," she said. "But how about County? The relief team came from there."

"No one at County knew the password. The officers were supposed to call here to get the password."

Julie shook her head. "I can't believe this. I just can't."

"Believe it, Jules. One of them is dirty." I stood and patted her on the arm. "Find us something," I said, and started down the hall.

Half an hour later, Julie called, and I went to her office. We went through the calls one by one, but couldn't find anything suspicious. "I'm not surprised," I said. "I'd have been shocked if we *did* find something."

"I'll keep looking," Julie said. "Maybe the finances will show something fishy."

"Check everything you can," I said.

As I walked back to my desk, I replayed the scenes in my mind. When we got the information from Ben about the autopsy, Herb and Charlie went outside to smoke. When we found out Tiffany's real name, they went to smoke.

The information about Griffin and the law firm—I remembered Charlie smoking, but couldn't recall if Herb was with him. When Roberts was going to put the picture on the news, same thing. And most incriminating of all, when we arranged for the Sniders to be moved to the safe house. Herb went with Charlie to smoke. I sat at my desk, running the images over and over in my mind. I didn't want to believe what I knew was true.

"Must be important," Tip said.

I looked up to see Tip and Delgado standing by the desk. "Sorry, Tip. I was thinking."

"You looked like you were trying to solve the problems of the universe."

"Maybe I was," I said. I stood and peeked around the corner, then moved close to Tip and Delgado. "I know who the leak is. But we need a plan."

Chapter 51

A Plea For Help

While we sat at the desk discussing how to spring the trap, the Assistant DA called Coop to let us know they were cutting Carlos loose. She said she'd hold him as long as possible, but if we didn't have anything else to charge him with, he'd be gone by the end of the day. She had no choice.

The bottom line was Cortes was going to be free again, and there was nothing we could do about it. The Sniders were gone. We had no other witnesses, and without *El Terrible* we had no proof of his involvement in the other murders. I slammed my fist on the desk. "Goddamnit."

"Easy, Gianelli," Tip said.

"Easy my ass. The son of a bitch is getting away with it again. After all he did." I was so pissed off I was shaking.

"We'll get him," Delgado said. "I don't know how yet, but we will."

I looked at Ribs. He was only trying to be nice. "I hear you, but Tip and I said the same thing last year, and Carlos almost killed me."

I got up from the desk and started down the hall.

"Where are you going?" Tip asked.

"To the ladies room, for God's sake. You coming?"

"I just might. Don't be surprised."

Tip waited for her to get out of sight, and then turned to Delgado. "Ribs you think you could get me a coffee? I have to call Renkin."

"Be right back," Ribs said. "I need one anyway."

As soon as Delgado left, Tip grabbed Connie's phone and opened her contacts. It took a minute but he found what he wanted. He copied the number and made sure to put her phone back exactly as it was. A few seconds later Delgado returned with coffee.

"Thanks. I needed this."

"I did too," Delgado said. "And I think we'll both need a lot more before the night's over."

"That's no shit."

Ribs peered down the hall and then said, "I'm worried about Gianelli. She seems to be taking this pretty hard."

"I'm worried too," Tip said, and then, "Renkin wants to see me for a minute. Be right back."

All the way down the hall Tip thought about what he planned to do. It went against every fiber of his being, everything he lived for. If he knew for certain that Carlos was responsible for the Sniders and Cruz, he'd do it in a heartbeat, but there was that damn reasonable doubt. Every time a logical solution came to mind, other thoughts did too. At the forefront of those were three important things: Carlos was the one who killed Tony; he was the one who tried killing Connie; and he was the one who killed Kassie and Kelly. The image of his dogs lying on the ground, blood pooled under them, and their eyes dead of life flashed in Tip's head. And then he thought about Connie. There was no doubt in Tip's mind that Carlos would try to kill Connie. And this time, he'd likely succeed. Tip took the back steps to the parking lot and dialed the phone.

"Pronto."

"This is Tip Denton, I—"

"Is Concetta all right?"

Tip heard the pain that came through in this man's voice. The worry. The love. Suddenly he knew why Connie felt the way she did about her family.

"She's all right. Kind of."

"Why did you call, Detective?"

Tip hesitated. He didn't know if he wanted to cross this ground.

"Detective, if you're worried about strings being attached to this call—don't. And if Concetta has ever spoken to you about me, I'm sure she's told you that despite my past, I'm a man of my word. I give you that word now."

Something about the way the man said it convinced Tip. "Carlos Cortes, the guy who tried to kill her, is going to get out of jail. If he does, I *know* he'll come after her again."

"How much time do I have?"

"A couple of hours if we're lucky."

"Can you delay it?" Dominic asked.

"I can try," Tip said.

"I am in your debt, Detective."

"Listen, I don't want anything from you. I don't even know why I called. I shouldn't have."

He was about to hang up, and then he thought of something. "One more thing," Tip said. "Connie doesn't know I called you."

"You are a true friend," Dominic said. "I'm happy she has you." A slight pause followed, and then, "You did the right thing. And you have no need to worry about a scene. Things will be handled discreetly."

Oh shit! Tip tried convincing himself that he didn't just order a hit. That he didn't condemn a man to death, even if the man was Carlos Cortes. He tried, but it didn't work.

Chapter 52

CALLING IN A FAVOR

Dominic hung up and gathered his thoughts. Decisions must be made, and quickly. He had no juice in Houston, and the head of the Dallas Family had sidled up with Dominic's enemy in New York. He'd get no favors from them. As he pondered the situation, something came to mind. A rumor was all it was, but Dominic had learned long ago that these kind of rumors were born in truths. Now he knew who to contact.

Before making the call, he went to the refrigerator and removed a block of Fontina cheese. It was an intense cheese, with a pungent aroma that drove most Americans to run from it as if it were poison. He leaned close and breathed deeply. *Heaven.*

Dominic looked up the number on his private cell, lit his pipe, and then dialed. It rang three times.

"Donovan."

"Detective, are you alone?"

"Who's this?"

"An acquaintance calling in a favor."

"Hold on, I've got people with me." A moment later, Frankie came back on. "Mangini, you don't have a favor to call in."

"This is about Concetta. She's in trouble and I need your help."

"What kind of trouble?" Frankie asked. "And more importantly, what kind of help?"

Dominic took a long draw on his pipe. "A drug leader from one of the cartels is trying to kill her."

"Carlos Cortes?" Frankie asked.

"The same one who tried to kill her before," Dominic said. "It's not often I say this, but I need help."

"What can I do about it? She's in Houston."

"I have information that one of your friends is in Houston. A man named Paulie Perlano."

"No idea," Frankie said.

Dominic remained silent for a moment. "I have nothing against your friend. I only want to talk to him."

"Don't give me that shit. How is *talking* to Paulie going to help you with Carlos?"

"It is difficult to express myself clearly when talking to a police officer, but let's say that I have a man in Texas. All I need is a guide."

"A guide? You're not asking Paulie to…"

"No, Detective. I won't ask him to kill anyone. You have my word."

"And after this is over with?"

"He will be in good graces—with everyone. He could even return to New York if he wanted to."

"I'll see what I can do," Frankie said.

"Please see to it quickly. My information tells me Concetta has little time."

***

Frankie kept a burner in case he ever needed to use one. Today he needed it. He checked to make sure no one was near, then dialed Paulie's number.

"Yeah."

Frankie couldn't help but smile when he heard Paulie's voice. It brought back such good memories. "I bet you're still wearing suits aren't you?"

It didn't take Paulie long to recognize the voice. "Bugs? For Christ's sake, tell me it ain't Bugs Donovan."

"How's it going, Paulie?"

"I hope you're calling to tell me you're in Houston."

"I wish. But I'm calling for something serious. Shit, I don't even know why I'm calling."

"Spit it out. What's up?"

"I don't know how to say this any other way. Dominic Mangini asked me to call."

"What? What the fuck is wrong with you? You didn't give him my number did you? Did you tell him where I was?"

"Easy, Suit. Goddamn."

"You don't know what you've done," Suit said.

"Calm down and listen. Things aren't like they were when you left. Dominic said there are no hard feelings. He needs a favor to help his niece. That's all this is about."

"What's going on up there? Are you hooked up with Mangini?"

"You're pissing me off now. Hell no, I'm not with Mangini. I'm calling you because his niece is a cop. I worked with her and now she's in Houston. And she's in trouble."

Frankie waited through the silence. After maybe ten seconds Paulie said, "What's he want me to do?"

"I have no idea. I've got a number. You can call him."

"Bugs, you swear this is on the up and up? I mean this is my life we're talking about."

"I swear on the oath we took as kids. I'd never do that to you. And I can vouch for Mangini. As much as the man is a murdering scumbag, from what I've seen he keeps his word. And he gave that to me."

"So you trust him?"

"I do."

"Give me the number."

***

Dominic put water on for espresso and placed the cup and saucer on the table, next to the cheese. Then he reached into the corner cabinet and selected one of his favorite olive oils. While waiting on the espresso, he began the ritual of slicing garlic. This was so good it could tempt a man to break his word.

The phone rang, and Dominic answered. "Pronto."

"Bugs said you wanted to talk."

"I assume you are wearing a suit?"

"Yeah, Mr. Mangini. It's me, Paulie 'The Suit' Perlano."

"We have shared many friends in the past," Dominic said. "And there is no reason not to share them in the future."

"I understand you want a favor," Paulie said.

"Sometimes a man needs things. If you can help me, you will have all of your old friends and many new friends."

"So you're saying, I'll be forgiven. Like the priests do in confession?"

"A strange comparison, but not wrong."

"What do you need done?"

Dominic explained to Paulie what he wanted. He asked Paulie for his phone number, and said a man would contact him with more details. When Dominic hung up, he called Fabrizio and told him the plan.

After he explained everything to Fabrizio, he finished the cheese, took a last sip of espresso, and dialed one more number.

"Si, Signore."

"Tell the Doctor to pack his bags."

Chapter 53

THE TRAP IS SPRUNG

Stenson had several of his guys set up outside, ready for whatever happened. We were all in the coffee room when Tip's phone rang. He answered and then signaled for something to write with. I tossed a pen to him and then grabbed a piece of paper from beside the coffee machine.

"Hold up, Chicky. I need to write that down." He scribbled an address on the paper, and then said, "You're sure about this? This better pay off. I don't want to look like a goddamn ass." Tip gave us the *thumbs up* sign. "All right. You're the best, Chick. I'll be seeing you soon. If this plays out like I think I might introduce you to Mr. Franklin."

Tip hung up, a smile as big as Texas on his face. "We just hit the mother lode."

"You must have if you promised him a hundred."

"Shit, I'll give him two hundred."

"What have you got, Tip?" This came from Charlie.

"Chicky gave us a lead on where Carlos is storing the meth. It's a warehouse down on Navigation. Hang on, I need to call Coop."

While Tip talked to Coop, I kept alert. I tried not to be obvious watching Herb, but it was difficult. I wanted to kick his ass. Herb showed no signs; in fact, he seemed to be ignoring us. He was good. As I thought that, I wondered what made someone do this? And I thought again about Uncle Dominic and the things he did. It was men like him that corrupted cops. Even as I thought it I realized it wasn't true. Men like Dominic simply found the cops who could be corrupted. A fine line separated the two, but there was a difference.

Tip hung up the phone. "Coop is coordinating this. She's got Narcotics involved but they can't put it together until tonight. *Son of a bitch*, I'd like to be there," he said.

"This will put a dent in Carlos' operations," Delgado said.

Charlie walked to the machine and poured more coffee. As he mixed creamer in it, he said, "Herb, you want to catch a smoke?"

"I'm good, Charlie, but thanks for asking."

We were ready to put the trap in motion. I had even been thinking about saying something to Charlie, and then he said that. I decided to test the waters. "Charlie, I need some help on paperwork for the Snider case when you get a minute."

"Sure thing, Connie. I'm gonna catch a quick smoke, and then I'll get on it. I won't be but a minute."

I looked back to Herb, who was occupied at his computer, then I turned back to Charlie, walking toward the steps to go outside. I almost fell out of my seat.

Tip and Delgado shot me looks as if to say, *What the hell is going on?*

I shrugged and shook my head. They had to be thinking the same thing I was—*it's not Herb. It's Charlie.*

I couldn't believe it was true, but it all fit. Once or twice, I recalled that Charlie went out for a smoke by himself. I thought maybe I'd forgotten about Herb. But now I knew. And the way Charlie always seemed to be lurking around the corner, asking questions, volunteering to help.

Son of a bitch. It is *him.*

All that was left was to figure out how he was doing it, and if he was working alone.

Charlie walked out the front door onto the sidewalk, the parking lot spread out before him. He leaned against the wall, took a cigarette from his pack, cupped his hands to shield it from the wind, and then lit it. A huge puff of smoke came from his mouth as he rested his head against the wall.

One of Stenson's men watched from inside his car near the end of the parking lot. He had binoculars trained on Charlie. Two more officers were waiting at the side in a van. It took a few minutes, but Charlie finished the cigarette, crushed it out on the walk, and then walked into the building. The man watching from his car called Connie on her cell.

"Yeah?"

"Nothing. He smoked a cigarette and went back inside. Didn't use the phone and didn't talk to anyone."

"What the hell? You're sure?"

"I'm watching him with binoculars, for God's sake."

"All right. Let me know if anything changes."

Stenson's man continued to watch. Within a couple of minutes, another officer exited. He stood in the same spot as Charlie and smoked a cigarette. When he finished he flicked his butt into the parking lot, and tossed his cigarette pack in the trash can. After that he walked inside.

Stenson's man waited a few more minutes, and was about to call it quits when what looked to be a homeless man shuffled slowly toward the building. He stopped, looked through the trash can, and pulled out the cigarette pack the other officer had thrown away. He didn't look inside, just placed the pack in his pocket.

Getting interesting.

Stenson's man called Connie. "We've got a new player and he just picked up a cigarette pack from the can."

"What? Who put it there?"

"Your other guy. Herb."

"Son of a bitch. Keep me posted."

The homeless man walked across the parking lot, but his walk was a little faster, and his posture a little better. He opened the door to a car parked at the edge of the lot next to a dark tan pickup, got inside, and pulled out a cell phone. Stenson's man called the other two men on the radio. "Wait until he's finished," he said.

"We're on it."

When the man put the cell phone down, Stenson's man signaled the others. "Now."

The other two men pulled in behind the car just as he was backing out of the space. They got out with guns drawn. "Police! Get out of the car. Now."

The man inside the car reached for something, but the officers were on him. One yanked the door open and shoved the gun in his face. "Don't move."

The other officer grabbed the phone and handcuffed him, and then they emptied his pockets. By the time Connie, Tip, and Delgado arrived the officers had the items laid out on the hood of the car. Connie reached for the cigarette pack. A folded piece of paper lay inside.

Meth is compromised. Move it before tonight.

"Son of a bitch," she said.

Tip looked over her shoulder. "That mother fucker," he said, and ran for the building.

"Tip, don't. Wait, damn it." Connie grabbed Delgado. "Come on. We have to stop him."

***

Tip raced up the steps, taking them two at a time. Charlie was at his desk, typing on the keyboard. Tip ran past him, grabbed hold of Herb's shirt collar, and yanked him out of the seat. He slammed Herb into the wall, the back of his head hitting with a thud.

"What the fuck?" Herb screamed.

Tip punched his face, and then tossed him across the hall into the other wall. People gathered around but no one interfered. Herb tried protecting himself, but Tip pummeled him, punches to the gut and face.

Delgado was the first to arrive, Connie right behind him. Delgado grabbed Tip from behind, but Tip shrugged him off. Herb broke free, but Tip came at him again. Herb reached for his gun.

Connie drew her gun and pointed it. "Drop it!" She moved forward, gun leveled at his chest, her finger on the trigger.

Tip was seething. "You motherfucker."

Connie moved in front of Tip, between him and Herb. "Lay the gun on the floor, Herb. Gently."

He bent his knees and set the gun on the floor and then he stood. Delgado cuffed him.

Coop came running down the hall. "What the hell is going on?"

"It was Herb," Connie said.

Coop balled her hand into a fist. It looked as if she would hit him. "Take that piece of shit away," she said.

Delgado got up in Herb's face. "You know what they'll do to you in prison? I hope you die in there."

Connie pushed him forward. "How could you do this? How could you betray the badge?"

"Who the hell ever cared one bit about me?" Herb said. "All I ever got from anyone here was a raft of shit."

"And you think that drug-dealing asshole cares?" Delgado asked. "I hope you rot in hell."

"This was hell," Herb said.

Herb moved back when Tip approached. "I'm gonna spread the word. I'll tell everybody you turned on Carlos. They'll be waiting for you."

"Fuck you," Herb said.

"No, they'll save that for you. Have fun."

Julie came rushing down the hall. "We just had a call. Someone spotted *El Terrible's* car in a parking lot not far from her house."

"We're on the way," Connie said.

Chapter 54

CARLOS IS FREE

Paulie hung up from Dominic and called his wife. "Hey, babe. I got something to do. I won't be home for dinner."

"Is everything okay?"

"Everything's great. I gotta go now. I love you."

"I love you, too. Be careful."

Paulie "the Suit" Perlano got into his car and headed toward the city. He made a stop at the Galleria, where he was to meet someone. He pulled into the lot and navigated to the back section. A man was standing against a car. Paulie didn't need a description to know this was who he was meeting. The man had the *look* all killers had. The same look Nicky had.

Paulie pulled up close and rolled down his window. "I'm Suit."

The man extended his hand. "Fabrizio," he said, with a hint of an Italian accent.

Fabrizio got in the passenger seat. Two men sat in the back seat. They nodded to him.

"What's the plan?" Paulie asked.

"The lawyer will call his driver to pick them up. We will intercept him and explain that it would be in his best interest to let *us* pick them up."

"And the driver?" Paulie asked.

Fabrizio shook his head. "If he cooperates, he goes home to have dinner with his wife."

"And if he doesn't?" one of the men in the back asked.

Fabrizio turned to him and smiled. "He will cooperate."

"And after we pick up the package?" the man asked.

"You will follow us and make sure there are no tails."

"Sounds easy," the man said.

"It will be," Fabrizio said.

Several blocks from the courthouse, Paulie pulled in front of the limo scheduled to pick up Carlos and his lawyer. When he stopped the car at a traffic signal, Fabrizio exited and walked to the driver's side. He tapped on the window. When the driver rolled it down, Fabrizio showed him a gun.

"I am going to ride with you, if you don't mind."

The driver unlocked the doors and Fabrizio got in the passenger seat. "Do exactly as we say or we will kill you. And then my men will kill your wife and children."

"What do you want?" the driver asked.

"Your job is easy. Do what you always do. When your passengers arrive, open the doors for them and then close them. We will take care of the rest."

"What happens after that?"

"You won't be hurt as long as you do your part, and you don't talk."

"I understand," the driver said.

Fabrizio smiled. "Trust me, signore. You will not be harmed."

A few moments later, the driver's cell phone rang.

"Hello?

"Yes, Mr. Griffin. I'm almost there. Maybe one minute."

The driver pulled to the curb. Carlos and two other men walked toward the car.

Fabrizio stood less than fifty feet away. *Be calm. Do what you always do.*

The driver opened the door and walked to the other side. He held the door open for Mr. Griffin and his guests. The big man got in first, followed by Mr. Griffin. The driver walked to the other side and let Carlos in. Afterward he shut the door and he signaled Fabrizio.

Fabrizio nodded.

Paulie approached the car from behind, Fabrizio from the side. Paulie climbed in the driver's seat, Fabrizio the passenger side. And then they locked the doors, put the car in drive, and pulled away.

The glass panel separating the driver from the back seat was soundproof and heavily tinted. Paulie rolled it down and Fabrizio turned to look at the men riding in the back.

Griffin's expression was a surprised one. "Where is Timothy? Who is that driving?"

"No need for concern," Fabrizio said. "You are in my hands now."

"We'll see about that," Griffin said, and pulled out his cell phone.

"Put the phone away," Fabrizio said.

Griffin said, "I'll have you in jail before—"

The shot entered Griffin's chest near the heart. He would be dead in a few seconds.

Fabrizio noted there was little reaction from Carlos or his man. "I see you are men accustomed to violence. That is good."

Roberto made a sudden move toward Fabrizio. Fabrizio shot him once in the stomach, and then he shot him in the groin. "Don't be too concerned about the pain, signore. I will end it soon."

Carlos looked at Roberto and then focused on Fabrizio. "From your accent, I assume Mr. Mangini sent you."

Fabrizio didn't smile. He didn't say anything.

Carlos stared. "I can make you a rich man. Very rich."

No response.

"You would never have to work again. You could live in a mansion anywhere in the world."

Still no response.

Carlos shook his head. "How can you refuse an offer like that?"

"I gave my word."

"Your word?" Carlos said, and cracked a thin smile. "Please, señor. How much is your word worth?"

"In this instance, signore, it is worth your life."

"I see," Carlos said. "Now I understand why Señor Mangini has such power. But no matter, I will have the last laugh, even if it is from the grave."

Fabrizio looked puzzled, but then it hit him. He searched for a number on his phone and typed out a text.

'She's not done killing. Be alert.'

"I am curious," Carlos said. "Why are you waiting to kill me? Why not get it over with?"

Fabrizio said, "I have orders. I am waiting for a doctor to arrive."

The smile disappeared from Carlos' face first. Then his color.

"Fear is in your eyes, signore. I see you are familiar with the Doctor."

When Carlos didn't say anything, Fabrizio leaned toward him and whispered. "I have seen him work. You are right to be afraid."

Chapter 55

A GUARDIAN ANGEL

We rode to the center separately—Tip drove his car, and I rode with Delgado. I didn't want to be in a car with Tip in the mood he was in. An officer had the scene secured when we got there, and we had already called a team to process it for prints and other DNA evidence. The most interesting discovery was in the trunk—a gym bag that looked to have all the signs of the one used at the safe house. It still reeked of gasoline.

Delgado closed his eyes and whispered a prayer.

I wondered if it was a prayer for Cruz, or a plea to let Delgado catch *El Terrible*. I *know* what mine would have been. Five minutes with her. That's all I'd need.

Tip had been tied in knots since the incident with Herb. I guess we all were. It really shook me.

"We're not doing any good here," Tip said. "I'm going to get drunk."

"Like hell you are," I said. "You're dangerous enough when you're sober."

"All right, I won't get drunk, but we need to at least have a few beers to celebrate finding the leak."

"If you can call that a celebration," Ribs said. "I feel sick about it."

"Me too," I said, "But I'm up for a beer or two."

"Follow me," Tip said.

We drove for about fifteen minutes, ending up in a joint off Westheimer that Tip swore had great food. We sat at a table by the window. Delgado ordered nachos and cheese, and we all ordered beer.

"I can't believe Cruz is gone," Delgado said. "He was a good man."

I lifted my mug and said, "Here's to Cruz."

For the next hour we talked about the case, and we tried to figure out how to track down *El Terrible*.

"Roberts is going to put her picture on every station from here to Mexico," Tip said. "Somebody should spot her."

"Maybe not," I said. "Remember how good she was at changing her looks?"

Tip's phone rang. "Denton."

He talked for a few seconds and then said, "Thanks, Bobby. I appreciate it."

"Stenson?" I asked.

A smile came to Tip's face. The first one since we busted Herb. "He got Tico and the drugs. At least those two will be going away for a long time."

"No chance they'll give up Carlos," I said. "And that means he's going free."

"We should have been there when they let him go," Ribs said. "If nothing else we could have told him about Tico."

I shook my head. "I couldn't stand to see him go free. I think I'd lose it if I saw that smirk on his face, or heard his taunting voice."

"I might have had to do something," Tip said.

"Nothing to do," Delgado said. "He's gone."

"I wouldn't be too sure about that," Tip said. "It's a long way from here to Mexico."

I looked at him, puzzled. "What is that supposed to mean?"

"Just what it says. That it's a long way to Mexico."

Delgado said, "On that note, I need another beer."

I laughed. "Me too." I signaled the waitress.

Delgado downed the last of his mug as she placed new ones on the table. "I hate that Carlos is getting away," he said, "but I think it bothers me more that *she's* getting away."

"If I had been there, I *would have* done something," Delgado said, and then he raised his glass in a toast. "For Cruz."

"For Cruz," Tip and I said.

A beep sounded from my phone. "Hang on," I said and checked my messages.

'She's not done killing. Be alert.'

I stared at it, and thought, *What the hell?*

"What is it?" Tip asked.

I showed him the message.

"Who's it from?" Delgado asked.

"I don't know. I've never seen this number."

"It's *El Terrible*," Tip said.

"What?"

"It's her," Tip said. "Somebody is warning you that she's coming after you."

Delgado stood and looked around the bar. Tip unbuckled his gun and walked around. I did the same. We cleared the bar and moved toward the exit. "She might be close," Tip said. "I don't doubt she'd try in a public place. Anyone else, I'd say no, but not her."

After fifteen or twenty minutes, we'd lost the feeling and decided to head out. We stood outside the bar talking.

"It could have been a prank," Tip said.

"I don't think so. It's too specific. And besides, not many people down here have my number." As soon as I said *down here*, it struck me. I remembered seeing the guy I thought was Fabrizio.

Holy shit! It was *him. He sent the message.*

"Tip, I think we need to take this seriously."

"Don't worry. If Carlos wants anybody dead, it's me."

"Why's that?" Ribs asked.

"Because I kicked his ass in the bathroom when we locked him up."

Things were coming together. "And he knows where you live," I said.

"That's it," Delgado said. "She'll be waiting for you at the house."

Tip ran for the car. "Flash and Sacco!" he said, and took off.

"Shit," I said and got in Delgado's car. "Drive, Ribs."

"What the hell is going on?" Ribs said.

"Last year Carlos killed Tip's dogs."

"*Dios mío.* Let's go."

I knew we'd never catch Tip. He'd be going 100 at least. "Delgado, I'm calling it in."

I had them send two cars to Tip's house, and warned them of what they might encounter. "Don't send any goddamn rookies. This woman's armed and *very* dangerous."

When we arrived, two patrol cars were in the drive. Tip's car was parked half on the grass and half on the sidewalk. The officers were standing outside. No sign of Tip.

I got out and approached them. "Anything?"

"He's inside. He almost ran me over when he came in."

I explained the situation, and then said I was going in. "Come on, Ribs."

Tip was walking out the back door as we approached the house. "Everything okay?" I asked.

"They're fine," he said. "I guess I panicked."

"With good reason," Ribs said.

Tip brushed it off. "Go on home. I'm fine."

"I don't think that's a good idea," I said. "She might show up."

"Bullshit," Tip said.

After arguing for what seemed like an eternity, I told the officers we were calling it off. They called it in, and then I got in Ribs' car and followed them down the driveway.

El Terrible watched from her spot in the woods as the cop cars drove away. She had been across the drive from the detective's house for more than an hour, waiting. It would have been so easy if those other cops hadn't shown up. But now they were gone, and soon, he would be too. She hadn't decided if she would take the partner. Her orders had been for this one, but the orders did not forbid additional targets.

She waited another half an hour, giving the cop time to settle down, allowing him to feel safe. If she waited much longer he might start to grow nervous again. *No,* she thought, *a half an hour is just right.*

The woods were full of sticks and leaves, and things that made noise. She evaluated the surroundings and decided to take a roundabout way. She backed out of the woods, going the opposite direction of his house, and then she circled around until she exited onto a spot far up his drive, perhaps 150 meters or more. The drive was dark, no lights, and the night sky was dim with a crescent moon. Gripping her gun with her right hand, she moved slowly down the drive, keeping as close to the trees as she could. She moved one step at a time, careful not to make noise.

It was another fifteen minutes before she reached the walk leading to the house. Lights were on in the kitchen and the room beside it. A television played from that room. She could barely make out the form of his head peeking above the sofa.

Perfect.

Dressed in black, with nothing to reflect light, she moved like a panther up the walk, each step a planned move. It took her a minute to move six meters. *El Terrible* allowed herself a smile. Skills such as hers deserved a smile. The next six meters took the same amount of time.

It is almost time, Detective.

Delgado lay on the ground behind a water fountain in Tip's garden. He breathed slowly to control his nerves. He had seen this woman's work, and he couldn't afford to leave Rosalee to take care of six kids by herself. Both hands gripped his gun. He moved it an inch at a time, following her movements. He had never seen a human move so silently. A twinge of fear coursed his veins. He fought the urge to shiver.

At first, he hadn't even seen her, but as she moved closer to the house, the light exposed her. He ran the checklist through his mind. Phone was off. Nothing on him that could make noise. Nothing to reflect light. She moved slowly, perfectly, like a cat.

Damn, this woman was good.

She was only fifteen feet away now. Delgado's body tensed. He feared his muscles might cramp or that his body would freeze up. He thought about shooting her with no warning. That's what he should do. Rosalee didn't deserve to be a widow. Fear crept into his bones. He shook. His finger pressured the trigger.

At the last moment, he found his moral compass. "Drop the gun!"

She spun and dropped to the ground, firing at the same time. Two shots hit the fountain. Delgado fired twice. One shot hit her shoulder. She rolled to the ground, flat on her stomach, and fired three more shots. One of them hit Delgado's arm. He popped up to fire again, but bullets sprayed the fountain. He ducked. She was moving toward him, continually firing.

Tip came out from behind the house. He moved quickly, his gun aimed at her. When she advanced on Delgado, he fired.

El Terrible had the cop trapped. She fired a few more rounds then reached for her other gun. A shadow moving to her right alerted her. She jumped left as three bullets barely missed her. She rolled, scrambled for the darkest part of the garden and came up behind a tree. She popped in a fresh clip, fired from the left side of the tree in the direction of the shadow.

The cop who almost shot her advanced, firing two rounds at a time. *El Terrible* crawled across the mulch, using shrubs for cover. Both cops were moving toward her, slowly splitting, approaching from both sides of the tree where they thought she was. Using her elbows, she inched a few more feet to a spot where she had a clear shot of the one called Tip.

With her elbows planted on the ground, she gripped the gun with both hands and took aim.

And fired.

Tip went down with the first shot. Two more were close misses.

Then the sound of rapid gunfire from behind *El Terrible.*

Then a curse. "*Dios mío.*"

El Terrible twisted on the ground, raised her gun.

Three more shots rang out. And then *El Terrible* dropped her head to the ground.

I advanced slowly, kicked the gun away from *El Terrible's* hand. Then I knelt to check her pulse.

"She dead?" Tip asked.

"Are you?"

"Not yet," he said, "but you better call an ambulance."

"Got one waiting down the road," I said, and called to let them know to come in.

"How's Tip?" I asked.

"Leg shot," Delgado said. "He'll be all right."

"And you?"

"Arm. I'm okay."

I stood above them, looking down. Delgado's arm was bleeding badly, and so was Tip's leg.

The sirens from the ambulance and the other patrol cars blared as they came down the drive.

Tip propped himself up on one elbow and looked over at *El Terrible.* "That was one tough son of a bitch."

"Rosalee thanks you," Delgado said, and kissed my cheek. And then he blessed himself.

I stared at *El Terrible*, lying on the ground. "Thank God," I said.

Chapter 56

CLOSURE

Cruz was buried four days later, the day after we closed the case on *El Terrible.* He had no family, so the funeral consisted mostly of cops and a few friends. Tip, Delgado, and I went to a local bar after the funeral. I was the only one not bandaged up. We sat at a table near the back, the dark corner seemed appropriate for the occasion.

I laughed at Delgado struggling with the sling on his arm, but seeing Tip on crutches was funnier. "How are you holding up, Ribs?"

He took a long swig of beer and said, "Considering who shot me, I'm glad it's only my arm. That was one nasty woman we put down."

"We?" Tip said. "I believe that was *me* who put her down, Mr. Delgado."

"I wounded her," Ribs said. "If she wasn't already bleeding she'd have gutted you."

"A lot of macho shit going on at this table. But to set the record straight, it was me who put her down...as she was about to rid the world of two detectives."

Ribs shook his head as he nibbled on nachos. "I can live with that, but I don't think your partner can."

"I still can't believe the body count on this one," Tip said. "Worst I've ever seen."

"What was it—11?" Delgado asked.

"If you count the two on her team, it was 13," I said.

"That's a lot of people that didn't have to die," Tip said.

I downed the rest of my beer and signaled for another. "And the worst part of it, is that son of a bitch Carlos got away. Again."

"Like I said before, it's a long way to Mexico."

I looked at Delgado and said, "There he goes again with that nonsense. What the hell is that supposed to mean, Ribs? Do you know?"

"Connie, the longer you're here, the sooner you'll realize that Tip's sayings usually don't make sense. And if you find yourself thinking they do make sense, it's time to go back home."

"I'll drink to that," I said, and we all took a swig.

"I wonder how the girl's doing?" Tip said.

"She's okay," Delgado said. "About as good as you can expect."

I stared at Ribs. "How do you know? Did you check on her?"

"I was waiting before I mentioned it, but Rosalee and I might try to adopt her."

A warm rush went through me. I got up and hugged him. "That's the sweetest thing I've ever heard of."

He blushed. "We talked about it. I figure what's one more kid when you have six?"

"You can always skim more drug money," Tip said.

"Or pimp out a few more girls," Ribs said.

I held my glass up. "To the Delgados. Damn good people."

We shot the shit for another half hour or so, before Ribs said he had to go. He reached for money, but Tip stopped him. "You're gonna need every penny if you plan on taking Marissa in." He called the waiter over and asked for the check.

"It's been taken care of, sir."

Tip scrunched up his brow and looked over at me.

"Don't look this way," I said. "I was counting on you to pay."

Delgado held up his hands. "Not me."

"Who paid?" Tip asked.

"Some guy at the bar," the waiter said. "A big guy in a suit."

"Do you know him?" Tip asked.

"I've never seen him in here, but he said to give you this." The waiter handed Tip a note.

"What's it say?" I asked.

"Your problem has disappeared," Tip said, and then his face sunk, as if he'd gotten bad news.

"What's wrong, Tip? Does that mean something?"

He shook his head. "I can't think of anything," he said, but I didn't believe one word of it.

We finished up and headed home in our own cars. I couldn't help but wonder what the hell that was all about, but I knew I'd never find out until Tip was ready to tell me.

Tip drove home under the speed limit. He felt sick inside, dirty, and guilty. If that message meant what he thought it meant—and he felt certain it did—he was responsible for killing a man in cold blood. On the other hand, considering what he knew, that text to Connie probably also came from the same man, which meant that Dominic had saved his life. How could he be upset about someone who killed Carlos, and at the same time, saved Tip's life. Now he understood a little bit about how Connie felt at times. How she struggled with her feelings about family. If nothing else, he knew one thing—he could *never* tell Connie what he'd done. She'd never forgive him.

Epilogue

Three weeks later

I was sipping espresso at the kitchen table and waiting for Tip to pick me up. A headline flashed on the TV and caught my eye. A sick feeling roiled in my gut.

Body parts found outside of Victoria.

I set my coffee down and turned up the volume.

The body of Carlos Cortes, reputed leader of a drug cartel in Monterrey, Mexico, was discovered in a shallow grave ten miles outside of Victoria, Texas. The body was in pieces, and according to the Medical Examiner, Cortes was still alive when the dismemberment of his body took place. His limbs showed signs of being stitched up after the amputations, and displayed signs of healing. Cortes seemed to have been kept alive for a long time.

The Medical Examiner said Mr. Cortes' skin had been peeled from his face and burns covered almost 30% of his body. Seven of his fingers had been removed, and all of his toes. Also his genitals. The torture appears to have been carried out by someone with professional surgical skills.

The newsman continued with graphic details, but I didn't need to hear anymore. I didn't *want* to hear anymore. From somewhere deep inside of me, I *knew* what had happened. I *knew* it. That knowledge made me come to grips with something that had been bothering me since I was twelve years old. For the first time in my life, I understood what the relationship with Uncle Dominic was all about. And that scared me. It scared the hell out of me. I cursed him, and swore I hated him for being a gangster, but something inside me respected him. And loved him.

When I received the text about *El Terrible,* a lot of feelings ran through me—fear, curiosity, the mystery of who sent it, but one emotion overwhelmed me the moment I realized it was from Fabrizio—pride. I was *proud* that Uncle Dominic was looking out for me. And I was thankful.

I finished my espresso, moved the dishes to the sink, and started washing them. All the while I tried suppressing my other feelings. The ones that had been keeping me awake at night, and haunting me for the past three weeks.

From the moment I realized that Fabrizio had been here—my dreams no longer belonged to me. The thought of Fabrizio in Houston, and looking after me…filled me with a feeling I hadn't felt in many years. That realization frightened me more than anything.

How can I be a cop and feel that way about a killer?

As I pondered that, the phone rang. It was Tip.

"I'll be there in half a minute," he said. "Pack plenty of bullets."

"Why's that?"

"Didn't Coop call? We got us a killer to catch."

ACKNOWLEDGEMENTS

The tough part of writing a book is not the writing, it's all the stuff that comes after that. I'll take credit for the writing. For the tough parts I am honor bound to thank the following:

My great copy editor, Annette Lyon.

Natasha Brown for the fantastic book cover.

Jason Anderson from Polgarus Studio, for the amazing layout and formatting.

And most importantly the beta readers who helped me get this book into shape: Missy, Otto, Chris, Nick, Rose, Joe Michalcewicz, Carrie Shepherd & Elizabeth Hull. If I missed someone, please shoot me.

It takes a lot of technical help to write a book like this. I owe a debt of gratitude to my good friend, Skip Oliver, Retired Major in the Harris County Sheriff's Office. Whatever mistakes are in here, are mine alone.

I also want to give special thanks to my niece, Emiliana, for making me laugh on many nights when I needed a laugh, and to Braden and Bella for all the wonderful video chats.

Lastly, to my wife, Mikki.

Ti amo con tutto il mio cuore.

ABOUT THE AUTHOR

I grew up in a large Italian family in the Northeast. No one had money, so for entertainment our family played board games and told stories. I loved the city—the noise, the people—but it was the family get togethers and the storytelling that stuck with me.

I still love storytelling, but now I write the stories instead of telling them.

My wife and I live in Texas, where we run an animal sanctuary with 45 loving "friends." One of them is a crazy wild boar named Dennis, who is my best buddy.

Sometimes I miss the early days, but not much. Now I enjoy the solitude and the noise of the animals.

CPSIA information can be obtained
at www.ICGtesting.com
Printed in the USA
LVHW090851200119
604567LV00001B/34/P

9 781940 313078